An

ANTHOLOGY

of

EAST AFRICAN
LITERATURE

8th House Publishing
Montreal, Canada

ISBN 978-1-926716-61-9

Published worldwide by 8th House Publishing.
Front Cover Design by 8th House Publishing

Designed by 8th House Publishing.
www.8thHousePublishing.com
Set in Garamond, Delicious Heavy, Raleway and Caslon.

Library and Archives Canada Cataloguing in Publication

Title: An anthology of East African literature / edited by Beatrice Lamwaka & Josh Mali.
Names: Lamwaka, Beatrice, editor. | Mali, Josh, editor.
Description: Poems and short stories.
Identifiers: Canadiana 20230222862 | ISBN 9781926716619 (softcover)
Subjects: LCSH: East African literature (English)—21st century.
Classification: LCC PR9345 .A58 2023 | DDC 820.89676—dc23

An
ANTHOLOGY
of
EAST AFRICAN LITERATURE

Edited by

BEATRICE LAMWAKA
& JOSH MALI

CONTENTS

FOREWORD   vii

Poetry

Beverley Nambozo Nsengiyunva
Since you attended my funeral, I'll also attend yours   5
Al Qaeda   6
Conversations with Her Breasts   6
Aquagasm   7
Flowers in My Rectum   8

Lydia Kasese
I Lost My Teeth in a Fight   9
C.A.G   10
Compass   10
Self-Negotiation   11
Forced Dreams   12

Bigoa Chuol
recipe for a wide gap between your teeth   13

Kagayi Ngobi
Poetic Justice   16
I Used To Shout My Poems   17
What I Dreaming?   18

Raïs Neza Boneza
Dinanga, the Ark of refuge   19
Urugo, HOMESTEAD   21
La Paysanne   22
At dusk to my Tate's home (Grandma)   22
Nandi   23
Tunda, the Flower   24
Second Dimension   25

Sitawa Namwalie
1984! A Lesson on How to Wear Jordache Jeans   26
A Father of Nine Children   27
How to Receive Aid?   27

Betty Kituyi
When I am Me   29
Pioneering Feet   31
Against the Unknown   32
Cloud Escape   33
Missed Communion   34
Painting the Colour of Light   35

Josh Mali
The Women are Here   37
Voices from the Sea   38
Talking to you   39
Who Will Marry Her?   40
Panda gari, in English   41

Gervaz Lushaju
In an Instant   42
Body Noise   42
Well-Meaning Fools   43
Black Mirror   44
Exist   44
Home   45

Prof. Laban Erapu
The Gift of Words   46
I Asked My Heart   46
Delicate Wings   47

Julius Ocwinyo
The Knell of Doom   48

Short Stories

World Pawa — Billy Kahora — 53
The Books of Judas — Sam Okoth Opondo — 70
A Place With Many Doors — Troy Onyango — 86
Yalla Nrooh Masr — Dennis Mugaa — 94
Falling — Aress Mohamed — 102
The Letter Writer — Dessale Berekhet — 113
Frangipani — Alex Teyie — 122
Raised by the Rod — Lucky Grace Isingizwe — 130
Streetlights — Barbara Oketta — 139
A Memorial for Bella — Lilian Akampurira Aujo — 146
Magic Invisible — Jameela Siddiqi — 156
Doom Harvest — Derek Lubangakene — 163
April in Kinoo — Rosey Ssembatya — 174
Goats on a Balcony — Sophie Alal — 177
Restless Souls — Ayeta Anne Wangusa — 186
Untitled — Carey Baraka — 197
My She-Husband — Muthoni wa Gichuru — 207
The Chicken League — Neema Komba — 213
Seed Sowing — Regina Asinde — 220
Fish Skeletons — Dilman Dila — 227
The Shopkeeper Is Melting — Dilman Dila — 233
Kissing Gordo — Muthoni Garland — 243
The Bigness of Littleness — Davina Philomena Kawuma — 256
In Transit — Abraham T. Zere — 267
How To Break — Tim Baroraho — 277
Nobody's Child — Bob G. Kisiki — 283
The Super Dancer — Josh Mali — 289
A Tale of Two Husbands — Julius Ocwinyo — 299
Ceilings — Acan Innocent Immaculate — 309
Chief of the Home — Beatrice Lamwaka — 315
Till We Find Our Voices — Hilda J. Twongyeirwe — 319

Glossary of common terms — 328

About the Editors — 331

FOREWORD

THIS IS not just a collection of poems and short stories; it is a granary of artistic abundance! For here, will you find a rich variety of masterfully crafted pieces in a range of style, including those that draw from the African oral storytelling tradition. It is a montage of pieces of literary art, curated in a manner that allows for the 'strict grammarian' forms of expression to coalesce with those given to poetic licentiousness.

The anthology's poetry is rich and sundry, mirroring the diverse spectrum of literary expression to be found across the East African region. Verb repetition – a familiar linguistic form often used to create a sense of frequency or emphasis in many Bantu languages – is at play as the persona in *Aquagasm* playfully draws us into her romantic entrancement with nature.

> *She dip dips in the Ocean with her toes,*
> *Smack smacks the waves with her breasts*
> *Lick licks the sand with her fingers*
> *Point points at the sky with her nose*

Ngonjera, a Swahili word for a conversational poem with more than one persona's voice, comes to the fore in *Who Will Marry Her?* This conversational form, a characteristic of many an African poetry recital rooted in the oral poetic tradition, is more overtly recognizable in the opening line of *Poetic Justice*:

> *First wait I tell you!*

It is an African storytelling format that is to be encountered shortly later in the lines:

> *What are you saying?*
> *First wait I tell you!*

Beyond the different verse forms that render these poems quintessentially African, one needn't look too far to find other features that easily lend themselves to that categorization, such as the imagery and symbolism peppering the pages that contain *Home; The Knell of Doom*. Consider this, from *Home*:

The taste of cooked plantains wraps my mother's love in salted banana leaves.

The anthology's short stories section features some of the finest writing yet, both in terms of form and meaning. Yet, like with its poetry, the prose writers make a deliberate departure from the strict English sentence; abandoning the text-book lexical and syntactical forms in favour of relatable diction and sentence structure that is easily discernible in day-to-day conversations across East Africa. Here, the African narrative voice is to be found in a story set in rural Africa as it is to be encountered in one set in America. For example, in *Restless Souls*, the concept of time in America is still pretty much the same as that of a village herdsman – relying on the position of the shadow in relation to the sun, instead of a modern watch.

"Situuma could see that it was getting late because the shadow of the Greyhound on the tarmac was growing shorter. But the sky was lit up because this was summer, and the daylight had a long life."

Thematically, the writings cover a range of issues, from the societal to the personal. This way, you have terrorism juxtaposed with romantic cravings; political disenchantment residing side by side with justice and gender equality issues; sexual exploitation and human/family relations finding acres of space in both the prose and the poetry, and an unmissable glimpse into racial and ethnic issues. In some cases, the themes have a bearing on the style employed. Sometimes the personal is also symbolically societal, as with the conservationist personification of a tree, complete with affectionate nomenclature in *Frangipani*, and the allegorical rendering of Uganda's tumultuous political history through dance in *The Super Dancer*.

Lucky Grace Isingizwe explores an issue that has increasingly become the subject of debate and public legislation. In *Raised by the Rod*, she lays bare the scourge of childhood violence familiar to many who grew up in households where parenting was guided by the Biblical dictum, 'spare the rod and spoil the child'. Denis Mugaa's *Yalla Nrooh Masr* is an eclectic menu of experiences, juxtaposing difficult choices of picking between a potentially financially rewarding traditional career and adventure; the familiar that is resident in one's own family vs the deep familial links we establish with strangers from different backgrounds, etc.

There has been growing concern about the stigma surrounding mental health, or about the fact that it's a neglected issue that is sometimes deferred to exploitative schemes of religious charlatans. In Falling, Aress Mohamed lets all this play out in a rather heartbreaking yet sobering way. Relatedly, albeit with a twist, in Lilian Akampurira Aujo's '*A Memorial for Bella*', a reader is treated to the complexities of interracial relations in rural Uganda and yet another mental health challenge, with a mother sliding into depression following a tragic ending to a forced botched abortion.

While this foreword provides a small window through which the reader may peek into the content of this anthology, it is in no way exhaustive, as it covers only a few pieces randomly selected for illustrative purposes. Their inclusion may, thus, not necessarily speak to their stylistic or thematic merit, nor may it point to their literary strength in comparison to the ones that do not feature.

Whichever your favourite genre is, this anthology of East African literature has delivered something that has not been served to readers in many years. It is a fitting gift to the lovers of literary art in this first quarter of the 21st century.

—Josh Mali

An
ANTHOLOGY
of
EAST AFRICAN LITERATURE

Edited by

BEATRICE LAMWAKA
& JOSH MALI

8TH HOUSE PUBLISHING

Beverley Nambozo Nsengiyunva	(Uganda)	5
Lydia Kasese	(Tanzania)	9
Bigoa Chuol	(South Sudan)	13
Kagayi Ngobi	(Uganda)	16
Raïs Neza Boneza	(Democratic Republic of Congo)	19
Sitawa Namwalie	(Kenya)	26
Betty Kituyi	(Uganda)	29
Josh Mali	(Kenya)	37
Gervaz Lushaju	(Tanzania)	42
Prof. Laban Erapu	(Uganda)	46
Julius Ocwinyo	(Uganda)	49

Poetry

Since you attended my funeral, I'll also attend yours
Beverley Nambozo Nsengiyunva

Since you attended my funeral, I'll also attend yours.
I'll arrive just before the coffin
Enters the church
And join the line of weepers.
Weepers, mind you, not mourners.
Weeping is the physical evidence for Facebook
That people actually cared about you.

But mourning…
Mourning is the spiritual evidence
That people cared about you.

I'll stand with the weepers,
dab my eyelids and sniffle
Make sure I greet the right people.
Your great aunt
The one who hugs me so hard
That she flattens my breasts
I'll hug your grandmother
The one whose weave gets caught in my earrings.
I'll hug your uncle
The one whose hands rest on my bum
Like he's kneading dough.
Since you attended my funeral,
I'll also attend yours.
I'll place a wreath on your coffin
Pluck out the petals and leave the thorns.
I'll deliver a eulogy
About how close we were as friends
And in the collection box
I'll leave a copy of my HIV results
And a photo of that passionate night.

Previously published in Expound Magazine, Femrite

Al Qaeda
Beverley Nambozo Nsengiyunva

I am an **Al Qaeda**.
Metal scanners are my foes; my friends.
The scanner rubs me up and rubs me down
It makes a sound.
I take off my metallic belt willingly.
Your scanner rubs me up and rubs me down again.
This time it is my metallic bra.
Please help me undo the clasp.
Your scanner is glowing red
As it rubs me up and rubs me down again.
The scanner makes a sound.
It is the metal in my garters
Your scanner begins to bulge.
You take me to a room.
The scanner beeps and beeps and beeps.
I am an Al Qaeda.
Metal scanners are my foes; my friends.

Previously published in Kwani?

Conversations with Her Breasts
Beverley Nambozo Nsengiyunva

She had a lump in her breast
It was a single rosebud
In a vase
It was a lonely lily
Floating in a pond
It was the beautiful ugly story
Of our friendship.

Her naked breast
Rolls off the pillow
Searching for a companion
Searching for me
Our conversations,

Now coloured with shades
That have no name
With colours that were
Once called friendship.
But now we speak
In sullen softness.

We are two pillows on a bed
That can no longer lay side by side.

We are a single password
Which enters decades of our friendship

Her eyes glint
And the single rosebud floats.
All I can do is watch through the vase
As it floats in her tears.

Previously published in EVENT Magazine

Aquagasm
Beverley Nambozo Nsengiyunva

She dip dips in the Ocean with her toes,
Smack smacks the waves with her breasts,
Lick licks the sand with her fingers,
Point points at the sky with her nose.

-her first love affair with the Indian Ocean.

She feel feels the ripples in her thighs,
Squirm squirms as water enters her eyes,
Wish wishes the boats would disappear,
She can't share this *aquagasm* with anyone.

-her first love affair with the Indian Ocean.

Flowers in My Rectum
Beverley Nambozo Nsengiyunva

I don't use the toilet anymore
because of the green leaves in my butt.
It has caused three months of forced constipation
and stacks and stacks of unwrapped toilet paper.

I wrote a prayer on the ground using a pen
made from memories.

My prayer.
"Someone above who is listening,
Make the leaves in my rectum
remind me of what they took from us,
When
They
Chopped
Down
Our
Trees
and forced us on our knees,
begging for the return of our stories."

We designed prose on the barks of those trees,
with our fingernails
stained with the love of our children and neighbours.

We sketched poetry from the memories
of love-making,
squeezing the shyness out of those gazing,
making them understand that open love
is primal
and pure
and undefined
and harmless.

Now we hide in bedrooms
and stifle the animal grunts
of pleasure.

We have forgotten how to make love
They say they will teach us.
They will turn the trees into paper
So that we write with ink.

They don't know that I have written with ink
and it stinks.

I throw the last bit of memory away.
It bounces off the lonely forest
back to the middle of my forehead.

A deep cut.
The blood.
Shaped like a tree.

Beverley Nambozo Nsengiyunva *is a poet, author, public speaker and long-distance swimmer. She is the founder of the* Babishai Niwe Poetry Foundation *and Founding President of* Bukoto Toastmasters Club. *Beverley holds a Masters Degree in Creative Writing from* Lancaster University, *with a Distinction. She loves to travel with her four children, to write and to dance. Her works have been published world-wide and translated in several international languages. Beverley is a 2010 joint first runner-up of the* annual international erbacce-press poetry prize. *She currently lives in Kampala and looks forward to living in different spaces in the world, with her family.*

I Lost My Teeth in a Fight

Lydia Kasese

I.
My father tries to kill me twice
before the age of twelve.
both times I'm a tiny thing on a floor.
He breaks the branch of a jacaranda tree on my skin
and I lose my voice.
In both scenarios he screams: I will kill you.
In both scenarios,
my mother stands by and watches me die.
In both scenarios I am unsure of the things I have done that deserve death.
In both scenarios I die.
I learn that there is no heaven for children that die at the hands of their fathers.
There is no heaven for children whose mothers stand by and watch them die.
Because maybe they deserved it.

II.
I tell my girlfriend of how my father has dreams of killing me.
She tells me when she was ten,
Her father stuck his hands down her clothes during afternoon naps
And held onto her privates.
I cry on her carpet. She says:
If men could rape us and get away with it, they would.
Every. Single. One. Of. Them.
I cry some more in the dark.
I spend that week in a suitcase.
A man touches my name as I introduce myself.
My father destroyed the fight in me when I was a child.
I think that boy only raped me because I lost my teeth in a fight.
I think, I think too much of the past.
I think maybe if I had the courage to leave this body my teeth would grow back.

C.A.G
Lydia Kasese

I cut my wrists in your bathroom one time when you were away at work.
What I meant to say in the time that you got home
And kicked me out of your house was;
You are not the man you said you were.
You made me cross borders,
Into a city where no one would hear me if I screamed.
Or said I was dying.
You enjoyed my invisibility and used it as the kindling for your poetry.
I looked as pretty and seductive as nothing.

Compass
Lydia Kasese

If you use a compass
As a metaphor for your father,
You will lose direction.
You will learn all the different ways
Your body can repel into itself.
You will become a raisin in his presence,
A mushroom,

Something made out of mold,
Something that rots for a living.
You will become a dying thing.
A bending thing.
A spineless thing.
A hiding thing.

Self-Negotiation
Lydia Kasese

The thought of physical contact has begun to scare you again.
One morning,
in the middle of breakfast making,
your mother's relative reaches out and grabs at your breast.
Your mind trips into your memory
And you are seven years old, and another woman is playing x and o's with your
privates.

Maybe it is because,
When for the second time in your life,
You attempted to tell your mother,
That someone had attempted to break into your body,
That it made you uncomfortable,
That it left an open box,
An untidy mess,
A drowning sound,
Awoke a hurtful space in your head,
All she had to say was,
"just ignore it".

Maybe the little girl that lives under your skin
Is finally tired of the wait.
Maybe she has stopped dreaming
Of homes that can be found in women
That birth you.
Maybe she finally stretches
Out of the cowering position she has become accustomed to
And assumes the position of a rabid dog
Protecting the things it still remembers it owns.

There are two versions of you in this body.
The first learns to survive intimate relationships
By not being sober.
The second
Constantly negotiates with the first,
Reminding her of all the reasons she should continue giving life a second chance.

Forced Dreams
Lydia Kasese

This morning,
You hurl words at me and I shrivel.
My anxiety awakens and drives my day.
My self-esteem rushes
To line up the insides of my stomach
And I become weak.

There is a child lining the bottom of my skin,
Every now and then she stretches herself
To remind me she still exists,
To remind me to breath,
To remind me to live.

I swallow my words more often
Than I let them see the light of day.
I swallow your words more often than
I can ever admit to myself.
But my anxiety,
It recognizes the sound of your voice,
It knows all the different octaves that disappointment
Disapproval comes in.

Lydia Kasese *is a Tanzanian writer, poet, columnist, and media director. In 2016, her first poetry chapbook,* Paper Dolls, *was published by the* African Poetry Book Fund *as part of their* Tatu *collection. In 2017, her short story, 'My Mother's Project,' appeared in the* Caine Prize's anthology, The Goddess of Mtwara.

recipe for a wide *gap* between your teeth
Bigoa Chuol

kɛl   my mother is hard things,
beneath she has infused *teak* splinters cautiously
      mimicking leathery skin
  she is heavy,   it has flattened her feet
toughened women do not soften,
          they rust

    rɛw
    my mother *is* rough handling,
     she says it shapes prudent daughters
livid, when it just presses them   wider and away

diɔk   she insists,
  the water *pi_hw*   is the most exquisite
    and profoundly sweet in *Manchom*
she means the memories,   her favourite brother is the one
    with the big gap between their top front teeth,
 like our *guand*ɔŋ   grandfather
  she declares they look most
alike when unbowed by
       calamity
this is when she speaks   about *nhök* about love,
  she loves him obscured by expanding   kilometres,
by gaps   as wide as between both

        their top front teeth

        ŋɔaan
   in 1997, we nuzzled into each other
  and took photographs in front of all the
       bougainvillea
   in Nairobi
    our favourite is the purple and pink
that april, head outside window   on a sunday,
vomit washed back onto the side of the *matatu*
   the conductor insisted   my mother clean it

I now try to sleep when I feel nauseous
    Inter-generational gaps are mature potholes

we will not arrive

                    cleanly

dhieer   when father is murmur in the night,
         I find a birthday card
      from my mother's brother, dated the year
                              1997
this one,   they look most alike in the hair
      In their *sorghum* sized coils
            he is fifth sibling and she is fourth but
he has no gaps   in all his clean straight white
         teeth
                  she compliments his gums,
they are a pale pink *bougainvillea*

                    bakɛl
              we presume *guandɔŋ*
      has not noticed the language   collapse
from the tongues of his grandchildren,
                              dispatched
to back molars to be chewed
                        occasionally

   we hope he thinks of *us*
            when he is weaving trinkets,
we hope there is some left to return
               home when we visit   very soon
   It hurts his hands   nowadays
they beg him to slow down   they mean stop

barɔw   your smile is a collision
your mouth is
                  catastrophe with   teeth
I am 17 years old; she asks me to   explain
why I want to leave the house when my father died
      only two years ago   *Duɔl*

         badek
my brave   brother boy, his tears fall faster
than he can ball his hands into fists

weep,   mourn

      reaches out to embrace
quicker than he can implode into rage
      recipe to compelling
                              softness
he looks like baba,   therefore, graduates first sibling
              an arch for flat feet

                    baŋɔan   come home and see the *okra*
bloom flowers,   clip *guandɔŋ's* toenails
      and stroke his white hair   with a *soft* comb
              he laughs with his spirit
quells our casual   scepticism with delicious kindness,
                    spit and   ceremony
puɔhth
      there are no children here of a lesser
          god

                                        we̱l
              there is rest,
snatch it from the   kilometres expanding
      prepare the place we can lay
      mother *sleep* long
              sleep long   till

              your sides *hurt*

Bigoa Chuol is a South Sudanese writer, poet and facilitator. An active practitioner in community engaged arts and creative project development. She is a fellow of *Melbourne University Social Equity Institute*. Her more recent writing explores the reverberations of war time displacement in the diaspora on gender equality, language and memory. She is currently working on a collection of essays.

Poetic Justice
Kagayi Ngobi

First wait I tell you!

Another political poem
Found me undressed
Ready to mount
My nakedness

…in a flash…
Everything went MYE!

Blind.

To open my eyes,
My conscience was in court
On trial!

What are you saying?
First wait I tell you!

A poem I once wrote
Was arrested
Brought to court
With its tongue tied to
Its twisted knickers

Naye
Kama mbaya mbaya
It was also ready to go to jail!

Then it began to speak
Its truth through the bailiff
It possessed the registrar
Spoke tongues through
The prosecutor and clerk
And the judge decided
To elope with justice

And the poem? Left
To address readers
In the national library
Of dust to dust

I tell you!
You don't know my country if you think
Poems care
What gets in their way
Of expression

Should I whisper a secret?
Freedom of expression is a round-about
Injustice maneuvers
Just for just

No wonder every day
My poems are on trial.

I Used To Shout My Poems
Kagayi Ngobi

before the gun on my forehead
buried the pen in my veins
before the words 'I spoke'
grew thorns in my throat
before the force of law
gagged my mouth
before my tongue was cut out

I used to shout my poems.

before the mic
was finally dead
and the stage we loved
to perform our art
was finally sold
before we lamented
our art was homeless

I used to shout my poems.

after my metaphors
in my eyes were burnt
in the fire of society's conscience,
after I drowned in swamps
where Bachwezi heard
the Babiito prophesy,
after I foresaw
what would happen here

I stopped shouting my poems.

What I Dreaming?
Kagayi Ngobi

The national flag
On a mugaire tree
The crested crane burnt   at a Police station
Black mambas hitting streets
The kob a special food menu   orders from above
Voters not counting their votes
Their fingers not enough.

What do I hear?

The tarmac
on   roads fleeing
Doctors dying   in hospitals   on burial grounds
Of military shoes   walking into
Stomachs of   loud-mouthed well-fed   voters
Demanding   CHANGE! CHANGE!
Voters not counting their votes
Ballot boxes not being enough.

What do I smell?
The law   for hire
MPs dancing   to Smart Wire-Wire
Parte-after-parte,   Amendment After Amendment
Voters not counting their votes.

What do I touch?

Time wall-clocked   counting time
Backwards
Justice yellow fenced around   national courts
Facial-make-up police   drinking   kitu-kidogo
                Soft-hand-holding-hard-ammunition
Because African taxes are never enough.

What is this taste?
Food   spread with teargas
And grass   from Ibingira's grave
Paper-poetry ordinances   for Karamoja
Saliva eaters   eating the eaten
Their appetite not enough.

WAKE UP!
WAKE UP!
WAKE UP!

Kagayi Ngobi is a Ugandan poet, performer and author of the poetry books *The (New) Headline That Morning* (2020) and *For My Negativity* (2019). He is the Founding editor of the *Kitara Nation Poetry Series*, a compendium of poetry books written by young Ugandan poets. Kagayi's works have been adopted for theatre performance by various dancers, vocalists, dramatists and theater poets. He lives in Kampala.

Dinanga, the Ark of refuge

Raïs Neza Boneza

Eighteen days since the ship began it voyage toward the distance capital town of Kinshasa-Malebo; on the majestic River Congo; sailing slowly and hesitantly on the vicious liquid leaving behind the foretold fall of a regime in disarray.

We have tamped everything down under the bags of cassava; the life conditions are unimaginable on the barges.

Solitude!

When the shadow of the night appears, the torrential equatorial rains choose to flagellate us with no leniency

During the day and under the torrid sun, the tsetse flies bite us relentlessly with no mercy.

Kraaaak!

Suddenly, once again, trapped into a bank of sand.
The roaring of the engine hangs over our weakened heart.

The Dinanga vessel is exhausted

Drifting over five hundred kilometers from *Boyoma city*, nearing *Lisala* the birth town of the eagle of *Kawele palace; Mobutu Sese Seko.*

The weakened Dinanga has thrown itself in the submerged sandbank.

Piled up with the merchandises, the passengers are grieving…

Yeah! Weeping and mourning such is our quotidian burden on this haunted ark of refuge.

The malevolent has arrived.
One or two departed par day.
Life is obscure.
The number of affected is yet to be known:

A death from dysentery,
A death from misery.

The time is suspended
Days have passed
Without fuel, we are helplessly stuck into the wet sand in the middle of the serpent river, Congo River

Meanwhile, things fall apart:

In front of us, in Kinshasa, the leopard has fled…
Moreover, behind us: the kadogo-child-soldiers have dismembered the giant one, Zaïre…

The light of our faith dissolves living us on the moist island of misfortune.
We are but a sample of what people from all corners of the land are enduring.

Grief –
Abandonment –

Now among the bags of manioc, under the trap of wealth, a new victim shies away.

A friend, a sister and brother, who yesterday was well full of hope,
 and dreams but vanishing today.
While currently in my reminiscence, his face remains forever etched into my spirit:

A soul who fight to survive.
Alone, a refugee on the boat,
Attacked by diseases …
His heart want to let go …

Along the River Congo; memory in the whispering winds -

Urugo, HOMESTEAD
Raïs Neza Boneza

Alone on the shore of the Tanganyika
Stands the kraal of drummers.
Above the plain of the Rizizi river,
Stands the empire of the Inanga poets.
They sing and relate.

But then,
The cadence of modern cannonade arises
Stifling these glorious songs and the rich poems!

The children of thunder against the bashingatahe wisdom
The ancient replaced by deviltry;
 Ancestral truths replaced by profanation.

In the paternal enclosure besieged delusion;
The words of the wise Bagabo, forgotten.

            –They violate and betray!
Now, raise the sun
On the great summit of the Bugamba.
Hope is piercing the heavens:
The gentle rain of a Kwizera raconteur
Falling once again on a parched earth.

The offsprings of the lightning return to the bosom of their ancestors
To revive the song of peace in the Urugo.

La Paysanne
Raïs Neza Boneza

After the deep silence of the night
A new smiling sun
Dressed in woolen cloth
Her jug on her head full of millet brew

As the path is so narrow
Early morning
She takes the strait
Going and ready for the harvest of spring

On the dew of greens
First knock of the holly
On the land for her family
She invokes the verbs of her forbears.

Nice smell of the sand
Soil comes from the anger of a volcano
As a flowering wisdom, a memory of fertility

Ready for the crop
Praise for the honor of the dignified women in the village
Songs of vintage

They flock from all the areas
And with the rhythm of melodies of fields
Women celebrate the season
Around the new seeds.

At dusk to my Tate's home (Grandma)
Raïs Neza Boneza

After a long day walking
between the gardens along the hills
Crowned of Bugombas banana trees,
When the air becomes still
And the insects begin to go chide,
I can hear "Tate" occupied;
And with pride making our dinner.

Later, when we have eaten well,
And are feeling content,
We sit down in the living room
Meanwhile, it grows dark outside,
While time to listen to the radio news is spent;
And to the west is where daytime is sent.

When this is fulfilled,
And most of our chores have been done,
We settle down at a table,
And play a « mancala » bead game.
–Whether one win or one lose,
it always is gratifying

After our amusement,
Then comes the time to sleep,
We go from room to room,
Closing the shutters with a final creak;

And for my last sigh I whisper :
"My Grandma Tates home, my paradisiac retreat"

Then all is silent,
And pleasant dreams are all that our thoughts keep.

Nandi
Raïs Neza Boneza

I have reached my destination; I trace calligraphies.
My quill seems to pour its ink unto the banks of the Tanganyika Lake.
The sacred place to which from the other side of the frontier;
I confined my boredom and worries when I was that youth.
Nevertheless, always along my way.

How have I arrived at the kraal of the oldest wisdom? *Hekima!*

These legendary drummers armed with virtues,
Keepers of tradition of tolerance and pride.
This is a story or yet another imagining.
However, I am as often inspired and consoled by the lake.

We always went there together.
We are from the lake, she and I.

She who freed me every morning from the prison of my subconscious that
shrouded me whenever sleep appeared on the horizon.

She writes too.

She colors verses in the sand of the beach,
or paint figures in the water on the lake.

We are from the lake. She and I.

We are very close because we had the lakes in common, our nuptial bed.
We are united, almost intimate, and love had never been so noble.

She and I

Together in the lake, that nourishes our desires, passion for freedom
Nandi belongs to the lake, a beauty that surpassed that of the muses.
Moreover, in her eyes, as on the shores of the Tanganyika Lake, I found my
liberty.

Nandi has fallen sleep and watch over her.

Tunda, the Flower
Raïs Neza Boneza

I am born from your eyes, Lovely sun
I take form
And live in your fertile heart
Full of a thousand fireworks
Fruitful of a thousand eternal felicities

Gently,
Gently and softly

I bury myself into your hidden lips
Rainbow coloured smackers
And I die to spring from a soft crash of breeze
I die to live

Second Dimension
Raïs Neza Boneza

Near his table rests a glass of water;
Through his window he glances at passersby;
He observes and always waits, waits, waits.

Bitterness nourishes his being;
Subjected to misunderstandings
And false airs of 'people'
He is a prisoner.

He sits, hands cupped around his chin
Solemnly thinking.
In his dream, his spirit escapes
The world of hardships
And travel in the expanses of the wild blue sky.

He leans on his table, half worried, half-contented.
In this place of his there is no compassion;
Evil prowls around its prey;
Rancor sings its melody of morning.

A stranger to his land,
He melancholically sips from his glass—
A sip of freedom.

Marginalized and needy,
Very far is the wind of liberty blowing for him
He is clandestine, always without address,
Not a nomad, but a recluse in the midst of humanity.

In his unbroken crystal enclosure,
He follows the echoes of his silent screams.
A rock of madness, only solitude answers him.

He startles! His heart rapidly beats!
He rises from his bed!
Ah! It's only a nightmare!

Raïs Neza Boneza was born in the former Zaïre, now Democratic Republic of Congo. He is the author of three poetry collections, two books of non-fiction and several articles and essays on transformative justice. He has travelled extensively in Africa and the world as a lecturer, educator and consultant for various NGOs and institutions. His work is premised on peace and conflict transformation and human-rights issues coming out of Africa and the Diaspora. Boneza is currently a freelance journalist based in Trondheim, Norway.

1984! A Lesson on How to Wear Jordache Jeans
Sitawa Namwalie

First buy a pair; two sizes too small,
Bring them home.
Next,
Find a bed,
Lie on it.
Lie flat on your back, with your feet touching the ground.
Pull on your Jordache jeans,
Squeeze yourself in,
Slowly, bit by bit, the opposite of a snake sloughing off skin.
Ignore the resistance, the push of living flesh trying to escape.
Pull them past your knees,
Slowly wriggle them up your thighs, all the time hold your breath,
Don't give in to the pain!
Fight your way into those jeans!

Once you have them on,
Zip them up gently,
Gently, I said,
Any sudden rush will have consequences!
Trust me,
You don't want to nip your skin in the jagged teeth, of the metal zip, of your
Jordache jeans.
Be patient, it's not over yet,
Beauty takes commitment.

Next!
Fill a bath with warm water, as if you are going to take a long slow soak.
Climb into the bath,
Yes, with your Jordache jeans still on.
Lie flat on your back in the water, relax,
Ten minutes will do the trick.
Lie back,
Feel the water, soaking into your jeans.
Lie back,
Feel the water mould your jeans to every curve of your body.
Lie back,
Feel the warm water,
You and your Jordache jeans are fusing, becoming one.

Lie back.
Feel!

And lastly, peel your new skin off,
Dry it in the hot sun.
Put them back on,
Step out, new jeans, thigh-high-six-inch-stiletto-boots.
And sizzle!

A Father of Nine Children
Sitawa Namwalie

I love all my children, all nine of them. The man insisted. But his eyes were hungry for sons. He sought out his one boy, mirrored his contours in his eyes. On his son's face, he traced the angles of his father's expressions; etched in memory. He dissected the arrangement of his grandfather's features; concentrated especially in the region of the eyes.

I love all my children, all nine of them. Yet, he remembered. He remembered how pride bloomed in his chest when he first heard; the drought had come to an end. At last. A son has been born.

I love all my children, all nine of them. But with eyes hungry for boys, he sought out his solitary son. His voice caressed the boy's name. "Kisilu." Each syllable stretched, held in the mouth, elongated, measured in time.

I love all my children, all nine of them. But, at night he dreamed he was a magician, he turned all his surplus daughters into sons. And, at last; quenched the hunger his eyes harboured for sons.

How to Receive Aid?
Sitawa Namwalie

How does one receive aid?
What a dilemma?
One word floats up clearly, flashes at me, teasing in a rather obvious manner.
"Obsequious," that's one way!
Bono and Bob Geldof are raising all that money for Afrika!
For the poor, the hungry, the sick, the suffering, for me and you. Get ready.
Get obsequious, ready.

Bend your knees, outstretch your arms, let your head lean to one side, the
right is good, but the left will do just as well,
Twist your features into a careful rictus of suffering,
Your face is dry, caked in a thin layer of misaligned dust.
Good, good
Eyebrows raised, slack mouth, eyes vacant.
There is nothing home but perpetual hunger and motley suffering,
Hover on your feet, between standing and falling.

That's one way to receive aid.
But that's the old way.

There is a new exciting way to receive aid!
One guaranteed to blur the distinction between giving and receiving,
After all, we now live in a unipolar world,
There is no third, second, first world!
East, west, rich, poor, Africa, no one is under-developed!
The word donor is passé,
We're all "partners",
It's so much cleaner don't you think?
#We/are/one!

So how to receive aid today?
Take it with belligerence, the money, the food, the clothes!
Be haughty, when you take it,
As if accepting all that aid is an insult, to you and your ancestors,
And it is, it injures your pride!
So, take it with anger!

To lend an authentic air,
Hover between taking and refusing,
Spit at the donor and thrill them with your swear words, loud and nasty!
*You idiot, you bloody fool, who do you think I am? I'm not poor, I don't need
your bloody hand-outs, your old shapeless clothes, your smelly left-over food, puh!
I am not your one story!*
Level the field!
Bite the hand that gives, bite it hard!

But. Don't break skin when you bite, it's only a charade.
Here is where those acting classes come in handy, the ones you took when
you thought you too could be the next Lupita,
When you thought indeed, all dreams are valid, like she said,
Act, act, act, your life depends on it, so act!

It's all a charade!!
Do remember, the donor is still king,
You want him to come back next year to save you?
Don't you?
He must save you, when your crops fail,
Save you when Ebola ravages the land and when next an earthquake strikes.
And, you will need saving when your dictator goes rogue, again.
Shreds your rights, threatens to snuff out your life!
So, don't overdo it!
Bite that saviour's hand,
But; make it feel like a kiss!

Sitawa Namwalie is a writer and performer. In 2008, her first dramatized poetry performance, Cut Off My Tongue, was successfully performed in Nairobi, and was later selected for the Sundance Institute Theatre Program's first East African Theatre.

When I am Me
Betty Kituyi

Silencing me,
there is interior,
she is young
and spacious.

She waits to know me,
she waits for me
to be me.

A silent waiting
on the core,
I meet this woman
who has grown to be me.

Because she is
I am,
because I am,
she is who she is.

Willing friend who waits
at mother's home
come,
come because I call,
I call because
you can come,

You are here with me,
here in me,
here for me,
here we are,

Knowing friend
who asks not
why I am,
and Knows enough
not to know,

Know me for me,
with too much light
blurring,
with little darkness in seeing,
with friendly nothingness that protects,
with dark nights that lure sleep,

Come,
scary darkness that attacks,
come full darkness that births babies -
me,

of hiding moons
and fleeing loves,
of blinking stars
at far glances,

Waiting mercies
that draw upon coming near,

A shy me
who met terror in the face,

The terror is not
knowing why
I know.

The questions
That wait the asking,

The answers that
cannot be heard,

And because
I do not want to
know the asking
of questions,
I am happy
knowing some
answers
do not exist
so I do not
ask questions,

So I will not
say
and she will not ask

Her nature is spirit
of nothing in the matter,

She is spirit
in the wholeness
of my being,

Spirit nature
of even flows,
flow
in the hollowness
of parallel tribes.

Pioneering Feet
Betty Kituyi

Walk dear feet
on the ground that shakes,
pull through the thickets
where no one ever walked before,

Be the first
to beat this path
into being,

Walk like a pilgrim
on long stretches of hardships
and hidden corners
of darkness,

Walk
the journey of life
though the ground beneath shakes,

You are brave
who is sinking
but chooses to walk,

Along this walk,
may you be led
into burning bushes
where you can hear the I AM.

Against the Unknown
Betty Kituyi

The fear of the unknown
brings my heart to a shuttering lilt.

Not knowing brings me to a surprise key
to my approach,
a stream of ideas flow
and wash my heart along with it.

The surprise key happens to be stored
somewhere at our home
mother feeds me on the konja*
which is the natural in her,
at an old age,
she beams a teenager's smile,
proof that inside me is a child waiting
for unknown adventures life brings.

With mother's presence
golden beams of light fall upon my face,
the fear in me softens and
I rebel against shadows of the unknown.
Flow

I am arriving at a safe distance,
because I stretched
for everything to become
the attentive clarity of choices I made,

Standing at ease with ease
without fear
and bathed in beauties unknown,
I am arriving at this landscape of easy control,
where flow is the name of things,
and joy is a pool I can play in.

Arriving here where mercy is a handshake
hidden in luminescent paths of peace,
I am at a place
where even I can unfold
In diminishing self-righteousness.

Flowing from within are streams
of healing contours
for all that is hard
and I am left,
bending to revere.

Cloud Escape
Betty Kituyi

What would happen to my view
if I let the clouds roll on each other in their moods?
what would happen
if I let then form dragons gods
in their formless flow?

If the gods were to build my house?
would I sleep on tree tops
and watch the world drift by
like a giant ship on this trip we call life?

And what have we done to our world?
have we created to free ourselves?
or created to confine us in our limitedness?

What if in this limited place
of terror and ugliness,
I chose to find habitation in the clouds
where I can be bounced from one cloud to another
like trampoline jumps
when I chose to tease myself
out of that settled boredom.

Will I stretch and role?
will freedom become mine
to stretch like a hunter with his spear?
will the savannahs shift to the skies
If mine is to let go?

How about dance?
do I need feet to dance
on the carpeted canopies of time?
Will angels become my dance partners?
or eagles my guides to higher skies?

And who is blocking my world view?
is it the sky scrapers
or myself choosing to stare at mud floats
or rubbish damps?

Like cirrus,
why choose to be condensed,
when I can stretch to conquer the skies?

Missed Communion
Betty Kituyi

I have to let go
I have to give of myself
I have to move into the circle

This isn't working,
it is a stiff wall between us -
That isn't me standing there looking wooden.

We are not an institution
we are not a cultural tribe,
you are not a man,
I am not a woman -
we are individuals unique in our flaws,

Let us harness our brokenness
let us bring the formlessness of it
into the circle,

The centre invites,
it is our leading that will reveal
the hidden rules to this game.

Bring in your height
bring in the whole length of it,
let us curl it in our circle
let us build a tower from the height
of our straight ways

We have to write new rules to this game,
but they have to be those that will allow us
to win at failing to play it well,

There is no single path to the stars,
the sky is floating with foamless clouds,
we too can become the tour guides
of each other's cloud to the stars.

It is not too late to start,
we have to record that the dew
on the grass blades in our backyard
are tears of missed communion
on our dark nights.

Painting the Colour of Light
Betty Kituyi

In a rare moment
you allow yourself time
to watch the tiny waves of chemistry happening
between toe touches,
when nothing is said,

You notice the parting darkness upon
a light morning
stretching into happenstance of a together.

For a longtime,
you relax your grip of things
and start to observe yourself learning
from un expected source
by un expected teacher.

The lesson points
have been arranged cautiously not
to scare the moth flapping around
the candle flame that has loomed out of the dark
onto a morning that is already overtaken
by the chirping birds.

You have gone on a trip
that seems safe,
illuminated with lessons in ways
to behold the other.

It is time to notice the breathe
coming in and going out,
lifting your chest in every exhale.
It is a moment
to paint your toe nails
with the colour of light
appearing in the far corner of your communion.

You are a drift wood in a current
relentlessly efficient,
to carry whole weights of burdening expectations
away from the current of streaming feelings.

You are a sailor
in this strange horizon you happen upon,
with a lifetime to learn
how to find yourself
in a light zone
that accompanies the intimacy you allow to happen.

In moment of dispersing thin clouds,
you dance lightly
with a wondrous haze,
loosing and gaining
at the same time.

In that moment,
you become.

Betty Kituyi is a manager at *Fundi Bots* an organization promoting scientific education in Africa. She holds a Bachelor of Education and a masters degree in Chemistry. She is the author of two poetry collections, one of which has been published in the UK. In 2009, Ms Kituyi left her lecturing career at Kyambogo University to head an informal science program, *Cafe Scientifique*, linking young people with working scientists. She is a mother and wife.

The Women are Here
Josh Mali

For ages you reigned and waxed strong
Clouding their being for a time so long
For years you rained unspeakable wrongs
Limiting their abilities with contrived thongs
Brother, the women are coming....

You kept them in the kitchen as you ate their chicken
You buried their dreams, so you could live your own
You gagged their tongues, so yours could wag
You covered their heads so yours could be seen
You made them lie to protect your name
It's all over now, man, the women are coming!

You used your muscles to find your way
You assumed it was the way to satisfy your urges
Ignoring their pleas for you to stop
You claimed they didn't know what they want
And took their NO for their unuttered YES
Your time is up, the women have come!

You maneuvered your way into powerful places
And made yourself the master of all
You surrounded yourself with your penile kind
And removed the rungs to halt their ascent
You stifled their tongues and drowned their voices
This you'll do no more, the women have come.

You rode a wave of bloated superiority
Nourishing your ego on traditional norms
You diminished their chances by tethering them
To domestic chores and lowly paying stations
You gave them crumbs while you kept the buttered bit
Your time is up, the women have come!

They're leaders running governments and managing trade
And auditors making sense of the books you messed up
They are directors and managers of companies and humans
And researchers discovering new ways to arrest global problems
Still find it hard to believe these lines?
There's a new game in town, man, the women have come!

They're campaigners seeking justice and equality for all
And communicators telling the world patriarchy was but a lie
They're doctors fixing broken limbs and saving precious lives
And engineers and architects with skills to tap into
They're teachers and professors imparting new knowledge
Get on board, bro, the women are here!

They're shaking traditions that kept them in bondage
And challenging dubious beliefs that sustained the injustice
They've taken charge of their bodies and their destiny
And reclaimed their space in the uneven human sphere
They've recovered their voices and now they speak up
Listen, it's real, man, the women, are here!

Voices from the Sea
Josh Mali

Dusk falls fast as the tide goes high
From the wondrous sea a breeze sweeps by
Bearing tidings of Mother Nature's approval
Of an age-long force that defies removal

There, in the wondrous expanse of the aquatic theatre
Where but a few play with creatures of the water
As the moon brightly smiles and the stars twinkly dance
Over lovers who laugh and kiss like it's their last chance

There, do we laugh at the miles that separated us
Chit-chatting and agreeing it was but a plus
Distance, they say, has a way with fondness
For there, by the waves of the sea, are we to witness

There, entwined, stand we, you and I
Staring, as whispers, birds and minutes fly by
Beckoning the imminent helpless longing
That comes with your departure's dawning

There, in the howling and clapping
Of waves that come surging and snapping
Emerge boats of whispers and jests from the sea
Reminding us of the distance that soon will be

There, in the roaring of the colossal sea
Are voices asking what else we can see
And there, in our eyes, see we what we seek
As we look on in silence, yet none shall speak

Talking to you
Josh Mali

Talking to you is the perfect ploy
To make a soul erupt in joy
For in your smile lie little bubbles
And ripples of laughter that disband all troubles
Talking to you is the joyful journey
That leads a man to gourds of honey
For in your words lies sweetness supreme
That flows down my being like an endless stream
Talking to you is the soothing lullaby
A melody that kisses all worries goodbye
For in the music of your words is the pill
That calms the mind and pays the sleep bill
Talking to you is the biggest trigger
That spurs a soul to seek something bigger

For in your words lies the sweetest dream
That rouses the mind to seek the cream
Talking to you is the poetry
Whose lines redefine our geometry
Giving the world an artistic thrill
And many dull things a better appeal

Who Will Marry Her?
Josh Mali

Like a giraffe in the wild
She walks with her head high
Stepping carelessly in the territory of men
Her dress hangs like a dancer's costume
Barely covering her thigh
Bereft of all morals, who'll marry her?

A giraffe walks with elegance
Seeking prime vegetation
She steps where she pleases,
Choosing her own dance tune
Her flanks may please your wandering eye
Yet her appetite lies not with the grass, I'll marry her!

She's read many dangerous books
And cares not how she looks
She sits and eats at the table with men
Raising her voice in unladylike fashion
Teeming with steaming noxious knowledge
She'll raise rebels of your girls

Draped in her shiny book armour,
She scoffs at your opinion of her looks
Creating her own place at the table
She amplifies her voice to drown the noise of men
Seeking to free her kind from bondage
She toasts to relishing the rebel label

She cares not for the old ways
And won't kneel for elders and men
Your place as head will be no more
You'll man the kitchen and tend the babies

Like a restless gazelle, her career outruns her maternity
You'll get few babies out of her liberal womb

The old tree shall not be cut down
Yet pest-infested parts must be removed
Two heads are better than one,
Is a saying from the good old days
The kitchen and babies won't define her
Her womb is no farm for my humanoid crops

Panda gari, in English
Josh Mali

They said they came to stop the blatant theft
Of voices of citizens once their foes had left
They said they came to end a dominion
So you and I could have an opinion
They said they sought to end political prisons
But made our homes prisons for ridiculous reasons
They said they came to stop the wanton killing
But now do it on camera and find it thrilling
They said they bore arms to free us all
But took our freedom and made us small
With laws that gag and guns that scare
They've forced the helpless to turn to prayer
They shoot to kill and, rarely, to maim
And hope that fear will make us tame
They said they came to stop the cars
That took folks away and left us scars
The infamous panda gari, they promised to banish
But now shout, "Get in the car!" ere they vanish!

Josh Mali taught Communication Skills at Makerere University, and high school Literature and English (at Aga Khan High School, Kampala and St. Joseph's Girls Secondary School, Nsambya), before starting a career in journalism with the BBC in 2006. He is the author of a children's book, *The Bad Friends* (Fountain Publishers, 2003) and three plays, including *The Betrothal* (2019), and *God of Small Hands*. His first collection of poems, *The Women Are Here* was also published in 2019. *The Super Dancer* is one among a collection of short stories he is currently working on. Besides a degree in Education (Language and Literature), he holds an MA in Communications, Media and Public Relations from the University of Leicester.

In an Instant
Gervaz Lushaju

In an instant
I looked up and our gazes got caught up
In an instant
And little bit of your soul pours into mine
As eyes lock briefly there it is felt,
A hunger
In an instant
Even destiny itself held its breath
In an instant
My need to know you more than i do screams to be met
In an instant
I am disembodied to gaze upon this moment and yet i am in it
in an instant
I am finished
in an instant
we run and leap forwards crushing past the walls we built around us
in an instant
we let our inner selves seep into each other rushing like rivers meeting oceans
in an instant
I cannot help but give all of myself
in an instant
anything less would not be enough
in this instant
I know
in this instant
I am
in this instance
we are.

Body Noise
Gervaz Lushaju

Sometimes my body talks too loudly
forgetting its manners when with other people
It let's slip something it wants
something it sees and just can't quite have
Sometimes my body is overcome with the urge to be pressed against another
to be meshed
to be indistinguishable one from the other

Sometimes in a casual conversation
you say something smart and in that instant, I am almost unable to any longer
be apart from your innermost being
A feeling
Sometimes my body won't let me sleep
making disturbing demands of me
I keep filling my fists with my sheets
and my mind in twists....

Well-Meaning Fools
Gervaz Lushaju

Look at you, thinking you know what is best
Telling me not to have that drink because red wine makes me unwittingly
promiscuous
And that I am prone to declarations of love and and unsettling confessions

Well-meaning fools the lot of you
Laughing at my bad jokes as you hide my cigarettes, so I don't kill myself and you
all with my secondhand smoke

Well-meaning fools
Telling me how to live MY life, telling me if I carry on this way I will die alone
and never find someone to marry

Well-meaning fools! keeping me occupied so I don't text my ex because certainly
they will text back and regretfully, I will regress into who I was
before you
before I started listening to all you well-meaning fools

why won't you let me be? surely, I will bear the consequences of my doing must
you really try this hard to stop my undoing and yet I have told you a thousand
times
I am fine
I am fine with my ruin
well-meaning fools all of you! You are lucky I have no one else to call "friends" and I
am certain our relationship will come to an end as soon as you all stop being right,
as soon as you stop accurately predicting the outcomes of my bad choices I will
leave you, as soon as I stop running back with regret, tears and sad noises
until then
I am stuck with all of you
my well-meaning fools.

Black Mirror
Gervaz Lushaju

You are only black at the roots not at the tips
You are not truly black because you lack a little flesh near the hips
You are black on your skin, but you talk like you are not black from within
You are black but not black enough because you do not have a certain mentality about certain things
You are black but to you it's a color but to us it is a state of being
We determine if you are black because we are what give black its meaning
You are black if you had a struggle
You are black because you were smuggled
You are black if in some way it has set you back you're not at your best because somehow it causes you to lack
You are black
You are black if you hold the same prejudice as we do
You are black because before you were born an injustice was done to you
You are black because someone else isn't
You are black because we now subscribe to the mentality of identifying as a color to protest years of being identified only as color
You are black because you can say a word that no else can
You are black because we have certain expectations of you as man
How does a color become a culture?
How does a culture become identity
Are you person
Or are you black?

Exist
Gervaz Lushaju

I needed to make you feel like you are more than the space you fill
So, I hugged you and held you close so that you can fill the space between my arms and my chest
And as our chests meet, I need you to feel my heart beat against yours and for you to know that you are here and you exist
If only for me
If only for this moment
If only enough to bear the pain of your own mortality
Though I press against your flesh, though I listen for the warmth of your breath on my neck, yet you are more than this

What makes you cannot be held
cannot be taught
cannot be said
cannot   be   touched
cannot be kissed
I will let you go now so you can leave me,
so that after you go, I can call you back
because I need you to know what it is
to be to missed

Home
Gervaz Lushaju

The taste of cooked plantains wraps my mother's love in salted banana leaves,
Here it will not go bad
It will stay warm until I need it
The feel of the calluses in my father's palms places my admiration in the strength of pulling the sisal edges of the fish nets
Everyday
This is the home I will always know

Long silver coloured lake fish
Red brown soil
The colour of soot above my mother's fire on the coral orange brick and mud walls of an elephant grass thatched house
The pale brown straw mats that have been worn out just enough to be comfortable and but not thrown away
This is the home to which I will always go

It is the taste of the water from the large clay pot
It is the smell of my grandfather's cow skin spread that is balding in the middle where we have sat more often than on its edges
The smooth wooden walking stick with a ball like end and the tap it adds to the rhythm of his footsteps
The caws of the hamerkop birds occasionally interrupted by chickens
Tall tales with cautionary endings
laughter
Love
This is the home I will remember

Gervaz Lushaju *is a Tanzanian photographer and graphic designer with a background in fashion and textile design.*

The Gift of Words
Prof. Laban Erapu

When others stand up
To count their blessings
I sit back and thank God
For giving me the greatest gift of all!

While everything else
Has been taken from me
At one time or other
I thank God that no one
Has ever thought of taking away
My greatest treasure!

Poor as I am in anything else
I have this that surpasses all wealth
This that gives me grace
Time and again
When all else has let me down.

The gift of words
May not count for much
In the reckoning of most people
But for me it is everything
That I ever wanted
It is all that I ever dreamt of
For it is my daily bread!

I Asked My Heart
Prof. Laban Erapu

I asked my heart
How will I know
That I've found the right one for me
And my heart said
Don't worry,
I'll be there I'll be the first to know
I promise I'll not lead you astray.

Then I asked my heart
What if
And my heart replied
Don't worry, I'll be there
We'll cross that bridge
When we get there!

But I wanted to know
And my heart said
Don't worry, I'm strong
Though I'm wounded and bleeding
I can stand the pain
And if I can survive it
So will you!

Delicate Wings
Prof. Laban Erapu

Step
softly
when you walk
on my dreams
for the words I write
are tender shoots
untouched by sun
unkissed by rain
like the delicate wings of a chrysalis
opening tentatively to test the wind
that blows
tenderly
buoyed
by hope
of tomorrow
when my time
comes.

Walk
gently when you trample
on my birthright
for the things I say

may seem trivial
but that is all I know now
and that is how best I can speak
so give me a chance
to find my voice
and I'll learn to sing in tune
with life's experience!

Laban Erapu *is Professor of Literature, Bishop Stuart University, Mbarara; an independent publishing consultant with* East African Educational Publishers; *and Managing Director/ Chairman Designate with* Creative Digital Productions Ltd.

The Knell of Doom
Julius Ocwinyo

Awash in moonlight
The owl hooted,
Screeched,
Enraptured,
Rupturing
The gossamer shroud of sleep
That uneasily I carried.

The screeching owl
Perched above,
Balanced,
At ease,
Ominous intrusion
Plugging that hole
In my roof,
Clicking its hoary feathers clean
As I stare up
At this weird presence
That has rent
The flimsy
Garment
Of my sleep.

The owl
Eerily, weirdly *hibou*[1],
As if on cue
Shrieks!
Under a spell,
I ask: 'What message of doom
Do you bring?'

Buffetted and stunned
In the swirling squall
Churning my mind
My bruised thoughts
Cast one look at Time:
>Montage of heart-searing nostalgia
>For yesterday
>For vanished youth, unthriftily spent
>Staling into dully leaden today
>Clouded in nausea,
>Spilling into baffling tomorrow,
>Ungraspable
>Receding
>Vanishing into patina'ed obscurity.

The owl screamed –
Again!
>And I think
>I hear the shriek of doom
>For the dead-living, the living-dead
>In this limbo, this zombieland.
Inspired, I ask God
To grant
My one wish:
>To spare me
>This soul-deadening grey-drab vista
>Of futility,
>Unendable, Unending,
>To snuff out the light
>In me,
>Transient slumberer.

1. *hibou*: French for 'owl'.

Julius Ocwinyo was born in Teboke, a township in Apach district, Uganda, in 1961. He trained in both a Catholic seminary and secular institutions. After qualifying as a teacher of English and French, he taught at various educational institutions. Eventually he quit teaching and took up book publishing as a career. Currently he is Associate Editor at Fountain Publishers, one of the leading publishing houses in the Great Lakes region, Africa. Ocwinyo is the author of *Fate of the Banished* (1997), a novel that has won national acclaim. It has also been on the Ugandan A-level Literature syllabus and is currently taught at a number of universities in Uganda and Kenya. Another novel, *Footprints of the Outsider*, has just gone on the Ugandan A-level Literature syllabus and is also taught at university. Furthermore, Ocwinyo has written works of prose targeted at youth and children and his poems have been published in a number of anthologies.

SHORT STORIES

Billy Kahora	(Kenya)	53
Sam Okoth Opondo	(Kenya)	70
Troy Onyango	(Kenya)	86
Dennis Mugaa	(Kenya)	94
Aress Mohamed	(Kenya)	102
Dessale Berekhet	(Eritrea)	113
Alex Teyie	(Kenya)	122
Lucky Grace Isingizwe	(Rwanda)	130
Barbara Oketta	(Kenya)	139
Lilian Akampurira Aujo	(Uganda)	146
Jameela Siddiqi	(Uganda)	156
Derek Lubangakene	(Uganda)	163
Rosey Ssembatya	(Uganda)	174
Sophie Alal	(Uganda)	177
Ayeta Anne Wangusa	(Tanzania)	186
Carey Baraka	(Kenya)	197
Muthoni wa Gichuru	(Kenya)	207
Neema Komba	(Tanzania)	213
Regina Asinde	(Uganda)	220
Dilman Dila	(Uganda)	227
Muthoni Garland	(Kenya)	243
Davina Philomena Kawuma	(Uganda)	256
Abraham T. Zere	(Eritrea)	267
Tim Bororaho	(Uganda)	277
Bob G. Kisiki	(Uganda)	283
Josh Mali	(Kenya)	289
Julius Ocwinyo	(Uganda)	299
Acan Innocent Immaculate	(Uganda)	309
Beatrice Lamwaka	(Uganda)	315
Hilda J. Twongyeirwe	(Uganda)	319

World Pawa
Billy Kahora

JEMIMAH Kariuki is becoming Chinese.

"Charity begins at work," she says at every desk she stops at in her workplace, Domestic Revenue, ExtelComms Inspectorate. She licks her lips—a nervous habit from childhood—trying to recruit members. A few have promised to join the Chinese venture, Kianshi Multi-marketing, that she has just signed up as an agent for: Mama Kitu, the Domestic Revenue manager's soon-to-retire secretary, who has a sausage and 'Buru Buru free-range' eggs business; Bob 'just call me Bobby' Onyango, who offers green card opportunities for a price, and who starts asking Jemimah whether she can hook him up with red cards to go to China—Bobby says he needs a new product and he sees potential in their working together; Assumpta from Engineering. Then there is Silas, the intern from Domestic Revenue, and Dennis Wafula from Wires and Cables, who needs something on the side to help him pay school fees for his twelve children.

"The new Kenya is Dholuo and Gikuyu. Working together. Kenyatta na O.O. Oginga Odinga. Kenyatta Mboya—Okuyu meets Kisum City," Bobby says.

Many at the office who have bought green card promises from Bobby are yet to go to the States and are disappointed. Soon, the office's informal marketplace can't stop whispering about Jemimah's new Chinese thing. Wires and Cables, who have *shiba'd*[1] from the bribes they have gotten from stolen copper cables, start deriding it. Accounts starts looking for small ways to deduct her salary and clip her wings because of this latest sign of Jemimah's irritating ambition. All the messengers want in but are unable to cough up the Ksh 500 they need to join the Chinese scheme.

This is how it works: Kianshi offers the best consumer products from China at very affordable prices based on flexible payment instalment plans; agents receive Chinese goods upfront based on how many members they can sign up. Jemimah is determined to be the number one Kianshi agent of all the twenty-five based in the city. She met the head of Kianshi Multi-Marketing in Kenya, Han So, five months ago and has since gained his confidence. Recently, Han So asked her to come up with a more identifiable Kenyan name for Kianshi. She was his choice for that select assignment among many other Kianshi hopefuls.

Later, at lunch, Jemimah stands in the queue with other junior clerks

---

1   Swahili meaning "to be made full" or "sated.

from her department, at Mama Jacinta's. The kiosk has a smoky stillness and midday sunbeams bullet through the recycled wood walls. Once in a while, there is a large crack as the iron-sheet roof suddenly expands and contracts from the lunchtime sun and a cloud of hot *githeri*[2] washes the interior. Bessie, Jemimah's work best friend, is closest to her in the line for food. Bessie's back is to the counter, so she does not notice she's holding up the queue. Assumpta, tall and beautiful as always, stands in front of her. As she listens to Jemimah, three cheap suits from Accounts breeze past her, get their lunch, hungry eyes on Assumpta.

One says, "Sasa Beejing?"

Accounts is all male, a hundred per cent juvenile. Beejing—their latest idiotic joke making fun of the International Women's Conference in the Chinese Capital—is now doing the rounds in Accounts, spreading to Wires and Cables, and will finally be legitimised in Field Division.

Jemimah is speaking to Assumpta, who nods, her eyes roaming in their perpetual panic. Jemimah's eyes are caught by Assumpta's mouth—large, large and soft and painted carefully, and never grimacing or stretching. Bessie laughs and says, "It's a private-sector mouth. The girl will never last here."

Jemimah says at Assumpta's mouth: "Not America, Chaina is the next world pawa—everyone knows. You need to buy new Made in Chaina. Thas why I'm selling Made in Chaina. Na-Sell World Pawa."

"Yeah, yeah," says Assumpta in her serious way, "I went shopping in Cheng Du last year. Their kitchen tiles are very good."

"Korea, Iddian, Firipino watever," Bessie says. "I forgot my purse in the office. Can you pay for me?" Bessie has been forgetting her purses and having her handbags stolen ever since she lost her Nigerian boyfriend two years ago and stopped living what she used to call *la vida loca*. During friendlier moments, like month-ends, Bessie commiserates on their present vertical immobility in life with a standard sigh.

"My sista mon, Jemmie," she says this in her slow, stalking and deliberate way, in a passably bad Nigerian accent that, with time, has acquired old Jamaican reggae lyrics. Bessie is long rather than tall—like a gawky giraffe calf. "Pay for me beans and *chapati*[3], please."

'Jemmie' suggests to just about everyone that Bessie is unlikeable because she is high maintenance. She hates it when Bessie calls her 'Jemmie', though her short quirkiness has learned to shrug this off—like many things about Bessie—because of her marketing training at Kianshi. Part of her understands that her plump, round-shouldered lightness is complemented by Bessie's dark, long features.

"Kwisha," says the young man behind the counter, with a smile, and

---

2   A Kenyan traditional meal of maize and legumes, mostly beans of any type, mixed and boiled together
3   Unleavened flatbread

a flourish of the *sufuria*[4] lid. He bangs two lids together, "*Chakula*[5]. Food *finito.*"

Accounts are already seated, enjoying what was supposed to be Domestic Revenue's *Chapati* Madondo.

"Aieee … Kijana, not again!" Bessie says with her elbows.

Kijana laughs, "Last month's money. Mama Jacinta *anakutafuta*[6]." He bangs his lids again, and a cheer rises from where Accounts are seated. Domestic Revenue has to do *chapatis* and Stoney Tangawizi. They all leave the queue. Bessie glares at Jemimah who stands, oblivious of their food disaster, still talking Chinese products to Mama Jacinta. Mama Jacinta owns the kiosk and is making her way to the till when she sees Jemimah. It's too late for Mama Jacinta to hide. She is tired of listening to this Kianshi *biashara*[7] every day.

"Kianshi is Chinese. They do multi-level marketing. Selling Chinese products. Wait a minute … here it is," she says to Mama Jacinta, as she riffles in her bag. "As it says here … I will photocopy this for you. No, you don't have to pay for photocopies. I'll do them at the office."

Mama Jacinta holds up her hand. "Ngoja,"[8] she says. She quickly scribbles on her receipt book: Photocopy—*Jemimah to pay.*

"Kianshi is a large-scale global enterprise group. Advanced biotechnologies. Advanced… you understand. Kianshi boasts a rapid average annual growth rate—270 per cent…" Jemimah suddenly remembers the video presentation on presentation, and juts out her chest to project her voice.

The kiosk has quieted down with all occupants masticating away their lunchtime. Light beams shooting through the holes in the *mabati*[9] walls slant as the sun moves across the sky.

"Three years minimum," Jemimah continues, still standing and explaining to an entranced but skeptical Mama Jacinta. "I plan to be Kianshi head marketer. You have the Ksh 500 to join for me? There will be benefits later."

"Chapo Dengu," shouts a late customer, pushing Jemimah aside from the counter. Jemimah remembers where she is, makes her way and sits down, ignoring Bessie's hangry glower.

Now Jemimah sips at her soda, too excited to eat because Mama Jacinta might finally sign up. Counting in her head everyone in the building they work in, she does not notice Bessie appropriate her chapati. Mlima House. She thinks of all those Ministries: Labour, National Planning and the defunct Heritage. Five askaris at the gate, the women selling felt-tip pens near the chain fence around the compound, the two police and four receptionists.

---

4 A flat-based, deep-sided, lipped and handleless cooking pot
5 Swahili for "food".
6 Swahili meaning "I am looking for".
7 Swahili word for business
8 Swahili word for "wait"
9 Swahili word for roofing sheets.

Eighteen storeys in the building, fifty people per storey.

She turns to Bessie. "Like the wheel of a bike, every ka-spoke is number one. With 10 per cent of kila mwananchi in our building—thas ninety people," she says, removes a pen from her bag, and starts making notes. "I need to invest in a scientific calculator," she says. Everyone sitting at the Domestic Revenue table removes their toothpicks from their mouths and laughs.

"Shock on you," Bessie says to Jemimah. "Aloe Vera products are better," she leans in to whisper, "the cream tightens it *down there*." Jemimah knows that Bessie is angry with her for making them miss out on madondo and chapati, talking up China. She will make it up to her when she becomes a senior marketer at Kianshi and take her to the Oriental restaurants she likes so much. Jemimah has not asked Bessie to join Kianshi. She fears that her sista will be highly successful. After Obi left, she thought of introducing Bessie to Han So's brother-in-law, Jin Shu, but decided he was too short for her.

Obi, the Nigerian boyfriend, was thrown out of the country leaving Bessie rich with a Yaya apartment, two hair salons in South B and West and a cyber café in Westlands, at least for a few months, till Obi started sending his associates back to Kenya for it all. The properties, as well as the dark platinum 5-series Beemer, the Hutchings Biemer furniture. Bessie was left with some Dubai 24-carat gold trinkets, a pair of Dubai Donna Karan outfits, a queen-size gold bed with a smaller mattress (concentric squares), her stocky puppy, Boss, who looked a bit too much like Obi, and an almost life-size poster of a Dubai Tiger, all yellow and gleaming and photoshopped and crouching in a mass of cartoon-like jungle-ness.

Bessie lived with Jemimah for a while and they became friends. Jemimah knows she is Bessie's only company at the office. But the days of doing Chinese, Japanese or seafood for lunch are long gone with Obi and his money.

That Friday afternoon there is no one in the Domestic Revenues' cardboard and mkojo-smell office on the fourth floor at Mlima House. Everyone is running around, collecting money for the coming weekend from their various office enterprises. *Saa nane na forty.*[10] It is quiet. Jemimah is relieved and exhausted after two hours of detailed calculations in Mama Jacinta's small, hot office kiosk and is now thinking about the potential in the Mlima House offices. Mama Jacinta, it turns out, is a member of GLD, Amway, Aloe Vera, Herbatronics, and five merry-go-round schemes. When Jemimah hears this, she tries to convince her: "Kianshi is special. All members are a FAMILY. Chaina is the next World Pawa. Everyone knows this."

Friday traffic, shouts and smells rise from the street, the burning blue saucer of sky outside the curtain-less windows, grit in her eyes and the perpetual smell of urine and chemical lemon toilet cleaner: the things she is

10   Swahili phrase meaning "9:40"

trying to get out of her life.

Jemimah remembers the last Kianshi video she received in her P.O. Box. VISUALISE, the video says: she daydreams, driving up Community, on her way to the office. But wait a minute—passing by, drifting towards the leafier Nairobi suburbs, further west into Karen, Adams or Hurlingham—a non-working and free woman unencumbered at 3 p.m. on a weekday afternoon. Following the setting sun in the opposite direction to her 5 p.m. reality, downtown Eastlands. She has calculated. With hard work it could take up to two years.

So, immediately she gets to work, she starts drawing up the generational multi-level mind map structure for Mama Jacinta and writing up her recent lunchtime projections for her sponsor, Mr Han So. She looks around the tired Extelcomms office she knows she will be leaving soon. Jemimah underlines beneath the projections she has placed on paper—IDENTIFY GOALS NOT NEEDS—then starts working again on the new name Han So has asked for.

"Chenya, Kinya," she mutters rolling her tongue. Enunciate the vowels. She does not see the slouching figure before her for a moment. When she opens her eyes the intern she is assigned to train that afternoon is standing at her desk. Both his hands are placed on her desk.

"… Er Sammy." Her head is still on the Kianshi figures and names, but she switches haraka. "In-this-department-we-deal-with-telecommunication-revenue. We - get - photos - from - all - over - the - country - that - show - pipeline - meter - reading. Edit - and - forward - to - IT," she says in staccato.

"Eh," the boy says, and stares at the front of her blouse.

She ignores his stare and, after they go through the meter counter photos for half an hour, looks around and, making sure there is no one within earshot, pulls back her shoulders and says a new tone that she has learned from the Kianshi video: "Ever heard of multi-level marketing? While everyone is doing silly tu-small businesses in this office there is money to be made."

The intern jerks back, "Is this part of my internship?"

Jemimah ignores the Friday lunch beers on his breath, notes with surprise the expensive patterned yellow shirt he is wearing. Han So has taught her to look for potential signs of new agents and members for Kianshi.

"Nice shirt. You are a dyed-in-the-wool multi-level marketer," she says and bares her teeth trying to smile.

"What you doing after work?" he asks. They are alone in the office—3.30 p.m. "By the way… my name is Walter."

"Si Silas?"[11]

He grins.

Even better, she thinks. A thick skin. Not easily offended.

"Skiza[12]," she says smoothly, "I can't join you. Marketing training seminar.

---

11   Transl.: "Not Silas?"
12   Swahili meaning "sketchy".

4.30 Westlands."

Walter walks away and picks up the phone at the next desk, dials and stares at her.

Jemimah fishes a small mirror from her bag and carefully moves it over the new red suit with padded shoulders that she is wearing. It is one of a batch she bought in Ngara after joining Kianshi. She has thrown out the chiffon dresses with erratic hemlines and balloon shoulders that she wore when she had moved to Nairobi to from Karatina. Out too, the softer skirts with shorter hemlines and white blouses bought from Wangari at Posta. Bessie had always made fun of her, saying the clothes made her blend into Extelcomms like a good Made in China weave. She purses her, and applies lip gloss over a cold sore.

Some men from Wires and Cables have joined the intern in looking at her from over the far corner of the partitioned office. One imitates her with a clipboard. She ignores them: decides that, after all, Walter the Intern is not going places with Kianshi and heads out to meet Han So.

✎⌘✎

THEY meet near Parliament at the C & A coffee house. Whenever they meet, Han So likes to watch how the establishment works and even asks her questions that make her feel good about herself.

"You think they make money here?" Han So asks. "Where do they buy coffee? Who are their main customers?" Silly questions, she thinks.

She pretends to study the C & A coffee shop. After the mandatory month's training, she has been judging everyone around her as either a multi-level marketer or a non-marketer. Or, even worse, the bottom of the marketing heap—the traditional marketer. Han So has trained her to be wary of these. Traditional marketers like the father of her eight-year old son, Kim. Traditional marketers like her parents back in Karatina. At first, even with Han So's training, the criteria she used to tell who were marketers, non-marketers and traditional marketers was vague and instinctive. But now she has watched Han So at work and she has caught on to some of his mantras.

"I think this coffee shop is in the shifting stage from non-marketer to marketer," she offers.

Han So looks at her blankly, like she is mad. When she tries to tell him about Mlima House he does not seem too excited. He instead asks her about Extelcomm products, and listens carefully. She asks Han So about the results of her latest test and he says the results are yet to arrive.

✎⌘✎

WHEN Jemimah had gone to the Kianshi opening seminar at KICC, she had been impressed by Han So's opening presentation, which she had paid Ksh 500 to attend.

"You must avoid the number one problem of Africa: thinking luck, not hard work, will solve your problems." Now, this is something she never tires of telling her focus group during the seminars Kianshi arranges. The twenty-five Kianshi Nairobi agents are split into five focus groups that meet every Saturday to discuss marketing strategies. After the strategy sessions anyone is allowed volunteer to give a testimony. Han So has said that she has improved in her testimony telling.

She never tires of playing what they call 'the testimony game' with the five other telemarketers in her Kianshi focus group every Saturday. Each session is Ksh1,000. All have undergone the one-month training period together. Jemimah can't always remember their names. They are a sight—an exercise in Han So's faith. An old, recovering alcoholic who lost his senior marketing position at one of Kenya's largest HMOs, some bright kid just out of International School of Kenya, Han So's ever-grinning brother-in-law, Jin Shu. The rest hover on the edges of Jemimah's memory. The nervous oddity of the group doesn't matter in the face of Han So's motivational speeches, "Magnifying glass catch sun, bring power, focus energy. Then fire! Catch potential!" They all cheer and become one but whenever they try to use the same words it doesn't sound right. They've all tried this public voice in the mirror. "Magnifying glass catch sun, bring power, focus energy. Then fire! Catch potential!"

At first, she used her experience from her time at the New Redeemer Church of Christ in Karatina where she had trained to become a pastor before she came to Nairobi. She had to leave while she was still training after she started an affair with Pastor Muremi who refused to leave his wife for her, even after they had been seeing each other for at least one year. She thinks that the Karatina church testimonies did not work at Kianshi because of these unhappy memories. Han So encourages the use of personal experiences to sell products. They also practice this in the focus group. "When I first arrived in Nairobi two years ago, I lived with my relatives ... Mbari ya Mundia[13]", she says. "They hated me, but I loved them. I know I will meet many people like the Mundias when I am out there selling." In reality, the Mundias she uses as a teaching guide were vaguely hostile and pleasantly indifferent to Jemimah. She finished the testimony by saying: "In the end, Mundia wa Steven got me my first job because I had sold myself and marketed my skills. I moved to a high-rise bed-sitter in Kayole. In Nairobi, you start small small, so I started saving for better things. And I am here now."

Presently, they finish their coffee at C & A and because Han So is still

---

13   "The best of Mundia."

observing what is going on in the shop, Jemimah removes her notebook. Han So watches: how fast the waiters go to new clients? How fast the orders are? What everybody is ordering? Jemimah thinks of how far she has come since she joined Kianshi. With her new expertise she now categorizes everything aloud to practice her marketing voice: national politicians, newscasters and people starring in TV ads as either traditional marketers or telemarketers. During such sessions at home, her current come-we-stay husband, Miano wa Miano, curses and mutes the TV.

"Sawa, let's listen to YOU, nye nye nye … nye nye nye," he says. "All the time. Nye nye nye … Go on and on. Endelea …" Miano wa Miano urges with a hardcore relish that he has developed from being a spare parts dealer on Kirinyaga Road. Miano wa Miano knows how to sell spare parts and makes a lot of money so she cannot understand his contempt for her new venture. "Where is the demand?" he asks, in anger. Miano wa Miano took care of her while she was still finding her way in Nairobi. But, a few months ago, there was a huge crackdown on spare parts as part of a racket of stolen cars in Nairobi and the cash has dried up.

Once, during these regular TV battles, Jemimah switched off the TV in a huff during one of Miano Wa Miano's favourites—*Nderemo ya Mabingwa. Win-A-House Contest*. She then watched him calculating whether her action warranted some form of physical action. He gave her a speculative look and all he said was: "Niki-win the house; you won't be coming." She ignored him as he walked out of the door and made him sleep on the floor after he came back after three days, drunk, meek and dishevelled. He becomes quiet when he drinks because of the lean days on Kirinyaga Road.

"Being multi-marketer, very challenge," Han So has told her when she tells him about the lack of support at home.

Jemimah recognizes the uneasy détente that becoming Chinese has created between her and Miano wa Miano. She finds him useless now that she has more money but likes the new sense of power over a man. She wonders what he'll say when she tells him about her son. For now, she is too busy to engage in a retaliatory aggressive short-term competition with him.

And so her son, Kim, remains undiscovered by him.

The after-work crowd starts thinning in the coffee shop, heading to the bars. Han So is satisfied with his observations and they leave.

ON Monday, happy and high after three weekend meetings with Han So, Jemimah comes to work wearing a dress from China that Han So has given her from the Kianshi products. He always says that the best way to market Chinese goods is also to use them.

"It is a Qipao," Han has told her, and she repeats that to all at work. It is a long flowing deep blue garment with aquamarine herons on the breast flowing over the shoulder to the small of her back. Jemimah ignores the snickers from Wires and Cables.

Han So explained: "Also called Cheongsam. Not only for Chinese woman but beautiful all woman. Come in many style. You can sell here in Kinya?"

Her boss, PK Maina, calls her into his office. "*Kama unataka kuvaa hiyo*[14] stupid national dress you do it in your home."

"This is Chinese silk! It is called Kipao." She storms out of his office. People stare and laugh through the glass partition of PK Maina's office.

"Mambo ya wanawake," he mutters, shaking his head.

Even Bessie is not as supportive. "Imagine me coming to work in a Nigerian *agbada*[15] when I was with Obi. If and when I could. And Jemmie, you know what I mean—I had the money and the man." When Bessie says this, she places her fingers on the sides of Jemimah's eyes and tugs upwards: "Chinese." Sideways: "Japanese." And downwards: "Portuguese."

Bessie then puts her hand flutteringly to her chest leans back and says: "Nigerian."

Both women start laughing hard.

❧

OVER the next month, Jemimah notices that Han So now asks her more and more about ExtelComms products—and one day he asks her whether she can get copies of shipment invoices, credit notes and local purchase orders from the office. When she manages to sneak away the documents he wants she is surprised at how happy he seems. He even promises her more Kianshi products over the next month.

Then one day he asks: "Your boss is good man… can talk?"

She pretends to think and says: "He's a traditional marketer." Two years ago, she had an affair with her boss, PK Maina, when he was not the present brusque top-heavy man given to picking his teeth to distraction in the afternoons at the office. She was still in the white blouse, tight skirt phase. Jemimah stopped sleeping with him when he started telling everyone he was "eating Beejing."

Soon after, Jemimah met Miano wa Miano and moved in with him, and she hasn't thought of PK Maina in awhile. She asks Han So about the differential margins between Kianshi cosmetics and golf equipment. His eyes glaze over from behind his thick glasses and he curses in Chinese. "No time for joke. Time for serious. You introduce me to your boss?" he says with a smile, tapping his chest, and almost pushing his hand into her face.

---

14   Swahili phrase meaning "if you want to wear that"

15   A traditional Nigerian outfit worn by men on special occasions, ceremonies and traditional events, it is an oversized, flowing robe with wide sleeves.

When he calms down, he asks: "You know… er how you say it… where government company you work for buys…" He pretends to be picking up a telephone receiver. Bessie always tells her that men will change after a certain period of knowing them and she wonders whether this is what is happening with Han So. She tells Han So about PK Maina's recent scorn at the Chinese dress he gave her and this time he laughs and says, "Time for serious. You introduce me to boss?" She decides to forgive Han So for his strange behaviour.

Jemimah invites Han So to her office and introduces him to PK Maina. She leaves the two of them alone and they talk for three hours. Now and then she turns, everyone does, and watches the two through the transparent government glass. Finally, they laugh and shake hands. When Han So comes out of PK's office she walks him out. She can hear Accounts making their loud stadium whispers, "Beejing, Beejing na Ka-Chinese boyfriend." She also hears Bessie's loud laugh.

When she comes back, Bessie says: "Now you know how I used to feel when you'd call Emenkua, 'Obi'."

"Your boss he good man," Han So says to her later when they meet after work at the open-air restaurant near KICC. She realizes, for the first time, that he's much shorter than her. She has always thought him as big. She can put her hands all around his upper frame. Until now, she has never contemplated physical contact with him. Now she notices his small tight thrusting hips, and a charcoal coloured mouth—smoke and beer and a certain knowledge. She wonders what their children would look like. Pink to medium-brown depending on the time of day, she decides. She thinks about her son and Miano Wa Miano.

Last night, she kept waking Miano wa Miano up with screams from a recurring bad dream. Her son Kim appeared in a field of maize in the dream. He wore his grey, black-and-white boarding academy uniform. Starting at the foot of the field he wandered into the long stalks and she watched as the lilting green leaves started to whir like blades as he walked in harsh sunlight.

Miano wa Miano woke up to her thrashing and, still semi-drunk from the previous night, found this arousing. She pushed aside his gropings. These dreams have been going on for weeks. Miano wa Miano has decided that Jemimah has *kifafa*[16]. He has also found a payslip lying around, full of scribbles and evidence that there is another budgetary presence in her life, but he has said nothing.

Han So is saying. "Your boss is good man. He agree to buy Chinese phone. We soon talk about computer. You do not listen. This is important." She wonders whether she should leave Miano wa Miano because her life with him is now affecting her concentration during these Kianshi meetings with Han So.

---

16   Swahili for "epilepsy".

"I am sorry," she says in her best Kianshi voice. "I have come up with a name that sounds Kenyan for Kianshi. Kenshi," she tells him. He nods.

"When are our products arriving?" she asks.

"Factory in Shanghai burn down. Six months."

Later that afternoon, PK Maina passes by her desk and whispers: "I like your *kajamaa*,[17] Anaelewa Kenya. He taught me some Chinese words." He leers: "You know what *tongoza*[18] in Chinese is?"

❧

THE moment Jemimah has been dreading comes. Han So is to visit her two-room high-rise bed-sitter in Kayole to see whether it is safe to store Kianshi products there in the future. She cannot remember what the pamphlets says about home storage and she is worried that her home will not be good enough as a Kianshi marketing outlet. She is scared that when Han So sees where she lives he will think she cannot make a good Kianshi agent because she is not ambitious enough and lives in a hole. She has postponed visiting her son Kim at his Academy in Athi so she can receive some goods Han So has said he wants stored as testing for a bigger Kianshi venture. The school no-visit she can tell will be another trigger on the escalating hostility from her mother, whom she has not spoken to for three weeks.

Jemimah makes sure the maid removes all the wet clothes hanging in the small corridor leading to her room. She removes the *vitambaas*[19] from the red velvet jumbo sofa set, looks at them and puts them back. She opens all the windows trying to make the room larger and removes a cracked mirror that hangs on top of the TV. She stares at the small pile of books from her days as a Sociology student at Maseno. Looking at a household list on the wall, an account from one of the local shops in which she has scribbled the little Chinese she has learned, Jemimah feels small and hopeless. She crosses out the Chinese words. They are from a book Han So lent her when she joined Kianshi. He has said that, as the most promising agent, when the time comes, she will go for training at Kianshi headquarters in Beijing. She takes her monthly shopping list down from the kitchen wall.

Mwangi Shop List—July
Mafuta Boy 1kg, Milk (30 pkt) niúnǎi, Bread (8) miànbāo, Ugari, Ketepa, Tomatoes, Waru, Boga, Degu, Beans, Bebe, Hey-Ho, Mchere

With nothing to do but wait till Han So calls her, she walks out of the door and, looking down from the dangerous balcony with the low railing, her phone rings. She can see the city in the distance, and when she turns she can

---

17   Swahili for "guy".
18   Swahili for "seducce".
19   Cloth covers

see the huge white emptiness of the quarry behind the block of flats.

"Haai," she says into the phone.

"Mathee," she hears. It's her son, Kim.

As she looks down from the balcony she is surprised to see Han So emerge from a small Canter parked outside the block of bed sitters. She had hoped he would call first.

"Mathee…"

"Kimani."

"I couldn't make it… this weekend," she says. "Sorry." She feels like crying and is not sure why.

"Mathee. *Una homa?*[20] You sound funny."

"Kimani. English. English. Argh… leave that Sheng, Daddy… How are you?"

She can see below how the neighbourhood kids have gathered around Han So, "Jackie Chan, Jackie Chan," they shout, chopping their hands and kicking in the air. Han So laughs and shouts and, with a flourish, takes a Kung Fu stance and kicks out in the air:

"Ha!" The kids cheer.

Han So looks up, sees her and waves her down. Relieved, thinking he might not come up after all, she clacks down the five flights of stairs in heels, still on the phone. Looking at the huge white quarry at a distance she feels a sudden heat on her face, the white dust it brings caking her face.

"Mathee. *Mi si mlami.*"[21] her son says. "*Sitaki*[22] English."

"Kimani!"

"Okay. When are you coming? Will you bring Kenchic?"

People are lighting *jikos*[23] everywhere on the corridors of each floor. Saturday maize and beans, *githeri*[24] gas everywhere, the smells of her mother's life. There is a burst water pipe. Water overflows from the third floor to the second in a stink.

"Soon. Soon." she says to her son. "Your school is so nice. Green, big. Like where I grew up."

"*Mum imejaa wa* Cambodia."[25]

"Kambas cannot be trusted but they are not bad people … Are there any Chinese children?" she asks.

"*Hakuna ma* Jackie Chan."[26]

Jemimah paces herself, tiptoeing through the last flight of stairs—she wants to finish with her son before she meets Han So. On the ground floor.

---

20   Swahili meaning "You have a fever?"

21   Swahili meaning "I'm not lazy."

22   "I don't want."

23   Charcoal stoves.

24   Kenyan dish made of corn and beans.

25   "My mother is from Cambodia"

26   "There is no Jackie Chan here."

She sees that some of the bigger kids are playing with him. He can't see her. The kids stare at her phone. If they were alone and at night she would lose it.

"Bye Dadee… I will call tomorrow." She straightens her dress. Her face feels tight with white dust from the quarry.

"They like leettle monkeys," Han So smiles, looking at the crowd of kids gathered around.

Jemimah is thankful that Miano wa Miano is not at home. He has not come in since last night, Friday. Han So's men start stacking boxes everywhere in the small house.

Jemimah is happy when Han So doesn't ask to go up to her house.

They watch the men carry the boxes upstairs. When one box falls down the stairs Han So curses furiously: "Carefle. Carefle." Small containers and packets of seasoning fall and flutter to the ground. Han So hands out an armful to Jemimah.

"For you. Good friend of Han So. Chinese seasoning. Like Loyco."

She laughs. "How long did it take for her to stop saying Loyco?"

As the men go up and down she notices an oil stain on one of the boxes. "For cooking. Chinese fat for cooking. Some for you. Good friend of Han So," he says.

He turns to the small kiosk metres away from where they stand. "Come, let us dleenk soda dleenk," he says, his hands fishing into his pockets. He waves the kids over and ends up buying over fifty sodas and thirty *mandazis*.

"Ha ha ha. For good fliend of Han So."

Han So leaves her and goes to talk to Mwangi, the owner of the kiosk, for about twenty minutes. Han So then comes outside and waves at the men. They bring over five cartons from the Canter. Jemimah sees Mwangi shaking his head.

"Angalia *hii* label. These Omo packets are torn and they are in Chinese."

"Half-plice. For good friend of Han So," Han So says. Mwangi stops when he hears this.

"Half-plice?" he asks. Then he laughs and shakes Han So's hand.

"Money half yours," Han So whispers to Jemimah as they walk out. She likes his lips near her ear, his hair tickles and his breath is strange and exciting. "If you can supply this area with these goods. Boxes have electrical goods from China… silk from China… Some to sell. Toothpick, clockradio. Big and small. Yes? Till Kianshi product come from Shanghai." Jemimah does not mind working with strange goods till the proper Kianshi merchandise arrives.

Han So never comes back to Kayole after his one and only visit. The Canter comes every Monday at 11 a.m. to Jemimah's house to pick up the boxes she is storing for him. Miano wa Miano says nothing when he notices the full shelves in their kitchen, their small bathroom laden with Vim and Jemimah's dressing table full of Lady Gay and Limara all written in Chinese.

Things are bad on Kirinyaga Road after the police crackdown.

Han So still comes frequently to the office to see PK Maina. He does not bother telling her of these visits—now he just waves from a distance. The days when he does come over to her desk are only when she has some money for him from the Chinese Royco seasoning, Chinese Vim toilet detergent, Chinese Kiwi shoe polish and Chinese Eveready batteries that she has distributed and sold for him in Kayole, Komarock, Umoja and Dandora.

After six months, Jemimah and her focus group are still waiting for Kianshi products. This does not seem to bother Han So, who has given her money to rent out the flat next to hers so that she can store all the Chinese goods that he is now bringing in. She distributes these Chinese goods to Jogoo Road, Bahati, Kaloleni and Burma.

One Friday, PK Maina comes in wearing a deep-blue silk shirt and a glossy tie with herons that shimmer in the office dust.

"Have you heard that your Beejing boyfriend bought Maina a car?" Bessie says.

∞∞

JEMIMAH first learned about Kianshi when a street vendor handed her a small promotional leaflet in a *matatu*[27]. "Make Money. Sell Chinese products. Call No. 0740444888 and attend seminar at K.I.C.C. February 5th" the leaflet said. That's when she met Han So. A small man wearing a flashy tracksuit and dark glasses with an even smaller identical half standing by his side. Jinshu, his brother-in-law wearing exactly the same clothes. There were about two hundred people at the seminar. Han So's helpers sent away all those without employment IDs—leaving about twenty-five people in the small hall.

Once, during these first meetings she asked him what China was like and for the first time since she had met him he grinned. "There is story of famous Chinese government official with heart of general. Name is Lin Tse-hsi. My father name me after him but I don't use that name here. In 1830… 1840; I not remember exact. He refuse British product but greedy Chinese government official agree. British then bring opium and people become weak. British first say they sell to China, world power. British say British products are world power. And that Chinese will become strong. But come opium. And then opium war or Anglo–China war. Me not like that. Want to make China strong and Kenya strong. Bring products that make Kenya and China strong. Bring Kianshi. Bring World Power."

Now almost a year since starting her Kianshi adventure Jemimah is the biggest supplier of local consumer products from China in the whole of Eastlands all the way to Gikomba. Though it is not through Kianshi Marketing as she planned, she has come far since the '97 El Niño floods

---

27   A minibus or similar vehicle used as a taxi.

when she moved there. The days of getting home at midnight after wading through half of Nairobi and squeezing into *matatus* are over. Now Kayole is no longer nights spent staring and listening to the rushed pounding of rain on her ceiling at three in the morning waiting to start the next day. She thinks that in another year she will be able to buy a small Daihatsu Charade. And maybe even move from Kayole and get a bed-sitter in Buru Buru or move to Umoja. She is now the one looking after Miano wa Miano.

One Tuesday morning, she climbs into her usual 5 a.m. *matatu*. As the *matatu* pulls into the city centre, a dirty brownish light fills the sky. It is August again and the cold months are behind Nairobi. By the time the *matatu* gets to Lower Hill, Mlima House, she is warm from FM 101.8's Breakfast Show offering cash prizes, and a climbing sun.

Before she settles down, three men in brown and grey suits and grim, bland, smiling faces show up at ExtelComms. They walk directly into PK Maina's office. Everyone can see something is wrong. Two of the men sit in PK's visitors' chairs and the third, a fattish individual with folds of skin for hair, sits behind PK Maina's desk. PK Maina remains standing, alert like a schoolboy with his hands behind his back. He never sits down even as the others stand and pace leaving empty chairs to sit on.

Very little work is done in the office that day. Wires and Cables is hushed— the department could be under investigation, being the most lucrative in Extelcomms. Jemimah doesn't even pretend to work after she notices PK Maina pointing her out to the men. The fat guy in the brown jacket fingers the folds of fat on his scalp, rubs the top of his head hard, all the time smiling through the glass partition.

Later, she sees the fat man stand and feel PK Maina's mauve silk shirt between his fingers. The other men laugh silently behind the glass. Bessie is full of information, "Msichana, they are coming for you! It is for you. I know that bald guy. I recognize him from when I was with Emenkua… he works at CID."

Jemimah glares at her: "This is China we are talking about, not Nigeria. Nothing will happen. I tell you. How can you compare a world pawa with a foo-foo drug culture?"

Lunchtime comes and goes, and the men are still in PK Maina's office. Chapati Madondo today. It's that time of the month. No one can afford *nyama*[28] and this makes the atmosphere at the office more oppressive. Finally, the men leave at around 4 p.m. carrying a phone handset.

"Nothing. Nothing is wrong," PK Maina tells her when she rushes in and asks what is going on.

"Where is your Chinese *jamaa*?"[29]

"Han So is in China. His mother is sick. Can I leave early?" she asks.

---

28 Swahili word for "meat".
29 A relative or family member. Swahili word for "friend"

PK Maina waves her away. She picks up the heavy bag of GUKKI designer clothes and PANASONIC electronic samples she brought for some people at the office on the way out.

The next day the three men come back. This time they carry a large paper bag and walk straight into PK Maina's office.

After a few minutes, PK Maina comes and calls her at her desk and leads her to his office, "These men are from the State Research Bureau." He introduces them. "Nyakundi, Kaboga and Rutto." They sound like a multi-ethnic Kenyan law firm in a small town like Eldoret.

The men look at her without a word and spill cans, bottles and packets on PK Maina's desk; Royco, Vaseline Petroleum Jelly, Cooking oil, Omo, Tea, Kiwi, Homecup Chai, Lady Gay.

"We are aware that you introduced the man you call Han So to your boss, Mr Maina. We have been trying to find him for months, but he fled when he became aware. We were lucky when we learned that he is supplying a government office with fake telephone handsets. These things are costing the Kenya Revenue Authority 1 pillion a year," the fattish man says. He is Nyakundi. Today, he is in a green metallic suit faded at the shoulders.

They hand her a *Nation* newspaper, opening it up in the middle: "FAKE OR REAL: THE CHOICE IS YOURS," it reads. There are photos of all the items on the desk. "Don't worry, Madam. This can go away, as we told your boss and our friend here, Mr Maina. The Trade Descriptions Act just needs you to prove that you did not know these are fake. That you thought Han So was a legitimate businessman. And I'm sure you did not know this was a crime. That is the law for you. Ignorance is your defence." PK Maina shakes his head in agreement. Droplets of sweat fly.

Nyakundi beckons to her to come to the corner. He whispers into her ear: "Nyakundi and Co understand. But the magistrate might not... Even your Chinese boyfriend, Mr Han-Chu. Good friend of everyone... We need to find him. Don't worry. He is our friend."

Jemimah tells them everything.

The verdict: Café TwendiOne. Kenyatta Avenue. 4 p.m. *Alafu tumalizane*[30]. Bring 40,000.

⌘

A WEEK later, early in the evening, there is a knock at the door. It is Mwangi, the kiosk owner. Jemimah has never seen him like that. Dishevelled and unkempt. It's time she brought up moving out of Kayole with Miano wa Miano. They can afford it—even after she paid off the three-man gang that sounded like a multi-ethnic law firm. She notices that everybody in Kayole nowadays either looks drunk or criminal.

---

30   Swahili which roughly translates to "And we have finished" in English.

"I've already paid for this month's milk," she starts to say.

"Ngoja… you know the police put me inside for one week for selling curry powder mixed with flour as Royco," he shouts. "Your Chinese Royco. Your Chinese Omo. Asking me why it is doesn't wash. Kiwi Chinese *yako* hardens my customers' shoes. I've closed shop. Njuguna and Kimemia also bought from your boyfriend and are still inside Buru Buru police. Wait till they get out and you'll see."

"Fake or real, the choice is yours," Jemimah shouts at his back, as he thuds downstairs. She can see the city's tiny lights in the distance from her balcony. She feels like she could reach out and touch them—the city lights are so near.

"That's why they were half price!" she shouts into the night. "Shenzi!"

Miano wa Miano comes to the door and drags her in when she continues shouting and reaching out into the night as if to grab the city lights. He closes the door and explains it's just a matter of time till the police pick her up even if they have already given Nyakundi and Co. Ksh 40,000. Miano wa Miano knows these things from Kirinyaga Road.

That night, they pack with haste. Jemimah puts away all her possessions piece by piece as if she is counting the years in Nairobi. They also pack all of Han So's remaining boxes and bags full of clothes and electronics. When they leave at daybreak all that is left in the small apartment are the Kianshi brochures.

As the *matatu* swerves past Globe Cinema, Jemimah pictures Miano wa Miano and Kim, who have no idea the other exists, sitting in a shop in Karatina town with her mother. She already has a name for the shop. She will call it "World Pawa."

Billy Kahora's short fiction and creative non-fiction has appeared in *Chimurenga*, *McSweeney's*, *Granta Online*, *Internazionale* and *Vanity Fair* and *Kwani*. He has written a non-fiction book titled *The True Story of David Munyakei*. His story *Urban Zoning* was shortlisted for the Caine Prize for African Literature in 2012, *The Gorilla's Apprentice* in 2014. He wrote the screenplay for the film *Soul Boy* and co-wrote *Nairobi Half Life* which both won the Kalasha awards and were shown on the European film festival circuit. He is working on a novel titled *The Applications*. A short story collection *The Cape Cod Bicycle War and Other Youthful Follies* was published recently.

The Books of Judas
Sam Okoth Opondo

I

I ALWAYS knew this day would come. Not because I, like everyone else has their appointment with death, but because just like many others who have gone before me, my day of reckoning has been postponed many times. Now that my day is here, I will do what I have always done; betray, pray, and hope that the end which awaits me may be delayed by hastening someone else's demise. Delayed by looking away where I know I could have helped or prevented their death. Delayed by waiting until the time is right and then watch as others—blinded by their desire to be led or the comfort that comes from knowing that they are not facing the end alone—walk into the abyss, the promised end for all of us.

I am Judas.

OVER the years, I have learnt how to listen and see things that beings like me are not meant to see. Some say this gift of prophesy comes from the cleaving of two hearts—my own and that of he who holds the reins and guides my path. Others believe that I, like the thirteenth spirit, am the cursed keeper of mysteries and secrets. But I know that I am not exceptional. I see that which is yet-to-come by looking at what has happened to my brothers and sisters in other lands. If it happened there, it will 'probably' happen here. So I wait. I eavesdrop. I spy. This is my way of living and staying alive.

Like the thirteenth spirit, I am friend, foe, and traitor. Like the son of perdition, I always get the job done. Though I may grunt in disagreement, bat my layered eyelids, or hold a grudge, I remain dutiful. Of course, my occasional smile conceals this enduring trait.

I am Judas.

WITH every passing day, and after all the years and tears, I still feel the pain and disdain that my younger sister Ameera endured at the hands of men like Jamal. Against all my advice, Ameera gave her whole being to Jamal and hoped that he would choose her just as she had chosen him. He was her first love and had taught her everything she knew about her own body. She spoke fondly of the slow and gentle dressage; the measured rhythm, their synchronized breathing, and the bodily cadence through which their lives were now bound to each other. Ameera let him ride her until he couldn't ride anymore and outdid herself rocking him until he snored loudly, farted wholesomely, and grunted as one would when they were puffing up their soft dulla. Unable to hide her feelings, Ameera shadowed Jamal and did not let anyone else touch her. She made excuses for him even when he shooed her away and stopped talking to anyone who criticized him. After saturating Ameera's heart, body, and whole being with his passions, Jamal rejected her. He said that she was too clingy and hoped she'd venture out and see more of the world.

❦

AMEERA'S world came crushing when Zaki, an old friend from Nairobi arrived with a large wooden chest full of used books that he had bought at a diplomat's sale in Nairobi. "You are the only person I know who reads such things…" Zaki said as he arranged the books on the floor; "Claude Sumner: *The Rationalism of Zera Yacob, The Gospel of Judas: From Codex Tchacos… Thus Spake Zarathustra…*Al-Jahiz's *Kitab al Hayawan…* and George Orwell's *1984…*"

Confident that his book display had whetted Jamal's appetite, he put the books back into the chest and snapped the lock. "You won't believe it. The diplomat even had a book bound in human skin. I gave it back to him but only after he went down on his knees begging me to take this watch instead." Zaki lifted his sleeve to reveal an expensive-looking watch.

"It's called anthropodermic binding." Jamal said as he shook his head in disbelief. "That one book is worth more than this whole chest of books and the lorry you brought them in. You just lost the deal of your life."

Then, as if he was measuring the strange book's value against Ameera, Zaki ran his rather small hand up and down her bare back. "No problem. After all, who, in their right mind buys such strange things? I just don't understand these *wazungu.*"[31] Still taking in her beauty, and realizing how uncomfortable Ameera was, he stopped stroking her and used the back of his forefinger to wipe the tears off her tender face. "I know where I can use such a beauty…" he said as his hand wandered off and settled on Ameera's back again. "Her long legs, long neck, and long eyelashes, make her ideal for the show. Do we have a deal my friend?"

Jamal did not need a lot of convincing. He gave in to Zaki's demands and ordered the turnboy and I to carry the chest to the veranda. We watched as he inspected each book before placing it on his oakwood bookshelf where they were meticulously arranged by subject. As soon as we were done, the turnboy and Zaki put Ameera into the back of the lorry and bid us farewell. Standing next to her and pushing his rump against her for most of the trip was a large male donkey. He had been blindfolded to keep him from seeing things as the truck drove past them lest he laughed himself to death. The donkey, the other passengers said, was named Chryssipus after the Greek philosopher who died while laughing at a donkey.

31   Swahili word for "white people"

If the trip to Nairobi was degrading, life there was doubly so. Used to only one man's rhythm, touch, and domestic work, Ameera now had to entertain Zaki's clients in all kinds of places. She had to endure being ridden by pot-bellied drunk men, high-heeled women, and undisciplined children. Sometimes she had to bear the load of two grown men keen on stretching their experience by co-riding this new exotic body that the city had put at their disposal. Shamelessly, they mounted her right there in the middle of Uhuru Park. Their sweaty bodies rubbed against each other as they both, overwhelmed by the newness of the mutual ride, laughed loudly as if to get rid of the awkwardness.

Ashamed of her new life, Ameera wondered how full-grown men could lack rhythm. How, just a few rocking motions would make them shriek and get off shortly after mounting her. She hated that Zaki made her do this ten, sometimes fifteen times a day and even tried to charge the voyeuristic crowd that had gathered to witness the spectacle of her misplaced body as it was used in this cold and cold-hearted city.

What had the world come to? Ameera who would never let anyone but Jamal touch her now had to endure these incompetent riders. She who only knew the rhythm of Jamal's breathing now had to bear the strangers' raucous laughter, beeping cell-phones, shrieks, and Zaki's demands that she get on her knees over and over again. "The customer comes first." She heard him say as he collected the money each time someone got off her. As a recompense, Zaki fed her on left-over vegetables from Wakulima market save for unlucky days when she, like most of the people at Uhuru Park, had to eat air-burgers.

Tired of the use to which Zaki was putting her body, Ameera went on strike. She refused to run away from Kanjo and watched gleefully as Zaki pushed the ruffled notes into the council askari's hands. She refused to put on the silly *shuka*[32] and when someone tried to mount her forcefully, she would bite, kick, and use her imposing height and long legs to ensure that no one got close to her. When Zaki tried to beat her, she pinned him on the ground and was almost biting off his arm but stopped when she saw the look of horror in his eyes. The next day, Zaki loaded her on a lorry and returned her to Jamal. As part of the conspiracy of men, Jamal promised to take Ameera to that place that is promised to us whether we were obedient or unruly; faithful or perfidious —the abattoir that awaits us.

The night before she was to go into the abyss, Ameera told us stories of that city that was both teacher and terrorizer. She spoke of its rhythms, smells, sounds, heightened excitations, and the deepest forms of inattention. I listened keenly and cried like a human baby when Jamal pulled me aside to give me my new assignment. I was to lead Ameera, my flesh, blood, and bones to the abattoir.

Luckily, Ameera had made peace with her fate. She had lost the will to

---

32   Sheets like a cover or comforter.

live after Jamal betrayed her and as a last service, she offered to take the load off my hump by leading all the camels to the abattoir. To prepare her followers, Ameera told them of Emirati camel Botox injections and the sweet and beautiful things that awaited them on the other side. Excited by Ameera's worldliness, the keen listeners-turned-followers walked behind her in single file. She watched as they were subdued and tied town amid groans, grunts, and fruitless attempts to escape. Then, she walked majestically into the abattoir and lay smiling as they thrust the blade into her long hairy neck.

For this one time, she too became Judas.

II

Kikulacho ki nguoni mwako[33]. Our humans assume that everything begins and ends with them. They believe that what eats you is either close to you, with you, or inside you. They love and suspect their neighbors in equal measure. They forget that enmity, just like neighborliness, is more than a matter of proximity.

I, having been the carrier of men and the things that they value and abuse; having seen what they can do to each other; I know that what eats you could come from any place at any time. Together with Gulaal, I accompanied the AMOCO men as they drilled for oil and buried that white powder in Chalbi desert in the 1980s. Gulaal was a loyal, hardworking, and good-looking camel by all standards. He never complained. Not only because he stammered a lot, but also because he wanted Jamal to like him.

Working twice as hard and twice as long as the rest of us, Gulaal soon developed sores on his back and his knees buckled under half the load that he usually carried. Disgusted by the mucus that perpetually dripped from Gulaal's nostrils, the hives appearing all over his body, and his general inability to work, Jamal moved him to the back of the herd and began bleeding him instead. He knew the same fate would befall the other camels in the caravan and asked me to lead them all to the abattoir. It was just a matter of time before the signs of their labor began showing on their bodies.

THE journey to the abattoir was slower than usual as Gulaal fell down a number of times under the weight of his now emaciated body. Amoco—a camel born while his mother carried the company barrels—walked behind Gulaal and supported him. He reminded his friend of the good old days and the future that Jamal had promised them as the hardest working duo. I too encouraged the other camels and watched their eyes light up when I assured them that Gulaal would soon resume work after our visit to the veterinary. I could not tell if they were happy for Gulaal or for themselves. They all knew

33   Swahili phrase roughly meaning to guard or take care of one's heart.

that their loads would be lighter as soon he recovered; I knew mine would be lighter as soon as he was dead.

I kissed Gulaal on the right cheek and ushered him in to the 'doctor's office.' He turned, looked me in the eye, nodded, and then walked in. It had finally dawned on him that this was a place of killing and not healing. I turned to the remaining six camels and encouraged them to go in to support our brother's healing process. Amoco went first. The other five followed graciously. After the last camel walked through the door of no return, I turned and walked away to avoid hearing the wailing that I was sure would follow.

I betrayed my kin. I was the bearer of orders. I did my duty. I just obeyed the law that Jamal imposed on me.

I am Judas.

⸎⸎⸎

THE people who ate of Gulaal's body and drank of his blood fell sick too. Those who drank from the same wells and watering holes he used are now sicker than he was. Only yesterday, I carried Abdourahman's son to the hospital. Born many years after Gulaal's death, his skin had the same hives as Gulaal's. Even though he was human, his upper lip was swollen and split in two like a camel's. Moving his mouth around as if he was trying to feel if it was still there deepened his uncanny resemblance to Gulaal. But it is those rheumy eyes that struck me. They reminded me of Gulaal's final stare. They were the eyes that one saw on a camel as the blade pierced its neck. Eyes that asked "Why?...How could you after all I have done for you?" They were also the eyes that one saw on humans when the hand that caressed the body yesterday was now wrapped tightly around their necks. They were the eyes of those who had the boots on their neck in 1984. I have seen these eyes of the betrayed many times before.

III

AYAAN, the child's mother, says he has cancer. She believes Jamal when he tells her that Abdourahman might have passed it on to the child from the wayward women he slept with when he worked for him digging holes alongside the white ghost-suited men from AMOCO.

Though Ayaan knows that Jamal is a traitor, liar, and survivor, she still has a soft spot for him. She lets Jamal send me to carry her child to hospital even though we all know that not much can be done for him. Ayaan understands how betrayals of the past made Jamal lose the desire to continue his father's bloodline or his father's commitment to changing the world. He now directs his energies and passions towards reading and surviving in the world as it is and it is for this reason that she loves him.

Before it became sexual, their communion had been textual. They were both lovers of books and she would visit and listen to Jamal talk about his latest book acquisition and the worlds that they brought forth. Ayaan wanted to access this world of words but could only do so through Jamal's lips. First, he whispered the books into her ears and then began whispering his own desires. Soon after, his lips nibbled on her earlobes, then her neck, nipples, and now…he wants to go lower. He sang to her the *Song of Songs* and told her how, like the poet king's southern winds, he would like to "blow on her garden so that its fragrance may spread abroad… as he tastes its choice fruits." Jamal told Ayaan about the Egyptian god Osiris who was murdered, cut up, and fourteen pieces of his dismembered body scattered all over Egypt by his resentful brother Set. Severed off and tossed, Osiris's penis landed in the river Nile where it was eaten by a fish. Isis, the ever so faithful sister-wife put Osiris's body back together and had to make a prosthetic penis out of clay or her thumb before blowing life back into him by sucking his member.

Ayaan listened keenly as Jamal moved from one tale to another. She wasn't sure if he was propositioning her, trying to make a case for her to reciprocate his having blown the flowers in her garden, or if he was laying out the scene of his life-long struggle against his cousin Abdourahman.

Sitting hand-in-hand, Ayaan and Jamal exchanged a Judas kiss. Whether or not they still loved each other was secondary. The moonlight shone on their sweaty faces as they looked into each other's eyes each loving the fact that they were betraying Abdourahman who they both accused of having betrayed them first. Jamal's tongue took leave from speaking and kissing as he blew on Ayaan's garden. The stirring in their loins grew stronger as Ayaan's fragrance spread. She arched her back, pressed her body against his face, and held him as they rocked each other into a state of post-coital bliss as I too began salivating and blowing up my dulla. Silent, their bodies came to rest against my abdomen and we all fell into *la petit mort.*

Together; the two lovers and I were caught in the rhythms of life and a stolen deathly embrace…we were Judas.

❧∞❧

JAMAL emerged from 'the little death' first. He took out a torch and began reading Orwell's *1984* to Ayaan who was still asleep. I could feel his voice vibrate against my abdomen and hear her cooing as his words caressed her ears. I was just beginning to enjoy the story when Ayaan woke up grabbing her bosom as she mumbled the words "truth…airstrip…1984." She struggled to breath as images of unmourned deaths from another time interrupted her 'little death' and my reading session.

"Truth, Ministry…Airstrip One…1984." She tried to catch her breath as tears of pain replaced the tears of pleasure that had caressed her face not too long ago.

"Macaan…shhhhh… Macaan… It is just a book. It is just a story. This is not our 1984." Jamal consoled her, hoping that she would forget the truth that no one spoke of so that they could go back to their homes without a trace of where they had been. I also wanted her to stop crying so that Jamal would continue reading to me.

Carried away by the moment of enjoyment, Jamal hoped that the first book he ever read to Ayaan would take both of them back to the time before she knew Abdourahman. That it would take her back to the time before the pain of seeing her father's hands bound behind his back with the same rope that he had used to tie his camels broke her brain such that she could no longer read. He hoped to carry both of them to the time of readerly bliss when their worlds were boundless or at least the books made it appear so.

But *1984* had stirred up memories of the old deaths that were still fresh in her mind. It brought back the things that we had thrown down memory holes. Today, *1984* had even interrupted their post-coital bliss and its little deaths. The book *1984* had awoken that year of betrayal that our minds had tucked away.

1984, this was one of the books and years of Judas.

❧◌◌◌◌❧

EVERY Friday, Ayaan, rubbed myrrh and frankincense oil all over her son's body and put a few drops of the oil on a warm cloth for him take in the relaxing fragrance. As soon as the child calmed down, she would draw her shawl over his shoulders using its hanging ends to wipe the sweat off his forehead and the tears off his puffy cheeks. She would hum the *Huuwaya huuwa* tune as the *luuban*[34] smoke from the ceramic incense burner enveloped her in its musky lemony fragrance with the same warmth and tenderness that she embraced her son. For the next two to three days, anyone who touched Ayaan and her son smelled of the *luuban* that her father and fore fathers had grown and the gum resin tears that they had collected and traded all the way down the old Frankincense trail and what became the Silk Road. It is this *luuban* that one could smell on Jamal's clothes and as well as my hide. This scent of a mother trying to stop her child from dying was written all over our skins. Its trace lingering in our nostrils as the child's illness turned him into an olfactory archive. A carrier of a fragrance that reminded us of the resin tappers and the camels that walked this land, and the healing that the now dying myrrh and frankincense trees had brought to the soul, the mind, and the soil. This fragrance of the love and healing was also a reminder of the knowledge that we had lost. It refreshed our memories of old friends and foes warned us of the betrayal that was to come.

The child's fragrance stung Abdourahman nose. Whenever he smelt the same fragrance on Jamal, it stung his heart. He knew it was the trace of Ayaan's love for their dying child and her undying love for his cousin. Being a

---

34 An incense made of olibanum; frankincense; gum or resin

man of depths rather than surfaces, Abdourahman insisted that the child get his weekly injections instead of the myrrh and frankincense bath. When the doctor said there was nothing more that he could do for the child, he began preparing a *Taweez*[35] for the frail child to drink for true healing, just like love and hate, came from the inside.

Every day, just after his morning prayers, Abdourahman would take a plain plate and write down an *ayat*[36] from the Quran in saffron ink. Knowing the weight of the words that he had just written, he would pour the water into the plate, shake it, and after waking up the child, make him drink the liquified holy words of the Quran hoping that they would bring the healing that had eluded him.

But the child was too ill at this point. Each sip of the Quran-infused water wet his chapped lips, rested on his tongue, and then spilt on the floor as nothing could go past the lump in his throat. Soaked in frankincense, myrrh, his parents tears, and Quranic waters, the child, like his father Abdourahman, moved closer to his forefathers with each attempted sip of the *Taweez*.

Then he breathed his last.

The scent on the child's limp body betrayed his parents' efforts to save the one thing that they both loved even when they both knew there was nothing they could do to save him or their love for each other.

With the mutual care that brought them together gone, Abdourahman and Ayaan withdrew into their worlds of words. Each was enriched by their pursuit of the words of others—One after the sacred, and the other, after the most profane.

IV

JAMAL whispered into Ayaan's ears telling her he felt no remorse for sending men whose names and families he knew to do a job that the nameless figures had paid him to do. In another life, they would have been the ones sending him into the desert to die. He who was never given to work. But today, things are different. These men are like Gulaal and Amoco. They were born workers and for that they suffered. They were resilient beings who diligently dug and carried barrels never pausing to contemplate on the scale of death, destruction, and time that had gone into creating the fossil sludge that AMOCO was looking for and the deaths it would bring in the future. They were survivors. They knew how death on an airstrip had turned men and women who come from a long line of warriors into workers who walked with their heads bowed down. These men had looked into the abyss. They had felt the weight of boots and bayonets on their backs before and knew that the past had already betrayed the future.

With no one and nowhere to turn to, they did not protest when company

---

35 An amulet or locket worn for good luck and protection

36 A verse.

men drilled for oil and buried barrels near their homes and watering holes. Then their bodies began betraying them. First it was the itching and twitching, and then the bloating and hemorrhaging. When they began burying their peers just as they had done with the barrels and their kin not too many years ago, they confronted the area chief who arrived for the *baraza*[37] dressed in a suit and shiny shoes in total defiance of the heat and dust that everyone else seemed to obey. His shoes and clothes, just like the speech that he read, had come straight from Nairobi:

"Brothers and sisters," he began softly. "We members of the Degodia clan are here today because some of you believe that any form of progress is the work of *Iblis*[38]. I am here to tell you that the government wants you all to catch up. Allah has heard our cries and sent us these men from AMOCO and our own son Jamal whose work will be our redemption. They are here to save us from those who laughed at us and our barren land. Everyone will see how this oil, this black gold, is the hand of god. He who heard our cries and saw our shame."

Abdourahman, even though he was the youngest at the gathering, stood up and interrupted the chief.

"This drilling for oil, it is not the work of god. Look at what it is doing to us. It is not a blessing. This is a curse." He stopped, cleared his throat violently and then, like a man possessed by a demon, spat on the floor.

"Beware my brothers and sisters. As they burrow into the belly of the earth, what they are pulling out is not black gold. It is, as many before me have said, the devil's excrement." With the exception of Ayaan who sat quietly throughout the meeting, everyone else nodded as Abdourahman spoke.

"Look!" He pointed to the ground where he had just spat. "This thing is already making us sick. The burrowing for the devils excrement, the barrels that Jamal makes us put into the ground, they are already choking us. We are now drowning in our own sputum. The phlegm, rolling deep in our lungs and throats reminds us that pursuing the devils excrement fills up our lungs, our camels lungs, with the devils semen. Many will hear me today and say that I am a young man thinking as young men are wont to do. That I am the enemy... of progress and development...Brothers..." He cleared his throat and spat on the floor again. "...Sisters and my dear parents, I am only warning you. *Iblis*'s agents are here among us. They stir the devil's bowels and he smiles knowing that soon, he will erupt. He will take over this land just as he did in 1984. Let us refuse this depravity and join the fight against this *Iblis*."

The crowd watched in silence as Abdourahman raised his hands as if he were in prayer, bowed, and then crouched under the tree as one does when they are waiting to attack or to be attacked.

The attack came from the chief whose forced smile evaporated from his

---

37   A place where public meetings are held; and the meeting itself.
38   The devil of Islam.

face as he retook the floor:

"My dear brothers and sisters…" he began, "you have heard what the young man has said. Those impassioned words, the careless invocation of Allah's name, the vulgar references to body parts and our land, and the attempt to scare you all back into poverty and dissension; that is the kind of thing that we will not allow." The crowd nodded in return. It is not that they agreed with what the chief said or how he said it, they had all noticed how quickly his mood had changed and knew what men like him were capable of.

"Our brother Jamal has the full blessing of my office. No one is forcing you to work with him. If you do not like the work, quit. However, be forewarned that anyone who tries to interrupt the important work that we are doing here will have no one but themselves to blame when my men visit them or if we have an operation."

The chief dismissed the *baraza*[39] and watched with his soul piercing eyes as one-by-one, the men returned to their digging. Abdourahman stood alone with his clenched fists knowing that he was now a target. None of the men looked at Abdourahman or the chief knowing that they were being forced to choose between two deaths—one immediate, and the other, drawn out over time. They chose to live today. They chose to die slowly and dug in fear and anger knowing that he who was betraying them today had a bigger traitor behind him. They had seen the same chain of betrayal in 1984 and were yet to heal from the wounds of that hot day in February when hell descended on them…on a barren airstrip. This death was not an aberration, it was how things were designed to work in a place where the law brutalized rather than protected these stepchildren of a barren yet-coveted land.

⚬⚬⚬

WHEN the job was done, Jamal asked that part of his payment be made in books. The eclectic collection of texts on his bookshelf reminded him of shadow worlds and shadowy figures that he had engaged over the years. The enlightenment coming out of the books reminded him of the dark souls that he had betrayed. Jamal, reader of men and the word, read the *Tchacos Codex*. He pored over the pages of the *Gospel of Judas* that identified Judas Iscariot as Christ's most loyal confidant who, having betrayed Jesus as was his destiny, was to become the first martyr. Jamal identified with this thirteenth spirit who was both friend and traitor. He felt relieved when he read how Judas, he whose name had been spoilt and soiled did not commit suicide, and how the returned silver was in fact used to buy the 'field of blood.' Judas, the only one who understood the true message this gospel tells us, was actually stoned to death by the twelve. He was killed by those who overcome with jealousies over his intimacies, could not help but betray him.

---

39   A meeting or council.

Jamal, reader of the word and its worlds, *knew the envious world would betray him and chose to become a Judas himself.*

JAMAL and I, we come from a long line of traitorous Judas figures. We trust each other knowing that one day, one of us will betray the other. For now, we betray others and take care of each other. His recent one-leggedness makes him a camel-man while turning me into something between a friend, a pet, and a beast of burden.

Losing a leg gave Jamal the appearance of someone with more interesting life story. He never corrects those who assume that he has known war or a much deeper suffering. He lets them commiserate with him on account of the siblings, spouses, and friends, who just like him, lost a limb in Wagalla in 1984. He nods along when people who have lost neither limb nor life appreciate that it was a limb and not a life that was lost on his part. He never corrects those who mistake him for his cousin Abdallah—a decorated UN soldier who stepped on a land-mine in Sierra Leone. Jamal wears his one leg like a badge of honor. It makes people assume that he, like the other men in his family, has broken bones and is willing to shoot or at least be shot at as they sacrifice for the greater good.

But we who know Jamal intimately know that it is a small prick from the thorn of the Mathenge, the mesquite, or Garan-waa shrub as it is called in Somali, that cost him his leg. Like Jamal and myself, this 'unknown' shrub betrays. It is a friend-turned-foe though some say that it is a miracle waiting to be discovered.

The *mathenge* shrub is seductive, sexually prolific, and gluttonous. It turned the desert green and after greening this dusty brown-land, it choked it. It ate at the ground as its thorns created deep tropical wounds in the feet of our humans and where they saw bitterness, we non-humans saw nothing but sweetness. Now, toothless goats roam the land having fed on *mathenge* day and night; its sweet pods sticking on their teeth like a toffee. Coated in sweetness, the teeth quickly decay and then fall off. Toothless goats now die a slow, painful, starving death. We camels on the other hand, are now like humans. Our diabetes-induced urination irrigates this once dry land hydrating the same devil's weed that chokes man, beast, and land. Our sister camels smell our sweet pheromones and think we are ready for action even without our dullas puffing up.

The sweet and prolific mathenge remapped our land and our bodies. Now, I am tickled by Jamal's stump bumping against my hump as he mounts and dismounts me. Ayaan's body tingles when his stump caresses her inner thigh as he mounts her. It sends the wind and waves radiating up her spine, down her legs, and into her curling toes. He reads poems to her. She jokes about him being Osiris—an amputee—and she, like Isis, will put him back together. They laugh because they both know that while this moment might recur, it will not last. Ayaan has been through this before and waits for Jamal to pull my reins and direct me away from her saying that it is I, his camel and his borrowed legs that has rejected her.

He will tell her that it is I and I alone, who is Judas.

V

PERDITION and hellfire. I remember the day that I was matched with Jamal. The day that his father took him aside and gave him a copy of Al-Jahiz's *Kitab al-hayawan* (The Book of Animals) with excerpts from the *Book of Misers* pasted on as an addendum. Jamal's father had hoped that by sharing the book he would have signaled to his son that they were now peers and therefore stir up something manly in him. That giving him the book while he sent out his cousin Abdourahman to take the camels to drink would make it clear to Jamal that he would have to do more if he wanted to carry the family name. That he was not going to make a name for himself as master camel herdsman or trader if all he did was sit around and read books and imagine worlds.

Seeing the excitement with which Jamal devoured the books, his father gave in. He asked him to chronicle the family line to ensure that the way of the land and the camel is kept sacred.

Even though he had not worked for it, Jamal felt that his old man had betrayed him by assigning Abdourahman who was many years his junior and with many sisters and cousins between them to carry the family trade and the family name. Embittered by the betrayal, Jamal vowed to slowly kill all the camels. He promised himself that he would master books and then turn all these camel people into book people.

Recognizing Jamal's grief, his father gave him one camel...Me. Jamal mistreated me due to my dented hump , long hair and slight limp from a childhood injury. He was irritated by my presence until he read about camels who looked just like me in Al-Jahiz's *Kitab al Hayawan*. As if he had just had an epiphany, Jamal read the passage over and over such that even though I do not know how to read, I now know the passage by heart:

When [male] two humped camels (*al-fawalij*) are bred with [female] Arab camels (*al-ibil*), you get these noble [*karima*] *bhukts*, and *jammazas* that combine the virtues of the Arab with the virtues of the *bhukt*. For the formation of these two species does not get any nobler, more glorious, more pleasing, or more costly.

By redefining me, Jamal redefined himself. He said that we were the product of the best and harshest elements of both worlds. What some considered a deformity, to him, was a mark of my lineage to both one-humped dromedary and two-humped Bactrian camels. We suited each other and had learnt to do little and expect much in return. Together, Jamal and

I became astute readers of human and non-human beings—books in the case of Jamal, and camels, the earth, and stars, in my case. Owing to our circumstances, we were haters of our kin and in our hate, we became one. Our hearts were cleaved to each other.

Jamal and I, we became Judas.

BOUND to his seat by his one-leggedness, Jamal trained me on how to take books from his bookshelf through the veranda window. I learnt that two upward tugs of my rein in quick succession meant I needed to go and pick a book from the top shelf while each downward tug meant that the book was lower down the shelf. Left and right tugs indicated which direction I was to move once I got to the window and the number of pats on my dented hump made it clear how many books he needed. The commands were accompanied by words of reinforcement as well as a crack of the whip or a small snack depending on how well I performed my task.

As soulmates, we learned how to communicate without the physical tugs as I now understood all his verbal instructions and even anticipated his requests. Duly trained, Jamal sent me to pick a book randomly from the shelf and would repeat this until he was satisfied with what I had picked. There was no need for Jamal to limp into the room or climb over shelves and he now spent most mornings seated at the far-end of the veranda reading a book as he sipped his cardamom and ginger tea. He waited for me to bring him the next book just the way he would wait for his wife to bring him another cup of tea. Jamal complained and sneered at her while rewarding me with morsels of food for every book that I put in his outstretched hand.

Not knowing beforehand what it was that he would read for the day and leaving it up to me—this illiterate beast—to feed him with the knowledge that he so much hankered after was a great honor. With time, I came to know the books that put Jamal in a good mood and those that dampened his spirit. I gave Jamal the books that brought out the Jamal that I wanted to have around. Whereas other camel herders sang to their flock, Jamal read to me in his soothing voice. I learned how to nod my head when I liked what he was saying and he, being the good student that he was, found himself grunting like a camel whenever he enjoyed a text.

Of course, we had our textual disagreements. Whenever Jamal read Nietzsche's *Thus Spoke Zarathustra,* he mused over the metamorphosis of the spirit from camel, to lion, to the child. I hated it when he spoke of the camel as a simple load-bearing spirit. He knew I did not like the passage and read it over and over. I, on the other hand, was elated when he turned to Zarathustra's musings on those people who '...*lack everything except one thing of which they have too much of—human beings who have nothing but a big eye, or a big mouth, or a big belly, or anything at all that is big. Inverse cripples...*"

I would rest my nose on his thigh and watch Jamal as he rubbed his stump as if my rough hair were tickling his phantom limb. We both grunted after he animatedly read about *"An ear! An ear as big as a man!.. tremendous ear was attached to a small, thin stalk- but this stalk was a human being!"*

While Jamal told me that his cousin Abdourahman was an inverse cripple. I always imagined that it was he, Jamal—the single-minded owner of an envious face, the resentful self-taught genius, the merchant who sold out, the abattoir owner—who was the inverse cripple. I knew that behind this genius; behind this man-friend of mine who would betray anyone and anything; behind this person who could very easily turn from friend to foe, was an insecure child who felt betrayed by his kin and only considered himself meaningful to the extent that he dominated or betrayed others. To the extent that he bit the hand that fed him and turned every secret into blackmail.

Where others only saw how Jamal had betrayed them, Ayaan saw how he had been betrayed many times before he learnt how to be a traitor. She understood how those who betrayed him had also been betrayed and hurt deeply. She knew what Jamal had trained me to do and said that it is from this chain of pain that Jamal learnt how to be and how to remain who he is today…*Judas*.

⁂

AS I advance in age, I hear Jamal reading Al-Jahiz's *The Book of Animals, Book of Misers,* and the *Book of Africans* and know that these books will not protect me. Like others who have come before me, Jamal will soon find a younger and more useful camel to betray me. He will train them on how to lead me to the blade and if lucky, they might learn how to be read to. If Jamal falls into Ayaan's embrace again, the lucky camel will have the pleasure of being the lovers' pillow as they rock each other into their small deaths.

I have tried to delay this eventuality by changing the way Jamal sees the world. Whenever he sends me to bring his books, I try, even though I cannot read, to bring something that would make him care for animals a little more. I often reach for the smallest book on the shelf for between those covers lie the pages of J.M. Coetzee's *Lives of Animals* which Jamal reads to me. He fell in love with the book's protagonist—Elizabeth Costello—and wrote her letters telling her how her lecture made him realize the entanglement between the plight of animals and those of men like him. As one who had trained camels to lure their kin to the slaughterhouse, Jamal spoke of man's atrocity against Judas camels like Duba Junior from Isiolo, and the feral camels of Australia fitted with GPS collars in order to betray other members of their herd even though it is these same camels that had been used to colonize the interior of this penal colony. I stopped listening to Jamal and felt betrayed by his praise for Red Peter—the literate Ape that Kafka wrote about and who Costello refers to in her lectures.

Even as he thought of changing his ways, Jamal still had to betray someone. *He was a literary Judas.*

VI

YESTERDAY, I was eager to have Jamal read to me and went to get *The Lives of Animals* from the bookshelf. Maybe reading Costello's words might make him write her another letter. The letters made him kinder to me, to his wife, and even to himself. I pulled the booklet from the shelf and hurried back to the veranda and put it in Jamal's hands. He looked at the cover and smiled. The kind of smile that I had seen in the old Jamal. He cleared his throat and read the title; *Kenya Bureau of Standards: Basic requirements for a Slaughter house—Specification.* "Aha!" He grunted like a camel whose belly was being stroked. I knew he would enjoy his read.

Jamal read through the pages slowly, smiled, and repeated the details that the booklet provided always raising his eyes to look at me. "My friend, I think we need an upgrade." Jamal said as he took out a pen from his shirt pocket and began writing notes on the back of the booklet. I had just dug my own grave and watched the glee with which Jamal read the 'Slaughterhouse Layout Plan' section.

To let him know of my disapproval, I got up and went to the window and brought back some of my favorite books which he did not bother to touch.

❦

"UPGRADE!" What did Jamal mean when he said "we need an upgrade"? Did he intend to replace me or to upgrade the abattoir? Whichever way, it was clear that I was destined to see the blade. This was the way of men. They always paid kindness with random acts of cruelty. Sometimes, they failed to pay you at all. They did it to camels and to their fellow humans. But I am Judas. I work towards delaying my own demise.

Today, I did what I was always meant to do. I acted like the camel that I am and did not bring the books when Jamal asked for them. When he began whipping me, I was reminded of Ameera and what she had endured at the hands of men like Jamal. I was reminded of how Jamal treated me before he found out what I could do. Pained by these memories, I walked to the shelf and brought him the rolled prayer mat instead of a book. I was sure that he would need it.

"Ngamia hii!" he called me as he dragged himself across the room. Using his good leg, he got on the stool and reached for his Al-Jahiz books and his new favorite text... *The Slaughterhouse Plans.*

"Ngamia Hii...' that was the straw that broke my back. Even I, a camel, had my limits. I waited for him to get down and then gently pushed the heavy oak shelf which toppled over as if it had been waiting for this moment.

The weight of books was evidence of Jamal's obsession with collecting books and the shadow dealings that provided the means of feeding his passions. As Jamal's frail body buckled under the weight of his passions, I felt an uncanny satisfaction. I had done more than betray him. I had avenged the indignities and pains that Ameera had suffered. Pains that I thought time would heal but, as my years of waiting revealed, it is waiting to heal that had come to ail me.

I ran to Abdourahman's house and tugged on his collar until he followed me to Jamal's reading room. There he was on the floor. Lying dead with that unmistakably irritated look on his face. In death, Jamal did not have the peace that you would expect to find on the face of a bibliophile who dies in a library. Maybe he was shocked by the weight of the pile of books as the shelf fell on him. Maybe he was irritated by the realization that I had beaten him at the game of betrayal. I don't know if he died instantly. His mouth lay agape and his good leg was contorted like Gulaal's back legs after falling down during that long journey to the abattoir. In Jamal's hands were two of his favorite books by Al-Jāḥiẓ; *Kitab al-Hayawan* (Book of the Animals) and *Kitab al-Bukhala* (Book of Misers). On his chest was the *Gospel of Judas*. For most people, his death by books looks like a coincidence. But anyone who knows Al-Jahiz's story knows that this is too perfect a coincidence for it to be a coincidence. As the story goes, the aging Al-jahiz, now himself a hemiplegic struggling to move his body had died the same way in Basra in the Arabic month of Muharram almost 1200 years ago.

LATER that evening, I moved into Abdourahman's home. I put my head on his lap and waited for him to feed me some morsels of food for having rushed to his place in an attempt to save his cousin. Even though they had fought all their lives, Abdourahman mourned our beloved Jamal. Ayaan consoled him as she consoled herself. She put some frankincense in the *dabqaab* incense burner enveloping all of us in the musky lemony fragrance. The notes reminding us of the child they had brought them together, Jamal who stood between them for a long time. The fragrance carried us all to time that camels and camel men ruled this land that now betrayed us. Abdourahman took a deep breath letting the *lubaan* of his forefathers relax his heart as he stroked my hump. He told me that I had now earned a place in his loyal flock. He reached out and pulled Ayaan to his chest and gave a sigh of relief as she returned his embrace. Little did he know that like his cousin who he had just buried, Ayaan who embraced him, and the people he is resisting, *I too, I am Judas.*

Sam Okoth Opondo writes on the often-overlooked amateur diplomacies of everyday life, postcolonial cities, the politics of genre, estrangement, and cultural translation in postcolonial Africa. He is from Nairobi and teaches Political Science and Africana Studies at *Vassar College*, New York.

A Place with Many Doors
Troy Onyango

SHE DIED like death meant nothing to her. Even forgot to close her eyes. As if she could—wanted to—see everything around her. But her thin legs that had been flailing in the air and the delicate hands that had been clawing the ground, gathering dirt under her bitten fingernails, stopped moving, and he knew she was dead. That did not stop the man whose face was crunching up as if he was in pain and then, his foaming mouth opened, and he let out a guttural groan while he shook like he was possessed by a legion of demons. The others stood around and cheered him on, grunting, chanting incoherent words meant to inspire pride in whatever they had done; satisfied by their violent, vile deed.

They were not supposed to kill the girl with the big brown eyes and skin the colour of dirty leather. They were not supposed to. But they said the man's victory in the elections had been stolen for the third time, and also, she was from the wrong tribe. What was she doing there anyway? So they took turns at her—all seven of them—and when she was too tired to fight, and no sound was coming from her parched throat, the one with the crunched face took a rusty machete and cut her throat, not because she had died long before he was done.

The boy was not supposed to be there, but he saw it all. His stomach turned as if his intestines were being knotted by a skilled weaver. And he knew if retched from the metallic taste in the back of his throat and vomited they would find him behind the tower of garbage and cut him up into tiny pieces of meat like the cow meat at the butchery.

Or maybe, because he was from the right tribe, they would have told him to run home and tell no one. But he didn't make a sound. And after they left, he walked over to the girl and told her that he was sorry as if he was the one who had done it, and that's when she closed her eyes. He said he was sorry over and over again, expecting her corpse to have a heartbeat, a pulse, start breathing, stop flailing her legs in the air, stop clawing the dirt, get up from the ground, shake the dust off her hair, open her mouth and tell him, "You are forgiven." It did not. Eventually, he walked away and left the dead girl's body there. He put the back of his hand to his face and wiped away the tears from his eyes as though that alone would wipe away what he had seen.

He never told anyone what he saw. His eyes had stared into a darkness that he could not capture with words. Not even when he got home, and his mother, who was sitting on the floor with her legs stretched in front of her and her palms rubbing her thighs in slow circular motions, told him that the girl's mother had taken off and left her shop open for them to do as they pleased. He was going to ask his mother if they did, but she was already calling his brother to go and fetch water for the *chang'aa*. No one knows where or when (if) the girl's mother stopped running. All over the country, they were doing the worst to young girls, old women, children, and old men and the whole country was like a hyena that was eating its own children and accusing them of smelling like goats. But then the two old men who had been fighting over the seat showed up on TV and shook hands and the whole country paused, arms mid-air ready to hit, and said, "That was bad."

The first time she came to him, he thought it was an apparition, a consequence of his imagination. And yet, he could feel her presence in the room, engulfing every inch of the stuffy house he shared with his five siblings. Her scent clung to the air and with every breath he took, he felt as if he was inhaling her and she was taking over him. How could this be, he wondered, when she died exactly ten years ago? It had been ten years and she and all the other young girls had become nothing more than songs whose words had been forgotten—lost—to everyone else, remaining only as tunes hummed when the nights were cold and the children could not fall asleep.

But then she came, bones and flesh, she came. Her head was no longer falling off her body and the red was not spurting from her neck like the gush from the neglected burst water pipes. Her hair was not tearing off her head from all the grabbing and pulling. Her skin shone, glowed when the sunrays fell on her. Her dress was not torn and the only stain on it was from her mother's lipstick she had stolen the day they were to meet. She was whole, just as he remembered her from childhood. Except she was grown. The body of a girl who was fast becoming a woman. Her face still looked just like the face she wore when he was thirteen and she was eleven. Like she did on the morning when she came to their window and peeped and said, "They have started counting the votes." His mother never liked her habit of holding on to the window rails and lifting herself up until her toes pointed and sunk into the soft earth. "Are there no doors where they gave birth to you?" She would say to her. And she would squeal and retort, "There are so many. Even doors that lead nowhere."

The boy always wondered where she was born.

A place with many doors meant that one was free to come and leave at will. It meant that doors were always closing and shutting, creaking at their hinges and clicking in the locks. He had always wanted to stay in such a place, and not this room with one door that had belonged to his great-grandmother, his grandmother and now his mother. Imagine living in a place where one door lead to another and another like there was no one to bark, "Don't leave that door open boy!" in the way his father used to say before the disease came to him and took his throat, leaving him with nothing but the mere whimper of a puppy. His mother said it was because he drank all her profits, but they all know it was something more; a dangerous kind of fire that reckless men swallowed from the building down at the secluded part of the town. Anyway, the day came and life closed its door on him.

Did the doors of heaven close on her, locking her out, and that is why she was here?

On the day she came to him, he was preparing the pots for the boiling of the millet and sorghum. His two brothers had taken the wheelbarrow to go fetch the water and his eldest sister was busy trying to save her fifth marriage. When she appeared, he wanted to scream but then he saw she was whole and grown and he thought maybe he had imagined her death ten years ago; an imagination so elaborate and complex it was, essentially, to him, the truth. He smiled and she returned his smile. He folded himself in her open arms and her embrace was so warm he wanted to stay that way forever and never leave. They were that way for a long time until the baby's cry split into the moment, lodging itself between them. He opened his eyes and withdrew from her embrace sharply, quickly as one withdraws their hand from a flame. That is when he saw the betrayal in her eyes.

The baby's cries rose and rose, and he wanted to turn and go pick it from the large bed, but he thought if he left the spot he was standing in, he would turn to find the girl gone, vanished like she had appeared. Therefore, he stood there until she asked him, "Are you not going to take your baby?" The question was deliberate and he tried reading her face to see what she felt but she gave him nothing. Her voice was as clear and shrill as he remembered it. It made him remember all the songs she used to sing to him in a language he never understood. It made him remember– the baby was crying. He turned and picked up the baby from the bed, and when he turned back again, expecting her to be gone, he found her there. Standing with her arms still stretched in front of her, like how they had been.

They stood there, facing each other, and for a moment, he considered he was imagining things. Yet, she felt as real as the baby he was holding in his arms. He wanted to reach over to her again, close the gap between them and fill up the years when she was not there. He wanted to put the crying baby down and have his hands free so he could hold her. Standing there, barely ten metres from him, she looked so alone, so lonely. The realization that this loneliness could have been her life for the past ten years made his insides swell with shame. Yet, here she was. Back. Wherever she had been, whatever she had been through, he was going to make it right by her.

"She is such a beautiful baby." Her voice, low and piercing.

"He. He is a boy." He let out a nervous laugh that did not convince him.

"Boys are trouble. Beautiful boys are demons."

"He is just a baby. Don't say such things." He had not meant for his tone to be that sharp and defensive. He wished he could unspeak the words, swallow them back into his stomach. But they were out there already, and he hoped she did not take it to heart.

"Mothers are meant to be with their children."

He wanted to tell her that his sister had left the baby with him so that she could go find her husband in whichever brothel he was calling home or whichever *chang'aa*[40] den he was spending his days. He did not. She stood there, staring outside the window, past the clothing lines with wet dripping clothes, all the way past the mountain of garbage with the children dancing on top. He could not see what she was looking at, but he knew the shirtless children dancing to made-up lyrics of Awilo Longomba's songs were not objects of her fascination.

"What do you see?" She asked him. The question caught him off guard. He hesitated, straining to look past her and see what she was seeing. The heat from the sun burned his eyes and the baby's low, muffled cries with hiccups that sounded like the pop of gum could not let him focus.

"Nothing." He responded feeling defeated.

"Those children up there, do you think they see what we see?"

"What do we see?"

She did not respond. Her large eyes darted, sweeping the side of the room she was facing, then stopped again outside the window. Her frame was rooted to the same spot she had appeared. He wanted to move closer to her, touch her and let her know that he wanted to see what her eyes were seeing—what the children could not see.

"The children, they don't see the hate in us. They are unable to." Her voice startled him in the way it was brittle and sharp like cut, unsmoothed glass. The baby had stopped crying and his head rested on his shoulder. He stared at the children dancing in the blazing afternoon heat without a care.

He remembered when they were children.

She, two years younger than him, but faster and quicker than anyone he knew. She outraced him, even when he started running when she was still saying, "On your marks, get set—" and his body was already tearing through the blazing heat, his shirt flailing behind him, his torso stretching and hurting, his legs pulling and pulling, the weightless feeling of joy, pause, then the fatigue grinding at his bones, pause, the wind slowing him down. He would start gasping for breath, and that is when she would dart past him like an arrow shot from an eager hunter's bow.

The children did not see them. They danced: their waist and legs becoming rubber becoming water becoming air. Their hands were unable to hold them, and the sound of the paint containers being hit with the thin sticks was what filled the air. They sung. No coordination, no harmony, no nothing except the blissful innocence of childhood.

The baby slept through it all. Burped once or twice, snored softly, dug his small head in his neck, did everything a child does when they sleep. He

---

40   An illegal, homemade distilled alcohol popular in Kenya.

stood there with her, careful not to say anything that would make her leave. Careful not to hurt her again.

"Do you remember when we were children?" He asked.

"Everything about it. It is the only reality I know. The only one I live."

"Were you happy then?"

"I suppose. But sometimes I wonder if I even knew the true meaning of happiness back then. Was I conscious of it? I wonder."

"Are you happy now?"

"…Or if I was confusing it with something else. Some other emotion?"

"Grief?"

"I am incapable of being happy now. I cling to the moments in my childhood."

"And grief?"

"What about grief?"

"Those children." He turned towards the window and the children had melted to nothingness; going, *gone*. The haze of the afternoon heat no longer danced. The wind blew gently from the lake. They were gone. They had disappeared. He would see them again, he knew, for they had made a home out of that heap of garbage, spending their days clawing through the used condoms, soiled pampers, polythene bags full of dog vomit and children's runny shit. They dug through, trying to find bits of metal to sell to the scrap dealers. Did they know anything about grief?

"Sometimes your entire life is a long, continuous episode of grief."

He did not listen to her, ignoring the words she had spoken. He trained his eyes and mind on the children. On their absence. The huge pile of garbage with flies buzzing around. With cockroaches roaming, searching, and being the filthy insects they always were—are. The sound of the street was the trill of a cricket. A prolonged sound that hurt the ears and calmed the mind.

It was almost evening. His sister, if at all she was coming back, was bound to find them standing like this, motionless in the middle of the living room. She would have asked, "Brother, have you lost your mind?" Her high, booming voice scattering his thoughts, and perhaps even, her presence. She must have sensed his fear and she turned to him, her face glowing in the orange light of the sunset, and she told him, "You and I have work to do. I will come back at dawn."

"Where will you go?"

She was gone.

The man in the green jumper took three steps forward, two steps back before his knees buckled and he folded like a thirsty camel. He was the first to go. And while everyone stood around and watched while saying, "Omera, let's get this guy to the hospital," he already knew that he would not survive what she had done to him. What she had made him do. He squirmed and wriggled on the dirt like he was a large headless snake. He was in so much pain. He tried to block the screams out of his head, but the incessant ringing that the screams left made his head hurt. He turned away from the crowd, and even though all he wanted was to get home and wash his hands, she made him turn back and forced him to look.

"He did worse to me."

"I was there. I saw it."

"You didn't stop them!"

"Is this your way of punishing me?" He repeated the question over and over and over until it replaced the man's screams, the eclipsed voice becoming faint with every boom of his own voice. He heard himself, the clarity in his voice, as if he was in a large empty room with closed doors and windows; the echo of pain mixed with something, something he didn't know how to name yet. He asked the question again. He already knew her answer: "You were just a child back then." That would have been her response. She had not said anything to him, but he understood that even without her telling him certain things, he could know them.

Like the day she had told him to find the man in the green jumper. He was not wearing a green jumper when he found him, and his face was no longer crunched as he remembered it; creases and folds ran all over it, and he knew, even then, that time and sadness had converged there. He observed his face, taking in his eyes that had the colour of marbles when hit with light at the right angle. He watched his mouth as it opened, his chapped, reddened lips parting ways, for the ball of *ugali* to get inside. He hated him. He walked over to him and stood over him like he was some god.

"Get me *ugali sosa*."[41]

"I don't work here." His own voice sounded different. It was still his own.

"Then get away from me."

That is what made him the first to go.

This is how he went.

He followed him from the restaurant and knew where he lived. He went back home and found her seated there waiting. When she asked if he had found him, he simply nodded. She smiled and told him he had to do it. She made him remember how he was the one who cut her throat like she was just some chicken. And when she was done, she told him he owed her this. And he nodded again and again as if to say he understood.

The deed was simple, a knife to his throat, blood spilling like water from a fountain, sound struggling to come out. Red, red, red. He looked in his eyes when he held on to his throat and walked outside the house, his neighbours seeing him and suggesting he be taken to the hospital.

That is what she did. That is what *he* did.

---

41 *Ugali* is a staple food in East Africa made from maize flour, typically served with stews or vegetables. *Ugali sosa* is a type of ugali made from a mixture of maize flour and sorgum flour.

He realizes now, what he did not know back then, that human beings change. Sometimes, for the better. Sometimes. Other times, however, they change for the worst. Not entirely but they become capable of actions that make one say, they have changed for the worst. And that is exactly what he thought of her after that first time. After she made him do what he did to that man in the green jumper. As he washed his hands, scrubbing with all the rage he could muster, seeing the water take on a new colour, he shook his head and the pain was unbearable. He wanted to shut it out. It was as if, in doing what she had made him do to the man, the pain had bounced back and hit him with more impact than he had used on the man.

However, she was not done yet. She made him follow the man with one bad leg who wobbled when he walked, the short man with skin black as tar and the wiry man with eyes that looked in opposite directions as if they had had a disagreement when he was a child. She made him find them, follow them and do to them what she had made him do to the first man. All of them cried and howled when it happened. All of them died a death filled with so much pain, a certain kind of pain that reached the depths of the flesh and yanked away everything that mattered. All seven of them, eventually, one after the other.

And when, three weeks later she told him she was done, he shook his head and fell down with exhaustion. He woke up on the bed in the house right next to the baby, a paste of vomit from him covering his face. He turned towards the door and saw her standing there.

"What more do you want?" he moaned.

"This is not what I imagined it would feel like."

"Have I not given you your revenge?"

"It feels empty."

"That kind of hunger and hollowness cannot be sated. It yearns for more always."

"More? Of what?"

"Of what you fed it the first time."

He got off the bed and walked towards her. She seemed terrified; like she was the day the men came for her. Like she was when they pushed her to the ground. He touched her face and she was cold. He withdrew his hand, turning his face away from hers.

"Why did you come?" It was only now that he thought to ask her the question.

"I had to at some point. My return, and that of all the other girls the world scarred, was inevitable. We were not going to let our songs be forgotten. Our fires would not be extinguished."

"But after all this while? Why now?"

"We lurked on the other side for so long, groping in the dark, scared, weary. We watched through the glass how the people who hurt us went on to hurt more and more people—young girls, little boys, frightened mothers. We watched. We screamed. We wanted to leave but there were no doors. You couldn't just walk away like it was a house. We screamed louder each day, our anguish growing into a song that chorused and swallowed everything. And at some point, our screams became loud enough that the glass shattered. Some of us crossed. Some of us were too tired to cross."

"The world burns and burns, charring even its own children."

"We ourselves burn the world."

She walked closer to him. He could feel the ice of her breath on the nape of his neck. He felt weightless. He wanted to turn and face her, but he did not know what he would see in her eyes. In that moment, the door creaked open and his sister and her fifth husband rushed in, shouting expletives at each other. Eleven months they had been together, the longest he had seen them. That was two months more than she had been with her previous husband. This one, she had sworn she loved with everything she held dear. She had once told him that she would die if he left her for another woman. Now, however, she called him a smelly cockroach, a wild dog, a crippled donkey and all the other names she could. It was over this time. She picked the child from the bed and when he started crying, she handed him over to her husband. Yes, it was over.

He stood there, watching them but not seeing as if his vision was fading. The baby cried louder and louder until he could not hear himself think. Still, he ignored the crying and the shouting and stood there, transfixed to the point she had left him. He listened. He listened to the sound of the girl going away. He listened, for something in the way her feet sunk into the ground. He wondered if she would ever come back.

Troy Onyango's work has been published in *Prairie Schooner, Wasafiri, Johannesburg Review of Books, Caine Prize Anthology, Kalahari Review* and *Transition* among others. The winner of the inaugural *Nyanza Literary Festival Prize* and first runner-up in the *Black Letter Media Competition*, he has also been shortlisted for the *Short Story Day Africa Prize*, the *Brittle Paper* Awards, and nominated for the *Pushcart Prize*. He holds an LL.B from the University of Nairobi and and MA in Creative Writing from the University of East Anglia, where he was a recipient of the *Miles Morland Foundation Scholarship*.

Yalla Nrooh Masr
Dennis Mugaa

A THIRST for self-destruction, I suppose, led me to remain unaffected by the gravity of having deliberately missed the flight back to Nairobi. As it was, my friends and I had travelled from Cairo to Dahab—considering it a fine decision in our pursuit of the absurdities of youth. My worry of being in a foreign country with fast depleting finances dissipated from the happiness around me. I was present, living in the moment with people I had come to love in the past month—perfectly in tune with the world.

I was seated on an intricately designed cushion with my legs crossed, in a café beside a promenade, smoking hashish and taking momentary pauses to inhale *shisha*.[42] Luiza was playing the guitar next to me, her dream catcher earrings dangling from side to side. The music wafted through the air—so sweet and savoury to the ears that I could almost taste it in my mouth. Rami had stood up with our new Egyptian friends, they sang at the top of their voices in Arabic, horribly out of tune. We all resonated at the same frequency. Our souls vibed: floating in a space of pure bliss where everything else was inconsequential.

The café owner had joined our circle: inhaling puff after puff and laughing with reckless abandon. Occasionally, he referred to me as "brother" in such a deep sincere way that I almost felt that we had known each other in a past life. We had tried to leave but instead, he insisted on having our company, so much so that he served us more *shisha* on the house. In addition, it turned out that he was an expert in rolling a joint; reaffirming his dubious claims that he had been a hippie in his younger golden years.

Beneath the midnight sky, the Red Sea glittered in tiny reflections from the stars and the moon. The waves beat softly against the shore, swirling in and out of themselves to a rhythm of their own making. I was flying into a cloud of deep introspection. The vibe: smooth, infinitely pleasing and peaceful. A Midnight High. A Midnight Flight. Midnight by Moonlight.

The thing about life is this: some moments can be thought of; some dreamt of for so long and others recalled from memory; but sometimes, even reality surpasses our greatest imagination. I had found a home so far, far away from home.

My phone beeped. It had been ringing over and over in the past half hour. It was my father calling but I could not bring myself to pick it up. Eventually, he gave up and sent a message. I looked at my phone to read it. My hands began to sweat and the previous composure I had faded.

I am at the airport waiting for you, which terminal will you come from?

42   Tobacco for smoking in a hookah.

I suddenly felt horrible for having lied that I would be arriving in Nairobi. But I didn't know what else to tell him. The fact that I had decided to prolong my stay in Egypt would have been beyond his comprehension: more so without his approval. I could picture him standing at the arrivals terminal in his brown cowboy hat, still stuck in what he termed as "the glorious eighties". His phone in hand and his fingernails tapping disapprovingly on the car bonnet: angry at my being late.

After I had completed my university, I applied for an internship position to teach English in Egypt. However, I did not do so in the most appropriate way given the friction between my father and me. In the years before, my mother played mediator, calming us down when we disagreed. But when she passed on, no one was left to pacify the storm and our fractious relationship was constantly on the verge of disintegrating.

I only informed him of my departure a day before leaving, explaining that it was an academic internship trip and that I would be back, in the hopes of placating him. By then, I had ensured to get my visa application approved and even borrowed money from relatives on the pretext of starting a business. My father was livid, especially after having gone through the trouble of securing a placement for me in a law firm.

Initially, I planned on saving enough so that I could move on to a different country. But that had proved disastrous in the past month. Despite things falling separately from my initial design, I was still determined to travel indefinitely: to see places and live out a lifelong dream of experiencing the world for what it truly was. I harboured an aversion to washed-up platitudes about how life was meant to unfold: going to school, getting a job, and getting married. A banal greyness to the spectrum of colour I saw and felt around me.

"Bro! Bro! Pass the blunt," Rami said, interrupting my flow of thought.

"We should start going to the club," I said.

"Yes, Kenya is right," Ahmed, one of our Egyptian friends, joined in. I was certain he had forgotten my name. Granted, he had only joined us an hour before. "I will take you guys to the best club in Sharm El-Sheikh." Luiza, Rami and I had wanted to go to a nightclub for a long time. It hadn't happened since it proved difficult to find a good place. Ahmed, however, had changed the dynamics drastically with an array of suggestions until we finally let him choose where he thought was best. There was something in his voice, a form of certainty about the places he mentioned as though he had been involved in the drawing up of their plans and knew each one of them by heart.

"Luiza, are you coming?" I asked.

"Yessssss," she said. Her Portuguese accent always drove me to exasperation; every time she spoke it was in the most excited of gasps as though she had never known sadness. "Let's goooo, it will be fun."

I don't know why we settled on going all the way to Sharm El-Sheikh just to get to a nightclub. It took us almost two hours to get there, by which time the effects of the hashish had worn off drastically. Luiza and Rami, however, were the essence of life. They seemed high on it, like they were made out of happiness—it radiated out of them, as if they were its centre-light.

It took us some time to negotiate the entrance fee as we were trying to be frugal with money. We got into Pacha nightclub after paying what was, to my mind, a fortune. Once inside, we spotted a large group of exchange students we had met back in Cairo. The excitement was immediate when we saw them as we didn't know they had chosen to spend their weekend in Sharm El-Sheikh. The club music was boring, stale, and hard to dance to; the DJ was only playing electronic music. It certainly wasn't the best club we were promised. Nonetheless, after a few shots of whisky, it was surreal, marvellous and immensely gratifying.

We stopped moving to the beats of the music. I asked Luiza to dance with me. Someone else joined in and then Rami came. Soon there was an inexhaustible variety of dance moves and the dance floor reverberated, full of excitement and exuberance. The club colours changed: Red, Yellow, Blue, Violet, and Green. An effervescent cheer leapt out of each one us: a certain *joie de vivre* I thought was beyond me. Everyone danced with each other (boy and girl, girl and girl, boy and boy). An endless amount of alcohol steamed past me. I lost Luiza, I found her again. Arms flared near me and far from me as we moved in graceful and less graceful circles, dancing in contrast to each other. We thought that we would live forever and danced like it was our last day.

Some people stumbled and others fell on their way to the bar counter. I kissed Luiza, someone else kissed another. The club security personnel surrounded us trying to get a hold of the situation to no avail. It just didn't matter. Our passions controlled us, lighting a flame inside us and we let it burn! An ethereal beauty to life connected us: it was euphoria! We were Young, Wild and Free; with a freedom of thought that coasted across the Sahara desert sand, never settling among the dunes but drifting on to the sea, remembering only what we wanted to remember.

THE next morning Rami, Luiza and I barely managed to make it back to our hotel in Dahab. I woke up at noon to more than fifty missed calls from my father. I didn't want to call him back, but I reasoned that because of the emotional turmoil he might have been through, the situation at the very least warranted a phone call. I left Luiza and Rami asleep on the bed and walked outside to the balcony, bracing myself as I dialed my father's number.

He picked up on the first beep.

"Where are you?" His voice had a trace of anger mixed with worry. It was dragged and tired as though he had barely slept.

"I'm still here."

"Where is here?"

"Egypt."

"I waited for you, how dare you! You lied to—"

"I know, I don't want to argue. I just—"

"Why do you always do this?"

"Do what?"

"Never listen to me!"

And there it was: the distance between our lines of thought, as though an ice-cold misty sea separated us. And there was no way to get to the other side.

"I have, ever since mum died."

"Don't bring your mother into this."

"I know it's a—"

"Know what. They are expecting you at the law firm on Monday!" I felt his irritation on the other end of the line. There was no winning with him. "The work you said you had isn't even happening. I have asked my friend to give you another chance to show up!"

"It has just been delayed—"

"Then," my father paused. It was too long to be the normal pause so present in international calls. "Then stay there, don't come back home!" He hung up the phone.

Even though I had anticipated such a response I was heartbroken when it came. I didn't want to go back. The thought was disconcerting: going back with nothing to show for it. I had arrived in Egypt a month before for a teaching position in Cairo. It turned out that the job advertised was false. I found out when I went to the school where I was supposed to teach. When I told the administrators they stared at me with surprise and a remorseful look. They explained they did not have any position available and that it was probably an internet ploy. I was extremely crestfallen wondering how I could have trusted an internet link.

However, it so happened that Rami and Luiza had also fallen for the same scam. We met outside the school on that particular day. Since high school, I had always found it difficult to make new friends. Puberty, it seemed, had dealt me a hard hand. I had to vibe with someone a certain way to consider them my friend. Therefore, by the time of completing my university, I was on the perceived sad end of the social spectrum having a total of five friends.

Hence, I was surprised that we got along well when the three of us decided to go to a café in Maadi to lament our horrid luck. I found both of them rather unfazed by what had happened given that they had also come from different countries. They seemed to somehow go with the flow. As if life was a river, and they, its water, flowing along in supreme serene calm. Luiza, I discovered, was my soulmate from Brazil. We understood each other profoundly. Rami was from Tunisia, he always wore bohemian hippie trousers and was fluent in four languages: Arabic, French, English, and German, which I found impressive. Over coffee, we decided to travel and since then, we had been backpacking all around Egypt.

I slipped my phone into my pocket and went back inside the apartment. Rami and Luiza stirred a little, savouring the last vestiges of sleep. I woke them up so that we would not incur the charges of checking out from the hotel later than expected.

Rami sat up on the bed and said, "*Yalla nrooh Masr.*"[43]

"What does that mean?" I asked; although I had been in Egypt for some time, Arabic still hovered over me without any coherence.

"It means let's go to Cairo."

"I thought it meant, let's go to Egypt?" Luiza asked.

"It's both of them Luiza."

We went to buy a few souvenirs at the bazaar in Dahab. I had found out from Khan El-Khalili *souk*[44] market that bargaining was an art form. The traders always started with the highest prices while at the same time adding "good price". Sometimes they got angry when we began at low prices which may or may not have been the actual prices. Later on, we boarded the bus to Cairo in the evening. Our Egyptian friends gifted us rolls of hashish. It was illegal, but they told us to transport it inside a perfume bottle—which was what Luiza and I did. The police and military checkpoints in South Sinai were several since it was almost the anniversary for the Revolution Day of January 25th of the Arab Spring.

❧

THE cold air inside the bus bit hard into my skin like sharp ice crystals. I woke up momentarily and tucked my hands into the thin blanket that the three of us were sharing. It was dawn and the sun was peering far out in the distance from the sprawling metropolis of Cairo. The orange hue would have been beautiful to behold on any other day, but I was tired: my back ached and my neck was cramped from having sat down for almost thirteen hours in the bus. Incidentally, we had come across such lame luck in the sitting arrangement—we were positioned right below a billowing stream of cold air from the AC.

There were signs that a sandstorm was looming. A few cars had been parked on the side of the road to wait it out. Our driver, however, never stopped. Instead, he adjusted his Arafat scarf to cover his mouth and nose and turned up the radio. A popular Arabic song played—El3ab Yalla. I didn't know what it meant but the tune was catchy and had a swagger to it. The song seeped into my subconscious and for a moment I felt like I was part of a contemporary version of Arabian Nights.

I struggled to ease myself back to sleep without much success. I glanced at

43   Arabic for "Let's go to Egypt".
44   Street market or bazaar.

Luiza and Rami, feeling a wave of sadness slowly rise inside me. We had been through a lot in the past month; we celebrated Christmas and the New Year together, which I had never spent away from home, and we had eventually become family. Porthos, Athos, and Aramis: The Three Musketeers. We existed in this space where everything was perfect, full of love and devoid of worry. No matter how much longer I wanted it to last, I knew it wasn't going to be forever.

We had been to so many places together. The best places were Luxor, Aswan, and Hurghada. In Luxor, we went to the temples from where the ancient Egyptian Kings used to rule. Its evocative ruins of a glorious past were immensely staggering. The city was a spiral, weaving ancient grandeur with lacklustre modernity. One got confused as to where the old ended and where the new began. We became famous on the West Bank of the Nile in Luxor. Mostly because of the contrast that we had, and it was so evident to the locals that we were travellers. They referred to me as Bob Marley because of my Afro which I found extremely funny.

In Aswan, we rode in *felucca*[45] boats on the Nile, cruising down the river propelled by not just the wind but by our thirst for adventure. When we got to the Nubian Village in Aswan, I noticed that the whole place was a sea of colour—predominantly blue. I had worn a dashiki shirt and I blended into it. Rami, in typical Rami fashion, coaxed us into engaging the traders in singing and dancing. He had a warm, welcoming feel to him—a genuine quality that made people comfortable in his presence. We were so engrossed in our performance that we did not notice when other tourists formed a circle around us, cheering us on. Afterwards, we got discounts in all the shops that we went to. And we even got matching henna tattoos for free.

In Hurghada, Luiza and I went snorkelling and free diving. Rami didn't like water and instead watched us from the shore. We found freediving to be a dream—a dream of different shades of blue. With one breathe, we dived in and became one with the sea; all our worry faded into oblivion. Inside the water, we found a different world. It felt like there was some part of the universe that was hidden from us before and we were seeing it for the first time encircled by a deep blue hue. The beautiful outline of the coral reefs and the fish inside the water existed in harmony that gave form to my desire for peace. Luiza, ahead of me, swam deeper and deeper into the sea, I followed her. And then I felt it that deep connection to the world that I had yearned for so long. How could I ever go back to my life before?

"I'm so tired," Luiza complained as we approached Cairo.

"I'm cold," Rami said.

The desultory exchange of words ended. I placed my head on the window and adjusted the curtains to block the sun from hurting my eyes.

---

45   A narrow fast lateen-rigged wooden sailing boat.

WE reached Cairo in the early hours of the morning. At the bus station, dust particles whirled from strong gusts of wind. A newspaper from a stand announced that the President's main rival had dropped out of the race for the March elections in unclear circumstances.

So much was happening simultaneously.

The call to prayer from half a dozen mosques in the station rent the air.

Hooting everywhere.

Arabic phrases.

Cars switching lanes at undesignated spots.

The smell of cigarette smoke.

More dust.

However, I had grown accustomed to the chaos and grandeur of Cairo during the time I had been there.

"Yalla! Yalla!" the bus driver screamed for us to alight. We drifted from sleep and lazily walked out to crowded streets.

The three of us had rented out an apartment in Nasr City. When we got there, we found that the landlord had locked us out and changed the locks. Our bags were locked inside as well. We were so tired; we needed to take a shower and rest. It had not occurred to us to remember to pay for the coming month's rent because we were travelling a lot.

Furthermore, I had little left to afford another month in Cairo. It dawned on me that I would probably not have a place to sleep, I had no more money left, my visa was expiring and my flight had left without me. Before leaving for Egypt, I had not considered that things would fall this drastically out of place. But I still had my family (Rami and Luiza) and somehow in my moment of temporary despair, it assuaged me.

Therefore, I didn't panic but I knew I had to get back home. Rami suggested that I should try and get deported as it would be a free ticket back to Kenya.

"How?" I asked him.

"Go and protest at Tahrir Square."

On some level, I was perhaps up for it. However, given the heavy army personnel presence, I was unsure of where I would end up. Chances were quite slim that I would be on a flight home.

Despite the setback and with all of us still heavy with sleep, we decided to visit the Pyramids. Rami offered to pay for me. It seemed like a good enough idea as the landlord would be unavailable until the afternoon. At least that was what he told us. Egyptian time, in our experience, dictated that he would probably arrive in the evening.

We took a cab to Giza which was not too far from Cairo. It was our fourth time to go there, and each time we were astounded by their splendour as though their majestic quality never faded to our eyes. We took photos beside the Sphinx and thereafter rode on camels. Luiza argued with our tour guide about whether the Pyramids were built by aliens. The guide disagreed explaining that it was ancient Egyptians. Regardless, she pulled out proof from the internet, but he didn't want to hear any of it. Eventually, he tried to sell her an artifact, but she declined.

The tour took us until late afternoon and we went back to Cairo. We ate *koshari*[46] in Downtown before making our way to a spot we had discovered in Zamalek beside the River Nile. As we sat on a bench, I couldn't help but think that I was wrong. Thoughts of my leaving home in the way I did came to me in a flood. I wanted to defy convention. To my mind, convention was irrevocably flawed. The idea of working in a law firm did not sit with me well. I wanted to see the world for what it was: be present, meet beautiful people, learn new languages, live without having money as an object of desire and for it to consume me in the way that it perhaps did to my father.

"Why do you look sad Tendwa?" Luiza asked. Rami had noticed too but I tried my best to hide it from them.

"Because I will leave you guys."

"Look at us," Rami said. "We had nothing in common before we met, neither religion nor culture, but here we are finding something similar in our differences, you two are the best thing to ever happen to me."

"I will miss you," I said as tears welled up my eyes.

I took a moment to be alone and called my father. Remorseful words tumbled out of me. He sounded exceedingly angry but after a back and forth that lasted forever, he finally had his way.

Luiza, Rami and I looked out at the boats as they splashed water, breaking the waves of the enormous river. A cold wind breezed past me into my past. And there I was in what remained of the day having lived out a dream and getting ready to wake up. I felt an odd sense of melancholy filled with immense satisfaction. The evanescence moment stretched out to limitless possibilities. Although I had failed, I had found beautiful spaces in invisible cities and met people along the way who taught me a lot about life.

I gave Rami and Luiza Maasai *shukas*[47] I had carried to give as gifts. We put our arms across each other's shoulders. I cried, unable to hold back tears. In that moment, it was they who mattered most. We were all emotional—promising we would never forget: the laughs, the hugs, the kisses, the adventures and times we shared, but most of all each other.

Dennis Mugaa *is a writer from Meru, Kenya. He was longlisted for the* Afritondo Short Story Prize *and was a finalist for the* Black Warrior Review Fiction Contest. *His work has appeared or is forthcoming in* Jalada, Lolwe, Isele *and* Washington Square Review. *He is currently studying for an MA in Creative Writing at the* University of East Anglia *where he is a* Miles Morland Scholar.

---

46   Egypt's national dish and a widely popular street food, mixing pasta, rice and lentils, garnished with chickpeas and crispy fried onions and topped with a tomato sauce.
47   Traditional Maasai blankets

Falling
Aress Mohamed

MAHAD alighted from the matatu at a stage along Thika Road. Crossing the footbridge should have been easy—it was a sunny Sunday afternoon and the streets of Nairobi were not swarming with people as on weekdays. But it was dizzying, even though the bridge was not high up, because his arms felt heavy and his gut was wrenching itself free. It was a constant, this feeling in his stomach, but ever since Ma and Uncle Hussen called to say they had brought Farah to *this place* two weeks ago and went back to Garissa (he was out of town for work) his stomach was falling to his knees and it felt like there was no ground under his feet. Inside, Mahad walked the ragged road down the big compound strewn with overgrown grass and garbage piles, past office buildings and wards that were old and overused. Ma and Uncle Hussen had given him the directions. "Look for Ward Five." Ward Five was an orange building with a concrete front yard fortified by a see-through fence made of wire mesh and wooden planks. Spread inside, like prisoners in a prison yard, were patients in blue uniform.

A tall, Somali-looking youth opened the door. As Mahad walked in several patients rose from the floor and gathered around him, like a flight of sparrows flitting off the ground to settle on a tree. They tugged at his arms and touched his face. They looked at him with the innocence of little children, but there was a cold, dazed stare in their eyes too.

"You've come to see who?" One of them jumped onto his path.

"Farah."

"Farah!" They ran ahead, tripping over the others. "Farah!"

On the floor a few yards away stirred a figure. Mahad made to walk on but the figure lugged itself up, lumbered towards Mahad and embraced him.

"Mahad bro."

A blindfold must have been wrapped around Mahad's mind because it became blind. When it came to, Farah's voice registered first; his *person*, much later. When it did, it could not reconcile Farah's voice and the speaker, who was obese, sluggish, slobbering, his mouth contorted sideways, his face and limbs twitching involuntarily, his skin covered with grime and flares, his body teeming with lice like ants on an anthill. Mahad would have sworn it was not his brother were it not for his distinctive facial features: the slanting forehead, the bushy eyebrows, the drooping lower lip, the patchy beard. Farah must have changed so much in the five years since Mahad had seen him, since *what happened.*

Mahad's stomach—no, the creature that it had now become—fell free. Like the way he fell in that dream in which he climbs up their childhood house by grabbing the blocks sticking out from its edges and he marvels at the world he can see from up there. Then the ground slips from under the house and he remains suspended in mid-air, gripping the blocks with all his strength, and his arms tire out and he falls through empty space and the scariest thing was not the falling but having nothing underneath his feet.

"Farah." Mahad sat down on the floor, dizzy. His lungs squeezed tight. The name came out as an involuntary whisper.

Farah sat, too. His belly floated about him, more like a life vest than a part of his body. It was a by-product of a year of taking old-generation antipsychotics prescribed by a psychiatrist at the Garissa Provincial General Hospital's mental wing. A year ago was the first time he received any psychiatric help, even though he had been sick for four years up to that point. It did not happen because Ma and Uncle Hussen believed in psychiatrists (they did not). It was the only option they had not tried. Also, Ma was afraid for the children. When she tried to take Farah's phone away because he was using it to watch porn, he clobbered her and tried to strangle the children— Osman and Ilhan—for trying to intervene. Ma took everything he threw at her, she watched him and washed him and cleaned the sheets he soiled and fed him and took his thumping and worried over him when he ran away and got lost and prayed for him every night, but when he squeezed his siblings' little necks tight, she was willing to try anything.

When he heard of the diagnosis, Mahad ran to google it. 'Schizophrenia' did not sound so ominous, until he read the words *permanent, incurable, delusions, hallucinations, jumbled thinking, odd movements*. Neither were the medications he was put on to "manage the symptoms." Aripiprazole. Haloperidol. Paliperidone. That is, until he read what they could also do: *weight gain, drowsiness, sexual problems, dizziness, anxiety, constipation, nausea, seizures, low blood pressure, dyskinesia…*

Ma had a different view on the source of her first-born son's new weight.

"This thing you think is flesh or fat is evil that resides in him. *What's* in there is liquid that needs to be purged."

Farah's face twitched without his noticing. He bore his eyes into Mahad's, creamy, wide open, unblinking. The Eyes, as Mahad called Farah's staring, appeared after he had started talking gibberish and just before he started shedding off his clothes. He would stare at you for minutes, hours if you could stand it, lips sealed, nostrils flaring, Eyes plead-accusing.

The indictment in Farah's eyes was creamy, naked, unmistakable—like a peeled banana. You let them do that to me! They screamed loud enough to scare chickens into frenzy. You went off when you were the only one who could help! You didn't fight for me! I tried brother, Mahad's eyes said. Allah knows I tried but I was a child whose word didn't mean anything. And I went off because I couldn't watch it anymore, *what happened*. But this never was enough both to Farah and himself. His eyes averted. No matter how much he tried to run, the guilt wouldn't abate; it overran him, like floods speeding down a plain and tearing down houses.

"Made any friends here?" Mahad cracked his knuckles for the fifth time that afternoon, and he squeezed his fingers.

Farah did not hear. He was staring through him. You would ask him ten questions and he would answer two. Mahad asked several times.

"Moha is nice." Farah nodded towards the youth that manned the gate. He caressed his cheek and spoke nonchalantly. Back when he was well, he would do this to appear confident; now, to demonstrate sanity, too. To Mahad, the cheek-caressing and the nonchalant manner of speaking were the last vestiges of who his brother used to be. "The rest are all crazy." Farah laughed.

Mahad noticed Farah's front teeth were missing. When he laughed, he looked like a baby. Mahad realized for the first time in five years that he had lost his brother. Even in the five years since he left home because he could not stand watching *what happened,* he never once considered that Farah may have passed that point in one's mental health where one still has hope of a normal life in the future. He was sure of the day when he would have enough money to take him to the best psychiatrists in the world and they would fix him anew. Now he was not sure. It seemed it was not *what happened* that would snuff out Mahad's hope. Not the diagnosis, not the permanency of the condition, not its incurability, not the long list of side effects the drugs could cause, not the obesity, not the scars on his skin, not the fact that he was at *this place,* not the lines of lice that were now checking patterns into his plain blue uniform, not the contorted mouth, not the dyskinesia, not his urological problems. No. None of that did. It was mere missing teeth that would break Mahad clean in half. His gut dived further. The order of the cosmos shifted without warning. Or maybe he realized the way he perceived that order was wrong, and with it the ground that held him, and it was a *falling*.

II

THE thing that roamed inside Mahad was not always big. When it came, it did not come fast, and it did not come *at* him, but *about* and *around* him, slow, the way the houses of growing town start enveloping its outermost house. It began as a flutter of hot wind inside his chest soon after he left home after *what happened,* maybe because his body could not forget it and could not accept it either, so the memory of it floated around inside him, unwanted, unsettled, like a spirit wandering between two worlds. Then it became a knot because the guilt he felt after *what happened* gathered and curdled. Then the lump sprouted limbs when Farah clobbered her and the kids. When it became a humanoid with arching ram-horns, eagle-claws and split snake-tongue, and it was all red and hot like a flame, he started to think it had become a jinn because that's how he saw the jinn in his dreams.

It had reached full maturity when he fell into a crippling depression, and he became a walking contradiction, bright on the outside but black on the inside. A few months later when Cousin Gedi and Cousin Raage fell into depression and began roaming the streets of Garissa, acting insane, Mahad googled 'genetics and mental illness' and was certain he would go insane too, and he became cloaked in fear of jinn possession and going mad. He was worried he would strip off his clothes without knowing what he was doing and walk around naked and talk to invisible people and get chased around by children who would call him "Mad Mahad" and he would couple with mad females right in the streets until the shopkeepers covered them with sheets of cloth out of discomfort, like Shimoy and Biif and other mad people in Garissa did. The creature then spread from his gut and took over other parts of his body; it squeezed his lungs tight, made his back hurt bad and his arms feel heavy. And when he told his two close friends they could not understand because they were happy people who chewed gum and whistled, and he wished he could do that—chew gum and whistle—but he could not and all he could do to cope was to crack his knuckles and breathe hard. His life became that dream: the ground beneath his feet was giving way and those blocks that were his sanity were slipping from his hands.

III

MAHAD opened a plastic wrapper he had brought and removed the contents. A dozen cupcakes and several little packs of juice. The other patients lingered closer. Mahad gave each of them a cupcake and a juice pack. Farah held his cupcake in his hand, unaware of it.

A patient said, "Farah never fights for plates." He laughed. "Here you must fight for plates."

Another said, "And he does not like eating porridge and cabbages every day. So we eat for him. He is our friend."

Farah had a look of interest in his eyes. "Bro, can I ask you something?"

"Of course."

"Can I go back to university?"

"Yes, you will." Mahad's back pained. He jerked his chest forward to ease the pain. The bones cracked. He sighed. "But you need to get well first."

"I like university."

"I know. I remember how you knew you wanted to be a psychologist back in primary school."

"I like to be a psychologist." Farah grinned.

"I didn't know what I wanted."

Ma liked to say, "My son has been eaten by people. That time he went abroad to represent his country in a foreign language competition, that was when they took the first bite. That news reached the remotest nomad who knows this family. First kid of an entire clan to top his class all through primary school, to reach high school, and to go abroad, to attend university. No, make that two clans, mine and his father's. The day he returned with a medal and some prize money, he was not the son that I gave birth to. And the day he won a scholarship to France to become a doctor, they swallowed what was left of him."

Mahad used to envy Farah for his brightness and the adoration he received. Now, the thought that he had blocked all these years stood right before him: if Ma was right, maybe it was *he* that ate his own brother.

Mahad squeezed his knuckles tight.

Farah spilled juice down his shirt. He laughed a toothless laugh. Like a tickled child, his cheeks were plump and his whole body shook. His body convulsed, like he did back during *what happened,* when they pinned him down and had him swallow the liquid with his nose pinched shut and he gurgled. Mahad looked at his brother, at least at what was left of him after the drugs and after *what happened,* and wondered if this was truly his brother. Wondered if he was still that boy in that photograph in the album back at home that Ma kept in her box, the one entirely composed of him—because he was the only one who had occasion to take photographs—taken with his best friend Liban back when in high school, in which he looks thin and tall, and both are wearing baggy jeans that were in vogue at the time. Or in one of the many other photographs of him abroad, holding a camera in his hands, the sun on his forehead, a look of assurance on his face, the world at his feet. If he was not that person, then was he as good as dead? If not, what or who was he? What did insanity really mean? Was it a return to a former state such as childhood and so his twenty-eight-year-old brother was a child? Or was it some liminal stage between life and death? Was it some death? *a* death?

Mahad mourned for his brother, for all that he used to be and he could have been, would have been and would never be. He moaned for himself too, for the loss of a brother, an older brother to talk to, rely on when he had no food to eat and share responsibilities with because he had no one except God to fall back on.

IV

WHEN he was ten years old, at different times, several girls from Mahad's *duksi*[48] would fall ill. They would faint, eat without stop and not sleep. The *duksi* teacher and other sheikhs would recite Quran on each girl, squirting spittle on her after every few verses, and they would press short pipes to each of her ears and blow *azan*[49] through it, and they would whip her. After a week she would be cured.

Abdi, one of the older boys, said, "Jinn had entered the girls."

They stood on the edge of the fence where they washed the Quran off their wooden planks.

---

48   An Islamic boarding school or madrasa.
49   The Islamic call to perform the five daily prayers, usually recited by a muezzin.

Mahad said, "What are jinn?"

"They are creatures like us humans, only we can't see them but they can see us."

"They sound scary." Mahad spilled water on his plank from the small plastic container. The water ran down its length in rivulets.

Another boy, Ahmed, said, "They are made of smokeless flaming wind. And they have powers like flying and knowing things we can't know."

"They climb on top of each other until below the first heaven and they listen to the secrets of God and the angels. That's how they can predict the future." Abdi bent down and placed his wet hand on the ground until sand clung to it, then he ran it up and down his wet plank until the ink dissolved. "Then God chases them away using the shooting stars we see at night."

Ahmed said, "I heard they can take any form like animals and objects and people. And if you annoy them, they slap you and you go mad. That's how people go mad."

Mahad gathered leaves from the trees that formed the thorn fence. He wadded them and used it to mark green horizontal lines on his dry plank, where he would later write with ink. His forehead creased. "I bet mad people like Shimoy and Biif became mad because jinn slapped them."

He became afraid of jinn. Whenever he was alone he imagined a group of jinn were sitting around watching him, planning to slap him and make him mad. When he talked to a stranger he feared it was a jinn in the guise of a person. He imagined they were red burning wind, smokeless, with arching ram horns, sinuous human-like body, forking snake-tongue and eagle-claws. At night, when the lamp went out, he saw dark apparitions with horns, hovering and swaying and reaching for him with claws. He would shriek and his mum would switch on the torch and say, "It is only the curtain dear."

"Ma, will I be entered by jinn and become like Shimoy?"

"No dear."

"Or will I become like those mentally handicapped children who are chained in houses and eat their waste?"

"That will not happen dear. Say *auzubillahi*[50] to the *shaitan*[51] and go back to sleep."

V

THIS place. Mahad looked at it. Some patients were sprawled on the floor, like dead soldiers; some curled up in fetal positions, like wounded ones; others fought and played. Some drove imaginary cars, their hands steering and their mouths making engine sounds. Others fought enemies no one could see and conducted military parades. One defecated on the floor and used his shirt to wipe himself. Another banged at the door, trying to get away, Moha at his heels.

"Paul, you must take your medication whether you like it or not!"

---

50   A common Arabic phrase that translates to "I seek refuge in Allah" or "I seek protection in Allah."
51   Lit. "the enemy" referring to the Devil.

Two patients joined Moha to subdue Paul. Paul hit out, but staggered like a drunk. They pinned him down easy and pulled down his pants and Moha injected him to a calm stupor.

Beyond the ward traffic whizzed along Thika Road, a faint reminder that life existed right outside these dead walls. Mahad was thinking about something people said: patients raped other patients, and it didn't happen only in the maximum-security wards over to that side where the state dumped its mentally ill offenders, but it could happen in any ward. What if Farah got raped? He would be too drugged to defend himself. The thought clawed at him. I know I have to take Farah out of this place as soon as I can, he thought. But where would I take him? I can't take him back home to Ma and Uncle Hussen because there he would have to stay quarantined in a hut to keep him from running away or beating the children and Ma to a pulp. And I certainly can't afford the decent private hospitals in the city. I can't even afford the thirty thousand shillings they charged here even if I wanted to keep him here. But I must take him out of here urgently…

Mahad scratched himself all over. Lice crawled on his skin. His chest tightened. He took deep breaths but the tightening did not loosen. The patients clamoured. They said things.

"Brathe buy me cigarettes."

"Waria give me twenty bob."

"Help us, Farah is our friend."

They touched him again. Touch so cold it made Mahad shiver. The air reeked of human waste. He scratched himself. Their Eyes stirred the anxious creature inside. They were sucking him into their world, and he felt cold and sad and his movements and speech slowed. He stood up and made for the door but his knees felt weak and he felt he was going to collapse. And the patients were on his heels, and there were so many hands all over him and they were all trying to drag him back down.

The place seemed to spin. His mind seemed to boil and fizzle, leaving his body. Mahad could see his body from a distance. It was as though he was being wiped away. It was a *fragmenting,* a *disorganizing,* a *disintegrating.* Mahad groped about the floor for his mind, trying to capture it. Before it was too late. With all his effort he looked at the floor, at the ceiling, at the patients. He tried to *see* them. He tried to touch the floor, his arms. To see if he was conscious. He could not feel them. The room felt as though it was there but not there.

My consciousness is slipping away fast, Mahad thought.   I feel lonely and terrified   what's happening to me   what am I slipping into I'm sure it isn't sleep   am i dying or going insane   or both   did people lose their minds when they died or they died when they lost their minds   and would it be better to die and so lose your mind than lose your mind and die a sort of undeath   is it better to have a healthy mind but a dead body like total paralysis than to have a healthy body but lose your mind   i'd rather

physical death than going insane   no no no   not in this country   not
in *this place*   but too late now   my worst fear's come to pass   this jinn
inside me has claimed my mind and my eyes   i'm already having the eyes
i'm staring at everything with wide eyes   this must be how madness starts
     what's happening to me?   why is my speech heavy and slow   everything
is happening in slow motion   i'm on my knees   i'm touching my face
i cant feel my face   im touching farah's face   i can't feel his face   i cant
feel the patients' faces   i'm staggering about   i'm touching patients' faces
     a thing is hovering over towards me   tall and wavy
     what's wrong, farah's bro?
     i'm looking at it with the Eyes
     this is Moha are you okay?
     i don't know
     are you feeling sick?
     i don't know what's happening to me
     more things are circling around me   i'm trying to breathe   i cant
breathe
     what's happening to me
     nothing is happening to you   just relax ok?
     i don't know how
      just try   i'll go get some help
     please don't leave me   why are you leaving me   i'm lonely   i need you
      i'll be back in a second
      please

VI

AT first Mahad saw it before his eyes, *what happened,* like an act playing. He
saw it the way it happened. Farah's friend calling home from Lille to report
Farah was "unwell" and that he is being sent back home "to recover." Uncle
Hussen leaving Garissa for Nairobi to get Farah from the airport. He and
Farah arriving back home two days later. Farah being taken into the thatched
house whose sand floor was swept clean and smelt of incense. Then it was no
longer Farah but he—Mahad—that was entering the house and lying on the
mattress lain on the ground. Then it was no longer an act playing before him
but something that he was experiencing.

Now, the following morning, they file in at ten o'clock just as the women
sling the slaughtered goat from a stump on the neem tree. This time it's not
Mahad but his little brother Osman who stands next to Uncle Hussein to
usher the sheikhs in. They eat. They place a pipe on the rim of each of his
ears, and read the *azan* into it. They begin reading the Quran at the top
of their voices and spitting on Mahad. The chorus continues late into the
evening. They pick it up the following morning.

On the seventh morning, they say, "We've entertained these boys enough.

Osman, climb that tree and bring fifteen of the best."

Ma raises her hands towards the skies. "May Allah make them the best cure for him."

When it begins, maybe Osman does what Mahad did back then and goes round the house and sits beneath the window. Maybe he feels the crack of the whip as though it were landing on his own skin. Maybe he'll wonder which is louder, the deafening incantations or his brother's howl. Maybe he decides there's no comparison, like pattering rain and roaring thunder.

They say, "Now *they* are feeling it."

Later they say, "Tell us where you came from. Tell us what you want from this young man?"

"I don't know what you are asking me."

"Tell us your name."

"Mahad."

"Liar!"

"Wallahi. Osman, tell them I'm not jinn."

On the fourth week, neighbours and relatives flock to the compound and sit under trees and in houses. More curious than concerned. More sheikhs join the team. They shift Mahad from the house and set up camp outside. They roll up their sleeves. Their faces sparkle with sweat, their beards with drivel. The whip cracks and cracks and cracks. Until the skin on his back is flayed, like a peeled tomato.

"Tell us your name."

"Mahad."

"Must be one of those *hafiz* jinn that recite Quran alongside people, blocking their supplications."

"Tricky fellows."

On the fifth week they say, "Tell us your name."

"Mahad."

"Must be *insi* then, the evil eye."

"Yes. Harder to remove."

They send Uncle Hussen to the market to fetch them. Rue, lotus, peppermint, senna, Indian costus, black seed, camphor and frankincense. They peel, grind, grate, boil, blend, mix, sieve. He drinks up. He retches. He disgorges. Over and over. They have him lie on his back to empty the bottle down his nose. The first droplet has him flying to the roof. He makes to bolt. They circle him. He knows he can't hurl men to the ground like Farah did. He shoots like a dart instead, aiming for the small spaces between them. They grab his arms. He tries to wriggle free, but they haul him to the ground and pin him down. The women and girls cover their eyes and turn away. The sun burns so hot and so bright the ground seems to shimmy. Farah had head-butted one of them in the throat but Mahad bites one in the breast until it almost comes off. They bust his mouth open. They pinch his nose shut and empty a bottle into his mouth. Then up his nose. He cannot breathe. He gurgles. Convulses. They tie his wrists and ankles and chain him to a tree. He sits in a pool of his own vomit. He hallucinates. He stops eating. He stops sleeping.

Weeks pass. The sheikhs start to leave. Some go back to the centres where they exorcised possessed people and rehabilitated addict Somali boys from America using whips and herbal potions.

The relatives say, "They say there's a sheikh in Wajir if he spits on mad people they are cured. And he only takes a hundred thousand only."

Sheikh Wajir comes and says, "Give me one week with him and you'll wash your hands off this problem."

When he runs out of whips and herbs he takes a paper full of money and says, "They need me in Banaaney now. May God cure him."

The relatives say, "They say there's a sheikh in Mombasa everyone he spit on is cured on the spot. And he only charges two hundred thousand."

Sheikh Mombasa says, "There's people living inside this boy."

The relatives say, "We knew it."

Ma says, "I've always known my boy was eaten."

Sheikh Mombasa says, "Give me ten days and I'll fling each one of them out." After two weeks he takes a paper bag full of money and says, "My family needs me now. May God cure him."

Mahad says, "Please untie me."

Uncle Hussen says, "I have to close down the shop because there's no money left." (Uncle Hussen had inherited from Pa both the shop and Ma when he died five years earlier.)

Mahad says, "I want to go back to school."

Osman says, "I know spitting Quran works if jinn enter you but there are no jinns in Farah."

Uncle Hussen says, "How would you know?"

Osman says, "I *just* know. We should take him to a doctor."

Uncle Hussein says, "The only cure anyone needs is the Quran."

Mahad says, "Please untie me."

The season changes. The heat gives in to windstorms. Mahad starts talking to himself. First Quran verses. Then a poem he read in high school. Some random French phrases that give way for gibberish. He howls them louder than the winds until he loses his voice. He threatens. Fights. Beats Ma and Uncle Hussein and the sheikhs. The chains grow bigger, tighter. He pleads. Begs. With no voice, he plead-accuses with the Eyes. He sheds his clothes, and the relatives stop coming, their curiosity filled. Nobody remembers to sleep. The little children are forgotten and lurk in the shadows, terrified.

Osman wanders through the woods out beyond the neighbourhood during the day starts and starts sleeping at friends' houses at night. Some random nights he comes home late at night and tries to sleep. He dreams of falling from a house with no ground beneath it. As the howling winds change into rain a letter of admission might arrive from a university, having only finished high school months before. He might jump at the opportunity and leaves his brother, without looking back. But the memory of *what happened* starts to flutter in his stomach like the wings of a sparrow. The guilt slowly curdles into a lump.

VII

The thing is back with two other things   they have white coats   the things hover in the air
their lips are walking
tell us what's wrong?
please help me
are you feeling pain?
i don't know what's happening to me   can i touch you
tell us what's wrong?
the jinn inside me possessed me   he's making me mad
there's no jinn inside you
i'm totally gone
looks like a panic attack
i'm no longer anyone
have you ever felt like this before?
i shouldn't have left him
what?
my brother   it's all my fault
how?
i've lost my dignity   how can i have gone crazy   i'm so young
we'll help you
i can't be gone
is there somebody we can call?
please god   why did you let me lose my mind
we'll take care of you
the things are taking my arms   they are dragging me away
where are you taking me   don't keep me in *this place*
don't worry, you will not be admitted here
i know they are lying   they are going keep me here
i see myself staggering on the cold floor of Mathari   bits of me i think
i have Ma's bruised face   Farah's peeled-tomato skin   my clay-hard gut
is falling free   clanging on the floor   my eyes are itching   something is
coming out   something wet   a lot of it   all at once
i am mad

Aress Mohamed is a writer, photographer and lawyer from Garissa, Kenya. Some of his writing can be found at aressmohameddotorg.wordpress.com, and his photography on Instagram at aress.mohamed.

The Letter Writer
Dessale Berekhet

"COME HERE, you lying bastard!" Semere beckoned me at full volume.

There was not a big distance between us to necessitate such an uproarious voice. I could have heeded to his voice at a much lower tone than this one. However, his exertions were intended more to instill terror than merely calling for my attention.

Semere was easily irate. What could have I done this time? I do not know, but I could feel terror surging in my bosom. He has been the leader of our unit for over a year now. I do not recall a day when he wore a sprightly spirit over his face. He inspired fear in every one of us, with his death stare and abusive name calling.

If it had not been for his lethargic disposition and abusive manner he was a soldier of good stature.

What was most intolerable about him was his disparaging language. He never cared to know our proper names, but called us by whichever insult that got into his mouth. Of his entire name calling I most disliked this "lying bastard", and it seems somehow, he was well aware of that. He might easily have noticed it from my countenance.

Oddly enough, Semere had a variety of good names for the stick he always carried. He liked calling his stick "Ageset". He firmly believed that only "Ageset" could discipline us into complete submission.

"Ageset" was dangling on his hand when he glared at me to approach him. No student ever escaped the scourge of Ageset. Semere himself believed that he inspired our respect because of this stick. The truth was, however, we never respected him. We rather feared him.

I could not remove my eyes from his stick. I dared not see his face. His bloodshot eyes came to my mind. He was struggling with fits of anger. I approached him with heavy steps.

I rummaged my mind with an incessant question. What could I have done?

"What could you possibly mean by writing this letter?" He waved a piece of paper on my face. Now, I learned what my cardinal sin was. Had my thoughts not been clouded by terror, I could have suspected what made him so fitful with anger.

I remembered my 'Sin'. It is the letter which still bore the fresh ink of my pen. When he confronted me with his terrorizing pitch I was left totally bemused; nor would he allow me to explain myself, had I been composed enough to give one. Semere cared not to hear what we had to say. In his eyes we were nonentities forever condemned to be on the receiving end.

"It was Hadgu who…" he would not have me finish what I had to say. He knew what I would to defend myself.

"Hadgu?! What does he know? He is a new student... If he can write himself why you are assigned to write letters for these students?" he cornered me with a volley of questions.

"Errr!" I groped for some words to save me from my position.

"You lying bastard!... Kneel down!" he beat me with the stick. The insult inflicted more pain than his stick.

"Now... Where is Hadgu?" He glared at me.

"He went down to the riverside," I retorted with a low voice.

He summoned one of the boys into the kitchen and ordered him to call Hadgu.

Hadgu is my schoolmate who led me to commit this 'mistake'. He was cultivating the petty orchard on the riverside. We used the harvest of tomatoes and green peppers as an input into the food we consumed. We were living the experiment of communal life.

I could imagine how Hagdu was petrified with fear upon being summoned by Semere. We trembled with fear when summoned by him, even when he meant no harm. Finally, I saw Hadgu arriving by the road from the river. He pulled his tattered shirt up. Terror was palpable in his pale, haggard face.

Semere, who squatted on a stone rose when he heard Hadgu approaching him. His nose bore tiny beads of perspiration, and his face was red with anger.

"What the Hell is this? What is this?!" he yelled at him.

Hadgu lowered his head and remained silent.

"I am talking to you dumb head! Is this some kind of contempt?" roared Semere.

Hadgu never said a word. He knew his 'Sin', and what actions would follow after this. Answering and remaining silent, were not good for us. Semere took the first for daring to challenge him, and the latter for sheer contempt.

My feet on the sand had already started shaking. The terror surging inside me however impaled my outside reaction.

There reigned a short silence among the three of us. Presently, I heard the sound of beating. I cringed as if the beating was received by me. Semere forcefully beat Hadgu with his stick. Hadgu never said a word. Semere seethed more with anger. Semere enjoyed our suffering like a good fragrance.

If I were the one receiving the beating I would have cried until the distant hills echoed them. But, at times I too was stubborn and would suffer any beating with silence.

I felt the beating no less than Hadgu did. Why! If Hadgu was liable for such punishment because of that 'Sin', then I myself deserved equal punishment.

The stick broke into pieces on Hadgu's back. Semere did not have enough. He kicked him with his boots.

"Worthless! Wet pants!" He wiped his perspiration.

We were brought up by a culture that saw pants as a symbol of courage and manhood. Wetting pants is then the worst form of humiliation.

Hagdu, while successfully suffering the shedding of many tears, wet his pants; and that was why Semere left his beating with great contempt.

I had dried up my courage. The terror surging inside me dominated over my dregs of courage. The stick Semere carried was broken into pieces on Hadgu's back. But our heads and teachers had had many sticks to lay waste on our poor bodies.

"You will see me in the evening," Semere menaced on us.

While passing by behind me, he struck me with his big palms. He still carried whatever remained of the stick and the letter I wrote in his hand.

Hadgu did not rise from the ground. He trembled with the severe punishment inflicted on him. He smiled ashamedly, touching the bruises on his hands and legs. We exchanged empathy, each other. That was all we were left with now. We had squandered any chance of not putting ourselves in danger.

He removed his threadbare shirt and clad it over his waist to cover his wet pants. I saw blood oozing on his calf and shoulders. He did not care to notice that. He saw it as a sign of his courage, as he had borne it without showing any signs of pain. Semere himself must have admired his courage in his heart.

He must however, cover his wet pants. His eyes seemed to entreat me not to divulge to anyone about his wet pants. I don't recall a single student who had pants to spare. There was no other way for him but to go back to the river and wash his only pants.

Semere's menacing words meant that our ordeal has just begun. Wednesdays evening, we conducted criticism and evaluation of our activities. Then will be decided what punishment is in store for us. We might as well wet our pants, with shit then. The punishments that are awaiting us will not only push us back into submission, but also serve as a lesson for other would be rebels.

Not a day passed without us experiencing violence and abuse of all sorts, since we came into this god-forsaken valley. We found some respite on Wednesdays. We considered Wednesday as a holiday. We spent the day on extracurricular activities, not playing but washing our laundry and on analysing our activities. I liked spending that day helping fellow students write letters.

I was pondering spending this Wednesday on the routine activities, as no one had asked me for help.

I saw Mokie Shifta come from his foxhole, raising his head to the sun and stretching his body out like a cat.

"Hi there! Would you please summon Anseba!" He got back into his foxhole without even waiting for a reply.

Though most were not wont on calling me Anseba, which was my moniker, at least Mokie Shifta always addressed me by that name.

I did not need anyone to tell me to go to Mokie Shifta, as I had heard him. Moke Shifta was another leader of our unit. His temperament was in complete contrast to Semere's, though. Shifta's upbringing made him more akin to herds than men. Before he joined this school, he neither saw a decent society nor school, except for the life of shepherding. He grew up in western Eritrea where banditry was rampant, and he liked talking about bandits and their exploits. He acquired the nickname Shifta (bandit) for himself because of such tales. Despite all these, he was the most amiable of all the unit leaders we had had. We all liked him.

"Does your exercise book have some blank papers," he asked me.

"Yes! There are about ten of them."

"That is enough for today. You have only five students today."

I nodded in response.

I knew what he was talking about. I am used to such orders.

"Go and prepare your papers and your pen." He pointed to our cottage.

I was not any older than the children in the school, but he addressed me like an adult pal.

I saw the five children coming to the stone I was sitting on. Hadgu was in front, in the beginning, but I saw him going to the back after their arrival. I could not understand why they did this. He was physically superior to most, and I least guessed that they could have cheated him.

The first student for whom I wrote a letter was called Hagos. They sat as a mere formality, though. I composed the whole content of the letter myself. They provided only the name and address of the recipient. They had, otherwise, no say on the content of the letter I composed. Everything was centralized. I for my part knew what was normal to write and what was not.

I hardly know the number of letters I composed in such a way. I enjoyed this particular task, anyway. Compared to the building of camouflaged underground houses and the cleaning of the environment, this one was much easier. Another advantage of this task was skipping the freezing shower of the morning. I used the opportunity for a milder shower in the hotter late mornings.

I and Hadgu stayed behind, after I wrote four letters.

"Who are you sending the letter to?" I asked.

"To Hadas," he replied.

I raised my face to him by way of asking who Hadas was.

"She is my sister," he said in a low voice, in a way implying what her father's name must be.

"Good"

"*My dear sister Hadas…*" I started writing the letter. I ensured that my words were not redundant.

If I am not mistake, the one who did this job before me was Andat.

He was 'fired' from this task because he used flowery words. He used too many poetic words to express emotions. *I miss you like the deserts do rain, I long for your loving memory more than I do for sweet honey, and you are to me like the distant stars shining in the vastness of the skies....*

He even addressed the recipient in similar poetic fashion. *May this letter reach your hands after roving through valleys and rivers and craggy mountains...*

That was too much for our leaders. This was a waste of resources. Here aesthetics has no place.

Presently, Hagdu, in whom I saw strange feelings on his face said, "I wanted to tell you something."

"Yes!" I said biting the tip of the pen with my teeth.

"The people here from my home village…" he stuttered with hesitation.

"What about them?" I encouraged him to proceed.

"You know they were forcibly conscripted. My parents are long dead, and I lived with my little sister. I came here by my own free-will. I feel restless whenever I recall that I left her by herself. She must blame me for this".

I respected how he felt, but I did not know what this had to do with the letter we were meant to write.

"What would you have me do?"

"I wanted to tell her so badly how I regret leaving her by herself!"

"Well… tell me what you want to say, make it short. I will write it for you."

"Dear little sister,

I made a deadly mistake for leaving you behind alone. The devil himself must have led me astray. Now, there is nothing I can do but regret it. We have already reached Sahel. In Sahel we are malnourished, and freezing. If I find a chance, I will escape and get back to you".

He stopped after looking at my face.

I was baffled by this strange manner of his.

Is he sent by one of the unit leaders to test my loyalty?

The unit leaders must read the letters before they were sent for their addresses. Words and whole sentences were erased and the letters were sent for revision. With time, however, I learned the limits of what is normal in our life, and the unit leaders built some trust on me.

"I fear the Devil that beguiled you has gotten us both now?" I responded in a humorous way.

He did not seem to note this. He was absorbed on how to persuade me to have his feelings written on the letter.

I saw tears swimming in his eyes. Seeing Hadgu, the child who bore the severe punishment of Semere shedding tears tormented me.

"Can your sister read anyway?"

I asked him lest his sister should ask one of the Jamaheer to do her that favor. The Jamaheer organized the masses, and did intelligence works. They would implicate enemies of the revolution, who were taken to Sahel

Mountains to be never seen again. Not a few others, who they did not bother to take to the Sahel, perished in the villages. And they are the ones who will take the letters with them to the villages.

"Yes, my little sister can read," he responded.

"Well   " I proceeded with my writing. I was deeply touched by his last words.

"I want to shed dome dregs of hope on my sister." I selected vocabulary to convey them in words.

"Dear sister Hadas,

I left you alone when I learnt that all the children in our village had marched for the revolution. I knew I had to think twice only later. The Devil must have beguiled me to commit such a wild decision. Dear sister, I would with all my heart's love to come back to live with you, but Sahel is very far from home. If any chance avails, I will escape and come back." I included in the letter.

"I have written what you wanted," I told him with a smile.

His eyes radiated suspicion. "Really? Can I hear you reading it?"

He did not dare to say these words. He may have feared that this would spoil any trust we have built. Pouring your message would suffice for now, no need to fret if I have conveyed your message into the letter. He thanked me and left without me reading him the letter.

I completed the letters and wrote their respective addresses for dispatch. The names of the senders were, normally, omitted. I guess they did this to dodge any suspicions from enemy agents that were at large.

As was customary, I had to go to Shifta directly. He wouild be the one dispatching them to the teachers' homes. The teachers will in turn staple the letters and hand them to the "Jamaheer".

Mokie was not there. Semere called me while I was on my way back. I felt an imminent consternation when I handed him the letters. There was nothing I could do to avoid this. I headed to the kitchen for breakfast.

Semere read the letters one at a time, and what transpired between me and Hadgu was revealed.

I could not help thinking what would have happened if the letter had otherwise been read by Mokie Shifta. It would most likely have gone unnoticed. If he had noticed, then the worst he could do would be to reprimand me for this offence. He would simply brush it off saying, "You are not supposed to say such things here!"

I FERVENTLY wished the sun of Nakfa would shine all night long. Pity, no one has power over nature. The sun set, and twilight and darkness reigned.

We fell into formation to be counted. Now was the time of reckoning. The squad leaders counted us and reported that no one was missing. In addition to Mokie and Semere we always had teachers acting as platoon leaders. This time Woldezghi Haile and Belay Gebremedhin were on duty. Belay's name was totally eclipsed by his monicker—Polis, and almost no one knew his real name. Woldezghi, for his part, was called by his namesake—Wedi Haile. Both were excellent teachers of the Tigrigna language. They were also notorious for their ruthlessness.

Wedi Haile had a severe nerve injury on one of his legs, which he received from wounds in one of the several bitter battles he had been in. When he was in the forefront his moniker was Tarik, and he was a heroic fighter they say, who valiantly stood firing before an enemy tank.

The weather at Nakfa around January was literally freezing, a condition that was not very welcomed by Wedi Haile, who felt the pain more severely than most of us. We had some respite from his ruthless punishment in those seasons, however. I surmised that Wedi Haile would be confined to his cozier habitat this freezing night. That would mean the punishment would be less severe, for me at least.

Semere ordered me and Hagdu to stand apart from the other children. That was an unmistakable sign of some iniquities committed. The other children glanced at us with sympathetic eyes. I saw Polis coming from beyond. He was holding a stick in one hand and a rope in the other. I also saw that the ominous letter was also held in one of his hands.

"Good afternoon; how was your day?" he broke the silence.

"Good!" we all said, habitually. That was how we always answered, while in our hearts we knew it was far from that.

"Get up—you!" he glared at me and Hagdu.

We were confused who he was addressing, as we two were sitting very close together. Hadgu stood up, presently. He was totally dejected all day long.

"Tell them what happened this day?" Polis ordered him.

"Mokie sent me right up to Dessale to have my letter written. I dictated to Dessale to write that we were freezing and malnourished, and that I was beguiled by the Devil himself to come to this place."

"And what did he say?" I interrupted him.

This confession alone would have sufficed to render him liable for punishment.

"He told me such things are not supposed to be said. He tried hard to persuade me otherwise".

"Why on earth did you not listen to him then?"

Hadgu did not raise his head. He remained silent.

I resented my not reading the contents of the letter to Hadgu. I still had the opportunity to talk with Semere when the letter was held by him.

Not all that he is saying in this confession was put into words in the letter. He poured it all thinking that I had committed them into writing.

"Are you saying it was you not him who is responsible?" he asked him for a yes or no answer.

"Do you know what verdict awaits for deserters?" He turned his face to the students with deadly purpose.

Some children formed some unintelligible words *sotto voce*[52]. No one answered him in clear words.

"Execution," they said in unison and terrorized voices.

He and Wedi Haile were the ones who read us the law that deserters would be dealt with by execution. He was invoking the law in a way of reminding us that we had fully sanctioned and cast them in stone.

Presently, Polis took a slight look at the paper and sneered.

"Hmm... and you dared to write the slogan 'follow the footsteps of the martyrs and not the renegade!'"

We normally put the slogan 'Victory to the Masses!' as the ending of any letter. But I had the habit of adding 'we will follow the footsteps of the martyrs and not the renegade.'

"Never mind, we will deal with you in time!" he cowed me with his stick and turned to Semere. They whispered some words over their ears.

Semere took the rope from Polis. He signaled to Hadgu to follow him. Hadgu did as he was told. Like a lamb led to the slaughterhouse they disappeared from our sight in the darkness.

We fell into formation and went to our tent house to sleep. A cold northern wind was blowing into the tent. It was a rather a very cold night! I could not sleep. I was torn between sympathy for Hadgu and fear that I would be summoned by Semere in the middle of the night.

I was wondering why they did not punish Hadgu in front of us. We were used to the agony and cries of students who were punished in public and afar. Hadgu was dealt with differently. Why? Where did Semere take him? I was tormented by these questions.

I DO not recall for how long I napped. I heard the routinely clapping of hands and woke up. The long night was gone; it was already morning.

"Wake up! Wake up! Fall into formation" he shouted.

It was the routine Thursday morning activity. An evaluation of the activities of the past day continued before we broke our fast.

All students were clustered around the place we called Teshkil. Two students from each squad supervised personal hygiene of every student. Mainly our hair was examined for any sign of nits. Those who had nits were severely punished.

I was one of these supervisors. However, Semere had already assigned Tesfom Abbaw to do the job.

After the hygiene examination we fell in line and marched for breakfast.

52   Italian for "low voice".

In front of Polis' house was a dead tree. It was a leafless tree with a black trunk.

From a distance I saw that there was some unclear figure next to the tree. His legs were unceremoniously lying on the ground. As I got closer I trembled with fear. It was Hagdu!

Both of his hands were tied to the tree. He looked as lifeless as the tree he was tied to.

He was surely dead. I was seized with deadening fear.

I considered my not looking at Hadgu's face as a betrayal to him. I overcame my fear and took a look at his face.

I saw his eyes struggling to open. His lips were dry from the freezing cold of the previous night. On his curly hair I saw dews defying evaporation. His barely naked torso was covered by some rag that resembled a piece of blanket.

Each one of us looked at Hadgu and moved on. They deliberately made us pass this way to terrorize us! It was not without effect.

I went to the kitchen as usual, but my mind had remained with the ghastly sight of Hadgu too weak to open his eyes.

Many years later, as I write this story, the memory of those poor eyes still lingers freshly.

Dessale Berekhet, *a former columnist in the Eritrean private newspapers and state-owned newspaper 'Haddas Ertra'. He is author and co-author of several children's books and researches on culture and traditions. He is the founder and Editor-in-Chief of* Tigre Youth Magazine 'Takiyat' (The Pilar) *and* Sa'eyob Children's Magazine. *After fleeing Eritrea in Sep. 2010, Dessale lived his most eye-opening couple of years in Uganda, from where he has organized a vibrant team of journalists and human rights activists and started to fight-back the most repressive régime in his country, Eritrea. Eventually, he was evacuated to Norway and became the core-founder of* PEN Eritrea in Exile. *Currently, he lives in Norway and volunteers for a Tigre language Radio for which he is also a founder. Dessale is honored by two international awards for both literature and his activism to promote Freedom of Expression.*

FRANGIPANI
Alex Teyie

I COULD hear him screaming. I knew it would happen, that the men, heavy-handed, with their tools would come; with their weapons, they would come. They would come for my tree. I knew it, I did. But somewhere in the back of my mouth, I didn't know it. This was the only place in my entire body that didn't know it, that wouldn't know that they would cut down my tree. This tree, *my* tree, was born before I was. My father told me the story. How I was born with a dark map on my leg, and mum thought it was a burn from all the hot porridge she drank while pregnant, but Baba knew it was a map. He showed me how to read it.

The place we found using this map, the place marked X, was where this Frangipani tree grew at the back of our house. After our great discovery, Baba gathered us all together—mum, Baba, the baby, and I—and we stood round the tree, solemn. Mum was smiling at first, but I stole the smile right off her face when I began: I love you most in the world, tree. I name you Azra. Baba poured holy water all around the roots, and we prayed it would grow even taller than it was, and fatter than the woman who sat at the front in church, and stronger than the ocean, and sweeter than the moon, and quieter than the baby's heartbeat. I led the prayers, because I loved tree most in the world. And so I knew, before anyone else, that the men, heavy handed, with their tools would come; with their weapons, they would come. I knew that any animal, any breathing thing, that grew as strong and gentle and brave as my tree, they would come for it, and they would tear it down. I knew because Azra told me.

Azra's scent, the inside of his heart, reached me across the air, through the glass of the window. Mum said not to go out, that it wasn't safe for little children. She said to let the men do their job, but I could smell Azra squirming, sweating. I could smell the heavy handed men, faces scrunched up, their arms and necks marked by throbbing veins, all of them drenched. I heard that metal animal of theirs warming up, then the *zzzz*, the *vvvrrrrr*, as it woke up from its sleep. I heard the krakrakra as it hit the side of Azra, and the *sssssss* as Azra began to bleed his sap out. Pharisees, that's what the men were. I learnt that word in church. And that's what they were, to cut into Azra's skin, to keep going until he started to moan, to bend, to tremble, to fall.

The sound Azra made when he fell, I won't forget it. The place in the back of my mouth, that's where I'll hide that sound. It was round, a round sound, round and angry. I felt the sound roll over the ground, shaking up the soil, burrowing, echoing underneath the earth, raging. That sound, I can't forget it. But the sight of Azra crumbling, landing violently, crushing the grass that had kept him company, that sight I must forget. I must forget the leaves weeping.

I must forget the branches waving at me from the ground, caught in a wave of seizures, coughing, pleading. I must forget the men laughing, opening beers, some leaning on Azra, others perched on his body, shameless. I must also forget that the sun wouldn't stop shining. I must forget the shape of the clouds, passing, unknowing, uncaring above it all. I must forget the green of the grass; what green though? Pale? Bottle-green? Black-green? Yellow-green? The green of the swimming pool near the basketball court? The green of the man's tongue upstairs who chews betel leaf? The green of our French teacher's eyes, like a sorcerer's? *Green.* Kale-green? Green-green? I must forget all green. All of them.

The men, with their tools, with their weapons, eventually leave. They chop Azra into smaller pieces. They load him onto wheelbarrows, and carry him away without a service, without any ritual. I sit and stare at the remaining stump, keeping vigil. By the time the sun sets, I can't feel my legs. I start to think maybe I can float away without my legs holding me hostage here in this living room. Azra is all roots, and I'm all torso. Maybe I can pull him out of the soil, and we can fly and leave for somewhere new.

– Junior, should I make you tea?

– No.

– Juice?

– No.

– A snack then? I made *maandazi*[53].

– Later, mum. Later.

– We need to pack up whatever is left in your room.

– *You* do it then.

Maybe I really can pull him out of the soil. I just need to sit here longer, until my body is completely separated from my roots, then I can carry Azra and we can find a new place to grow. I would start all over again with Azra. It would be difficult, and it would take a long time, I think, but we could get him strong again. I know I can do it. I know I can leave my body. I've done it before.

◈━✕━◈

THE first time I left my body was exactly a month ago. It was the day the maid came to school still in her house dress, with her eyes swollen from crying. I could see Annie through the doorway, wringing her hands as she spoke. Teacher Susan looked at me with a strange look, like I was a small bird by the side of the road. Everyone in class was whispering instead of doing their Composition. I was called outside, and then Teacher Susan told me I must go home. That it was urgent, and that I mustn't worry. That it would be alright. That there really was no need to carry anything. So I left my book bag. I left my lunch box. I left my jumbo pencil with a pink rubber at the top.

Annie said nothing on the walk back home, but I could feel my spirit folding, folding until it was squatting in my left ankle. I somehow knew to see

53   A small cake made of fried dough.

everything, to memorize the jingling of coins in the blind man's tin near the gate of the school, and the laughing of the woman drinking Coca-Cola outside the canteen, and the humming of the flowers outside the house belonging to the rude woman mum hates, and the crunching of the gravel underneath my Bata shoes, and always always the clouds gossiping above us all.

⧜

I HEARD them before I saw them. The wailing women. Women I knew from our picture album, women I only saw at church, women who dropped by for Sunday supper, women in mum's prayer group, women who taught at the university with Baba, women who congregated outside the local shop whenever someone's child was expelled, or someone's husband was sacked. It felt like all the women in the world were gathered in our estate, each trying to out-weep the other. Immediately they spotted Annie and I, their crying rose higher, only broken by someone cursing at the devil, until the air, thick with their tears and shaken by the force of their hoarse voices, began to waver, and then, finally, the tears began to fall back down, beating against the red dust of November. My wet uniform clung to me, and my feet refused to listen to the rest of my body. Annie tried to breathe through the current of sobs, and pulled me forward, my small hand in her rough, shaking one. In the corner of my ankle, I could feel my spirit rocking, singing the alphabet song in its inside voice.

Hands rained down on me, everyone so sorry, so sad, all of it so sudden, and God will make a way, but for shame, the children, and *woi*[54] what about their mother, with such a small baby! Some of the hands were gentle, caring. Others soothing, rubbing up and down my back, be a good boy they said, be good, you're the man of the family now, yes, and, take care of your mother. Many more were urgent, forceful, eager to pass on their discomfort to me, take it, they said, take our condolences and let us be done. I got separated from Annie amidst all the hugging and patting, but someone eventually thought to take me to Mum.

⧜

I HAD never seen her look so small. The sun pushed through the rain outside and fell around her sitting on the bed, unmoving. Aunty Jane, Aunty Judy and Aunty Mumu sat at the corners of the bed like sentinels, sucking in air loudly and sniffling in turns. Aunty Jane held the baby over her shoulder and was the only one who seemed to notice that I'd walked in. Mum didn't look up. I didn't know what to say, or how to say it. So I just stood there, hoping she would look up, and that when she did, I would know what to say, and how to say it. While I waited, I moved my ankle a little to see if my spirit was still there, and it was—just quiet now, watching. I took one step. Then another. A bit louder now. Then she looked at me, and I wished she hadn't.

---

54   An exclamatory sound made by women when crying/wailing.

– Come here, come! Come, Junior.

– Mum... everyone's outside, and Annie, she just—

– Just come, OK?

The three women turned to me, nodding and patting the bed. I didn't know whose face to look at. Aunty Mumu wouldn't stop crying, and Aunty Judy kept shaking her head and making clicking sounds. Aunty Jane was the calmest one and insisted that I be a big boy and listen to mummy, so I turned to Mum, but I couldn't bring myself to look at her face again. I focused on a loose button on her blouse and tracked its swinging as she talked.

– Junior. Do you know what 'dead' means?

– Not breathing?

– Yes, good. I mean, no. Not good, but Junior, listen.

– Mum?

– So, I mean. Look, Baba, he...just...Janey? Janey, please...say something.

– Fine, yes, sure. Junior.

– Yes, Aunty Jane?

So what your mum is saying—Wait. Mumu, please, quiet! OK, I was saying, Junior, there are some things in life you can't expect, alright? Some hard things. It's not a punishment, but it's life, alright? God is always good, you know that. But he gives and takes away, alright? We're all angels but some are called back to heaven early, alright? So basically, what your mum was asking, you know, it's just...so, I mean... Look, you're a man now... I... well, maybe... Judy? Judy, what do you think? This is a man-to-man talk, right, Judy? Mama Junior, no? I'll just... let's get someone in here... Judy, where's your husband?

– He's with the van. Where's yours?

– With the in-laws. Mumu? Mumu, where's yours?

– Look, look, he's getting nervous. It's fine, Janey, it's fine. Junior, just go to the neighbours for now, OK?

– OK, Mum.

✎∽✎

SOMEONE must have called to tell the neighbours I was coming. I hadn't even knocked, and Brian's head greeted me.

– Come on! We want you to see something.

Mike was stretched out on the couch as usual. The TV was on and the PlayStation out which meant their mother wasn't home. Brian stuck me between the two of them. There was something brittle in the way he patted my back, and the way Mike wouldn't stop smiling.

– You're turning into a real man, Junior. Eleven is no joke, hey! So we have a gift for you.

My spirit was jumping up and down in my ankle, shouting, dead dead dead dead dead. I tried to smile, because they were smiling so violently, and the only answer to a smile is another smile.

– Good good! Good boy, Junior.

– See? See! I told you he'd like this!

– Yeah yeah. Just put the tape in.

– OK. You're going to love this, Junior.

– Really, it's great.

– OK, OK, *shh*. It's starting!

The opening song sounded like the sickly music they played in lifts. I was not in the mood for a movie.

A really pale woman is dancing alone, wearing only bright pink panties. Mike hit me on the back, look look, are you looking? A man knocks on the door, and the woman opens, still wearing only bright pink panties. The woman traces the man's face with her nails. Her lips are red, very red, which reminded my spirit of its song, and off it went: dead dead dead. Brian was nodding, and looking at me more than at the screen. The man takes off his shirt (are you seeing this, Junior?), and *his* skin is orange. There are lines on his body like he is made of bricks (ehe!). She blows over his chest, but he doesn't fall down. He leans in and smiles with all his teeth. I could see all the way to the back of his mouth. Then he takes off his trousers and he isn't wearing anything else. This is when I *knew* things were going badly. I turned to look at Mike and found him already staring.

– What is this?

– We're your big brothers OK? You come to us for anything, you hear?

– Yeah, Junior, anything!

The man makes a strange sound, and the woman goes, Yeah Yeah!

– Look, I know it's hard, but you know…

– Yeah, you know…

– Oohhhh. Argh. YESSS!

– Turn down the volume, Mike.

– It's not that loud, Brian.

– Oh, what were we…Oh, right. I mean, it's life…right? And, yeah…

– Life, exactly! You just need to be strong.

– And don't cry. For your mum. Be strong!

– You want a beer?

– We have Pilsner.

– Warm and cold, whatever you want.

– Or crisps? Popcorn?

– Have you had dinner?

– Yeah, food is important right now. Mike could make you something?

– We could eat together? And play a quick game?

With the woman's voice stuck in my ear (fuck yeaahhh), I stood up and left. I heard them calling after me, but I just wanted to see Azra. I just wanted to be with Azra.

I HAD managed to sneak past the teams of wailers, but someone pulled my arm, and, of course, it had to be Uncle Jim. Mum hated Uncle Jim. He drank before 4pm and slept past noon. He only ironed the front of his shirts, so he was forever in a coat, regardless of the weather. He always dropped by close to meal time and never knew when to leave. He laughed with food in his mouth, and beat his wife. He had children with other women, but pretended he didn't. He had no job and no manners. He dragged me to the steps near the side of the house and stretched out beside me.

– Your dad ever take you driving?

– No.

– Want me to take you? (DEADDDD)

– No, I'm fine.

– It must be tough, hey.

– What?

– You know…

– I… sure.

– You know what's good for that feeling?

– What? (deaddeaddeaddeaddead)

– A cigarette. Smoke one with me?

– Uncle Jim, mum wouldn't—

– Your mum's not here, and neither is your dad, so have the bloody cigarette. It'll make you feel better. I promise.

– Okay then.

– Listen, one day you'll look back and think this was the worst day of your life. But you're wrong. You'll wake up tomorrow and in that first moment, you'll have forgotten. Then you'll remember. That's the worst you'll ever feel in your life. Don't think about it yet though.

All I wanted was to sit with Azra, and I said so.

dead

dead

dead

dead

dead

– A tree? You want to go see a tree? You know the story of the king with a long nose? He whispered his secret into a hole in the ground, and then the reeds in the water began to sing his secret to the world. No? Really? What do they teach kids nowadays? Anyway why talk to a tree when your uncle is here, *hmm*?

– Uncle Jim, please can I just go now?

– No no. Look here, I got you a scooter. You know, for your birthday?

My birthday was in February.

– Just say thank you.

– But, Uncle Jim…isn't that Cindy's from the next estate?

– It's yours now.

– I don't think—

– Who left *you* with the kid?

– Well, why not? Anyway, what's your problem, Timo? Your wife let you loose for a few minutes? Don't meddle. I'm teaching the kid.

– Really, Jim! Junior, are you good? Do you want some milk? Or we could—

– The kid's not five! He's fifteen!

– Actually, Uncle Jim, I'm eleven. You came to my party, remember?

– Oh yea, sure.

– Junior, you come to me anytime. Your Uncle Timo is here for you.

– What do you know about anything? What kind of man is always running around after his wife... Janey, dear, and Janey this and Janey, please…It's embarrassing.

– Jim, not now. Not in front of the kid. Junior, I'm so sorry about your dad...

The wailing became dense, packed tight with my spirit's chant (dead dead dead), bursting in short spurts, and bouncing off the walls of the house. I knew in the place in the back of my mouth what this meant. The hearse had come. The crowd gathered so close to it that the doors couldn't open. More and more joined the chorus, howling and marching around the hearse. When they finally got the doors open, everything slipped away from me. I vaguely felt Uncle Jim gripping my shoulder (don't cry don't cry don't cry), and Uncle Timo patting my head (it's fine, it's fine, it's fine), but the people faded as all of me tried not to cry, not to cry, not to cry, please just not to cry.

That's when it happened.

My spirit shifted, stretching only a little at first, then a stem extended up from my ankle, past my knee, folding a little, hesitating, then with renewed fervor, broadening, boldening, and upwards still, reaching past my abdomen, winding round my ribs before traveling right by my heart and out through my mouth, finally blooming into a bright yellow heart, which faded into a clean clean white—just like Azra's flowers.

Wreaths seemed to materialize out of nowhere, and hands, so many hands, passed roses overhead all the way to the coffin. Since the body had finally arrived, and the coffin was draped in flowers, the crowd seemed momentarily at a loss; had they fulfilled their obligation, was there another duty still unattended to, some protocol forgotten that unobserved might uncover a lack of decency, or simple courtesy? Someone called out my name from near the front of the crowd. I couldn't respond. Uncle Jim's grip tightened on my shoulder (stay here, boy). But another person recognized my face, a friend of Baba's cousin, and tried to pull me forward. Murmurs of Junior Junior Junior slid across the group, rousing them from their sudden diffidence, bestowing them, once again, with purpose: Junior. Once more, I felt the hands descend upon me, urging, pleading, go pray for your father, and, don't cry, you're a man, pushing me forward, all the way forward. Faces I half-knew loomed above me, nodding, mouthing something or the other, expectant, demanding. My body wouldn't obey me, but when my palms rose and lay flat on the wood of the coffin, smoother than Azra's, fresh wails escaped from the crowd. Holding my breath, I bowed my head and ran through the wall of people. My spirit hovered above me as I ran, bobbing up and down, now linked to me only by a few powdery threads, threatening to float away altogether, but eventually slamming back into my body when I stopped short under Azra's branches.

❧∽✠∾☙

I DON'T know how high my spirit can go. There is somewhere I would like it to reach, yes. That place is where Baba is. Where I think he is. The map on my leg hasn't been able to take me there. I've tried. Where else could we go, if we left, Azra and I? I pressed my face against the window and waited to hear if Azra would say anything; he always knew what to say, and how to say it. Maybe if I got closer? I ran across the sitting room, up the two steps to the main corridor, past the moving boxes, out through the door, left across the balcony and down the fourteen steps in the stairwell, round the house and all the way to the back. I could hear mum's high pitched Junior, Junior!, but I ran anyway, without turning even once.

I knelt on the grass near what was left of Azra. I made the Sign of the Cross. *Kwa jina la Baba, na la Mwana, na la Roho Mtakatifu, Amina.*[55] I stretched my arms around the stump and felt Azra's scratchy skin rub against mine. I waited for him to speak, but he said nothing. I looked for my spirit to see if it was getting agitated, preparing to leave, but it was also still.

I would like to cry. I can feel the place in the back of my mouth tingling, itching. I would like to cry forever. I would like to stretch out in the street, pull out my hair, wear sackcloth, and pour ashes all over my body—like in the Bible. I would like to run through the entire estate, shouting AZRA! AZRA! AZRA! But I know I won't cry. I won't make a fuss. I mustn't cry. I'm too big to cry.

Alexis Teyie *is a Kenyan author, feminist, co-founder and poetry editor with* Enkare Review. *She has co-authored a children's book,* Short Cut *(2015) and published a poetry chapbook,* Clay Plates: Broken Records of Kiswahili Proverbs *(2016), through the* African Poetry Book Fund *and* Akashic Books *(see on LitHub). Her poetry, short fiction or non-fiction have appeared in collections like* Routledge's Hand-book of Queer Studies (2019); 20.35 Africa; Queer Africa II (GALA); ID (SSDA); Water (SSDA); Anathema Speculative Fiction. *She has also been published by* Jalada Africa, Omenana, This is Africa, Writivism, African Feminist Forum, *among others. Past prizes include: the* Armstrong Prize for Composition, '13; *the* Collin Armstrong Poetry Prize, '13 & '14; *the* Corbin Prize, '13 & '15; *and the* Asa Davis Prize in Historical Scholarship, '16.

---

55 Swahili for "In the name of the Father, and of the Son, and of the Holy Spirit, Amen."

Raised by the Rod
Lucky Grace Isingizwe

Julia

WE DIE TODAY. My sisters and I. Nadia swears they'll lay us all face-down on the carpet and split open our skins with a twisted electric cable, turning our buttocks milky grey, tattooing our backs with several deep oblique lines that reach the curves of our shoulders, and marking the backs of our will-be-swollen hands with little shapes that resemble the teeth of a dog, just like father did to Nadia's body seven years ago. Lydia reminds her that father hasn't hit us since that horrible incident; that it's unlikely they'll hit us. I, for one, think they'll hang us. Well, that's not true; they can't hang us. But what do church people do to teenage Christian girls gone bad? What will she do? She is going to punish us in a much worse way than beatings I tell you. And by she, I mean the church lady. The prophetess who offered her hand to this woman in a wheelchair and made her walk.

She is going to once again declare me an adulteress "from the top of my head to the tip of my toes" isn't she? Even though I'm still a virgin at nineteen and I only had my first kiss in March this year. And the people will take her words to the heart. When we arrive at her house, a throng of people will surround us and listen in while we are sentenced. She is going to declare Cynthia a disobedient maniac, *umunyagasuzuguro.*[56] A girl who turns her back to you and makes a cast down eye contact while just gazing at your feet when you speak to her, swings her head and stomps off without word. Actually, because of those pictures that are going to end our lives, the church lady is going to revel in her claims from last year that my sister is a seductress. Poor girl.

And poor Lydia! Last year she was labeled a thief, and now she is actually the one who will be declared an adulteress because there is that one picture of her in skin tight red pants around her massive butt, a white tank top that clung to her bosom and lay her melons on display, and Martin—who wasn't even invited to the party—held her by the waist and had her bottom lip in his lips. Picture of the year! One of Martin's eyes peeked out almost frowning into the camera.

I'm sure dad dropped a few tears after he was called to see the pictures. After all he is a preacher, and if we are caught robbing a neighbour's house, it is testament to either how he trained us to steal or his failure in convincing his family to adhere to what he evangelizes in church ever so compellingly. I'm sure he felt embarrassed by his family. The family he's abandoned for his

56   Literally, "the scornful" in Kinyarwandan.

church people.

Sure, we'll never forget the hundred times he hit us for meaningless and meaningful reasons claiming that the Bible instructs him to beat up his children, but when he finally stopped right after he had turned Nadia into raw meat and blood, he transformed into a lovable person. One whose raised voice didn't make my heart start dancing around. One who came home at the end of a workday and we didn't run into our bedrooms and slide under the bed once in a while. One whose voice didn't sound like thunder when he was upset. But one whose voice thinned and choked on words you could almost hear the cry of his wounded heart stifled in his throat. It's the voice I heard a few minutes ago when he called.

"You and your sisters need to come to Maria's house right now," he said to me on the phone. Something in my stomach twisted. My heart pounded. I'd been dreading the call all day. I turned to my side and I said (I don't know to which sister), "Dad just called. We need to go."

On a typical Friday evening, things are usually flying about: dishes clinking, water splashing, dust skimming, and above or below that, voices chattering or quarreling. As soon as they all heard the word "Dad" leave my mouth, everyone paused as the voices and movements died down except for the flames licking a pot on a brazier in the kitchen, the smoke high above the pot, and the simmering of *imvange*[57] inside the pot. Potatoes with beans, onions and tomatoes—dad's current favorite dish. We looked at one another and our faces contorted in fear of what was to come, some of us throwing their hands on their heads.

"I've been praying all night for this not to happen," spat Nadia.

"That was just a desperate prayer you know. There is no way we could have gotten away with it after what Julia did," put in Lydia.

"True. Julia, this is all your fault," accused Nadia.

"Do you really think I wanted this? It was an accident, it -" I sighed and couldn't find words to finish. Then Cynthia concluded, "Well, your little 'accident' is going to cost us everything! Our lives are over. Baratwica." *They'll kill us.*

At this moment, my sisters and I head to our deaths. All for a stupid mistake. We hosted a goodbye get-together at my house a few weeks ago, just for my class. Not in secret, dad knew. We had just finished the national exams for Advanced Level and needed to hang for the last time. Guys and girls arrived at sunup to cook or help out. Once our bellies were nourished and our hearts content, the guys played Fifty Shades of Grey for movie time. Thirty minutes in and all who hadn't watched it before started leaving the room, so we switched the TV set off and played music to dance instead. My friend Ganza did a little deejaying and people went nuts. A circle was formed and Lydia stepped in the middle on her turn; she shook her butt this and that

---

57   Kinyarwandan for "mixture".

way, practically twerked, and she slowly did sliding up and down motions as the boys hooted. Afterwards, she danced in the arms of nearly every boy—we had never seen her act so wild. She is the most timid of all four of us. Then, some guy and Cynthia sneaked out and locked lips. As for me, I met my all-time crush in the corridor, took his arm and pulled him into my bedroom, and led my tongue down his throat. I had instructed the guys not to bring alcohol in the house but they did and a few got a little tipsy, then they took poses with their shirts off and their boxers showing.

Ganza later copied the pictures on my flash disk. A few days later, completely forgetting I had the photos on my flash, I gave it to a church person because I needed a Microsoft Word setup for my ugly laptop. Such is the tale of how I sealed our fate.

Cynthia

WE journey towards hell. To the church lady's house, or as we like to call it, the courthouse. All cases involving members of the church are tried by her. Under her roof, people receive punishments and names are exonerated. Being the worst sentence one can get, when the church lady shuns you from the church, members of the church won't speak to you ever again. They cast their faces aside when you fall on them abruptly, their eyes won't meet yours even when they begrudgingly answer your questions. If you see them at the market, they take a different path. Yewe, when they see you on the bus, they will sit as far away from you as possible, leave the bus if they can or get away from the bus if they were about to enter. You become a contagious disease to them.

We violated a cluster of rules women from the church must adhere to. I wore a grey loose mini dress for the party—church members aren't allowed to wear mini dresses or skirts. Julia wore a pair of blue jeans—pants are a man's garments thus women and girls should never wear them as a verse in Leviticus instructs. I, Julia and Lydia all wore make-up and some cheap jewelry for the party—a woman member of the church does not take part in such activities because that is what heathens do. Doing something wrong is not what terrifies us, we knew what we were doing. We knew if dad ever set eyes on our faces with lipstick applied on our lips and eyeliner below our eyes, he would-actually he wouldn't anything because we would never allow for him to see us like that. We had broken such rules before only we'd never been caught.

It is a twenty-minute walk from our home to the church lady's house. Terror unlike we have never known fills our hearts to the brim. We walk in silence, our heads filling with worst of things that may happen. We were raised by the rod, *inkoni*[58] might have been baptised 'frequent visitor whose stench clogs up the passageways of our noses'. It is a past we don't talk about amongst ourselves. Even in the privacy of our thoughts, we like locking up those memories. Now we loosen up the strings of our memories and let them

---

58   Kinyarwandan: "stick"

become a bit fresh in our minds. We let the reminiscences of our hurt gnaw at our brains.

For a small mistake such as insulting a neighbor kid or disobedience or fighting with a sibling, mom used a slipper to punish us when she was still around. For something bigger like stealing sugar or being caught with your fingers in the pot, mom would send you to go get a stick she'll beat you with. Then she would beat your hands because they did the stealing.

Ordering a child who's been bad to go get a stick they'd be beaten with is a thing that father would do too. When he did, one would go and bring a small stick. Father would give her an are-you-kidding look, and then he would go get one himself. Most parents liked euphorbia tirucalli sticks. Most of the sticks were damp making them heavier they struck to the blow and kids everywhere in Kigali hated them. Most people in every neighborhood we have ever moved into grow euphorbia tirucalli plants around their houses, serving as the fence for people who cannot afford to build a brick fence or a bamboo one around the house. So the sticks/plants were everywhere. Father always choose a long, very thick, and sturdy stick.

Father would sit or stand and hold my head between his knees so that I don't move around when he beat me. My buttocks would be getting redder by the second and my head would be suffocating. I would scream but I could feel my scream being useless because I was surrounded by these walls of flesh sometimes even above my ears. Possibly like being caught in the teeth of a wild animal and not dying right away. Father never played when he beat. With the euphorbia tirucalli stick, he would whip and whip and whip until the sturdy stick broke and turned into shreds. At worst times the *inkoni y'umuyenzi* shredded before he was done punishing. In which case he would go bring another one and keep whooping.

Things like wetting the bed, failing a course at school, not doing the dishes, having an unclean house, having an untidy living room, *agasuguro*[59], loosing money on the way to the market, falling asleep with dirty feet, or failing to understand when father was helping with homework, these things we did and he would bring a stick, a belt, the floor broom, or the radio cable. *Ikabure disi!*[60] Kids are kids, a week wouldn't go by without him beating. When the Nadia incident happened he finally stopped hitting. He would do as little as once a year or not at all. Now we are all grown up and have done much, much worse. Ayi weee! Baratwica![61]

Lydia

WE arrive at a place we hate the most and are welcomed by a handful of people, unlike we had feared. Good! They have conceded to keep the trial a

---

59 Kinyarwandan: "clean".
60 Kinyarwandan: "It's crazy!"
61 Kinyarwandan: "They kill us."

family matter even though by end of tomorrow, all the choirs, the deacons and part of the congregation will be able to recount the story as if they had been around. The matter is still being handled with secrecy their expressionless faces act as if we don't know why we've been summoned. We are shown seats on one side of the large sitting room on the big sofas whereas dad, Maria, the man whom Julia gave her flash drive and who obviously reported us, the pastor and a few other church men sit on the opposite side on long chairs. Dark brown and somewhat shiny curtains hide long windows exactly behind the maroon sofas we sit on and part of the cream coloured walls. The floor tiles look as every bit worth a bundle as everything in the living room alone. For a woman who doesn't have a job, it's an eyebrow-raising kind of wealth if you ask me.

Maria speaks beautiful words to us as if we are her children. No one has said a word to us alluding to the fact that they have seen the photos. We only know because when Julia's flash was returned she realized that the photos were on. So Maria says there is something they found out that they would like to show us. On the far wall on our right, a flat TV screen is attached and turned on but nothing is playing. The man who reported us is told to display whatever the surprise was, and then there we are. In a slideshow of the pictures from the party. The men shake their heads, turn their lips upside down or merely exclaim as if helpless. Dad just stares at us. We keep watching as we have been told. The slideshow ends and is replayed. The church lady pauses at the picture of me locking lips with a guy. Here we go! Let's hear the worst.

I close my eyes to prepare for the lecture and decisions that will break my back. Locking me in the house? Making me fast for 30 days while I only drink water? Taking me to prayer groups all year round? Maria speaks, but then my mouth hangs open as she's not addressing me. Julia is on the stand. The party was hers. The guests were hers. Maria rebukes Julia for leading us to hell. Her speech goes on as she says how Julia broke her heart. Then she concludes, "Today, I wash my hands off you and your siblings' souls. From now on, their souls is your responsibility. You're nineteen and clearly, they look upon you and what you do they do. From now on, *ibyo bakora uzabibazwa*[62]. Your father washes his hands off your souls too. It's all on your head now, Julia."

When judgment day comes, God will try all the nations for what they had done. However, anyone who have been given responsibility such as ruling a country or a church will be in trouble if they led wrong the sheep they had been entrusted with. Tonight, Maria declares that when judgment day comes, all the sins that I, Cynthia, and Nadia do will be on Julia's head and she alone will answer for them.

We did not come to be tried. Julia has. When Julia opens her mouth to speak, she says, "You can wash your hands off our souls all you want, but dad cannot wash his hands off my sisters' souls."

"You think your father is your only parent?" Maria glares at her. "How

____

62   Kinyarwandan: "They will be held accountable for what they do."

could you do this to me after all I have done for you? After all of the prayers I have sent above for you? After all the good I have done for your family?" Maria almost barks.

"Dad," Julia addresses dad instead, "I have done wrong, I accept. But punish me for that instead of abruptly and insensitively putting a massive burden on the head of a nineteen-year-old. Why are you not even saying anything?" Julia ends with a lump in her throat her final words came out tingly like.

Maria's mouth works out like she's swishing water in her mouth after a meal. She is pensive for only a second. And then it begins. Walls start falling.

Nadia

WE wept that night. My sisters and I. No one raised a hand on us. No one told us to go get a stick to beat our bums with. No one told us to take our clothes off and lay face-down on the floor to be chastised. On the day that was from then on known as the worst day of our lives, we sobbed together.

We had only said that once before. Just on the day that dad found out I had wet the bed. It was a Saturday. The stink from my and Cynthia's room had crawled all the way to his. I already knew I was in trouble. I was five turning six. When he reached home from a day of preaching, I couldn't bear the thoughts of being beaten again. I willed myself to be anywhere else or in a dream. I was wide awake, but I could be anywhere else. So, I tiptoed out of the house and out of the compound and ran. Father and Cynthia looked for me. On my way to I-don't-know-where, a man rebuked me for being out at so late at night. I pleaded with him that my father wants to kill me, to literally snuff breath out of me. Unamused, he took my hand to take me back claiming I would meet worse if I stay out as late as I had. What is worse than death? It was around eight o'clock. Down the scariest road in all of Remera, we walked and turned left only to come face to face with dad and Cynthia. The stranger pleaded with father not to punish me. I was just a child and wetting the bed, even though an ugly and smelly habit, was natural. And I was just too scared, so I had run away. Father smiled at him with gritted teeth.

One mistake of wetting the bed had multiplied into: running away from home, causing father to worry—filling his head with all sorts of horrible things that might have happened to me, making father look like a monster in front of a stranger, and wasting his time when he was tired. He grabbed a hard-wire blue electric cable and twisted it, just like a single braid of a two strand twist. Then, my howling blasted through the house. I opened my mouth as wide as I possibly could and dug out my entire voice with a glint of hope that someone, anyone, may come to rescue me just like that stranger who had asked my father not to beat me. No one came. My face swelled. My slim buttocks blackened. My lips doubled. Cynthia and Lydia wept for me when they saw. They heated some water, dipped a cloth in and gently pressed on me to ease the swelling.

Julia had been sent to the pastor's house to learn how to cook when the incident occurred. She was twelve. She had thinned and had a forlorn look when she returned. She had gone over in her head all of the things that happened to her at the pastor's house and was ready to share her pain with us only to find us with something much, much worse. We were sitting outside on a mat in the dirt space outside our house when she arrived. We stood to go hug her, but she laid her eyes on me before really looking at anyone else. Tears rushed outside as if they had been waiting impatiently for that one poke of a needle in order to scurry out. Her bag fell on the ground as she bent to hold my scarred hands in her trembling ones. At a light pace, she traced the scars from my hands, up on my arms, down my back and my bum and finished at the back of my thighs. She stood seemingly lightheaded, entered the house and whimpered from her room for some time.

When the sadness was past, Julia's fury would rise by the minute, but she would be helpless. The following day, we would go to school on my first day of primary school. Because the wounds would still be fresh, I won't be able to sit comfortably on a desk my teacher would notice and ask. I would tell her what had happened, and she would call my older sister Julia. Finally, she would have someone older to tell and beg to do something. She would explain to my teacher, other teachers and school authorities what had happened in tears and she would see the women amongst the bunch touch their faces to dry their own. My own teacher, Mama Prince, would speak in frustration and everyone would realize how red her eyes had gotten which would be a surprise, with her being the sternest teacher in primary one.

Julia would go with Mama Prince to a photography studio where pictures of me would be taken for the police. We would hear rumours that father had been called to the judge to be sentenced. Amongst the chaos, Julia would see for the first time a frightened look on his face which would quickly disappear she would wonder whether she'd imagined it. The judge would let my father go free because was he to be arrested, no one would be around to raise us. But that would be the last time father had raised a hand on any one of us with similar vehemence.

Now, at the happenings of the second time in our history we'd mark as the worst day of our lives, the church lady hid her fury at Julia for not acknowledging her as a parent to us. But beneath her adamant expression, she opened her mouth and butchered our souls with words. By prophecy she claimed, but we could sense she was cursing us she might as well had held out her pinky finger and spit on it making it known she was cursing us.

She spoke with such intensity it might have rattled the picture frames on her walls had she a microphone. She shook with what she said next. And like she liked to say during her shapeless, obviously spontaneous sermons, her voice rang through the living room and she began with, "*Imana irambwiye iti*[63]. When she begins with God tells me, more often than not, you know you are dead. So, my heart leapt to its feet. She said, "*Imana irambwiye iti,* the moment you let those shirtless boys into your house, you had just given a big *karibu*[64] to demons. The boys left a multitude of them in your house and now they live in each one of you they are actually merging with your souls to the point of inseparability." As we stared at her, Cynthia gave in first, tears rolled down. She's the most sensitive.

Unlucky for Cynthia, the church lady turned to her. "Cynthia my child, you reap what you sow. And from that party you reaped a hundred demons that ingest an ounce of your brain every day. Little by little, your intelligence will shrink until your teeth are unable to utter your name no more than your mind will be able to know what your name actually is," she proclaimed.

"Lydia my prodigal daughter. The demons you reaped that night will drive you to prostitution. They will fill you with lust for ambiance like you have never known you'll settle for sleeping with rich married men who buy you clothes that your body will rot in when disease finally strangles your last breath out of you." At this point everyone had let go.

"Nadia little girl," she turned to me, "You only live because I pray for you. You were not supposed to be born. I told your father not to have you. You were not born in God's will. If you break yourself from me, you are defenseless and prone to immediate death." What woman, who is a preacher, who is also a mother, tells a twelve year old that she was not born in God's will?

"Julia. A big host of demons surround you Julia that if you don't repent, in a few days' time they will become part of you getting rid of them will quench life out of you." She sat down in a chair. "I can see them right now Julia. You left them at the gate when you entered my house for mine is protected by Holy fire. They await their new host impatiently. They will be part of you. And since you brought destruction upon your sisters, the girls will each die before your eyes, falling one after the other like flies sprayed with pesticide. You won't be able to safe them," she ended.

Growing up, our father taught us the Bible and what it says about loving your neighbor. Once the church lady finished her "prophesy," it was the moment each one of us on her own accord decided that she hates her. Hate is a strong word, they say. Yet she had fed our minds with worse, watched our backs hunch lower and lower and she kept punching us, blow after blow, until we hit the ground with our foreheads, and she stomped on our backs with her heavy right foot.

From that moment till many years to come, the hate we felt for her became consolation to our wounded hearts and eyelids.

To all our surprise she said, "Of course there is a way out. You can choose to stay in the church, become once again Christian girls who do not wear

---

63   Kinyarwandan: "What did God say to me?"
64   Welcome.

pants, short dresses and skirts and tops that reveal their bosoms, who do not wear jewelry or makeup, who do not party, dance with boys, or kiss them which is all revolting to look at. Imagine what you would have done after this!! If you girls yearn to do what heathens do, you can leave the church, no one is stopping you. The door is right there. All up to you."

We had seen what happens to people who cross her to her face. So one by one, we wiped our faces with palms of our hands (and I sniffed some stuff back up my nose) and we said out loud, "I choose the church." *Mpisemo itorero.*[65] Julia lingered for a moment. Her body still heaved from anger or sobbing. When she finally let it out, we were told to kneel for prayer. The men and the woman stood up, laid their hands on our heads and filled the room with raised voices in prayer to destroy the "demons" we had left outside, to beg the Lord for forgiveness of all the abominations committed away from the glare of a camera or a judging human eye, and they begged the Lord to vanquish what had just been "prophesized."

Julia

BUT what do church people do about teenage Christian girls gone bad? They prophesy.

Lucky Grace *is a recent graduate at Mount Kenya University, Rwanda with a First Class Honours BA in Communication and Mass Media. Since June 2017, she's been working with Huza Press, a publishing house based in Kigali, in content creation and communications. She interned at* The East African, *a regional newspaper in 2018 as a reporter. And she is also an Amplify II Fellow at aKoma Media as of October 2017. Her short story* The Weaving of Death *is part of* Redemption Song and other stories, *won the 2018 Caine Prize Anthology. She was a participant in the 2018 Caine Prize Workshop. Her creative non-fiction piece* Losing Your Mind *was recently published in* Centre *for African Cultural Excellence's* Unbreakable Bonds, *a 2019 Writivism anthology. Her short story* Beyond Repair *was shortlisted for the Huza Press 2016 Short Story Prize. She participated in the 2018 African Writers Trust Publishing Fellowship which took place in Uganda and was facilitated by Ellah Wakatama Allfrey. In 2019, she was part of the Human Rights Cultures Workshop for photographers and writers that took place in Somaliland as part of the 2019 Hargeysa International Book Fair.*

---

65   Kinyarwandan: "I choose the church."

Streetlights
Barbara Oketta

MOTHERS are all knowing.

When I went home for holidays, I went to another type of routine. Wake up in the morning, make breakfast, clean the compound, and fetch water before putting lunch on fire, but mother was not convinced.

On my second day at home, she waited until we had had our evening meal and were preparing to sleep.

A curtain still separated the single room that mother and I lived in. The inner side of the curtain constituted mothers' bedroom, and the outer side was the sitting room that later converted into my bedroom at night.

She pulled the curtain. "What has happened my daughter?" she asked.

"Nothing mother."

I knew what she would say next. She always said it whenever she wanted to make me feel guilty into admitting something,

"You know that I am the only person who has the best of interest for you in this world. If you cannot confide in me then I don't understand you."

"Nothing about me has changed mother," I insisted.

I hoped we would then sleep but she was not yet done.

"Is it a boy?" she asked.

I kept quiet. I hoped she would let me be. Mother and I were close, yes, but we never discussed such things. How was I to tell her that a boy at the university had proposed marriage to me and I had said yes? She would probably think that all I went to do at the university was to fall in-love other than concentrate on my books. And what about Dan, could I bring myself to tell mother that I was seeing a man who was twice my age and that I enjoyed his company?

When she realized that I was not about to speak, she pulled down her curtain and spoke through it,

"When you are ready to talk about him, just know that I will be here waiting to guide you."

I had to hide my ring further now. There was no way mother was going to find out.

Life in the village was becoming more and more new to me and that of the city was becoming more and more of mine. I no longer had any friends in the village save for Frank. Titi and I had long since accepted that we could not be as close as we were. Occasionally when we met in the village market, we greeted each other but that was about it. There was nothing more to say to each other.

Frank had completed his studies but was still waiting to graduate. Since his parents were hard working people who had taken all their children to school, mother allowed him to come and visit. He however could not enter the house. He always remained on the veranda where everybody could see us. I on the other hand, was not allowed to visit him in his home.

Frank had learned to accept me more like a friend than a lover. I also valued our friendship although sometimes I wondered whether he still nursed hopes of me ever being in-love with him.

The secret that I was keeping was too large and I needed to let someone know. Frank was the most appropriate person I could think of. So, when he came to check on me one afternoon I just blurted

"I am engaged."

He seemed not to be getting it so I went inside the house and came out with the ring.

"See," I told him, "a boy at the university has proposed marriage to me and I have accepted," I said.

"Do you love him?"

I did not know what love was. All I knew was that O.N. was a faithful, honest, and hardworking man who would make a wonderful husband for any woman. I also told him that I had known him for almost two years and that our relationship had been steady so far.

"Well you asked the wrong guy about love. You would not want to use my experience to define your love. *All I know is that when the person is the right one, you feel it in your heart* whatever that means we laughed it off.

All I needed from Frank was for him to listen. I did not need any particular advice from him then. I was just glad that somebody else knew that I was engaged.

From the night that we had had that little conversation, mother always made sure she chipped in something about marriage whenever the opportunity arose. For example, I would be peeling *matooke* when she would mention;

"A married woman does not sit like that while peeling, your knees have to be tightly closed together."

Or sometimes I would put the food on fire and go to the sitting room; she would then complain that if the food burnt, my husband would think that she was the one who taught me how to cook like that.

"A proper woman always remains in the kitchen until the food is ready."

I wished she would stop but knew better than to ask her. I had refused to talk about my 'boyfriend' and that was the price I had to pay.

On some evenings, mother would slip in and tell me that I could only marry a man from my tribe. She said that she could not tolerate a non-Catholic since that was the faith I had been brought-up in. She also said that she did not mind about wealth as long as the man respected and supported me. If a man did not meet her approval, she warned me not to bring him unless I wanted to be embarrassed together with him.

O.N. fit in her standards well save for the fact that he was not of my tribe. I knew when the time came I would introduce him to her anyway and face the embarrassment but for now it was better to enjoy the peace while it lasted.

In her better moods she would talk of how a mother's joy was to hold her grand-children in her arms. She wanted me to have as many children as possible.

"You are a doctor after all; you can deliver your own children from home".

Whenever I visited Titi, I found when her life had taken a new twist.

This holiday, David had come back from the city with another wife. It was the woman whom she had always known existed but was glad they had never met. At-least if she was with him in the city, she had not had to worry about that shame of being the unwanted woman, she confided in me.

"David rented a lodge for themselves in town where they slept every night. During the day, they would come to the village and have me tend for them."

I was angry at Titi for allowing herself to be manipulated thus.

"Can you imagine, I had to fetch for them their bathing water, prepare their breakfast and lunch? I would then have to give them privacy like any other servant should."

As she spoke, I kept wondering when Titi had lost herself worth.

This second wife was lucky; Titi had told me. She had been accepted in the home.

"My mother-in-law and all the other in-laws treated her like queen. She had brought for them a son. It was as if the two sons I had had with David did not exist."

Maybe it was because she was from the city, or that she was a working class, better still, it could have been the dressing code. She was dressed as a city girl. I was jealous she had gained the approval of the entire family, as for me, I could leave there home on any day that I wanted.

I listened to my friend as she narrated her tale. That was all I could really do. That was all she really expected me to do. I had listened to her stories for seven years now and nothing had changed. Nothing was ever going to change. The in-laws were never going to accept her, David her husband was never going to love her.

What therefore that could not make sense about this entire story was the fact that Titi remained in the marriage knowing very well that she was not wanted.

"If you are mistreated in this marriage, why do you continue to stay?" I asked her.

"Shame," she replied. "I am ashamed that I will be a laughingstock in the village. People would say that my husband chased me out of the home when he got a replacement for me. Besides, where do I go to? My parents cannot return the bride price that David's parents gave them."

I still could not understand. If I were in that same situation with or without shame I would go back home; by mother's side where I was sure I would not be humiliated.

Titi told me that other women in the village suffered a worse fate than hers. There were women in the village, whose husbands beat them on a daily basis, and yet they had not abandoned their marriages. David had never laid a hand on her, at-least not yet. Some women in the village spent years without seeing their husbands and yet they had never left their homes. There were others still, whose husbands had brought home up to a fourth wife and they persisted in the marriage. There was no way she could leave her husband. She was lucky that for her the other woman was a city woman, very soon, she would be going back to the city and then her life would go back to normal.

I still did not understand.

Visiting Titi had become more of a responsibility than anything else had. I knew I had to visit her even though I always left her place with a heavy heart.

Titi said that she was suffering from shame, but the truth was that, more than shame, she was suffering from fear. The fear of facing the unknown, the fear of the knowledge that if she left the husbands' home, there would be no going back, that was what was laying her back. Not the fact that other women in the village were facing more problems than hers. That was a truth she had made-up so that she would not feel guilty remaining in the marriage even when she knew there was nothing much she was doing there. The same was true for all the women in the village, *they were hiding from reality.*

⚖

DAN was at the bus station waiting for me when I got out. I suspected Jude had told him about my arrival in Kampala since apart from O.N., she was the only other person who knew about my journey. He was pleased to see me. We entered into his car and headed for the hostel. I had a lot of luggage with me and I was glad that he had saved me the hustle of having to move in Kampala with them.

When we arrived at the hostel, it was still deserted.

Dan escorted me into my room. I was thinking of buying for him a packet of *splash* when he requested to leave. He told me he would be coming to pick me later in the evening.

I thought of my engagement ring but quickly reassured myself there was nothing wrong with me going out with a friend. I promised myself to tell Dan that I was now an engaged woman.

Hotel Africana had left a lasting impression on me. I liked the food, the ambiance, and the service. Later on when Jude showed me hotels that she said were better than Africana, I still preferred it. That evening, we went to Africana as I had requested. We stayed late but I was not worried since I knew Dan would drop me.

When it was time to leave, Dan went to ease himself before we left. I planned to tell him about my engagement when we arrived at the hostel.

On the way, I however noticed that the car was taking a route that we had never used before. I asked him where we were headed, to which he replied that there was something that he wanted to pick from his house before proceeding to the hostel. Something was not right.

Dan lived in a storied house. The windows were illuminated such that during the day a person from the inside could see you but you could not see them. He had black leathered sofa set in the living room and a flat screen television that was fixed to the wall. His kitchen was largely bare, a betrayal to the fact that he was still a bachelor. There was a kettle, electric cooker, toaster, microwave and a huge Samsung fridge, a sign that he mainly ate fast foods.

I wondered how many girls had entered that house. It was my second time. The first time, I had come with Jude who had felt very free in the house. She had even entered his bedroom, whereas, I had insisted on drifting between the living room and the kitchen.

Immediately we entered the house, I felt trapped. It was as if I was in Mr. Asiin's room again. Dan switched on the music player that greeted you immediately you entered the house. He then went into his kitchen and came back holding a glass of red wine. He gave it to me, switched on the TV and disappeared into his bedroom. For a moment, I felt like running away. I gave up on the idea because the television was already showing the eleven o'clock news and I did not know my way to the hostel.

Dan took his time. When he got out, he had changed into a pair of shorts and vest. Taking me to the hostel was the last thing on his mind.

He sat next to me and probed what it was I was watching.

"Kadaga has made history. She is the first female speaker for parliament in Uganda," I told him.

"I think she deserves it," he said and switched off the TV.

The wine was playing tricks with my feelings. I felt weak and lazy. When Dan started kissing me there was no way I could resist it. His kisses moved lower to my ears and neck; he then began unbuttoning my blouse. I knew it was time to repel but I did not have the will, I just let him go on until his hands could touch my sprouting breasts. They were small and I did not like them. I wondered what Dan thought as he gently squeezed and kissed them.

I remember Dan carrying me to his bedroom and laying me on his bed. I remember laying naked on his bed. I remember him covering me and wishing me a good night.

I woke up to the scent of fried eggs. The details of last night were not clear. I knew I was at Dan's place. I was angry at myself. I knew I had had sex with him. The inner part of my thighs felt sticky. We had not even used a condom. The same fear of pregnancy that had eaten me as a young girl at St. Theresa's Girls school engulfed me. A new fear of contracting Venereal diseases or HIV was alive. I made up my mind that as soon as I reached campus I would look for the university nurse and report rape. She should be in a position to give me emergency tablets.

I was glad for my profession at least I was not as naïve as I was back then.

Dan came back to the bedroom holding a tray in his hands. There was a glass of orange juice, a plate of fried eggs and some *britannia* cookies. He was happy that I was awake. He called me to breakfast as he laid the tray on a stool that was beside the bed. He had not served himself.

I got out of the bed and went to the bathroom to clean-up. I then realized that I was very hungry. I devoured my breakfast.

Dan only looked at me.

"Did you sleep well?"

"Yes."

"I will be working in the living room. In-case of anything just call me"

It was ten a.m. when I finally got out of his bedroom. I had bathed and felt that I was ready to go to the university. I hoped Jude had not yet come back from home. O.N. was also supposed to be arriving later in the day and I hoped that I reached the university before him.

Dan and I behaved as if nothing had happened the previous night. It was okay by me. I was not in the mood of discussing anything.

When I arrived at the university, I was glad that Jude had not yet come. Dan did not kiss me goodbye. He only wished me a good day and said that he loved me. The way you would tell a friend who had done you a favor that you loved them.

I locked myself in my room and cried. I felt used and dirty. I was angry with myself for having taken so much wine, and now I was sure Dan would want nothing to do with me since he had got what he had always wanted. He had said nothing while we were in his house or even as he drove me to the hostel.

I knew that the university nurse opened the clinic half day in the first days of the semester and that she was about to close. I gathered the little strength I had and went to the clinic. I was lucky the doctor was still in. After I narrated to him that I had just been forced into sex, I knew he had not believed the story. Maybe he had heard so many of them, he was tired.

"You should report this incident to the police." He said as a matter of procedure. He knew, like all the other students who came to report rape cases to him what they really wanted.

He sent me to the lab to have my blood tested for HIV. In case I was already infected, they would not have to waste their emergency treatment on me. I tested negative. I was lucky that the nurse at the dispensary was my friend. She gave me the emergency pills and explained how I was to use them. I was supposed to return for another test in three months' time. I asked the nurse to keep my secret and she assured me not to worry, I had no choice but to trust her.

The sun was unbearably hot as I climbed the Makerere hill back to my hostel. I was too sweaty I thought of undressing myself in the streets. I was happy that I was HIV negative. I however had to wait for three months to ascertain that Dan had not infected me.

When I got back at the hostel, the door to my room was open. I knew Jude had come back. We hugged because it had been such a long holiday. Jude had a lot to tell me. As she unpacked her bag, she told me of how Mike had taken her to Mombasa and how she had bought many clothes from there. She kept asking whether she still had a tarn; something I did not understand and didn't want to know. To me her skin was the same as it were two months ago when we parted for holidays. I was too upset.

She eventually stopped focusing on herself and asked whether I was sick. She was sympathetic and told me that she was going to call O.N. for me. Apparently, he had earlier on came looking for me. I was grateful but asked her not to call him; I did not have the face to meet him. I just needed some silence and sleep.

__Barbara Oketta__ was born in Mombasa, Kenya before relocating to Uganda where she resides today with her husband and three children. She teaches English language and English literature, volunteers at FEMRITE and is a freelance editor for Fountain Publications in Kiswahili.

A Memorial for Bella
Lilian Akampurira Aujo

UNEVENLY, a white blanket was spread over the island that February. Our tiny forest of bark cloth and eucalyptus trees formed an enclave around Bella's bench. The bench and enclave were tethered together by a criss cross of webs. In the webs, the lake flies, mosquitoes, dragonflies, and all manner of floating debris lay defeated. A little way from the bench, on both sides of the path, swathes of guinea grass leant in sections of milky hillocks.

I kept to the footpath, ducking every now and again to avoid the webs that stretched across both sides of the path. Still their threads stuck to my skin with a voracious clamminess. They reached for my face and threaded into my nose, which no doubt made for a more interesting destination. I sneezed and grabbed for my throat as my breath shortened. I felt caged in. This must have been how Bella felt when the spiders colonized the island that first time, four years ago. It seemed so much longer than that since her death.

Bella had a laser eye but the moment you started squirming, she retreated with a blink, only to return with a gaze so impatient that you were convinced you had only imagined the invasion, after all. But I, with 17 years of studying her, knew better. Even then I could never let on that most times I knew what her reaction would be, even before she showed it; I queued in like everyone else to indulge her because it was much simpler that way. The only people she looked at like she was seeing them were her mother, me sometimes, and Erias, for all the time they were together; and that had not lasted. Then Dr. Okello, who, according to her, was the most important person in her life.

When I reached the steps to Bella's house I stopped and stamped my boots on the flagstone patio, out of habit. I had turned to my left to brush out the webs in Bella's hair before I remembered she was not there anymore. Always carefree, she had let them tangle in her hair as if they were jewels, and it had driven me mad looking at her auburn curls matted with them. She walked the Island barefooted and no matter how I pointed at her cracked heels she simply shrugged and declared, 'Mother earth does not judge those who come to her with their naked feet.' Yes, there was both a carelessness and a meticulousness to Bella, and she enjoyed the deployment of each with an obsessiveness that bordered on psychotic.

I stood for an awkward ten seconds, brushing my fingers through my blonde bob, wondering how I was going to spend another summer break without her, how I was going to fill the twenty minutes with Marilyn, and if I was being observed from the Eastern balcony of what used to be Bella's room.

I found Marilyn was propped up on white pillows in what used to be her daughter's bed.

"Aunt M?" I said. Bella had called her 'Marilyn' as if she wasn't her mother, and even though I thought of her the same way, I could never bring myself to call her Marilyn as if she was one of us kids. I settled for what my mother called her and added the 'Aunt' for respect.

"Aunt M?" I said again. She did not stir except to trail a finger after a tiny brown translucent spider. I stepped in and sat on the bed. I picked up her leathery hand and patted it, but she did not acknowledge me. The caretaker, Paul had told me she was having more of such days, over the phone, in the months I was still at Kings College, London. The flesh of her fingers had withered so much that her liver-spotted skin sagged from the bones. I rubbed her hand in circles, watching for a reaction, but she was taken by a tiny grey spider crawling over the Fela Kuti poster. It eventually disappeared in a ripped spot, in Fela's right nostril.

The iconic musician had been Bella's newest obsession that gap year, and she had plastered blown up pictures of him everywhere in her room. We had listened to all the albums she managed to pawn off a Fela collector during her last semester. Up to now, the details of what she gave in return for the albums remain sketchy, since she hadn't been forthcoming with the details of their encounter. I like to imagine that at Bristol College, she had skived class and attended an African Music History class, for the fun of it. That would have been classic Bella.

The pictures had not been removed to date, no doubt on Marilyn's instructions. Bella treasured the picture because it was said to be one of the last ones he took before he died in 1997, which was also the year of Bella's birth. It did not matter that I was born the same year as well, because everything had to be about Bella.

Paul came in then.

"It is you Miz Sandra."

"Yes Paul. I didn't see you so I just came up. How are things here?" I asked, glancing at Marilyn.

"Oh, you know how things is." He sighed with the bulk of his chest. "Madame Marilyn she don't like to talk. Or walk. Or anything. She only lie there, looking."

"Is she eating?"

"Few times a week. She only allow porridge."

"And her medicines?"

"I have to force her like baby. Powder the tablet, mix juice, hold her nose and her mouth open, I keep holding until she swallow. That only way."

"And Doctor Okello, does he still come?"

"Yes, but he say we should get a nurse. Today is her day off."

"I see."

"I don't like nurse business. Bring a stranger in house, as if Madame

Marilyn has no one. Now see, she want day off and I have to pay her. Miz Sandra, does she not have a sister, another friend not sick sick like your Ma, there in England to come and see after her?"

"I am sure there is someone. But we don't know them. Marilyn never talked about her family back home. As far as we know this Island is home for her."

"Eeehh! You right! Even when Miss Bella go I ask her to start sending me to government doctor I go get death certificate, start to process her for bury in England. But you know she give me bad bad eye and shout me at once, 'My Bella love the sun and the Island, she going here, no where else.'" He holds his chin and shakes his head. "I was surprise! Eeeh! For us here they bury you in your own soil. Miz Sandra, sometime I worry."

"Yes, Madame Marilyn's condition is worrying."

"No, I don't mean that. I mean yes, it's worry, and bad, may God help her. But what I say is what if our black soil refuse the *muzungu*[66] skin?"

"What!"

"I know Miz Sandra with your university book. Even Dr. Okello say I not worry my head."

Like all people native to the Island Paul had his superstitions. My mother and Marilyn had smoothed over them when Paul brought in such anecdotes, especially when they were hiring new help or dealing with the locals. His motto was generally one: if Marilyn, my mother, and the rest of the white people on the Island observed local rituals like libating the floor of the house with wine every now and then, then the gods would be happy. Equi-Resort House would prosper.

"I know what you mean Paul, but Marilyn has been good to the Island, not so?"

"Of course I know, but what I mean is the soil knows its own. It will not drink *muzungu* blood. Not even I fool soil. Not even my grandfather who see and talk with spirit fool soil."

"That isn't true. Like the doctor said there is nothing to worry you. Apart from Madam Marilyn's sickness."

"That what exactly worry me Miz Sandra. Why you think Dr. Okello and all other doctor we take her to, all that doctor who know white medicine, all them not know what is wrong with Madam Marilyn?" I start to say something but Paul, eyebrows rising to hairline, puts a finger to his lips. "Shhh! I tell you now Miz Sandra, the sickness is spirit sickness. The gods are no happy about Bella in this ground." He stomps the floor several times. My body jumps in spite of myself. "Bella's spirit not happy being in black land. So all those spirit attack Madam Marilyn, that why you see she like tree with no branch, no leaves, just there like she forget her head." I could feel my patience trickling out, yes, I knew that Paul was semi illiterate and believed

66   Kinyarwandan: "white man".

in all sorts of mambo jumbo but it was somehow disrespectful bringing it up especially in Marilyn's presence.

"Paul, she has good doctors. Very soon she will be herself again."

"Even white medicines bring back forgotten head!" He shook his head again. "I never see it. Maybe she better, maybe then I believe. But four years, Miz Sandra. Four. One, two, three, four! All those she just sit, lie, I clean, I clean. Even to see Bella's bench and remove weed and put flower, she stop. I go. I tell the *shamba* boy to keep it nice nice. Then I check it. Four.... "

"I know Paul. Thank you very much. Marilyn will be happy with you." It was just like Paul to have handled everything like he was her child. Even before Bella's death Paul had seen to everything in the Equi-Resort House; he withdrew and banked money for Marilyn, he paid the cooks and stable boys when she had other things to do, and most importantly he rode the boat to the mainland, to pick and drop guests who were coming to holiday on the Island. He knew what Marilyn shopped, and where to find it in Entebbe or Gaaba town. He changed bulbs and fixed short circuits and toilets. He made sure the meals were running on time when there were guests at the house. Once, when Paul had to go all the way to the airport to pick up a honeymooning couple from Kenya, my mother had remarked, "Wouldn't it be nice if they were all like Paul? So hard-working, that Paul of yours."

Before Marilyn could answer Bella had turned from our chess board, glancing over her shoulder from the dining where we sat to the living room where our mothers lounged enjoying Chardonnay,

"She doesn't own him, you know."

"Bel dear, you know that's not what Marcella meant. She just meant as an emp—"

"And othering them because they are black, Ugandan... "

She had trailed off to let everyone fill in the blanks. My mother tittered nervously and Marilyn held her by the elbow.

"Come on dear, let's go for drinks in the cabana."

As usual, Bella was not to be upset; I wondered about this, how she wielded so much power over everything in her life, her own mother being no exception. Our mothers had shuffled out heading to the pool area, mumbling and giggling. Bella had kept her eyes on them until they were out of sight. When she turned back to our game her brown eyes had hardened and she kept staring off into space. After I had won the game and she was putting away the chessboard she looked at me and said, "Why are they like that?"

"Perhaps they don't know any other way to be. You have to understand, they are older. And my grandmother grew up on a huge ranch in India. And your great grandfather was one of the last governors of the empire."

"You would think they would at least try to hide their 'superiority'."

"Don't you think your being too harsh on your mother? Who would do all this conservation stuff?"

"Really? So you think no Ugandan is intelligent enough to protect the lake from pollution and over-fishing?"

"I think none of them is interested in doing it."

"So we white people should come save the day, as always?"

I fell silent. Paul cleared his throat, cutting into my memories. I sighed.

"Is she taking her medicines?"

"The doctor increase dose. Then he reduce it. Then change to another one. Still no change. He said to just sit, wait. Be like her, but I cannot Miz Sandra! I don't know what I do if she not come back to us."

"You tell me if you need something."

I nodded and he eased the door shut behind him. Then he ducked his head back in,

"Maybe time we ask Dr. Okello who father of Bella be. Sure he knows. Then we go tell them to come for their blood. Then Bella spirit be happy. Then our land spirit be happy. Then no spirit make Madam Marilyn like doll. See! We all win." And he shut the door before I could answer him. I did not know what I would have said if he hadn't left just then.

My own mother was lying weak in bed. She had just returned from her third round of chemo in South Africa. My father, after trading her in for a lithe ebony skinned Ugandan fifteen years older than me, had divorced her when I was fifteen. But he still paid for her health insurance and travel expenses and let her keep the beach house, where I stayed with her every time I came for holidays. The cancer seemed to have timed Bella's demise perfectly; stage two of the breast, we learnt, a month after burying Bella. The numbness that had already started eating into Marilyn seeped into my mother as well, almost instantaneously that day, in the private clinic. When she came out of the doctor's room she somehow looked like a chicken without feathers, and I knew it was bad even before she sat next to Marilyn and said, "It's really bad M, the old devil got my left boob."

I was stunned I suppose, but then my mind jumped to what Bella might have said: she would have tried to make light of it and failed by saying something like, 'Little wonder that a fancy private clinic cannot cure it!' I supposed I would have shut her down, I would have stepped up to Bella and told her that she didn't have to be everyone's commentator. I would have told her life is life, life is not a soccer match where she has to be the winner all the time. I would have told her all that if she had stayed alive long enough for my mother's cancer diagnosis and if she had made even one acidic remark I would have told her, 'It stops with my mother, with me, it stops with my mother. I was still thinking all that when Marilyn, taking both my mother's hands in hers said matter of factly, "Let me ring up Dr. Okello, he will know what to do." As if he was not only the best fertility specialist in town but also an Oncologist. She had made no move to know other Ugandan doctors. Whenever she was sick she called Dr. Okello first, then he recommended another Doctor to her, then she asked him to call ahead on her behalf, just in case. Bella hated what she called her mother's 'prissy Englishness', and she told her mother so in such terms. In turn Marilyn pretended she hadn't heard her daughter, or she defended herself by saying, "Anyone can ask for a favour, I am sure even Ugandan's ask him for such favours. And he is a well-mannered man."

But Marilyn's attitude to Dr. Okello immediately changed when Bella called him her father; he had overseen Marilyn's fertility treatments and finally the successful IVF procedure that had resulted into Bella. She referred to the donor as the sperm whenever we talked about him.

Marilyn had bristled whenever Bella said, "Marilyn, when is my father coming to see us?" A redness appeared beneath the tanned skin of her cheeks as she fought not to chastise Bella, which would only have encouraged her.

"I could ask Paul to come with me to Gaaba, you know, drop in on him or something."

"For God's sake, he's a busy man, Bella. You can't just walk into his clinic to chat!"

"Well then, I am sure he wouldn't refuse a dinner invitation to our nice Equi-Resort."

"I don't know what's got into you these days. You know very well he's always welcome here. And we've had him over recently—"

"—not since I got back. Will you ask him, please? Mom?"

And that was that. The next week, Dr. Okello was over for dinner. Marilyn was humming *Coward of the County* by Dolly Parton, as if she was priming herself for the doctor's arrival, "Shall we put on some music, then?" To which he nodded and she asked what it would be, as if she didn't already know. "Sweet Dolly Parton, would be nice," he would answer with his large smile.

Bella, with all the irritation she could muster asked, "Do you have to hum that now? You know it's what he will ask for. Plus, you're off tune anyways."

Marilyn, determined not to ruin her mood, ignored Bella and only paused to ask me, "Would you please find me the lovely table mats?"

She meant the ones that were woven with beige straw and embroidered with elaborate patterns of 'all sorts of tribal paraphernalia', as she liked to say. I pulled open the drawer in the cabinet and handed them to her. She arranged them on the table, with the meticulous care of threading a needle.

"The long stemmed glasses, you know he prefers white to red, Bella?"

She came over to the cabinet and opened the upper glass door compartment. She placed two glasses in my hands and I handed them to Marilyn who set them round the table. I grinned, thinking how a black Ugandan man could quell bickering between a white mother and her daughter, without even trying.

I shouldn't have celebrated so soon because Bella, voice honey sweet turned to Marilyn and said, "You never take out the 'tribal mats' and the rustic mahogany table for anyone else."

"Dr. Okello isn't just anybody, honey. You're looking for a fight, cut it out before he finds us at each others' necks."

We all knew that would never happen; Marilyn would back down, if it came to it. Bella was her precious and only child after so many IVF trials. On days when she was feeling more affectionate than usual she called her, her last good egg.

"Yeah! I bet you you think you've earned a spot in heaven for letting him stick his charcoal hands up your cervix." Bella spat.

Marilyn blanched and her mouth flew open but no words came out.

"How many nightmares did you have that you would give birth to a burnt local?" Bella's voice low and sharp, cut into the heavy silence as if her previous remark hadn't drawn enough blood. The last we had overheard one random afternoon, as Marilyn and my mother chatted over tea and tarts.

❧

I SAT with Marilyn for thirty minutes and still she did not glance my way. She had been diagnosed with severe depression. It was understandable that Bella's death was the trigger that brought it on, but one had hoped that it wouldn't be as bad as it proved to be. I thought she would be out of it maybe three or six months after the funeral, but Marilyn had not shaken the gloom off. It seemed to me that even in the grave, Bella still held the strings. Even I was a puppet, being plagued by specific memories towards the anniversary every year, it happened like clockwork.

The strangest thing was that the autopsy report came back inconclusive. I imagine they splayed her on a metal bed, with a thin Macintosh mattress, beneath a white bulb encased in a dish like aluminum holder, the better to see her bits; that the marks on her body were examined under a magnifying glass, that the colour and weight of her lungs, heart and kidney were noted; then they would have placed all of them back into her, just like we had done with anatomy Jane when we were in fifth grade. Marilyn had bought her for Bella when she refused to play with boring Barbies. She refused all food and drink until Jane was handed to her. Of course I had joined in on the hunger strike.

The next time she tried it was when we were seventeen. It was after the spider craze, after the ornithology and zoology craze, and right during the Fela craze. Bella was so taken by Elias that she believed he was a Godsend from Allah. Even for Bella, her new interests were extreme. I knew Marilyn would forbid it as soon as she found out that her daughter was glued to the laptop all day because she was researching Islam with the intention of becoming Muslim. Elias was not only Ugandan but also a school dropout; all he had managed was three years in secondary school before his father had run out of money. From then he had gone fishing with his father.

For speaking better English than the rest of the local youth, Marilyn had assigned him the duty of patrolling the lake for illegal fishermen. She had forbidden all the Islanders from fishing unless their nets were big enough to let the small fish through. Their boats had to be at least 6 feet long to prevent them docking in the shallows, where the small fish came to eat. Every Friday, Erias had come by the house to give a report of who was not following the conservation guidelines. Then Marilyn would summon them and pardon those she gauged as repentant; truants and repeat offender were jailed in the Island Police cell. The cell was four by six feet big. Occasionally, she banished the fishermen who found themselves in the cell more than two times.

Erias had laughed when he told us this story, saying that the banished returned to the Island two or three weeks later, and re-introduced themselves to Marilyn with different names. She never noticed the difference, and even hired some of them to do odd jobs in Equi-Resort.

Bella had laughed and said, "That's Marilyn alright, she thinks all dark skinned Ugandans look alike. That's so lame, don't you think so Maj dear?"

She called me 'Maj dear' as a reminder that I could not repeat any of what we were discussing to anyone else.

That day remains vivid in my mind as if it is playing on a loop and I can pause it to study our expressions, I can smell the air, I can hear our voices. It was one of the few times that Bella had come to my house. She came in dragging Elias by the hand and craning her neck to shout up the stairs, "Marjorie! We're here."

I had thought she was with Marilyn and came down the stairs saying, "You've just missed mom. She—" and then I stopped when I saw Elias and how their fingers were laced. He tried to pull his hand away but Bella held tight, "Don't worry, it's only Maj dear, she would never tell anyone. Not so Marjorie?"

"Tell anyone about what?"

"That Elias is my boyfriend."

"Oh! Okay," I added before telling her that it was just wrong and Marilyn would just kick him off the Island when she found out. I got a Fanta orange from the fridge for Bella and handed it to her. She gave me one of her looks but I remained rooted to the spot. She patted Elias on the chest, "What would you like to have my dear?"

"Nothing really. Maybe next time. And I need to go check on the nets anyway."

Bella drew her lips into a mock pout and then pecked his cheek. He waved at us as he walked out of the front door. When it was shut Bella came straight at me.

"You can at least pretend civility to Elias for my sake."

"I am civil with Elias the errand boy. I don't know how to be with whatever that was."

"*Is*, Marjorie. It is a relationship. How is it any different from you and Matt?"

Matt's father owned one of the houses on the Island. Their family vacationed there at least once a year. But he wasn't there that holiday. I was certain he had chosen something like skiing somewhere in Europe instead of being around me, stuck at second base.

"Matt and I broke up."

"Oh! Did you want to?"

"Not really, but he's bored I guess. Everyone else from his family came."

"Maybe it is for the best. You don't want to be with someone who doesn't notice you anymore. That's why I like Elias a whole lot, he sees only me."

Three weeks later she came running up the front porch of my house. She hurried to my bedroom and closed the door and turned the key.

"What is it, you look flushed."

"I am a week late," she whispered.

I did not know what to say. I had underestimated their relationship, I had not expected it to go in that directions, if at all.

"First we have to make sure. Then we go with Paul to the mainland when he goes shopping, then we sneak away to a doctor who can do it."

"I don't want to kill my baby. I am not even doing any tests. I'll just wait until it can't be hidden anymore."

"And then what?"

"And then it will be too late for Marilyn to try and make me do something."

I tried but I could not change her mind. A month passed and she got a little pouch. She hid it well with her old jeans and her mother's cardigans that were three sizes smaller than her. Marilyn would never have seen it if she hadn't walked in on them in her house, on the sofa, Elias with an ear pressed to her stomach saying, "I cannot wait for my *muzungu* baby."

What followed was a blur even for Bella. She later told me that her mother screamed for Paul who came running from the stables. That Marilyn was upon Elias swearing obscenities and scratching at his face by the time Paul arrived on the scene. That Marilyn screamed like a rabid dog, over and over again, "This fucking black ape imbecile defiled my daughter." And then Paul locked all the doors so that Elias would not escape as she called a policeman. Then Dr. Okello whom she told over the phone, "Please come with a pregnancy test kit."

When the policeman came, he handcuffed Elias and dragged him away. Bella was kicking and screening when the doctor arrived. Together with her mother they restrained her. Paul brought two ropes, one for her feet, the other for her body, then she was placed on a wooden chair. A plastic basin was brought and pushed near the edge of her chair, where her pee would trickle when she got tired of holding it in.

⁂

THE ropes were removed the following morning when my mother allowed me to see her. She recounted the whole ordeal dry eyed. I wondered at that. Her mother came in, to tell us that she had booked Bella a doctor to take care of it.

"It's the only option you have Bella. I will not be shamed like this. The case against him is defilement. You are not yet an adult. That scum is going away for life."

"Mother—" and she collapsed into her mother's hands. She did not wake up.

When her body was brought back from the autopsy, they had placed the coffin on a long table in the veranda. The spiders made a bee line for her coffin and surrounded it. We had never seen so many spiders on the island.

Lillian Akampurira Aujo *is a poet and fiction writer from Uganda. She is the winner of the* Jalada Prize for Literature 2015 *and the* BN Poetry Award 2009. *She has been shortlisted for the* Gerald Kraak Award 2019, the Brittle Paper Anniversary Award 2018, *and longlisted for a* Nommo Award 2018. *She is a 2017 fellow of the* Ebedi Residency *in Nigeria. She has presented poetry at the 2017 GIMAC meeting in Addis Ababa. Her work has been published by the* Caine Prize, Prairie Schooner, Transition, Jalada, Gerald Kraak Award, Babishai-Niwe Poetry Award, Bahati Books, Omenana, Enkare Review, Brittle Paper, and 20:35 Africa, An Anthology of Contemporary Poetry. *She has been a mentor in the* WritivismAt5 Online Mentoring *program. She has co-facilitated a creative writing workshop for South Sudanese women with Oxfam Kampala.*

Magic Invisible
Jameela Siddiqi

YOU KNOW, I believe in magic. I was born and raised in a place where magic happened daily. The smallest thing could make my heart soar with delight. The flutter of a butterfly's wing or a ray of afternoon sunshine that turns pebbles to diamonds could momentarily take me out of oneself and connect me to other worlds. But the magic lies in the eyes and mind of the person who wants to believe. It's something everybody has—initially—but once you go too far from the place that nurtured this sense of magic in your being, the feeling begins to fade. Life does its best to take that magic away from you. You don't know it but one day you feel you've lost something vital, but you're not sure what it is. You vaguely remember feeling what you once felt and you remember the place where you last felt it. And you wonder if revisiting that place would bring back that feeling, however fleetingly. Does the place still exist?

It does. Like Rome, it is built on seven hills and named after the antelopes that enjoyed grazing on those hills in the very old days when this settlement was the capital of the ancient kingdom of Buganda. We still have a king and he is held in very high esteem, especially by the Indians, because he studied at Oxford. In the 1950s, this city was said to be clean, safe and full of surprises. There's something for everyone here—or so claim the travel guide books—but, for me, it is really only divided into two halves: that which is within the school compound—where we live—and that which lies beyond. There is a clear dividing line between what we do on our compound and that which goes on outside the compound.

When we socialize with our neighbours—all teachers or school administration staff—we are interacting with like-minded beings who share our values, whatever their race, language or religion. We value education, as depicted by school grades and we take pride in our westernized airs and graces. When we go outside the compound—and particularly when we visit shops—it is understood we are tourists. Our world of education, education, education and neatly manicured gardens and flower beds with tea poured from a teapot at four pm sharp, stands aloof from this other world of trade and commerce where, my mother is convinced, a person would happily stick their head down a filthy lavatory pan to fish out a one-cent piece. There was a tacit agreement that when we ventured into this other world, we had to work hard at not appearing to be snobs. We had, after all, been entrusted the task of educating the offspring of the trading classes, to transform them into better human beings just as the British had undertaken the task of improving our characters. My father, of course, scoffed at this but my mother never ceased to remind us that the Brits had given up their temperate climate and cozy cottages covered in trellises of pink roses, to put up with the mosquito-infested heat of our country just so we could be more like them. It wasn't done to appear ungrateful.

Our compound is set in a lush valley at the foot of one of our most famous hills. At the top of the hill there's a world-class university, said to be the best university on the whole of the African continent. We often see the fashionable university students walking down the hill into our valley in small groups when they're setting out for jaunts into town to spend their monthly allowances. The main road cuts through the valley and then carries on up another hill leading into the city centre. But we seldom venture there. Each morning, I run across a small field to go to primary school alongside which stands the rather grand secondary grammar school building where my father is employed as Headmaster.

There's our house—the white one with the pretty red roof and red door surrounded by a border of marigolds and daisies. It's the second largest house on the compound, the largest being reserved for the school buildings and compound manager, Mr Ralph Jenkins, because he's White, supposedly, although every time I've seen him he's rather red faced and carries about his person a piercing aroma of boiled cabbage and stale beer. At the far end of our compound, opposite Mr Jenkins's big house there's a three-storey block of flats facing the main road, built for bachelor teachers and the women teachers who are single and some of whom live in groups of two or three—all except my mother's best friend, Miss Behroze Chopriwalla the cookery teacher, who has a ground floor flat all to herself because she cannot abide the habits of others.

"No civic sense, these people," is one of her favourite lines. Miss Chopriwalla is still cut up about the end of British Raj in India but consoles herself with the fact that she now lives in a British Protectorate and never misses an opportunity to remind us all of that fact, especially when we, the children, are being unruly.

"But who are they protecting us from, exactly?" I ask. She never bothers answering that vital question and instead informs me about major deficiencies in my character, two of which she describes as "insolence" and "impertinence". It is impossible to have an encounter with Chopriwalla without having to come home and consult one of my father's fat dictionaries.

All the compound children play outside in the communal gardens while the parents, usually both teachers, sit outside marking school exercise books and being served tea and cake by grim-faced houseboys. The golden, early evening sunshine provides a backdrop to this idyllic life of grown-ups working and children playing. If it's been raining then there's usually a crystal clear rainbow against a deep blue sky once the rain clears up. Early afternoons are very quiet but from five to six—everybody's play time—there's mayhem all over the residential side of the school compound. At exactly six o'clock we are all summoned back indoors. Under no circumstances are we allowed to be out at, or near, sunset. The evening chill starts to gather pace and the spirits are said to take their repose in the trees.

This was my world and I was Queen of The Compound. My company was eagerly sought by various cliques but I was always something of a loner, preferring my many books to idle chit-chat with children who I felt were still hopelessly immature. The school compound offered a secluded existence with very little reason to step beyond it. In my mind, it had become the safe, predictable territory while everything outside of it was likely to erupt, at any moment, into the most unpredictable chain of events. This possibility proved both exciting and frightening. Outside the safety and predictability of our neat, well-tended school compound, lay the city which was strictly out of bounds for us children of The Compound. It said to be much hotter than our compound, more crowded and nearly always choking with traffic. Grownups were often heard to say that there were more cars than people in this city. That, by itself, made the city sound most exciting because cars were still something of a novelty for us. All the teachers only had to walk across a small field to get to work—it took less than five minutes—so it was considered something of an extravagance to own a car. Cars were something that belonged in the "other" world—outside the compound.

For us kids, even a close-up view of a stationary car was something of a treat. So just imagine the excitement caused by the first car on our compound. It was in 1960, or thereabouts, when the newly-arrived South Indian maths teacher, an eccentric bachelor by the name of Mr George drove home one Saturday morning in a shiny black VW Beetle. He drove into the compound at the majestic pace of about three miles per hour and circled the gravel drive that ran through the compound a full five times to ensure that everyone had had a good view. Faces peeped out of curtains as Mr George finally brought the car to a halt, got out of the door on the driver's side and then walked right around the car several times to check that both doors were locked before proceeding to examine each of the four tires in great detail. Finally, just as he looked like he was done, he suddenly turned around and went back to the car. He unlocked the door, got inside, checked something again and then proceeded to go through the whole routine of lock-up and tire-checks. By this time, a few reluctant neighbours had begun to approach the car although there is an unspoken rule on the compound that any new acquisition by a neighbour should not be acknowledged with too much eagerness. According to Miss Chopriwalla, it showed a lack of breeding and etiquette to get too excited at somebody else's material possessions. Even so, there were those who could no longer hold back.

"So, Mr. George! New car! Is it yours?"

"Yes, of course it's mine."

"Why do you need a car? You only work across the field," they pointed out, stating the obvious, another speciality of our compound.

"There is so much to see in this country. I want to make a few safaris. Go to the National Parks. Murchison Falls. Explore the countryside… see wildlife…"

The handful of neighbours who had been unable to restrain themselves from making such a direct enquiry exchanged knowing looks with one another that meant that the car wasn't so much to tour the country's many attractions but more to attract a certain highly refined, single lady-teacher by the name of Miss Behroze Chopriwalla, then aged thirty-something. It was clear from the start that although George had lost his heart to her, his heavy South Indian-English accent didn't quite come up to scratch where that discerning lady was concerned. Even so, it was generally known that he would've gone to any ridiculous extreme to woo her, even something as ludicrous as actually buying a car. Satisfied with their general consensus on why the car had been purchased, they started ambling back to their houses. But we the kids remained, waiting for George to go back to his block of flats so we could take a closer look at the car.

No sooner had we started looking through the windows with awe and wonderment at the various instruments on the dashboard than George came out again, waving his arms and making hissing noises:

"Get away! Don't breathe on the glass! Those windows have just been polished. Keep your grubby fingers away from the paintwork!"

He ran back into the house and emerged with a piece of cloth to wipe off our fingerprints. A few minutes later, he emerged with a bucket of water and gave the car a wash.

The general view on the compound was that George, not having a wife or family to absorb his energy during his leisure hours, had become far too obsessed with this black metal box on four wheels. In time, it also became known that although he treated it like a brand new, immaculate object that had just emerged from the showroom, the car was actually an expertly re-buffed specimen of a fifteen-year old model. In those days, people kept their car for years and years. Cars themselves were built to last a good thirty or forty years as it would've been considered the height of vulgarity to buy more than one or two cars during an average lifespan.

Every afternoon George would return from teaching and after downing a hasty cup of tea, jump into his car and slowly crawl out of our compound— but not before doing two full rounds of the circular gravel drive so that all and sundry could see him at the wheel. When he'd completed circling, he'd finally approach the end of the driveway which led to the main road and, just before turning to the left, a little orange light stick would jut out of the passenger-side door. This phenomenon was the height of futuristic technology, as far as I was concerned: "It always juts out in whichever direction he's going to be turning. How does the car know where he wants to go?" I ask my bemused father.

We assumed he would be driving around town, showing off his car. Where else could he go? It was a fairly small place and he would return some twenty minutes later and go through all the usual checks and double-checks after which he would proceed to lovingly wash the car in soapy bubbles.

We would await his return and eagerly look forward to the treat of watching him splash water all over the car before lovingly drying and polishing it with a cloth.

"Does it with as much care and attention as washing a baby," observed Miss Chopriwalla, fully aware that the car had been purchased for her benefit and, secretly, extremely flattered by the gesture. Even so, she flatly refused to accompany him anywhere on the one or two occasions when he'd summoned up enough courage and forced himself to sound casual about it:

"Good evening, Miss Chopriwalla! Would you like to come for a drive?"

"Too kind. But I think I'll wait until you've had a bit more practice on that thing," she would say, jovially.

So all George could do in the meantime was to keep practising his driving and to keep on repeatedly washing and polishing his latest and most expensive possession.

Every twenty minutes or so, he would come out again to make sure that the crows hadn't had the audacity to use the shiny black roof of the Beetle as a lavatory.

In time, it seemed George had grown pretty fed up with his lone drives. One evening he beckoned to a few of us playing by the guava tree: "Hey, children! Do you want to go for a drive?"

We stared at him in stunned disbelief. George? Actually asking us if we wanted to be taken for a drive? We started to run helter-skelter towards the shiny black beast when somebody mentioned we ought to have permission. Hesitating, in case he changed his mind while we ran back indoors to check with various mothers, he put our minds at ease by saying: "Go! Go quickly ask your parents if you can come out with me for a drive."

Permissions duly secured, eight of us piled into the little Beetle—two in the front passenger seat and six in the back. George performed his start-up ceremony with a great deal of rancour. We gasped, open-mouthed, at his every move. He had the demeanour of a wartime bomber-pilot rather than a small-town second-hand car driver who had nothing better to do than go round and round in circles. He pulled up his sleeves, sat up straighter, surveyed the controls, took a deep breath, quickly looked over his shoulder, then into the mirror and turned the key causing the engine to gurgle a bit and then grunt and stop. He smiled nervously and turned the key again. This time it started and he revved it up, as though for encouragement. At that point, one of the boys in our gang said something and George hushed him down as though the slightest sound from us would distract the engine from doing its job.

George ceremoniously released a lever and then manipulated another one. We lurched forward and came to a grinding halt. At that point he asked everybody to get out of the car. We stood on the side uncertainly, wondering what would happen next. He tried to start it again but it wouldn't. He asked us to get together—two on each side and the rest at the back and push the car. We were thrilled. Our excitement reached fever pitch as we had never, ever, pushed a real car before. This was a brand new game and we pushed with all our might and soon he was rolling off, speeding away.

He didn't come back for us. So much for taking us for a drive. Having made such a ceremony of securing parental permission, we felt sheepish about going back indoors to admit that the adventure was cancelled. So we hung around outdoors wondering whether George had just taken the car for a brief spin to get the engine going or whether he had, indeed, abandoned us.

Some twenty minutes later he was back, being pushed by a group of African men, women and children who had had to get him all the way up the hill for him to roll down and then get stuck again.

From then on, George's black car became the proverbial white elephant. It was the same routine everyday: it had to be started up with a lot of pushing and then, each time, he returned with a number of bedraggled people and shoeless urchins pushing him back. In time, he also gave up the daily washing routine. He no longer came out to check on the crow droppings. The roof and bonnet were now covered in white stuff, solidified for weeks. Gradually, the once-black car gathered many patches of white interspersed with dust. It just stood there, a sad, derelict monument of unrequited love.

Soon, George had even stopped locking the doors and then the seats started disappearing. One of them was reported to have been seen in the gatehouse *jumba* of Imrozi, the school *askari*[67] watchman, who had always fancied owning a sofa. A few days later, the wheels had been taken, one by one.

Soon, the car became a playhouse for us and we came and went from it freely, without anyone batting an eyelid. We took it in turns to sit at the wheel and pretend to drive. George would walk past us as though the car

---

67   A Swahili word meaning "guard" or "soldier".

had nothing to do with him. Never in the entire history of possessions had an item once so cherished fallen into such decay and neglect. I now hated George's car because it had taken all the romance out of cars. I preferred cars when they were shiny, distant objects, belonging to no one in particular. George's rusty heap lying so close and so easily accessible had quite taken the magic out of everything. Yet, in my later years, the memory of Mr George and his disused car was to become one of my most magical childhood memories.

I stand at the edge of the compound, my gaze fixed on where the neatly trimmed lawn, dotted with flower beds and surrounded by well-pruned hedges had stood. It was now just overgrown grass with patches of earth. The circular gravel drive which George had circled so often to show off his car, had now given way to a rough, muddy path, now squelching and full of puddles. That's what happens now when it's been raining. No more rainbows. No more magic.

Jameela Siddiqi *is an award winning broadcaster and journalist. Born in Kenya and raised in Uganda, Jameela was an undergraduate student in Kampala at the time of the Asian Expulsion in 1972. She continued her studies at the London School of Economics and Political Science after which she worked as a television news journalist and documentary producer for several years. She has written and lectured widely on Indian music and culture and also taught on a degree course for Indian music in conjunction with the Trinity College of Music and Dance in London. She has produced and complied numerous albums of classical music and has translated poetry and songs from several Indian languages while also acting as language consultant for the reference section of Oxford University Press. Her first novel,* The Feast of the Nine Virgins *was published by* Bogle L'Ouverture *in 2001 and her second novel,* Bombay Gardens *was published by Lulu Inc. in 2006. She is the author of numerous short stories and essays published in various international periodicals and she is also a regular contributor for* Songlines, *a leading publication on* World Music.

Doom Harvest
Derek Lubangakene

ON WHAT should've been his last day—the full scope of 'last day' varying from last day on the island or last day on earth—Akena Sydney suffered what he'd later learn was the serendipitous (mis)fortune of meeting Hadiya and her husband's son, Omari. Without meaning to, he crashed their grief soiree; their 'doom harvest.' That only he could've come up with this phrase is probably worth noting, but that'd draw away from the generalised melancholy stifling the island. That low-grade hum of delayed hazard broadcasting as silent anxiety, as atmosphere of disquiet. Of course, he was romanticising. That's one way to look at it. The other is, if the other grievers had the words, they too would've thought like him. Or worse, let their grief eat at them like he was letting it eat at him.

Sydney had, yet again, woken passed out on the beach. That was the third night running he'd wandered so far away from the pier, ended up sprawled on the beach. It was late afternoon now. He'd slept through the mid-morning buzz. His back sun-burnt to a crisp.

Bwejuu was where Hadiya and Omari spent all their time. Sydney couldn't blame them; Bwejuu, even for a touristy seaweed-fishing village was rather deserted. Lots of the other grievers flocked here too. The ones like him, and Hadiya. Those who couldn't move on. There were no spectators here. Unless of course you were making a fool of yourself. Like Sydney was. Sydney didn't mind making a fool of himself. He hid in plain sight. It's one of the things *she* loved about him. His wife, that is. His present shame. Yes, shame. No, it wasn't a Luo thing (his wife thought everything quirky about him was a Luo thing—he was her 'first Luo' and she'd say, "Once you go Luo you can never go back.") Sydney equated grief to shame. This way, he could compartmentalize (this is a Luo thing). Technically, this was cheating. Seeing as over the years he'd developed quite the threshold for shame; from shrugging at being called derogatory tribal disses like '*muchope*,' '*northie*', to his premature balding, to not being able to speak his native tongue—his cultural heritage had been erased by a 20-year-old insurgency, to this now: making a fool of himself in front of all these grievers. He couldn't work up the nerve to cry and wail (this too was a Luo thing. Luo men are hard *jamaas*. "We are the Vikings of Africa" he'd joke every time *she* nudged him to be 'more sensitive.').

FYI, making a fool of himself was his tolerance for grief. Though one might aptly say intolerance. He chose not to watch his life taper to nothing, he actively destroyed himself. All that drinking and provocation.

In any case, his nightly wandering was his highlight. Watching the Indian Ocean all black (not technically true! He was being romantic, 'more sensitive' after the fact) the still-*ish* waves catching the light of the full moon, the jangling glint of the faraway lanterns. making the whole beach shimmer with prickly points of light. It was the only thing that didn't remind him of *her*. It wasn't even that beautiful, but it drowned out all reminiscing. The silence of it muffled all his other silences. A silence like driving through a tunnel in the Alps, like holding a shell to your ear: hollow—a mirror of his presently unadorned heart.

It was the perfect counterweight to all his 'lack' of grieving, his tolerance of shame.

Sydney had only travelled back to collect his wife's ashes and spread them over the Indian Ocean and be done with Zanzibar forever. But despite going everywhere with her urn, he couldn't get himself to spread her ashes. It wasn't what she would've wanted, being spread in the ocean. If it were any consolation, he found solace in the fact that his wife wouldn't have approved of his drinking either. So in light of things, the lesser evil triumphed.

Like him, Hadiya and Omari, had lost someone in the MV Unguja fire weeks ago. The survivors all received a municipal-issue ivory-hued urn which supposedly contained the ashes of their beloved. Urns filled with ash, beach sand, but not the people they lost. Some survivors got more than just ash, but Sydney didn't fancy scrapping for nondescript watch-straps, dental fillings, hairpins that might or might not be his wife's. Some of the survivors who'd secured these articles, soon returned, bemoaned their flawed perception. They begged to return the piece of bone, the hairpin, the toenail: in fact, during one of the many memorial services at Christ Church Cathedral, the Priest restrained one survivor whose husband's supposed watch left black rings around her wrist. She kept yelling she felt marked, singled out by doom.

Worse still, the official inquiry into the fire hit a dead wall. Largely handled by the mainland police, those bastards only appeared a week after the fire. By then the survived had suffered all kinds of speculation. Sydney hadn't lingered like the rest; he couldn't take any more of the *freakery*. Freakery, that was one of her words. It was to Africa, what magical realism is to Colombia. His wife didn't like the obvious African synonym, not *dog'o* (her native Luganda,) not *jok* (his native Luo,) not *juju*[68]. Freakery stood for everything she found odd, speculative. She was a little out of touch that way.

On confirming his wife's death, he'd chartered the first plane home. In their little flat (a wedding gift from her father) he settled to grieve alone. He'd returned three days ago because Zelda, his wife, deserved better than to have her urn lay unattended in the Municipal office. Or worse, some shifty survivor claiming it.

That's how he staggered upon Omari, who though only eight, had a scruffy disposition of someone much older, someone much accustomed to

68   A form of traditional African magic or witchcraft

being ignored. Sydney didn't ignore him. Not since the little bastard had stolen Zelda's urn and was using it to build a sand castle. Sydney snapped at the boy and trampled all over his sandcastle, rousing the ire and disdain of the clutch of grievers laying on the beach. Omari wouldn't let go of the urn, and Sydney, drunk-ish, unbalanced, stumbled while wrestling for his wife's urn. Omari's squealing helped best the drunken fool. The weather too bright, the squealing too loud, Sydney all but crawled into a ball.

This tussle lasted an embarrassingly long time. Long enough for Hadiya, dazed herself, eyes puffy from watching the shoreless horizon, make her way to the dueling pair. She was a solemn dreadlocked woman, slight, but tough looking.

She snatched the urn from Sydney and returned it to her son. Sydney could've protested, but the look in Hadiya's eyes stayed any dissent.

"Let him play, he'll return it soon enough," she said. Returning to her bright orange *kikoy*[69] mat.

Sydney returned to his perch—a section of the sand carved into the lanky shape of his body. He was within earshot of Hadiya. Kept staring at her. She never regarded him. Not once. He tried to recall where he remembered her from…

Right. The Municipal Office.

Like him, she didn't accept an urn. She was certain her Annan was still out there. Denial. There's a fine line between that and faith. Technically cheating too. But *c'est la guerre*. This is war. All is fair. He admired that.

Sydney followed her gaze. Soon got bored. He wished he were somewhere else. Preferably watching the divers off the wharfs, and the languorous bobbing of the dhows docking at the pier alongside the MV Kilimanjaro. Too bad his quest for distraction had led him here. Perhaps she, Hadiya, was a distraction (a v. non-Luo thing this. Still…) He cast the thought away.

According to the Mainlander's report, the MV Unguja was last serviced when Zanzibar was still a constitutional monarchy. There was no way the pilot could've avoided crashing into that island especially in such low light. The coastal guard (what passes for one anyway) located only the ashes. They sifted out the metal parts then tinned the ashes and contacted the survivors using the ferry's manifest. The manifest was why Hadiya held onto hope. Annan's name wasn't on it. Even though he was supposed to be on that late ferry.

Sydney, tired of waiting for Omari to return Zelda's urn, walked over, sat beside Hadiya. They sat a long while, Omari playing silently by himself, yards behind.

"Are you hungry," she asked, after a long while.

Hungry? Sydney couldn't remember the last thing he ate. Much less how long ago that was.

The Forodhani food court. Sydney's kryptonite.

---

69 A brightly colored, rectangular piece of cloth often worn as a sarong or shawl.

Zanzibar, as a resort, never had much of an off-peak or peak season. It made it hard to blame, to attribute this black-cloudedness to off-season blues. Everyone was grieving, except the grillboys at the food court. There are no hagglers across the whole of Tanzania, they're all here. A cluck of hens the lot of them. Rushing, grabbing, snatching. It was quite touristy, and took all the taste out of Sydney's mouth.

Food was never much of theatre for Sydney (a Luo thing! More her, Zelda's thing actually.) Still, no one should be this happy about food. Yes, the shawarmas, the seafood, the 'Zanzibar pizza' were worth dying for; the clouds of smoke wafting suspended above the grills, the incense and aroma, intoxicating, but still. . .

The trio sat by the waterfront, a platter of too-colourful *Orojo* to share. If there was ever another reason to hate Omari, it's how he ate. Snatching all the dumplings and skewers. Hadiya couldn't have cared less. Sydney reckoned she was in that grief phase where it made no sense to keep your strength up for anything. Where there's an indigestible dampness in your stomach, like something's gone and drowned there. Sydney had been there before. You just have to let it run its course.

Beyond the food court, twilight sunk the beaches over the waterfront. Omari and other kids, run after the stray cats. Such unformulated glee was refreshing. Sydney and Hadiya, meanwhile, mopped around the pier, avoiding the stares their lone urn invited. It wasn't enough that their platter had been discounted, on account of being survivors, the pity from the food court staff, the few tourists, insufferable.

Hadiya and Sydney perched on the bamboo railing. Stared wordlessly at the starless night.

A waiter later tapped Sydney's shoulder, said their son was asleep in one of the chairs. Hadiya regarded the waiter sullenly, too tired to protest the misapprehension. Sydney retrieved the boy and asked her where they were staying?

"Not yet," Hadiya said, taking the boy from his arms. Cradling Omari (he was too big for cradling) she sat in a plastic lounger, all but disappeared into it. All but forgot Sydney existed.

Sydney could've walked away and that would've been that, but he had an irrational fear of being forgotten. Zelda had the opposite, she lived in terror of never being forgotten. She was the artistic type, a ballet instructor (in Kampala, no less!) so Sydney chocked it up to artistic delusion. His pathology, though, was founded on a childhood trauma—his mum, one nippy Thursday, forgot to pick him up from kindergarten. He didn't have any friends because he mostly ran them away. Painstakingly calling them dozens of times "just to say hi." Zelda didn't mind that, she thought all that needling sweet, until it killed her, until it drove her to get on the MV Unguja, a last moment adjustment just to escape his nagging. Her name too wasn't on the list, but he knew. He just knew.

He could've walked away, but he hadn't even told her his name. He hadn't (yet) told her his story, his traumas, his overcomings... how interesting she'd find him. Maybe not, that version of him was very morose, incontinent. But it'd impress indelibly on her.

Above them, a crack in the sky, the rumble of thunder a way off. A collective silence, the charged pier waiting on the promise of rain. Something to damp the stifling night.

Sydney lingered.

The next morning, he woke at the Waterfront pier. He wasn't drunk, but the front of his head rang slightly, his bones stiff from sleeping crammed in a foetal position. Wait a minute, he'd actually slept. He couldn't remember the last good sleep he'd had. He felt overjoyed, until he groped around and couldn't find Zelda's urn. He'd forgotten it at Hadiya's. She was the last person he wanted to see. A shared sentiment, obviously.

At Zelda's budget hotel, Sydney couldn't remember which room he dropped them off. He walked the third floor knocking on doors. On the fifth random door, opened Omari, with a beamy smile that shriveled the moment he recognized Sydney. Sydney wondered if he knew what had passed between Hadiya and him? How this time it wasn't him who made a fool of himself, but her, which in a way broke down to him acting a fool by bringing her to his level. So, crap, no escape from the role he'd cast himself. There was a victory in that. Perhaps.

He shuffled into the room. Hadiya was in the bathroom. Sydney tracked dirt all over the rug as he went for the urn next to the flower vase. Hadiya emerged from the bathroom wrapped in a towel. They matched gazes for a second, before he tore away and bundled for the door.

Wait, she called out.

He didn't turn, but stopped. He owed her that, at least—the opportunity to apologize.

"I'm going to change into something more covering. I want you to promise you'll be here when I get back," she said. "Promise me?"

She picked a few clothes from her bag and retreated into the bathroom. Hadiya returned a while later, a beige-ish, willowy shirt plus faded jeans folded at the hem. They were his clothes, her Annan. She went over to the drapes and opened them. Omari shuffled to the windows, stared at the pier.

Hadiya apologized for last night. She looked puffier, paler.

"I can't explain what came over me. I thought it would make me feel something other than this. . . emptiness. . . I'm not even that kind of person, y'know, like, I just, oh—"

He said nothing

"I'm tired of feeling like a shadow." She looked up. "You were right, I have to be more there for Omari, but I just can't be that person right now, you get? I can't make any sense of it. All my ideas have been cut lose, my ideas about death, about will, about life itself. Everything has been exposed, even my sanity feels as shallow as my presumptions. There are things deep within me that've been dislodged, things that surprise me with the memories and feelings they awake, things I thought long buried. I feel like a rudderless dhow, bobbing along, aware of the changes, letting the waves hit me, my only buffer against the recollections is that I'll crash against some sandy bank and it'll all be over."

Her English wasn't native-poor (that soft and muffled English—unfinishable English, the one absent any suffixes.) Hers was a little posh-ish, but clear.

"You're very different today?" she said.

"Yesterday was supposed to be my last day here, and I don't know, I feel great that it didn't end like that."

She stared at him the way Zelda did, like what the hell are you carping on about?

"If I hadn't found you, I'd have most likely drowned in a bar or in some ill-fated attempt to spread my wife's ashes over the ocean."

"Oh," she pouted. "That's what you're doing with that."

Sydney sniped, "Yeah, like you're doing anything more interesting than sitting on a beach."

"What I do has hope in it."

"What you do is the end of hope. You just confuse it with being hopeful He's not coming—"

"Don't you think I know that?" she lowered her voice. "He's not coming back, but I'm not accepting loss. I see it as something that happened to me, not to him. If I think of it as death happening to him, I won't be able to reverse it, take the loss back. If I sit there and wait for him, he'll just sneak up on me and surprise me."

"I have no right to tell you how to grieve for your husband,"—off her look—"or whatever, but this isn't it. I didn't realize it until this morning that even though I can't move on, I refuse to get stuck—and stuck is me holding onto these fragments, these memories, these hopes that I can change things. If not, at least right what I can't change. You can't. No one can. And we have to live with it, me especially, the last words I said to her—to my Zelda was that she was the most selfish person I've ever known. I can't take that back but now I'm the one who's selfish—I'm not allowing myself to live. So, I'm going to see Stone Town one last time, like I should've with her. I'm going to confront my fears and spread her ashes in the ocean, because until I do that, I'm not going to get over my hydrophobia,"—Sydney sniffed his armpits—"*Whwwww*, I can fertilize the Sahara."

She laughed.

"If it wasn't for Omari here stealing my urn, I'd never have broken out of my cocoon, I'd probably have lived here forever because I lack the courage, even now, but only now I'm stronger—I'm more afraid of my own smell than I'm about drowning. That's a step, granted it's the first in a million steps, but it's progress in the direction of something conquerable."

"You really believe that?"

"I have to. The way I see it, grief is a language, like Luo, no, not Luo, like my Zelda's Luganda: sometimes one word can be either a verb or a noun. You decide which."

She gave him a half-shrug that was open to all kinds of misinterpretation.

"You can come if you want?" he added.

They walked through narrow chocked streets, where Hadiya had an idea of how great it would be to race *daladalas*[70] through the cobbled alleyways, like the *Il Palio* horse-races in Siena, Italy. The streets scattered with women in rainbow-coloured *kitenges*[71], overflowing *hijabs*, their slippers pattering across the streets. Donkeys loitered, tardy men slept in their rickshaws, others quietly played dominos. There's something very Florentine about Zanzibar.

Wafts of drifting incense, spices and smoke from the endless clutter of food shacks and open grills. They stumbled through streets filled with auto-rickshaws, sputtering *bajajs* and beat-up Toyota Carina's. Hadiya and Sydney barely spoke despite occasionally brushing hands. Omari ever quiet, dogged their heels, broke free of them when they reached Darajani Market off Creek Road. Omari, all enthusiasm, led them through the rows of market stalls, leaping over stagnant gutters and wooden crates, and poking at everything that looked strange to him: prickly king of fruits, cloves, vermilion, dried octopus. Such richness and bounty, the whole place teeming with texture and scent.

Omari's zeal reminded Sydney too much of Zelda. Of how she enjoyed talking to artisans and craftsmen wherever they went (Dakar, Kigali, Goma, etc.) How she'd lose herself down similar-looking narrow stallways, down the maze of wooden stalls, carefully studying the different fabrics, the wooden masks she'd heard the woodworkers buried to make look older. (This she didn't particularly like anymore, not after Sydney told her how the same way you bury a mask to age it, you have to bury monkey meat to make it palatable—he'd repressed memories of eating monkey meat.) Like Omari, Zelda had the innocent wonderment of discovering new things. Hadiya and Omari, despite looking local, were actually from the Mainland, from far north in Arusha. This too was new to them.

Zelda had this thing of asking about the process of things. Sometimes speculating about her intention to get into the trade. Sometimes she'd do this to drive a bargain, sometimes just to talk to someone (Sydney wasn't much of a talker, or when he talked, he talked too much.) Most times they ended up with things they had no application for. Same way Omari got Hadiya to buy

---

70   A type of minibus used as a form of public transportation.
71   A type of brightly colored, printed fabric.

bikapu of fruits and spices they'd never consume. Still they paid full weight, and didn't haggle. Relying largely on her Swahili, they didn't do anything to expose them as strangers here.

That he'd known her only one day seemed quite strange, fateful.

They left the market and walked south to open-air restaurant for lunch. Nothing else seemed more interesting, certainly not the Anglican market or gawking at the Madarasas and old dispensary, those ancient edifices, that rustic Oman Sultanese architecture. Hadiya wanted to check out the Harmamni Persian Baths at Kidichi, but didn't force the issue on account of Sydney's latent hydrophobia. Yes, *jamaa* smelled awful. Neither did she do the bitchy thing of trying to talk him into 'facing his fears.' It was too soon. The roles seemed reversed. He was grateful for that. After much deliberation, she told him she'd go and collect her husband's ashes.

Sydney uncharacteristically made it all about himself. "You don't have to."

"It's not what you think I mean," she said.

Minutes later, they left the restaurant and headed for the Zanzibar Municipal Council in the Malindi Quarter.

Later, the trio got back to the hotel cradling the urn the way you'd expect an exhausted couple returning home with yet another stillborn. They nevertheless visited the House of Wonders, the Livingstone House, and the Canons at Ngome Kongwe after ZMC. They looked wan. Sydney had to carry the worn-out Omari all the way back to the hotel. Hadiya was silent, like she'd run out of talktime. She didn't invite Sydney into their room, but told him to wait. She gave him her urn to hold on to.

Standing in the hallway, dirty, besmudged, waiting on Hadiya's return, Sydney thought how he'd differentiate which urn belonged to whom. Hadiya had gone into the room to return with his urn. Omari couldn't be parted with it last night.

Sydney didn't know what she planned, whatever it is, he knew he'd in some way regret it. Smart thing to do was to dump the urn at her door, and flee.

He almost did it. He went as far as the stairway, but returned like a bad case of *esprit d'escalier*. There was a deep nudging within his breast, something deeply layered beneath all his misapprehensions. Zelda deserved better. Hadiya too. Him scurrying away preserved the latter's vanity. Zelda had too much of that already. Even in death. She always wore these jacaranda braids, these billowy scarves, hard-pressed parkas and long stripped stockings. Her favourite colour was orange, because orange was the only word in the English language that had no rhyme, or something like that. She didn't have any tattoos or piercings, but encouraged him to knock himself out. She was there for all of his seven tattoos, which let's be honest, is too much for any Luo. She met his mother once. His mother never approved, but then again, she'd never liked any of his girlfriends. Zelda was the only one she couldn't guilt him into leaving. They wedded a year after dating, in a civil service while visiting her sister in Brussels (this, too practical, even for a Luo.) After the wedding he started to notice the shift in her moods. There was something off, freakery about her eyes. Despite all her outward eccentricity, all her character, her smile was in the eyes. There was always a warm fizz in them, that curiosity. After the wedding it seemed to burn now. Some wolf-hunger replaced her brittleness. Well, thinking about it now, an unmarked urn in his hands, an urn which could very well contain some of Zelda, he wanted to take on all her guilt. Claim she left because she couldn't stand him. He was too nice, not sturdy enough, incapable of sufficiently detaching. Sydney was a snuggler, yes, but everything else, even up to her getting on the MV Unguja was a story he couldn't invent reliable plot-lines for. He was slim in the way only Zelda could've fancied. He had no attachments. A sister he didn't speak much to, his mum and dad distant, aloof as any Luo parent is—that is, once the social contract of raising you is fulfilled. Once you've become 'your own man.' Sydney wasn't his own anything. He was just a well-preserved thing inhabiting a man's body—an empty soul occupying visible space. A lost, shifty boy on the verge of using up all his inner resources. If he ever had any.

As any Luo will tell you—it's difficult to emote. Luos are largely ceremonial, leopard hides and ostrich-feathered caps and songs of wars and woes they'll never overcome, for women we'll never truly want. He loved her, but it was never enough. Or she made it that way, gave him something to strive towards. There was victory in that. Perhaps.

Hadiya returned thirty minutes later, a red *shuka* and Zelda's urn in hand. They carried both urns to the beach. The Waterfront was full, cheery, so not their scene.

They were the only people on the beach. Hadiya sat at the same spot Sydney found her the day before. She told him how it was the spot Annan proposed to her a night before he had to get on the ferry for an emergency meeting on the mainland. No, it didn't hurt being here. Least of all with Sydney. It gave her some closure.

They stared at the tar-blackened ocean. The lights from the docked ships shinning like stars across different skies.

Hadiya, after a while, "I used to think death was easy. Going to funerals and *mkesha*[72] came easy for me. Now the only person I ever loved is dead, I look back wondering where I got the stupid idea that death was easy?" She scoffed, "The pain is nothing like I thought it'd be." She looked at Sydney, "I sit waiting, feeling like if he comes back to me, I'll ask him to ask me again, to propose. But you know what's scary, I'm still not sure I would say yes."

Grief makes amateurs of all of us, he reckoned. It's a game we learn and play at the same time.

He's never been much of a sportsman, so he's lost to these idiosyncrasies.

---

72   "mkesha" in Kenya means "someone who goes to funerals as a profession" or "professional funeral attendee".

Silence nestled between them.

"Annan was safe, predictable, a good man. I loved him, but. . ." Tears in her eyes. "I wish we'd taken the time to learn how to talk to each other."

Sydney turned, regarded her as though she'd stolen his lines.

She wiped her eyes, breathed in deeply, said, "Do you ever feel like it should've been you instead?"

"You only ask yourself a question like that because you're wondering if they'd be in the same sour state you're in right now. I can't trust something like that to my imagination."

"Your imagination won't betray you, isn't that a good thing?"

"No. Protecting me from the truth is a bigger betrayal."

Silence again.

"What're you going to do with your urn?" Sydney asked.

"I don't know." She turned to him, "I know you told me already, but remind me again?"

"I've to spread her ashes in the sea?"

"Why?"

He looked away. "Do you think Omari's okay, all on his own? He might wake up and wonder where you've gone to."

There was so much he wished he could tell her. So much she could understand, or not. He wanted to tell her about Zelda. If Hadiya knew her better, she'd understand. How despite feeling inadequate and knowing it wasn't really his fault couldn't stop him from feeling like it was. How all this striving was an attempt at *La danse des ombres*. The dance of the shades. That moment in classical ballets where an abandoned lover tries to resurrect the other lover.

No she'd never understand. He wasn't sure he did, himself.

He got up in a huff, carried the urn nearest him and hobbled to the water. She got up and followed him. Sydney objected.

"You coming along would cheat me of something," he said. "We both can't go."

"Neither can you go alone."

"I mean, I'm scared for you," he mumbled.

Smiling: "I'd think you heartless if you weren't." She took his hand and they waded into the water."

The water was cool.

He felt weak against the tug and pull of the tide. They waded until the water covered their chests. Facing each other, she stood on his feet, the moon glistening on her lips, her eyes nebulous.

"Any last words?" she asked.

He shook his head.

They popped the urns and spread the ashes on the surface of the water. A tide swept in and slapped the ashy water on their faces. They dipped into the water and lost grip of each other's hands. She swam against the tide, playfully kicking every time he grabbed her feet. They swam clumsily, weighted in their clothes, back to shore, and dropped onto the sand, shed their wet clothes and crawled into the *shuka*. Their lungs burning. Toes tingly. Sand going everywhere.

Hadiya lay next to him, her warmth wrapped around him. Nestled in the hollow of his arm, her head on his shoulder, her breathing shallow but regular, he'd forgotten how calming the simple act of breathing could be. He started to drift. The heat between them contained somewhat, like a car with bad A.C. A bit stark. Bare, stripped of everything but the primal.

No words were said. None needed to.

Nothing would be different in the morning, but at least this way, he wouldn't be afraid of his own shadow. Though lying still, he felt animated by this sustained unease, this unsaid thing nestled between them. Not really erotic, but not really not-erotic either. And though she'd made a fool of her that first night, thinking he'd attached to them because he wanted an easy target, a quick violent seduction. How she'd led him to her hotel room, in anticipation of some threat which never breached the surface of his own state of emergency. How he'd walked away, shamed for her. Shamed by her shame. This thing, this now, was a poor harvest. It was doom, yes, but all for the wrong reasons. Still, now that he'd discarded Zelda's ashes, and had not drunk for a while, he wondered if being with Hadiya could count as something Zelda would wish him strive against? Or maybe he better let go of the idea of pleasing her. Her menace was done, that feat of endurance art. The hope of not displeasing her had made him audience of his own life. Now he could… he could what? Live? Move on?

They lay there a long while, the warmth dissipated. Much like the ashes, carried away by the waves. A slight shiver had taken over her feet, teeth starting to chatter. A dim moon, no stars.

Sydney turned to her, "We better leave?"

"Just. A. Little while longer," she said. "Let the tide wash the ashes back to us. Then we can leave."

Sydney scoffed, nestled her closer to him and they waited. Waited for their harvest moon, their harvest doom. In his waiting, he realized the worst may not have passed, the worst wasn't out there waiting to happen, but just like Hadiya saw Annan's death as something happening to her, not him, Sydney's sense of relief, of letting go, felt like a big betrayal. Of him, not her. There was victory in that. Perhaps.

Derek Lubangakene lives in Kampala, Uganda. His work has appeared in Escape Pod, Apex Magazine, Omenana, Enkare Review, Prairie Schooner, River River Lit. Journal, and the Imagine Africa 500 Anthology, among others. In 2016 he received the Short Story Day Africa / All About Writing Development Prize. He was also shortlisted for the 2019 Nommo Short Story Award, and longlisted for the 2017 Writivism Short Story Award and the 2013 Golden Baobab Early Chapter Books Award.

April in Kinoo
Rosey Ssembatya

FOR CISSY, Kinoo was more than the little drowsy shops, the muddy roads when it rained and the immense cold. It was an experience with a man who had lured her with the promise of plenty.

They had met at the Makerere Arts copier both looking for an excerpt from *Artist, the Ruler* and the copier minder too tired to make another had asked them to share the lone copy. Back then, his belly was as flat as that of a workout addict. Now his arms sagged in the vests and his breathing came out laboured, and uneasy.

Her confessions of unchanged love seeped in from one ear and escaped through the other as he asked why he keeps looking well and her, thinning.

Their five years anniversary came on the heels of April and the present that she gave herself was a resolve to stop crying. His was the black beans.

Mwangi's craze for black beans had leaped off the pages of *Adam* Magazine onto his plate. The article had appeared on Page 23 with a blue bowl atop it, followed by a list of reasons why every man had to be friends with black beans. Since then Mwangi had those for dinner, a blue bowl accompanied his morning meal, and Cissy thought of packing him some to work; only they are too black, she had said.

She stopped those whispery whys that came after every clinic visit, and now a feeling of anger left her stomach and rose with its bitter bile up her throat, choking her. She had promised never to shed a tear ever again; she kept caressing her neck like she was dissuading an eminent cough. The tears that were welling within settled, leaving her eyes pepper red.

Mwangi had learnt to quench his words before he came home. He lay untalking, facing the wall, tapping at his phone. Six months since the black beans, this routine behavior had got him into a pattern that had him walk up the stairs and knock once before inserting his key in the lock. He would then put his rolled socks in his shoes, walk to the eating table, then the bed and fiddle with his phone before he slept.

❦

11:00 pm was always the hour of sobs every when his mother visited. For one who slept away from them, the sobs seemed to be right at their bedroom door, through the keyhole for they came through clear like choreographed. Mwangi's mother brought with her tears of delay that she had started by speaking about with calm, and then with insinuations of how it is real that a woman in her 30s would start watching her eggs drying, one by one like she were ticking them off a list. And in the night, with her sobs as clear as laughter, Cissy and Mwangi would not dare try for fear of offending her.

Cissy would instead dream of how much she wanted their baby's birth to coincide with their Wedding anniversary. Conceiving had taken a detour, even though the herbs that Mwangi's mother had carried from Meru had started coating the edges of the bathroom. Whenever she checked that Cissy was taking the herbal baths, she would be filled with anticipation and glee that at last Cissy had decided to listen to reason, her reason.

Everything would have remained the same that April if Mwangi's sister had not cheated on her husband. The cheating bore fruit—a white, curly haired bundle of joy. One look at the bundle and one would know for the baby was the colour of a blush, like a fruit, Cissy mentioned to Mwangi.

From then on Cissy knew that Mwangi was wasting their potency elsewhere. These are genes, she would say. She was livid with an urge to discover.

Stalking him at Sailors and watching him down his beers with the boys, Cissy lurked in the corridors, often having to barhop in an attempt to catch him red-handed. Back home, she snooped through his two phones, a sleek red one that he slid down his shirt pocket every morning and a black Nokia that he loved holding in his palm.

It was convenient to hold the black one there for it carried his busiest line, a safaricom line that he had bought while at University ten years ago. Its buttons were intact but all the digits had disappeared with frequent touch, and the more he kept promising himself to replace its housing, the more he forgot. The sleek red one was for meetings, the kind he knew rarely rang but it sure looked posh on the meeting table. It is the first thing that announced his presence for it got to the table before his notebook or diary.

Cissy knew that she would find answers in only three places. She rummaged through the red one first, and then the black Nokia. In prying dissatisfaction, she checked his trouser pockets looking for the genetic resemblance to his sister's wandering ways—chewed pieces of paper fell out as did a toothpick, prickly at one end. Then she discovered the diary entry on the 12th April, '*Monalisa*'.

One new to this household would not miss the dust coating that now covered the table. Or the multicolored lesu that seemed out of place on the black velvet cushions. Before, the mother's visits would cause a change in the grey colour of the curtains, but today the lesu lay in the same place it had three days ago.

Seething, Cissy could not be comforted by Dr. Kumba's confirmations that they were both fine enough to have enough children to fill their home; a two-bedroomed flat from whose balcony one could see the point at which the Malaba—Nairobi highway runoff down the Kinoo tunnel. At the bridge one could see the Nairobi skyline as high far off places where Mwangi said he worked as an Insurance broker.

As Cissy prepared the entry confrontation, Mwangi's sister escaped. She left her husband and the curly haired baby and went away. No one knew.

Not even Mwangi's mother. When the sister's husband packed the infant and took it to Meru, there was no expletive note but a suitcase full of SMA Milk formula, feeding bottles, bibs and little baby shoes in pink.

And that is how the practicals started for Cissy and Mwangi. In the place of the mother in law sobs, the baby's late night squeaks and screams discomforted them out of their obligatory trying and saw them creeping, sneaking, sign-speaking and turning the knob stealthly while whispering, looking forward to moments when the baby would take a rest before they would take refuge in the TV room and cuddle.

Nights of sleeplessness puffed beneath Mwangi's eyes and the haste showed in the double creases in his shirts. The rush to make use of the time when the infant would be sleeping saw him abandon his nights at Sailors and forget to delete the messages in his phone. Cissy too was preoccupied with attending to the baby's whims that her pink chiffon blouse had a dull patch near the armpits.

The house had been completely transformed with the arrival of the baby. The cleaning and cooking was done in haste and general whisperings had taken over. The sobs never visited again and the confrontational urge that had pervaded Cissy's mind was replaced with a need for warmth, a need for support, a need for a soul to whom to recount how the baby smiled when Cissy tickled her.

No one could explain the drastic shift from forlorn to adorable that their relationship had become. Most nights, they sat staring at the baby sleeping in her cot, and when Cissy would succumb to the heavy weight of sleep and lay her head onto Mwangi's shoulder, it was with fondness that he would wrap his arms around her and hers him. And there they would wake following a demand for attention that came in a shrill cry and then a hush, hush…

Mwangi's sister returned the same way she had left.

Mwangi's Sister, Beth appeared at her husband's door. The worry that appeared like frowns on her husband's face never left even when she came home. And it's in this that she blasted her Black Street album and danced to celebrate her return. Cissy stood at a distance looking at her, the mind tending towards certainty that indeed something is not right in her head. And she cooked. And danced. And sang.

Beth's eyes did not have the daze of delusion but she never mentioned the baby. She never sought to find out about her and Cissy's ears kept to the ground for the moment when Beth's husband would bring up the story, asking, interrogating, angry.

He never did.

Rosey Ssembatya *is a teacher who also runs a children's mobile library. She loves books and writing, and her current project is writing a non-fiction comic. Rosey spends her free time looking at picture books with her daughter.*

Goats on a Balcony
Sophie Alal

SUCH A CURIOUS sight it was. Drawing crowds. They craned their necks and strained their excited eyes, just to catch glimpses of the third-floor balcony. In those days it went drop, drop, drop with the gentle flurry of coffee coloured round turds. Some people laughed and some jeered, but all of them were curious about the industriousness of the oaf who kept goats, in a flat of all places, in the city. Not a dog or a cat, or a little bright bird in a cage for children to play with as was normal among city people who lived in rooms stacked one over the other. But of all things to keep in the world, smelly bleating beasts. A stony eyed woman said that the people up there must miss village life so much, so that the poor family was stuck in those ways. So eager to bring the countryside into the city. Bless them. An odd job man who lived in the compound said he could already taste the tender meat, come December. What a fine feast it would make on Christmas day when the music would be louder and everyone would be dressed in their best. That mood worked up a good appetite. Good humour rang out as they teased the odd job man. In that moment, the sure-handed Firmina Aber, was making her way up, laden with a bag of groceries and a small sisal sack filled with grass. She stopped to catch her breath, nervously, wondering if someone would heckle at her. Retaining a good sense of herself, and still so curt and determined, she set about trying to disperse the crowd.

"People! You have never seen goats before? Ho! This is 1992," she said panting.

"Not this type, I hear they even have a room and like watching TV," said the stony-faced woman. "We hear that they serve their food on plates. Is it true? Meanwhile, when are you inviting us to eat?"

"Any day now," she humoured them. "In fact, I'm going to make them fat right now. You just wait a little bit."

"Naaweh! Even you? All the time a little bit a little bit. You must be tired, let me help you," the stony-faced woman said in a tone almost bursting into song. Help was normal like laughter or rain. Up there was the big Afande in uniform with his family, in his nice flat, and everybody else was down there looking up with lingering eyes. Firmina had long ago resolved never to invite anyone in, because it was only a matter of time before they expected tea with sugar and escort, or at the very least a coin for their troubles. Not only that. Every thief and devil first came gently and politely.

In the block of flats, she was noted for the nearly heroic act of cutting huge bags of grass which she hauled up four flights of stairs daily. One time she even accidentally snagged a thief who tripped on the sacks of grass, so that the watchman and an odd job man had time to give him a good hiding. By the time the police arrived, he was well inflamed and his feet were bound with a curtain tie.

Feeling pitched against the world below, her muscles flexed and tensed until they burned under the weight of green grass. Her skin was damp, perhaps from sweat just as much as the light rain as she ascended the stairs on that hot afternoon. In the few months that she had lived there, everyone came to learn of her, and to call her by pet names of their choosing. And she was never under any delusions about the wicked curiosity of strangers. Many times they asked her, 'What was it like up there living inside the house? Did they have a big fridge? Is the sofa real leather? Can my children come and watch the cartoons on tv? Can I borrow the new Michael Jackson cassette? I've heard it playing from your side.' People of a different language made her nervous, especially these lake shore people for she had not yet learned to unravel the context of their proverbs. They were so easily insulted by simple gestures and too quick to demand redress. She pursed her lips and drew her thoughts in while passing them on the landing, noting their muddy feet. Her breathing relaxed only when she laid her bags and sack down on their own landing and inserted the key in the lock. She closed the door behind her. Out there, anyone could saunter in and out of the building without having any business, if they wanted to. Maybe they were sheltering from the rain. Maybe they were waiting for someone, but you never quite knew, and it seemed almost always rude to ask. She feared that one day it would bring hell to her because all those goats on the balcony were valuable stock.

So long as the busy din of city life continued, so sure was she that the landing would be muddied at the end of each day, and there would still be food to cook and children waiting to be cleaned up. The maid closed the door behind her and went into the sitting room where she had earlier left with the madam, then crossed over onto the balcony and began to pull the grass out of the sack. The goats' eyes shone with their square pupils, as they shoved and butted their way greedily into the green grass with small weeds spilling out onto the grey cement floor.

Madam was at work, the two children were at school and the Afande was upcountry attending to business. When you work indoors, you learn the ways of arresting deterioration, sometimes seen as dust, other times leaks and stains. It feels almost futile, so you work on yourself too. Firmina took this chance to lay down on the sofa to stretch her legs and rest her back. It felt good. So good that all her troubles seemed to be tucked far away. Everything was quiet. Everything was nice. Operation Simsim was raging up north, and she was supremely glad that there was no clap of gunshots, the fury of blood rushing into the head, falling debris or the constant fleeing into hills, woods and bushes, where they kept warm only by the heat of other people's bodies. The place that she was not meant to survive was a whole day and night's journey away, in fact it was so far away that she wondered if it was a fantasy that she made up. As she closed her eyes and drifted off quietly, to nap, immediately the image of her father resolved to come to her mind. He had been so-so, then gravely ill, but did not show it. One day as he sat under a cool shady tamarind tree, puffing on a Sportsman, he clutched at his chest, fighting with all his might to draw a single breath. The cigarette fell from his lean veiny fingers. All the breath in the world failed to fill his lungs, and he dropped dead on the cool black earth like a bird from the sky. No one bothered to lift him up and rush him to Lacor hospital; after all, they saw that he was an old man and he had had a long life.

It must have been his time, they said.

Before the man was even buried, Firmina's auntie wailed loudly wondering how she would feed her three sisters and four brothers. Before Firmina understood how life could unravel so quickly, the relatives set about organizing to parse out the children among their many relatives down south, in the city. Because they knew she was good, and steady, and spoke English well, she would go down to Kampala and help. Better still, she had not yet peaked in years or beauty and so that was reassuring of humility.

As things came apart up in the north, down south and in the surrounding areas the forces of neglect had made their mark on the landscape. In Kampala, great hulks of construction lay fallowing with moss and lichen year after year, since their owners were long settled in exile. As the weeks folded into months, armed with only patience and grace, she had neither asked for her money nor made her employers feel indebted to her. She simply worked. In their eyes though, there seemed to be little for her to do—a simple village girl, used to labouring in the fields, weeding or picking the harvest on top of chores. Madam wished she had a shop too. But Firmina saw it in a different way; withstanding tantrums, avoiding curses and the serious matter of blunting threats was hard work on her mind.

She was shivering when she woke up and there was sweat on her brow and the undulating spaces in her chest were thumping with a familiar effect. The shadow of the curtain was long on the floor, and by the weakness of the light, she knew that madam was somewhere near home—her two children Joseph and Maria by her side, with bright lollipops sticky in their hands. Three demanding people, food to reheat, spots to clean up, toys and books to put away.

"Ayo yah, I've slept but I'm still tired," she said picking herself up as a cushion slipped to the floor. "Welcome to city life, isn't it nice here?"

She tipped on her toes and with a lightening heart, swung her hips from side to side, mimicking a fancy lady with a handbag. As she got quite close to the dining area, she could see through to the balcony. The sack lay slack. All the grass had been eaten, while the three goats folded their legs on the floor and placidly chewed the cud.

The place that she was never meant to survive was a whole day and night's journey away.

So far away.

IT was not unusual to have several bags of charcoal and a chicken or two tied up in the railings of the balcony, waiting to be dispatched for Sunday lunch. One evening some weeks later, that ritual changed for better or worse. The Lt. Colonel unloaded two goats which he led up the stairs on leashes— the children were so thrilled that they barely slept that night, and spent all evening trying to get good goat names. In the morning the maid was sent down into the valley where people's shambas grew, with a kitchen knife to gather feed. For the goats. When she reached some good-looking bushes, the slim blade turned out to be inadequate for the tough strokes needed to bring down elephant grass, so she asked for a panga instead, which they borrowed from the watchman. Later on, they bought their own from a hardware store downtown in Kiyembe lane. From then on, the brisk rhythm of slashing green stalks was bracing and swift against the rumbling mechanical sounds of the city. She gathered the piles of wilting green grass into heaps, and stuffed armfuls into jute sacks till her hands prickled with the fuzz coming off the blades of grass.

Nobody in the village would believe her, if she told them that in the city, people kept livestock in high rise buildings. Nobody ever. For dwelling in flats was regarded as the epitome of modernity.

Nobody in the village would believe her, if she said that in the city, there were islands of bush and fields that used to be well lit gardens. Now vervet monkeys marauded all the way to the university, where the professors also grew food crops and herbs and flowers on their compounds and back gardens.

As the rains abated, down in the valley, the storm drain held on loosely to treasures stuck in the sleek brown mud on its bottom—a broken doll, bunched up black trousers, a bottle of cough syrup and feathers of an indeterminate bird. Firmina would be sent on errands, mostly to the shops and to deliver packages to their favoured neighbours. Because the father of the house received rations, which he was entitled to, as an officer with a big family, whenever there was a surplus of maize flour, rice or sugar, she would be sent out with a kilo or more for a neighbour. One day it was the turn of the watchman, but she did not find him at his post which was a simple clapboard box with a corrugated iron sheet roof. Long enough for a lean man to lay inside and as wide as an armchair with some leg room. It was shelter enough from the elements, but no comfort from extreme heat or the tearing fury of a tropical deluge. Outside the watchman's box was a chain-link fence much unravelled in places. Along it stood a line of gnarly old cypress of more than a quarter century. Ordinarily the shopkeepers broke off fragrant small branches, to whisk away flies from sweet bananas. Every Christmas season, the sturdier branches would be lopped off, trained with thick cords and decorated with tinsel, cotton wool and festive paper cut outs. Far back, where the cypresses ended, the shambas began. There grew bananas, vegetables and root crops, where the weeds had been beaten back from taking over the landscape. Eventually Firmina spotted the watchman seated on a boulder, next to two shamba boys, sharing a glass and roasting fresh white cobs of maize by the fire of twigs and branches. As they spoke, she noted that the watchman's eyes were irritated by smoke, on top of the usual malaise of watching days roll into months. They were speaking in their language, which marked them as coming from far away lands. So when they sat together, gravity of their camaraderie went deeper than eating or drinking. She drew close enough to greet them without having to raise her voice.

"*Ssebbo*, madam wants to give you something small. To thank you for your panga."

"You could've just brought my things, like you do for everyone," he complained and she could pick out a latent arrogance in his voice.

"I was going to. But you see..."

"But you didn't," he said, biting on his maize. She could tell that the liquor had singed his thoughts and released parts of him which were locked up by sobriety, so she became afraid. Men drinking made her feel guarded and she could feel annoyance rising in her head, percolating into the soft dregs of hate and she neither liked it nor wanted to be there. Plants in the nearby shambas fattened on strange manure. That made her think, what would happen if she said the wrong word or fixed her eyes in the wrong way? The watchman was the kind of man who could have done much with his mind, but for those times, he had degenerated into someone of lesser status. She crossed her arms on her chest and looked away, at no place in particular. These men were smirking with expectation, and to her it felt like they were waiting excitedly, for the moment when an untamed fowl puts its foot in a trap. The last time she had felt menaced this way was far back in their village, during an operation when army men cordoned off the camp for displaced people that they were in, sorting families away from one another like they were beans about to get cooked. Men who used fear as much as contempt, to get their way were erratic. So much frustration, hope and endless rounds of disappointment made them hate even themselves; they yelled their complaints on the radio and at village meetings you could hear the iron and fire in their voice. While the big men with new wealth had come from their villages, promising humble folk a share in the spoils of war, they ended up in the city, watching over the estates of their erstwhile neighbours.

If it were not for the goats she would not be standing there. And she wouldn't have borrowed a panga. Oh how she began to hate the goats, and prayed that they'd fall down from the balcony and die! Everything not lived well became regret.

"OK, I will go now," she said.

"Ah huh. How do you just go like that, eh? Without even greeting us."

She felt exhausted, from being ill at ease. Then he raised himself up, and lay his hand on her shoulder. She shrugged. He staggered, knocking over a small windup radio on a handkerchief.

"Heh, it is looking like you love yourself too much. I'm not going to eat you now, am I? Also you, be a little friendly. Why no manners? Some of us just want to greet you properly."

"You're right, forgive me," she said stepping back lightly, avoiding a rock. "I am going now. Madam is waiting for you when you are free."

She felt their gaze reaching out to her like tendrils. She had sought some kind of kinship with them but found none, for the life on an inside doors worker was so different to that of an outdoor worker. When gentle suggestion did not suit the function of their work, it was almost always forceful solicitations. At any rate, working outside, being battered by rain and wind chill hardened them out of softness. Her own life was like taking holy orders, and easing into a life of renunciation. Firmina was talk tired. An old lady passed by and observed them. For a long moment, this gave her a certain amount of relief. Gratefully. After passing through a fragile past, you hold your tongue right back as a matter of survival. In hard times, nobody is stalked by loneliness like the one who has many enemies.

Soles of feet carried dirt and vileness which were invisible to the naked eye. And for that reason, public thoroughfares were not supposed to be mopped by hand, or swept with brooms for indoor cleaning or laid down upon, like vagrants and drunkards sometimes found themselves. Every time the Afande returned, the mother of the house told Firmina to take special care as she mopped the landing and to sweep the whole flight of stairs. For good neighbourliness, she said. It unsettled Firmina, because to clean after strangers was a seemingly cursed job, but there was nothing she could do. In truth, the mother of the house was anxious about the landing never being clean enough, because the Afande would scold her—and her position in his life could come loose. And now with the goats, keeping the house pristine was a struggle. Firmina thought that if she would maybe tell the watchman to stop people from coming to the top floor, there would be less mud. But when they thought about it further, that plan was practically impossible.

The roof hatch was open.

"Get me a bucket of water," she said.

"Eh?"

"Just get it. I'm tired now."

There was an aluminium pail which perennially sat under the water heater in the bathroom, collecting drips all day long. But for that incongruity, the high-ceilinged rooms were passively cool and spacious; it made the flats a marvel of engineering. Constructed during the heyday of the Common Man's Charter, to house workers in the civil service, it was every young comrade's dream to be assigned one of those units when they returned from training in the USSR. Outside, the brutal sturdy walls were enviable, so much so that life seemed to be safely hemmed in, like the insides of a barracks.

In the dry season, the old pipes ran brown, especially when the reserve tanks on the roof were low. For the mother of the house, nothing was more calming or peaceful than the sanctity of a clear torrent of water, flowing evenly on the once white porcelain sinks; they were now stained a dull reddish brown by iron oxides. So red and muddy did it look that in low light you could be mistaken for thinking that a throat had been slit in the cisterns.

Firmina returned a moment later.

"Mummy, it is here," she said, setting the pail down on the blue linoleum flour. "Good," she said sighing deeply. Fatigue had deepened the lines around her eyes and the veins on her neck were throbbing prominently. Of late she had been eating so little that she could not fit into the sizing of the suits in her wardrobe. "Now take it over there and tip it out on those fools. That will give me some peace." She sat down and raised her feet, stretching them on the coffee table. Fermina looked at the pretty red polish, and could not help comparing them with her own feet—sturdy heels and toes splayed by a long childhood of running barefoot on the hard ground.

Pouring water down from the balcony grated her nerves. But she had to forget her thoughts. Forget her feelings. Work. Out she went, into the balcony past the goats on their bed of straw chewing the cud placidly. She hauled the pail to her waist and looked down below, then she set it on a nook as she steadied herself and flexed her arms under the weight of water. A few people were milling about when she stuck her neck out. She was terrified that the water would draw a poison out of the veins of anyone it touched, and they would look for her after that. So she waved and made it appear like she was cleaning, and warning them. And they waved back. Then she tipped the first bucket and heard the water fly down below.

Down below, the stony-faced old lady was watching the laundry of her clients dry, and also tending a clump of maize crops and bushes of small bitter *entula* down under the gutters. Big bushes of heirloom cherry tomatoes were in bloom, evidently sprouted from grey water or the droppings of birds coming from far away in the outskirts. Everything had taken root so beautifully and set about flowering in the stress of the long dry season.

"You're trampling my crops," the woman cried in a voice made hoary with complaint. She dropped her hoe and her hands were flailing in frustration. The distress in her eyes was enough to send the people on the compound shuffling to the side. Everyone's eyes were trained upwards, seeking a better view of a little goat that sat sweetly on a ledge. One little boy caught sight of the little brown goat.

"There, I see it, I see it," he said excitedly shooting up a finger, "UP. Up. Up there." He paused to hastily stuff a ribbon of fried flakes of pastry into his mouth. The goat on the ledge, leaped off the edge of the grey metal and scampered off onto some trees. "Take cover," he yelled. In that very moment, a second stream of cold water rushed down to the ground, missing its target. The children squealed with happy excitement and fled a little distance away.

"Now they're pouring water like in an irrigation scheme," a little girl with a big red ribbon said full of amazement. "My daddy says that is modern farming."

"Zero grazing," said her brother as he wiped his greasy fingers on his shorts.

"I hear goats multiply fast. How many do you think they have now?"

"I don't know but they must be many—like ten."

"Don't be a *zonto*. That tiny balcony?" said their friend.

"Ha, wouldn't it be nice to have your own goat? Take it on a walk. Play with it in the green grass," the girl said dreamily. It would be better than a dog, or a doll with real hair and eyes, she said.

The boys stared at her and decided it was time they went home.

Peace and quiet would have been possible if hunger was not always stalking. And that's why the Lt. Colonel timed his arrivals in the evening or at nightfall, so no one would study the goods being unloaded out of the foot wells and boot of his sky-blue Peugeot 405. Gone were the days in the city, when curfew started at sundown until sun up the next morning. Yet nobody really knew exactly when operations ended. Sometimes even when the hot bright sun was already high up above the trees, a roadblock of knotted wood, car tires, rolls of barbed wire and scrap metal would spring up on a main road and the straggly verge of grass which grew wild at either side. For the men in uniform, that was no inconvenience. On a good day, a roadblock yielded a nice chicken or decent fistful of cash in exchange for passage.

Whenever he was not at home in the city, the Lieutenant Colonel could be at his duty post in Luweero, with fellow officers of the Coffee Marketing Board. The Lieutenant Colonel now wore a full moustache, just like most of the cadres at the party Secretariat where he had been transferred from. In those times the presidential portrait bore a neat trimmed square above his chin, rather than the earlier full moustache, and the otherwise jovial Lieutenant Colonel also took the cue and trimmed his.

Gunshots in the evening were as normal as songs playing on the radio—sporadic and difficult to miss. They usually came from any direction, at any time of night. So when the Lieutenant Colonel approached his building, the sharp reach of his army green fatigues caught the attention of the people in the compound. He detested seeing people idling about. According to him, only small children were supposed to play. And if it were up to him, he would bring down the tough sole of his boots on them, get some discipline into place. But he loved the shine of his shoes more.

Afande rang a few dummy shots up in the air, a deterrent to those who did not know him and a cue to those who were waiting for him. The deadly sound echoed on the dusty white walls and dissipated into nothingness; at that sound the maid and the mother of the house came rushing downstairs with baskets and their wrappers flying about their strong legs. It often took more than one trip to unload the boot. And it was quiet and still again in the landing, and down below in the garden where the plants matured, the silks and tassels swayed gently on the maize plants. In under a year, the goats had doubled in number. They also learned to scale the walls like no other urban goats ever had, after all it was their instinct. They were not afraid of heights. Flight could have been possible if they had wings, and as Christmas day approached, it was as if they had read the air and learned of the fate that awaited them. That very night when everyone was asleep, they flexed their sinewy legs and leaped out onto a nearby candlenut tree, and it looked as though they were playing, but they never went back to the balcony, and neither the watchman nor the odd job man, or even the wind and rain could bring them down.

Sophie Alal was born and raised in Uganda, a place full of vitality and spellbinding stories. She has written both fiction and non-fiction, appearing in *The East African*, *Kalahari Review* and *Lawino Magazine*, among others.

Restless Souls
Ayeta Anne Wangusa

Chapter 27

SITUUMA MET a Russian woman at the artist-lover house, who reminded him of Martha, his wife's best friend. The Russian woman was a writer and was attending the three-month International Writers Programme in Iowa. She planned to stay on and join the Writers Workshop at the University of Iowa, which was a two-year programme. She was visiting San Francisco and was living in Oakland with some Russian friends. Natasha Gorbachev was strikingly beautiful but was surprisingly reserved when she was not tipsy. Situuma realized that her silence cloaked her terrible English. But her presence was so robust that it seemed to sap the energy of the guests at the party. The party had been thrown in her honour because she was about to leave San Francisco and return to the cornfields of Iowa. Situuma had wondered why Iowa was known for potatoes, yet all he saw was corn. Kirk had made everyone laugh when he said, "Well, the potatoes are underground, aren't they?"

Natasha was six feet tall, blond and had soulful eyes. Her presence was on the walls of the artist-lovers living room. Natasha was not only a writer but also an abstract painter. The artist-lovers had told Situuma just before she arrived that Natasha had written to them from Iowa, complaining that she was suffocating from the other female writers' jealousy. She was too attractive for their comfort and they could not stand it when all the men swarmed in on her, once she walked into a room. No female writer wanted to share a kitchen with her and she became the first writer in the writers programme to share a bathroom and kitchen with a male writer. The nose ring, gave her a sophisticated look. Natasha seemed to be in control of the world around her but not the life in her heart. She drank a glass of Chopin Vodka and threw off the cloak of her bad English. The topic, like it usually is, when a party of friends get drunk, was love.

"Ivanov, Ivanov... He walked away from my aparta-ment, He came to America. I wait... six years... Ivanov tell, he return to Moscow... I wait six years!" Everyone was now roaring with laughter. Kirk the cheeky one was the first to throw in a naughty joke.

"Oh, come on Tasha. You are such a confident and beautiful woman. How could you wait that long!"

"He tell me, he marry me... I wait," she spoke with the soft Russian accent.

"I'm sure you've written a play about this," Riya the actress made a professional comment.

"Me write five plays," she spoke in earnest and sent everyone cracking.

"Well, have you thought of doing a film, with the scripts," Kirk the artist-lover also turned professional.

"Yes," then she began laughing and the innocence in her eyes was awash with tears.

"Let's share the joke," Situuma joined in the conversation. All this time he had enjoyed looking at this attractive woman, wondering what her voice was like and then understanding why she only spoke when she was dipped in booze.

"I go Portland... and this woman, director, she wants make my play, film... I say yes... I quiet about money... I don't know about American agent... I go home think money... I, Russian friend, we smoke grass... we laugh... I write to woman about money," she says while demonstrating how her fingers worked hastily on the keyboard.

"What's grass?" Situuma asked Natasha.

"Marijuana. I love Marijuana... In Moscow Marijuana very cheap. It make me high and I can laugh away my misery. Something about Natasha really reminded Situuma about Martha. She too had waited for her so-called boyfriend for eight years. Now she had resorted to drinking to numb herself from the pain he had caused.

"But don't you have a literary agent in Moscow...you mention that your plays have been acted in many countries. Bulgaria, Romania, Paris, how is this?"

"They take play and act, me no invited, I hear play acted in Paris, Bulgaria, Romania. Funny, I get ticket, air ticket to go Romania, see my play *Tasha Tasha*, I say bye to me luver, I go Romania, to theatre. Receptionist, she tell me, Play in Bulgaria. I have $100, no ticket to Bulgaria. I speak Russian to woman, to help. She say, me no speak Russian," Natasha imitated the snobbish flare of the receptionist. "I see poster with my picture, I tell her me Natasha Gorbechev, Play Write *Tasha Tasha*. She shake her head and tell me in Russian, 'Me no understand Russian. I know she hate Russian communists but me no communist, me Play Write. I stop woman on the street, she knows me as Natasha Gorbachev, Play Write! ...and directs me to train to Bulgaria."

"What do you write about, Natasha?" Situuma involved himself in the conversation.

"Me write about love," she raised her hands in the air and said, "No more death. I want a peaceful life. A woman, she dreams about cutting off rival's ear. I like her story, I make play. Then my ear, it begins to pain. I go hospital, get surgery. Me no write about death again!" She said as she showed everyone the scar behind her left ear.

Kirk couldn't help laughing at his young friend's philosophy of life.

"Well, isn't life about love, sex and money, look at what is happening to Bill Clinton," Kirk said. Everyone nodded, before they sipped their wine and stretched to the tray of Buffalo wings, served with spicy barbecue sauce, dipped in blue cheese to taste.

"There's a joke told in Uganda that Russian prostitutes killed Sani Abacha who was experimenting on Viagra," Situuma sent everyone wild with laughter, drowning the classic music, Mozart to be precise that was playing in the background. "But getting back to Clinton, there is a Professor at Berkeley who believes Clinton was framed because he is seen as a black man."

"Oh, come on George, you can't be blind. Bill Clinton is clearly as white as my darling Kirk."

"It's more about his philosophy. Look at him. He is the only White American President who has been sympathetic to the African American. He is the only president who has gone to Africa, during his term, stood at the door of no return, at Goree Island and he acknowledged the evil of slavery. His footsteps have made many White Americans turn against him. The world saw his pensive silhouette at Goree, off the coastline of Senegal and they believed he was sincere. In a way, Clinton surprised the republicans on this issue. They didn't expect him to come out so clearly on the issue of slavery and Africa. You see, it in this way that Clinton is seen as a Black man. Unlike most white men who think in a straight line, Clinton thinks in circles; in proverbs. That's why they wanted to pull him down. This was a story about politics, not love, sex and lies!"

Situuma surprised the party by his analysis of the political environment in America. The laughing ceased and they were all thrown into a pensive mood. Situuma thought it was time to drive back to Berkeley. As they walked out of the house, Kirk said, "You know what, I'm a Democrat but I had never looked at the Clinton scandal from your point of view."

"Well American politics is really about race. This Thomas Jefferson story is really funny. They are saying he fathered a Black woman, yet he was the harshest president on record against the mixing of the Black and White races. But how can a White man father a Black person...well, unless they are trying to acknowledge the power of Black blood!"

Kirk and Situuma parted while laughing. Kirk could not believe Situuma's ingenuity.

⚮∽⚭

SAN Francisco had made Situuma see how slavery had dehumanized Africans on the American continent. Two hundred years after slavery was abolished, he could see that many of the Blacks were still enslaved by poverty. They lived on the streets and pushed trolleys along the streets that contained their filthy earthly belongings. Their faces had been numbed with drugs and did not feel the sensation of sleep. Their brownish-red eyes were restless. They hang in groups along Market Street and played cards and gambled with Hispanics under rain-age stained umbrellas.

There was an old man who brought tears to Situuma's eyes. He was old enough to be his father and wore an old grey tattered coat that was too thick for San Francisco's warm fall. He had a trumpet and played music for the tourists who waited for the Cable Cab to take them to the Fisherman's Wharf. The jazz gave the waiting a romantic flare as elderly couples tugged onto each other, while a young couple fed the pigeons that crowded the entrance of the American Bank. The line was long and tidy, everyone waiting for his or her turn to enjoy this fun ride, up and down Hilly Cisco. But none of them thought the grey-haired man wasting away his lungs, blowing at the trumpet, deserved to be paid for the melody that was feeding their hearts.

Situuma looked at the rusty bowl that was at his feet. It had a few quarters, dimes and cents. He saw a man walking out of the American Bank at the corner of the street, with a businesslike face, drop a quarter in the bowl as he raced off and disappeared in the thick crowd of human traffic.

At Berkeley, Situuma helped some professors as a tutorial fellow. The professors were busy writing project proposals for research grants and did not have time to meet all their students and mark their scripts. This is how teaching assistants became relevant. Situuma needed the money because he wanted to save and build a house when he returned to Uganda. He met some Black students, although there were very few at Berkeley. When he arrived at Berkeley, there was a strike at the university after the state threatened to pass a law restricting the registration of minorities, by special admission to the university. In comparison to other races, African Americans had the lowest graduation rate in many American universities because many were ill prepared for college and did not like the subjects that they were majoring in. They dropped out of school and stunted their intellectual capacity.

Situuma was able to meet a few during one of the classes. He introduced himself and told the class that he was from Uganda. He was surprised at the attitude the Black students had of Africa. They only wanted to associate with Africa because of history, however, they also were very American in their outlook. They looked at Africa as a continent that had to learn values from America and not the other way round. They looked at Situuma with suspicion. They wondered how he could be so intelligent, yet he came from Africa. Was he really from Africa? Situuma noticed that his Black and White students were all the same, they were all American. The difference was just the skin tone. However, he found one ironic difference between the two; he could understand the Whites accents better than the Blacks. For the Blacks

he had to be—'sorry, I beg your pardon'—before he learnt to listen carefully
when he was spoken to in a southern accent. The Blacks from Kentucky
or Mississippi made him feel jittery in class. Situuma spent valuable time
in the library. When in San Francisco, he went to the main library to use
their computers. Once, he went to the fifth floor because the computers on
the lower floors were very busy. He went to the shelf and picked a book as
he waited his turn to surf the Net. He sat next to a woman, who seemed so
engrossed with her computer. She was grinning at the screen, while hitting
at the keyboard roughly. Then she started laughing, sniffing, while hitting
the computer keyboard like it was a piano. Situuma threw his eyes at her
screen at intervals and noticed that she did not scroll the page down. What
was making her excitable? She continued giggling for about ten minutes
before Situuma confirmed that she had a missing wire in her head.

The disgusted woman suddenly screamed, "Fuck you!"

Situuma turned sharply and examined her more critically. He noticed
her pale long brown sisal hair that covered her face. She looked dangerous,
like a psycho who could suddenly jump at him with a knife in her hands
and yell, "Got you!"

She was fat like someone with an induced appetite from drugs.
Something about her neck reminded him of Namarome. He wondered how
she was. They had spoken over the phone and she sounded happier. He
did not understand his wife. He did not really know what made her happy
because when he was with her, she seemed depressed most of the time. It
was odd that he had not felt sexually attracted to any woman yet after a long
spell of abstinence; not even to the blond beauty at the artist-lovers house.
Strange, he did not even desire Namarome either. It felt awkward that he
had never got round to visiting Chief Cassandra Chinewezu and not gone
back to see the strippers at Adam and Eve! It was weird, Situuma mused, he
was not being adventurous enough.

Chapter 28

A YEAR had gone by and he had another to go before he could get back
to Namarome. Summer was coming to an end and fall was setting in. The
Bay Area was still warm and Situuma could not tell the difference between
the two seasons. Situuma itched to leave the western coast. He had spent
summer travelling southwards to Las Vegas and tried a hand at gambling.
He sobered up when he lost a few dollars. Situuma had plans of going to
the East Coast, America's other face during Christmas to visit a former
Fulbright professor who had taught Law at Makerere University. So he
decided to go to the Mid-West to visit Natasha during the summer. He used
the Greyhound-luxury coach to have a tourist feel of the various states in

the Mid-West before finally turning round to Iowa. He had a short spell in downtown Chicago dwarfed by the mighty Sears Tower that he learnt was the second tallest skyscraper in the world. Situuma was wrapped up in layers of wool because of the chilly wind from Lake Michigan.

The sparkling nightlife was tempting but Situuma had to move on because of a strong wind that made him lose balance because he was walking against the wind. His nose running, his fingers numb, his ears frozen, he felt the arrow of pain, shoot through his mid ear. The warm tail of pain tickled his nerve ends. His teeth sipped in the cold air and he sensed which molars needed fillings. He dreaded the thought of visiting a dentist. The cost of seeing an American dentist was like having his bad tooth removed without having his gums numbed with anaesthesia. The grey fog shielded Chicago's face that day and she looked like she was mourning. Situuma hated graveyards and he hastened his footsteps away from the rainbow flags at half-masts, behind him. Some people were mourning the death of David Shepherd, a twenty-one year-old homosexual who had been killed by two angry teenage friends in the town of Laramie in Wyoming. He had watched it on NBS new. The two blond lads felt it was shameful; it was dirty to hang out with a gay fellow.

"Christ! Perhaps they too were gay and were just mad that David was coming out of the closet!" Situuma mused.

The Greyhound coach raced southwestwards from Chicago, Illinois to Iowa City, Iowa. He saw the yellow smile of the Midwest cornfields come to surface as the warmth of the eastern sun touched them. The houses here were isolated farm bungalows, unlike San Francisco's storied terraced houses that were stuck together with seashell glue. Iowa houses came like fraternal twins, with wooden pouches patterned with the shadows of Maple trees. Situuma could see that it was getting late because the shadow of the Greyhound on the tarmac was growing shorter. But the sky was lit up because this was summer and the daylight had a long life.

Natasha resided at the May Flower on Dubuque Street. The coach pulled over on Market Street and Situuma found a Yellow Cab round the corner. He could have walked to May Flower, he thought because the metre, read $5. Situuma's wallet read $6 because he had been oriented into the American system of giving tips. Situuma was shocked once when he went out with Kirk and saw him calculating the tip in terms of percentages. Situuma looked at the menu and it read, "The tip is 15% of your bill."

Situuma had asked the artist-lovers whether the waiters did not earn a salary.

"They do but this was some kind of gratuity," Kirk said as he dropped the dollar bills on the saucer.

"How do you extort gratuity out of somebody!" Situuma had wondered.

He knew her room, 831 C, but he did not like May Flower's appearance.

What was such a beauty doing staying in a campus hostel! He felt awkward misplaced seeing the freshman faces dash up and down the lobby. He felt like he was going to visit a nineteen-year-old teenager not a thirty-year-old writer. He got off on the eighth floor and the long dimly lit corridor gave him a scare. He halted a few steps away from the elevator, when he noticed the dull grey carpet that was rolled below his feet to the far end of the corridor. Did Natasha really live here? It was so silent... He stood between a pair of grey doors that faced each other. The first door had a name written in bold ink.

He read loudly: "Mary of Nazareth." He looked again; off course this was Mary Nazareth, not Mary of Nazareth. He smiled. This wasn't Jerusalem. Fear evaporated from him after he read the name aloud. It exuded a sense of human presence and exorcised the ghosts on this floor. He held his black hat under his right arm; his left shoulder held his travel bag while his right hand-held a note scribbled on 'room 831 C', in a feminine handwriting. Halfway down the hall. He stood at the grey door with her name. It had been typed by an electric typewriter.

Natasha Gorbachev
Russia

Before Situuma could knock on the door, he heard running footsteps on the roof. Wasn't this the eighth floor, the top-most floor of May Flower? His heart was pounding and he pounded on Nastasha's door with a rhythm that equalled his fear. Natasha rushed to the door and opened it after identifying him from the peephole in the door. Her big brown eyes matched her chestnut hair.

Situuma was relieved to see her and greeted her with a comment about her new look. America had taught him to compliment women and expect them to appreciate a compliment. He had also learnt to be careful with women because you never knew when a comment like the one he was about to make, would be branded sexual harassment. In America a man had to know when a woman meant yes and when she said no. In Uganda, when a woman said 'Noooh,' in most cases there was an orange light, saying 'Go but you better be slow!'

"You look lovely tonight! Does your hair change with your mood?"

"Yes, mood... Me bored Andras go Hungary to see his family. His wife get baby girl," she said while smiling. Andras was the Hungarian writer in the Writers' Programme who had agreed to share a kitchen with her. She had smoked a packet of Newport cigarettes and her hair was rough but she remained as attractive as ever. She had invited Situuma to visit her because Andras was leaving and had allowed Situuma to use his room.

"You look restless, anything disturbing you."

"Tired of writing love...and you, why you look down?" she was curious about Situuma's scared look, when she opened the door. Situuma was embarrassed that she had read fright in his eyes.

"Well she uses her senses to understand people," Situuma reasoned

"Your roof... something was running down the hall. Isn't this the top floor, or do you have a Penthouse," he laughed sarcastically. He didn't expect May Flower to have a Penthouse.

"Penthouse other side... but you hear wind blowing off roof not ghost," she started her cheeky chuckle again. "Many writers, panic, run to Mary Nazareth, say they hear ghost walking and she laugh, she say, wind from Iowa river blowing," she continued laughing.

"But her husband, Peter, funny man. He Goan, he believe in African ghost. He say behind May Flower, in the big caves covered by maple trees, there lies the tracks where Black slaves tiptoed to Canada. Some of them caught, Whiteman slice their throat. Their ghost lingers there. Yes, he believe!"

Situuma brushed Peter's idea away. He couldn't imagine that a ghost could live for more than a century. It was bound to get tired of scaring the living.

However, something clicked in his head, when she talked of the wind. He remembered the wind that had blown off the roof of his house in Butiru. A strong wind filled with red dust, had filled his house with pressure and blown off the roof. A neighbour who was outside the house almost had his head cut off by the flying iron sheets. Namarome was shaken to tears when the village women started spinning tales that Situuma's mother's ghost had come to visit him.

"We in Butiru have brown earth that red earth is from Bugobero where his mother hails from." Word had gone round and round and gotten to Situuma's father's ear. Situuma's father had sent for him from Bugobero and told him to make a sacrifice to the ancestors but Situuma had refused saying he was a Christian.

"Can't you see it is your mother trying to speak to you? You ignored the sign from Wanzira when he spoke in his sleep calling out to his grandmother. Do you remember when he would sleepwalk in the house?"

"Come on father, Wanzira will out-grow these habits. He is just missing his grandmother, who was fresh in the grave.'

"No, my son, I think the ancestors are trying to tell us something. Watch your boy for any sign."

Although Wanzira stopped sleepwalking and sleep talking, something about his personality did not feel right but Situuma could not put a finger on it. When Situuma learnt that Wanzira suffered from autism, he explained to his father about the boy's mental condition. Namarome would not agree. "You did this to our son! That day when you planted a kiss on my breast, you bewitched your own son!"

Situuma had ignored her and hoped the city lifestyle would help her shed her superstitious beliefs.

He joined Tasha in the laughing over Peter before changing the topic. "What play are you writing?"

"Not Ivanov... He out of my blood... me through... he has wife. He live in Washington. I go to East Coast. My heart no say... go see Ivanov. My heart... Moscow... Me luver, wait, *waaaiiit* for me. Marry me in Spring!"

"What are you going to write then?"

"No Ivanov, I wait six years, each year, write play. Me write five Ivanov plays, this year, me meet my luver. Me has nothing to write. Me scratch my head, dye my hair, me don't remember the colour God give my head," she said scratching her head and looking like the nineteen-year-old down in the lobby.

Tasha walked to the kitchen lit the gas cooker and lit another of those Newport cigarettes.

She yelled from the kitchen and asked if Situuma wanted something to drink. "Red wine!" Situuma yelled back. She pulled out a bowl of corn chips and salsa from the fridge and placed it before him. Dinner will soon be ready, she alerted him. Her white ashtray was black with ash. She offered Situuma a cigarette.

"These cigarettes, lovely, they make you high and taste like mint chewing gum."

Situuma declined the offer. Tasha sucked in the cigarette and before blowing out the smoke in an elegant manner. She sat cross-legged on her bed, her long legs teasing him, then shocked Situuma with her next sentence.

"I like your smell."

"Oh my God Tasha, what do you mean by that!"

"You crazy, you blush like a white man!" She threw her arms in the air before she dressed the phrase that had made Situuma shift in his chair. "Your hairy... armpits—they suck up all the smoke from my room!"

Situuma was laughing uncomfortably. For the first time since his arrival in America, the warm sensation returned to the other place. He did not want Tasha, it was something about the hairy armpits that warmed up his blood.

"You have such an incredible sense of smell," Situuma decided to compliment her so that his mind would shift away from the bottom half of his body. He was responding to Tasha in an erotic manner and he was afraid that this would interfere with their friendship.

"Yes, Me Play Write. I put, feeling in my play. I, know everybody's smell. My sister's hairless armpits, my brother's oily armpits. Yes, I know their smell. I know me father's smell. I know when he leave toilet for me. He leave warm human smell. I love my mama's smell. She smell like breast milk. I know your smell now because you walk in and your hairy armpits suck all the smoke of my room; fill it with your smell. You smell like a man; tell me about your story."

"What story?" Situuma was not sure whether Tasha was not smoking grass; he didn't know the difference between the scents. He wondered about this six foot-once-blond-now-brown haired woman! She was odd. What did she want from him?

"I through with writing Ivanov plays. He has Russian wife, me have Russian luver. You see last year, I meet him in Las Vegas. Me have money, I meet Ivanov. Surprise! Surprise! I'm crazy. I'm happy. I want to gamble. He say no, me keep money. He go. I learn he married. He married! I learn he don't want my money. He married! I find me luver. I get married in Spring. You see, why write Ivanov plays? I find luver. But Me Play Write, run out of stories! Ha!" She sucked at cigarette and blew into the air. "Me drying up because writing plays, my life. That's why I invite you here to hear your story. I dry up, if I have no play to write this year."

Situuma understood why Tasha's scalp was sore and he had empathy for her role as a writer. It was her life and she felt suffocated because she had narrowed her scope of interest. She needed fresh air to breathe because writing was her way of breathing. Stranded in her room, thinking of her next play, she had felt trapped, like a woman who was living in a small town, yet she was used to the Moscow nightclubs where strippers danced in gigantic aquariums. She could not stop dyeing her hair because she was searching for the image of herself, which made her happy. She was not happy because her life was disappearing. When she stood in front of a mirror, she did not see the beauty that Situuma saw but a body that was losing its outline. She was gradually fading and becoming part of the atmosphere. She needed to find her soul, so that she could value the curves that attracted all the men to her when she walked into a room. She needed to get back her creativity that was slipping away. Situuma wondered how she expected him to just reel the thread of his life just like that.

But Tasha knew how. She took Situuma to the Japanese restaurant on Gilbert Street for dinner. She dropped a ten-cent coin in the pond at the entrance for good luck. Situuma had never eaten Japanese food and so Tasha recommended what she thought he would like. Chicken Teriyaki. She ate Sushi and sea food, accompanied by Vegetable Japanese rice. Situuma drank more red wine. It had not crossed his mind that he had never discussed his private life with anyone. Not even with the artist-lovers. It felt awkward talking about his love life with another woman. But the red wine made him tell HIStory.

He smiled when he thought of the first time he met Namarome.

"She was pregnant and married to another man. If it wasn't for the bull accident, Namarome would never have been my wife."

"Ha! What bull?" Tasha asked.

"The bull that had been her bride price had gored her private parts as she squatted to urinate in a makeshift bathroom."

"Lord God! That is evil!"

"She had returned to her father's home because she had trouble with her first husband. Her husband had come over to plead for return home, when the bull messed up the negotiations."

"Amazing story, you have in you heart!"

"Anyway, her two brothers run after the bull and butchered it to death. They believe they were exorcising the evil spirits in the bull. And that's how I came into the picture. I was responsible for having the two brothers arrested. There was a nasty scene between her family and me, but the attention was soon back to her, when the village women accused her of being a whore. She sought refuge at her father's home. She was now a free woman because her first husband had demanded back his bride price. That is when my opportunity came by."

"You buy her, also?" Tasha with her hands cupping her cheeks asked.

"It's not as cruel as you put it. Yes, I paid the bride price because that is what defines marriage in my culture. We got a son called Bernard Wanzira and moved to the city when I got the opportunity to do an LLB at Makerere University. Now I'm in America doing an LLM. A happy ending to a grim beginning," Situuma grinned as he rounded off his story.

Situuma thought Tasha would never get to know his silent story. But he was wrong for she was a playwright and she could feel his unsettled spirit. She could see in his eyes that he was not content with his marriage. She could smell his misery that sipped into the room from his hairy armpits and stained the walls, grey.

"Your wife sleeping around?"

Situuma, who had a mouthful of food, shook his head from this way to that way.

Ayeta Anne Wangusa is the author of the novel *Memoirs of a Mother* (1998), a children's book, *Don't Play with Fire* (2003), as well as short stories in *FEMRITE* anthologies. She is the Executive Director of Culture and Development East Africa (CDEA) and a member of the African Cultural Policy Network. From 2009-2012, she served as East Africa's representative on the Commonwealth Civil Society Advisory Committee (CSAC) and advised the Commonwealth Foundation on its programming work on Culture, Gender and Governance & Democracy. Her interests are in the areas of: African literature, cultural policy, creative economy, cities and the environment. She holds a Masters in New Media, Governance and Democracy from the University of Leicester, UK, a Masters in Literature from Makerere University, Uganda and a B.A (Hons) in Literature and Sociology, Makerere University, Uganda. She is currently a PhD student of Media and Communication Research at the University of Leicester.

Untitled
Carey Baraka

SUZANNA WAS singing the song of Kondele and Bayo was struggling to hold in her excitement. Her mother had told her that Misore was on his way to Kisumu, and while a part of her was hurt that he hadn't bothered to tell her himself, a bigger part of her was trying and failing to hide her joy at this piece of news. Her mother liked Misore, always had, but these feelings had been fading as her daughter grew older, and, as she got more and more into warning Bayo about the ways of men, Bayo made sure to betray less and less of her feelings about Misore to her. There was a verse in the Bible Bayo was thinking of now. How did it go, something about how when the writer was a child they were foolish, but as they grew older, they did away with the ways of childhood? Bayo couldn't remember the exact wording, but she knew her mother would, and hoped for a way to express that very sentiment to her. Bayo hoped and her mother frowned and Suzanna sang about *bodabodas*[73] in Kondele and Misore was coming home.

Bayo hadn't seen Misore in months. She had barely been home in August, so it had to be earlier than that, maybe during Easter, that they had been together last. Bayo thought she could remember their last conversation, something about the truth of music, Gidigidi Majimaji rapping in the background, Misore's face giddy and sweaty with excitement, Bayo swaying to the Dholuo of the music, Dinah A. smirking at their candour. Or was this a dream she had, a dream that she was confusing for reality? Bayo had been having strange dreams throughout the year, her last year of high school. She would be walking in a field, when the chameleons above her head would start talking to her. Or she would be moving, flying, above Kisumu, when God would appear next to her and they would fly together. Bayo didn't know who God was, or what he looked like, but, in her dreams, God was a woman, a woman with a voice like Suzanna's. Or she and Misore and Dinah A. would be in a room that looked like a feeling she used to smell, and she would start wondering why in her dreams Suzanna didn't have a voice, why it was God doing the singing. But none of this mattered at this moment, this moment when Misore was almost in Kisumu and they would be together again.

The night before, Bayo had been in her room reading an old collection of O. Henry's she had found in the house, when her mother swept in, dumped a thin booklet on her bed, and left without uttering a word to her. Bayo had kept on reading, fetal in her bed, but after a few minutes had coiled herself out of her position of warmth and opened the booklet. The story

---

73 A type of motorcycle taxi commonly used as a form of public transportation.

of this pamphlet is what she longed to tell Misore, would be the first thing she would tell him when she saw him. She felt a deep glow inside her as she imagined how this conversation would go.

She would say, "M2, here's a funny story."

He would turn to her, his chin rough with a few weeks' worth of stubble. "What is this? Is this like, is this like your mother, is she, this is like an embarrassing thing for her?"

She would grin. "This is my sex education, a booklet, M2. This is that funny story you wanted."

And M2 would roll back his head and laugh, laugh that deep vibratory laugh that was so laugh-inducing she would join in, and they would laugh and laugh and laugh and Dinah A., if she was in the room with them would wonder what was wrong with her two best friends, until she would tire of resisting and join in the laughter and the three of them would laugh and laugh and laugh. Bayo had missed Misore and he was coming tomorrow and how they would laugh and laugh alafa!

Listen.

Bayo was children-bring-water-to-wash-my-hands years old, she had long decided, and while her mother was unable to discuss the intricacies of sex with her, preferring instead to hide behind the *Women in the Community Humanizing* pamphlets, Bayo had no such scruples. As she cut and diced the pineapple on the table in front of her, she thought back to her high school, and how sex had been dished out like a priceless commodity. Once, when she had been in her first year of high school, she had stumbled into the fourth form block after dark, what she had been doing there she couldn't remember, and, there, discovered two fourth form students in flagrante delicto in the dark recesses of one of the classrooms. Even as the two—the boy with his back to her and his trousers down at his legs, and the girl with her skirt hoisted up to her belly and her legs entwined around the boy's waist—scrambled to hide what they were doing and cram the student's face so that they could threaten her into silence, Bayo was fleeing already, her eyes giddy with the excitement of witnessing something she shouldn't have, something she knew was wrong, something she had no wish in taking part in, yet something a part of her desired, for she had seen something in the senior girl's face, a wild bliss whose meaning she didn't know, but which she decided, in the single second when the girl's face was visible to her, that she must have, soon, but not too soon.

Four years. The red uniforms so conspicuous during funkies at other schools. Four years of reading and cramming and reading and cramming and reading and cramming. She would come home for her holidays and complain to Misore that she was not machine, that she couldn't go on like this, with all the reading, reading, reading. *No, ayam tired.* She would threaten to quit school, to drop everything and stay home, but Misore, the only person to whom she confided these thoughts of hers knew that she wouldn't quit, that she wasn't him. And she knew that he knew this. She knew that he knew that despite all the ayam tireds, she would go back to the reading and the cramming and the reading and the cramming and the being told by the teachers that their rivals, the national school in the bush, were not resting on their laurels, not sitting on their asses, and who were they, akina Bayo in their red uniforms, to think that they had arrived? So, she went back every time and read and crammed and read and crammed and went to mass every day in the mornings. Oh, the masses, at five in the am, every day, nine months a year, sometimes eleven in the years when holiday tuition became mandatory. Hail Mary, mother of God. Hail Mary, mother of God. Hail Mary, mother of God. Bayo hailed and hailed and hailed until she felt that she had hailed Mary so many times that she, the blessed mother of God, had to be inside her. Still, the sing-song voice of the priest bade them to hail. Hail Mary, mother God. Reading and cramming and the masses and all the sex. Every week Bayo seemed to find a new couple having at it like a pack of jackrabbits. In the classrooms. In the library. In the hall. In the chapel. Everywhere she turned, she saw it. Hail Mary, mother of God. Every night, at nine pm, after evening preps were done for the day, two of the boys in her class would hustle her out of the class, her and the other unwanted parties. Whose idea was it to build a mixed boarding in the middle of nowhere and keep five hundred teenagers locked up together in close quarters anyway? The two boys called themselves The Bodyguards, though what they ran was more of a pimping service than a security service. Wanaendesha danguro, their Kiswahili teacher would have said. The system was simple. Each night, The Bodyguards would rent out the classroom to whichever couple was raunchiest and had paid up to reserve the room. How it had been decided that The Bodyguards had the right to rent out the classroom like it was their personal fiefdom Bayo didn't know, but that was the way things were. Three sock an hour, they insisted, an exploitative amount, but what could the other students do? The dorms were out of the question, since they were too far from each other, and a slew of matrons had been hired by the school to live with the girls. So, the raunchy ones paid up, and The Bodyguards hustled the rest out of class and stood guard by the door to make sure no one interrupted the pair. In the morning, there would be a smell in the classroom that everyone would smell but not talk about, not the boys, not the girls, not whichever couple had been at it the previous night, not The Bodyguards, not Bayo, not the teachers who would come for morning classes and having a tough time instructing the students to air out the classroom. Instead, every month, a class or two would be ferried out of the school at random, the girls only, never the boys, and one or two or three of the girls would be discovered to be pregnant and they would be escorted to the dorms, have their things packed, their parents called, and that would be last their classmates would ever see of them.

Four years of this and still her mother thought her unable to handle a conversation about sex, preferring instead to ambush her with her *Women In The Community Humanizing* pamphlets. Is this what it meant to humanize? Bayo was tired. This year, her last one in school, one of The Bodyguards, Cassius – the other one was called Brutus – had planted a salacious rumour about Bayo, that the reason Bayo did not have sex with her fellow students, the reason she thought herself above her fellow students, was because she was having her needs taken care of by the teachers. The boy, Cassius, had been sending her texts during their April holiday, texts that Misore had seen and teased her about endlessly, and Bayo had ignored each of them with the cold indifference that was her *modus operandi* with this type of thing. Her, Bayo, daughter of Mrs. K, one of the fine young people of The Tabernacle of the Current-Day Saints, ati having sex with some of her teachers, heh, imagine. If her classmates had understood who Mrs. K was, they would have found Cassius's claims hilarious. They didn't, and some of them believed it. *Look at her, Bayo, walking around thinking that she's better for us, too good for us. Kumbe? Kwanza that Mr. Majiwa looks like her type.* Bayo heard them whisper as she sat in class, her head inside her History textbook, her eyes unable to move beyond the chapter on the history of the African National Congress in South Africa. The ANC was founded in? Even the girls in the corner, the ones who threw themselves at the young university students on teaching practice who joined the staff for three months every year had fun at her expense. *Ebu mcheki, vile anajidai.*[74] *Kumbe this is how she gets all those A's?* Every night, after evening preps, while The Bodyguards collected their due, while that Cassius collected his due, Bayo walked to the workshop, and there, amidst the broken-down chairs and desks, the chairs and desks in various states of disrepair, the chairs and desks abandoned after breaking under the collective wait of students doing Godknowswhat, Bayo put her head in her hands and cried. For ten minutes everyday from May until she finished school in November. Ten minutes, never more than that. It couldn't be more than that; a girl had to read. *Ayam tired.* This bit of her student life she didn't tell anyone, not her mother, not her father, not Misore, not Dinah A. with whom she talked from time to time. *Ayam tired.* Bayo would not miss those people. She would not even think about the people at that school. Forget it, that was then. Yamepita. Now, she was children-bring-me-water-to-wash-my-hands years old. Now, she was cutting pineapples in Kisumu.

Listen.

Pineapples were beautiful. Bayo remembered a story she had somewhere once, a story about the history of the pineapple. That, in the beginning, not in the beginning of time kabisa, but at the beginning of the people doing the recording, the apple and the pomegranate had been the fruits of choice, the fruits whose sweetness stood out above all the rest. But the two fruits suffered

---

74   A phrase in Swahili commonly used to invite someone to witness or to observe someone's behaviour, which translates to "Come see, how he is behaving" in English.

from PR problems: one from its association with the fall of man into sin; the other from its association with how winter came to the world. Then, to the New World Columbus was sent, and there, he had discovered the pineapple in all its glory. A hue of greenish-yellow, crisscrossed with multitudes of squares and rectangles and triangles, a crown of loud spikes on its head, and inside, flesh the colour of the sun. Columbus and his men had tasted the fruit and realized that this was the real reason they were in the New World, not any gold, not any diamonds, but eating this fruit with the colour of the sun, and the taste of Dionysia. They had packed their ships with pineapples and sailed back home. There, presenting what remained of the pineapples (most of them having either been eaten or rotted away) in the royal court of Spain, the king had proclaimed them heroes. In the years to come, as the pineapple spread its way through the royal corridors of Europe, usurping the apple and the pomegranate in the hierarchy of fruits, it ceased being a food and became a royal ornament. At balls thrown by the kings and the queens and the emperors, the pineapple was taken out to be shown off to revelers? The Diamond of St. Some Place? Fuck that. Here's a pineapple. Pineapple cartels developed in Europe. This was Bayo's favorite part of the story, and she swooned every time she thought about herself as a pineapple bandit, stealing pineapples from the rich to feed the poor, smuggling pineapples across countries. The pineapple became the royal mark of one of the English kings. King Edward Something Something. Only available in the tropics because it was unable to grow in the dreary cold of Europe, the pineapple was *the* fruit. An apple with a crown on its head. A pomegranate bright like the sun. Then the Dutch had invented the greenhouse, discovered they could grow the pineapple in their country. The Brits had threatened war, but one marriage later, it came to naught. The pineapple lost its glamour. It became available to the non-royals, the peasants. The British embarked on a wild adventure of colonization, hoping to discover the next pineapple from the tropics. For centuries they tried, The New World and The Far East and The Dark Continent. They discovered spices, but were spices the pineapple? The pineapple remained king. And it spread. Through the little hamlets and towns in Europe. Spread through the centuries. And now, in the kitchen of her parents' house in Kisumu, Bayo sliced and diced the pineapple into little cubes. Little cubes and vitamins and all the other things. Balance your diet, jothurwa. Mrs. K obsessed about having a balanced diet with every meal. In fact, it was one of the projects *Women in The Community Harmonizing* was passionate about. Fruits in every house. She told Bayo, every day, cut the pineapples. And the oranges and the sandra and the passion fruit and the maembe and the avocados, which Bayo despised but cut anyway because Mrs. K was her mother and what could she do anyway? Say no? Heh. In whose house? *Timbe magalagala,* saying no to your mother, and Bayo was in no mood for being accused of timbe magalagala. She cut because they had to have fruits with every meal and she blended the fruits into juice which she put in plastic bottles and put in the fridge, pineapple juice and mango juice and avocado juice and passion juice and beetroot juice and all the other juices.

Every evening, she would go to the market at Kondele to get more fruits. Fresh from the market, that's the way her mother wanted them, and that's the way Bayo wanted them too. She got them from the same stall every day, Akinyi, Akinyi Nyar Gem, one of the women *Women in The Community Humanizing* was helping, one of Mrs. K's projects. Go to Akinyi Nyar Gem, her mother advised, and Bayo went to Akinyi Nyar Gem. Bayo liked Akinyi Nyar Gem. She was one of her Hallelujah People. Fruits at Akinyi Nyar Gem. Fish from Apiyo Nyar Kochia at City Market. Hair at Gladys who run Marvellous Everlasting Salon at Nakumatt. New jeans and tops from Essie at her stall in Kibuye on Sunday mornings, early-early, before church. Conversations with Dinah A. every time they met in town, or after church. Mama Atoti down at the local shop. Atoti with his bodaboda, who Mrs. K sent to get gas from them. Oginga, mtu wa maji, who was called when KIWASCO was misbehaving. Jane, to whom Bayo took her dresses, so she that she could shona for her pockets into the dresses. Onditi in the village, her grandparents' boy. Samson, the caretaker of the Tabernacle who lived in the Tabernacle's compound, and who many expected to be ordained as an Elder of the Tabernacle soon-soon. The guys at the shack by the road, manambas, who even though they cat-called other women, respected Bayo because of who her father was. Instead, they asked her for money. *Siste, gony wa*. And Bayo, gonyo'd them. Fifty bob this time. A hundred bob the next. Fifty bob the next. Her Hallelujah People. Her ordinary people. Smiling at the bodaboda guys by the roadside. Staring at the girl at the counter. Spare change for the man on the corner. Keeping an open mind with her hair full. Collecting love where there was none. Her Hallelujah People. Her ordinary people. The faces of her Hallelujah People. Noticing the people whose faces meant they deserved to be her Hallelujah people. *Hello Min Odhis, how are the people?...Don't worry, Mama Truphena, The Lord will provide...Eh, a girl baby, I see you looking fine-fine...I know, I know, his fist is a voice he is used to raising.* Spreading her love to the people whose faces communicated that they needed it. Bayo was a woman, so she noticed these things. Bayo was children-bring-me-water-to-wash-my-hands years old, so she noticed these things.

Listen.

Bayo was listening. Suzanna sang. *Ayayeeee, itera adhi ane Kisumu*[75]. The strong smell of the pineapples in front of Bayo filled her ears. The simmering of the heat was loud, and there was a strange buzzing that accompanied it. Or was that her phone? Bayo put her hand in the pocket of her jeans. Strange number. She hang up. She put the phone back into her pocket. Cut-cut the pineapples. Cross-section the shape of the sun, the colour of the sun, the smell of the sun. Buzz buzz. The same number. Hello, who is this?

75   Ayayee, it's so hot in Kisumu.

"Bayo?"

Bayo knew that voice. She would know that voice anywhere. "Eh, finally, to be blessed with a call from The Great Master in Nairobi," she said.

Misore laughed. "Ha! Me, who said I am even in Nairobi?"

"But you are in Nairobi, ama? Kwani where are you?"

"Niko Nakuru. Listen, I just heard this, and I was like, this I have to share with Bayo. A man said, 'By the way, me none of my sisters are idle; they are all married.' I had to share this."

"Ati idle, wow. Me and my sister are both idle, can you believe? Haiya sawa, after he said this, what did you say?"

"Nothing…si ati I was talking to him?"

"Ah, The Great Master in Nairobi becomes The Great Eavesdropper in Nakuru. How the gods doth fall."

Misore laughed. His slow, deep, rolling laugh that Bayo loved and had missed so much. "You are silly, you know?"

Bayo laughed. "*Haiya, ushasema*[76]. So, why is The Great Master aka The Great Eavesdropper doing listening to the conversations of men whose sisters are not idle in Nakuru?"

"I'm actually on a bus, on my way to Kisumu. I've never understood why people stop in Nakuru, because, it's not like it's halfway, ama? Anyway, yes, niko Nakuru. I meant to call, to tell you nakuja, but things happened…" His voice trailed off.

Yes, things happened, just like things had happened all the times Bayo had sat herself in her little corner in the house and called him, or all the other times Bayo had called him while on the way to Kondele for fruits, or all the other times Bayo had called him while waiting for her turn at the salon, or, at midnight, when she ventured out into the balcony and called him, or after church on Saturday, or in school when she had borrowed teachers' phones to call ("Why else does Majiwa give her his phone so easily?" Cassius had sneered.) from school, or when, immediately after coming home after finishing high school the first thing she had done when coming home was to listen to a song she had been thinking about for three months, and the second thing was to call him, or all the other times, after Tabernacle on Sunday, or when she had a new song she had been listening to, or when she had missed him and wanted to listen to his voice and find out what was happening with him in Nairobi, or all the other times she felt locked out and couldn't understand why or how that had happened and had called and called and called but had been told *mteja wa nambari hapatikani kwa sasa*[77], please try later. Things had been happening for a long time, she wanted to tell the mteja wa nambari, but she didn't. Instead, she asked, "You're coming home for Christmas, ama?"

"Yes, yes," Misore said. "Christmas, but not quite Christmas. Pastor

76   Come on, speak up.
77   "The customer with that number cannot be reached at the moment."

Tiberius called, halafu he came down here, so I'm coming because of him."

"Oh."

"Listen, I have to go. But *nitakupigia*[78] when I reach. The bus announcer is saying that the bus is leaving. *Itatuwacha*[79] Immediately I'm in Kisumu I'll call you, sawa?"

"Sawa."

"Bye."

"Bye." Bayo said. She didn't hang up. Neither did Misore. She could hear him breathing on his side. She could hear the sounds of Nakuru. The bus announcer. Didn't Misore have a song about bus announcers? *Wasafiri wa kuelekea Kisumu*[80], *bus number 242, this is the last call.* Was this the last call? She didn't know. Misore came back on the line. "Oh, you're still here? Sorry, forgot to hang up." He hang up.

Bayo put her phone back into her phone pocket. She went on cutting the pineapples. Salad to accompany the food. Mrs. K. would cook lunch today, for that Bayo was grateful. Cut cut cut. Dice dice dice. The different yellows; this one yellow meant the pineapple wasn't quite ready, but what did it matter? People would eat it and get their vitamins. Cut cut cut. The sun fruit. Suzanna's voice on repeat. *Ayaye, itera adhi ane Kisumu.* Take me I go and see Kisumu. The Kisumu of all her Hallelujah People. Yesterday, when Bayo had gone to Akinyi Nyar Gem, the fruit seller had told her something that Bayo had thought about all the way home. "Nyako," she had said. "You know I love you. Aheri like my child. So I must say, that thing inside you, don't let it eat you up. Go to the Lord in prayer. He heals everything."

He heals everything. The great healer. No one goes to the Father except through me. Ask, and you shall find. Knock, and the door shall be found. How did the face of Christ look like? In the photos Bayo had seen, the face of Christ was of a white man, swathed in an all-consuming holy light. Did Christ eat pineapples? Bayo did not know. Such knowledge was not in the Bible. The Bible only had things about miracles and turning water into wine and calming the storm and declarations by Christ to the effect that he was the water of life. Christ was obsessed with water, Bayo had been thinking for a while, but he was also obsessed with life and the things that gave a person life. Be born again, he had offered to the Jewish politician who had come to him in the night to ask how his soul got be saved. And Christ had told him that the way to give oneself a new life was to start one's life again. Was this what Akinyi Nar Nam was talking about, this new life that Bayo could get?

Listen.

Misore was on his way home, he was coming *home*, and Suzanna was singing the song of Kisumu, the song of Kondele, the song of Kibuye, the

---

78   "I will call you."

79   "I will leave."

80   "Travelers heading to Kisumu"

song of bodabodas and Bayo was listening. *Ayaye, itera adhi ane Kisumu. Kisumu ber, Kisumu. Itera adhi ane Kisumu[81]*. Kisumu was good, Bayo agreed, but had she seen Kisumu? In the dreams she had been having, Christ did not have a face. Or, he had one, but Bayo couldn't see it. Instead, he had a voice like Suzanna, and he would sing to her, and Bayo would get life, the life that, like the woman at the well, she had been seeking. When she woke up, the life would be gone, and she would be her usual self. However, she would remember the songs that Christ had been singing to her. Every time she thought about him, Christ, she thought about him as a musician, his voice singing to her. I am the way the truth and the life, he would sing, and Bayo would agree with him, that he was the way the truth and the life. Jesus Christ and His Twelve Disciples. The Temptations, they would call themselves, thirteen men, a lucky number, singing in the rain in suits and afros and bellbottoms. *We are the way, the truth, and the life*, they would sing, *they are the way, the truth, and the life*, their backup singers, also in afros, and in matching outfits and left legs in the air, would sing, and *they are the way, the truth, and the life*, the crowd would chant along, waving their water bottles. At the centre of the crowd would be Bayo, her face aglow with rapture, looking at the leader of the group, the Diane Ross, the man whose face Bayo was unable to perceive, the man whose voice sounded like Suzanna's but also sounded like Misore.

Once, before Misore had gone off to Nairobi and disappeared from her, they had been in her parents' house, in her bedroom, Misore reading a book, Bayo lying on her bed, her head at the foot of the bed, her legs suspended midair. Ayn Rand, Bayo thought Misore had been reading, though, now, in the pressure of the remembrance of things past, Bayo wasn't sure she could remember anyone. It wasn't important. What was important was that they had been in her room, and her father away at work, and her mother somewhere in the house, whether cleaning or hovering outside Bayo's room trying to decide whether she wanted to risk opening the door Bayo couldn't remember, but Misore had been reading.

"Bayo," he had called. "Listen to what she says. So, all art works by concretizing things into concepts. Then from concepts we get emotion. Poetry, painting, sculpture, poetry, theatre, film, zote. *Kila kitu[82]*, that's how it works. You *elewa*?[83] Like, you read a book, and it has words, and it paints a scene, or a person, or a moment, or a mood, or politics, or an action, *kitu chochote kile[84]*. And then once you get this thing, this concept that has been concretized. *Halafu[85]* emotion. If it's *sijui[86]* football, then if *unapenda[87]* football, then the

---

81   "Oh wow, it's so hot in Kisumu. Kisumu, Kisumu. It's so hot in Kisumu."
82   "Everything"
83   "Understand"
84   "anything"
85   "Then"
86   "I don't know"
87   "you like"

emotions for enjoyment, whether joy or sorrow, or anger, or whatever. *Kama ni*[88] a film, and Rose and Jack are clutching on the wreckage of that boat, and Jack dies, you feel sad, you start to cry. It's the concept of the two of them on that piece of wood, the concept of Jack dying, that brings this emotion. Like, it dooon't come pelee yake. Lakini music, it doesn't work like that. *Hii siasa ya*[89] concretization and all the other difficult words, music doesn't work like that. Music has no time for all that. With music, it's boom, we're at the emotion. Which is why we listen to songs, *na hata kabla ianze vizuri*[90], before the first word, we already feel something, pain or sorrow or joy or anger, whatever. We feel it without the concept. That's something, isn't it?"

Emotion, maybe that's all people wanted from music. Sometimes, on Thursday evenings, Bayo would go to the tabernacle, and sit there. Choir practice was on Thursday evenings, and the head of the choir was the son of the father of Benga, *yaani* he was Benga itself, and Bayo would sit there and listen. Would Christ's mission have been different if had been a singer himself, and his disciples his backup singers? Or his band? Peter on the drums, John on the second mic, the other son of Zebedee with the electric guitar, Andrew on the bass, Doubting Thomas on the keyboard. How would they have sung? Would they have sung the beatitudes? The Lord's Prayer? Bayo had been wondering how The Lord's Prayer would sound like in song. Would it be better? Misore had a song about how he had been writing his own Lord's Prayer. Bayo had been curious about the song, and she had asked him questions. "M2, this thing of yours, why are you writing your own Lord's Prayer? What does it do for you, having your own personalized version? How does it help?"

"My music, why do you assume that's what going on in my life, that's it's fact? Can't music also be fiction?"

Bayo had been silent for a few seconds. *"Sijui."* She didn't know. She hadn't known that night, and she didn't know today, just like she didn't know whether these pineapples would be enough for all the *Women In the Community Humanizing* members who were supposed to have dinner in the house tonight.

Carey Baraka is a writer from Kisumu, Kenya. His writing has appeared in *Jalada Africa, Electric Literature and Gay Magazine,* among other places. He sings for a secret choir in Nairobi.

---

88   "If it is" or "If that's the case"
89   "This politics of"
90   "and even before it starts well"

My She-Husband
Muthoni wa Gichuru

THEY ARE here. They have come led by Gachibi, the man who had carried the twenty cows to our home, stuffed inside his socks and tied with rubber bands against his legs. There is Thige, who had followed with the *njoohi* in the breast pocket of military coat. My father had received the cows, wetting his fingers and separating them in twenty heaps, then counting them again making sure they were ten in each pile.

"Two hundred thousand Kenya shillings, I call them twenty cows," my father had said and spat on his chest. Tutu tutu tutu, "May they have sons, may they have daughters." The other had elders also wet their chests.

Through the crack on the wall, I could see the gleam in my father's eyes even though this marriage had been vehemently opposed by the church and my father was a church elder. He had asked for twenty cows instead of the normal fifteen and my husband had obliged him.

Thige gave Father the envelope with Njoohi. My father wet his finger again and counted ten thousand shillings. "I call them two guards of beer," he said. Tuutu tutu tutu. "May their fire never go off. Gakenia! Bring your new husband a calabash of *uji*[91]."

My belly was just beginning to strain the waist band of my skirt and my feet could not skim the ground as quickly as my father wanted. His walking cane caught me just above the ankles and I stumbled and almost fell.

"Enough!" I heard a shout and looked up and met the eyes softened with sympathy. For that I would have followed my husband like a faithful dog. My own mother never stood up for me although perhaps she too was cowed by the man who would never bend his will. A man, who stamped his authority by the whack of his walking stick or kimanyooko—a back handed slap that caught one from the ear to the chin.

My husband sits with the elders, a hunched figure not quite comfortable on the seat of patriarchal power like the ones who were born into it. Chege, the man who has caused discord in my home sits in front of the elders. His thin buttocks only occupy the edge of the seat, an insubstantial figure, the only substance of him his height which he has collapsed into a C. He sits with his hands clasped together in his lap and I find myself staring at those long fingers with a tapering tip. My desire is an elastic band. When Chege is out of my sight it shrinks and I can think clearly, knowing Chege and I are supposed to be transient. It was easy with other men even before I got married. A fumbling in the dark halfway undressed, a bumping of hip against hip, touching of a leg here and there and then a sandwich of thighs.

91   Swahili meaning "porridge."

A few groans and moans, and then the release and a quick separation. Chege, however, has become a craving, an insatiable thirst that has to be slaked.

The mind has the ability to lie to itself, bending to our will. I must have known from the moment Chege first touched me. When he put his hands under my skirt, past my knees and up where the flesh of my thighs meets, I felt I was being peeled. It was as if he was working the folds with his fingers. Heat suffused my body, his fingers trailing tendrils of fire. I wanted… Oh I wanted to…his fingers were inching up, slowly up and I felt myself opening up, like the petals of a flower. Later on, when Chege pulled down my underwear leaving me naked from the waist down I felt raw, my senses like the thin layer of a healing wound.

When I go to him, I spend the night instead of going back to my husband. When he finds me in the *shamba*[92] gathering the crop, I leave the ear of the maize half peeled and the cob still attached to the maize stalk and go into the bushes with him. He plays me like a *nyatiti*[93] and I emit a sorrowful moan that carries to the village path. His long fingers, as supple as young twigs, strap my nerve ends. When my senses return to me, I find the birds have plucked all but a few grains from the maize cob.

I am guilty. I am guilty of disobedience and going behind my husband's back. I am guilty of neglect and abandonment. I am guilty of talking back and being wasteful. I have insulted the hand that feeds me, scorned the protection accorded me as a married woman.

My grandmother says I spell trouble with every swing of my hips, every lifting of my backside and every jiggle of my breasts. Her words have the potency of seers for not only was I pregnant with my firstborn at sixteen but at nineteen I was carrying my second. My present husband took me in when my midriff was becoming taut with the pregnancy. My husband has been good to me. My body and that of my children have not been bared by torn clothes and our bellies have known no rubbles of hunger.

For six years we have lived together. I have learnt to laugh in the face of women who spit from the side of their mouths when they see me. I have learnt to fight off the men who try to pull me into the bushes assuming that my thighs are open for anyone. My husband and I have chosen carefully. No blood relatives, no history of strange diseases and strange customs. Together we have two children. Our son can round up the sheep and our daughter totters about the compound, chasing the chickens and falling on her fat bottom.

I don't know what first attracted me to Chege. Perhaps it was the newness of him, this man who came with red dust on his shoes marking him as a traveller in the ash coloured soil of Laikipia plains. He asked me for directions to his aunt's house which turned out to be just two *shambas* from ours. I met him a few days later, a filterless cigarette between his thin fingers. His direct

92   "farm" or "agricultural land"
93   a traditional stringed musical instrument, similar to a lyre, played in the traditional music of the Luo people of Kenya and Tanzania.

gaze was a challenge and his mouth, the upper lip turned as if in a sneer, held a hint of scorn. I knew he had been told about my marriage. The news about my marriage is the kind that stirs a village, staying at the tip of the tongue so that it is easily passed. Then it settles like soot on the rafters of a smoky kitchen until someone new comes along. Have you heard? People ask and enjoy the pleasure of the re-telling.

"What do you have to say for yourself?" Gachibi asks. I wiggle my bottom. The seat I am sitting on is too small for me and my hips push against the arms rest. "Did you? Have you?" Gikandi asks. His eyes linger on my bottom half. Gikandi owns one of the matatus that ply Matanya, our village to Nanyuki town. He carries a comb in his dashboard which he keeps running through greying hair. He never allows a man or an old woman in the front seat of his vehicle. He has made clear he would not mind sharing a bed with me but he was circumcised the same day with my father and there is a history of incestuous relationships in his family.

"Have you made your decision?" Thige finishes Gikandi's question. I draw figures on the ground using my big toe. I cannot lift my eyes and face the reproachful eyes of my husband.

"Well?" my father asks in that deceptively soft voice that I know so well. A voice he uses before flipping his wrist into a face so fast that the blow makes the head snap.

"I don't know what to say," I say.

I hear the scrapping of a chair and I look up. Chege rises to his feet toppling the chair he is sitting on. His walk is a shuffle, as if the shoes he is wearing are too heavy for him. He stands before the elders, a tall gaunt figure, like a stick in a field of potatoes. Hooking his fingers on the waist band of his jeans, he thrusts his pelvis forward. The wind balloons his thin cotton shirt behind making him look like a scare crow.

"You don't know what to say? What do these *wazee*[94] want you to say? That you will stay married to this She-husband?" Chege asks, pointing at my husband, "Does she do you?" Chege's voice is explosive, like a boy who farts loudly during a ceremony to draw attention to himself. I see my husband flinch, her dark face has turned a dark grey, the colour of rained-on ash. The elders sit up and my father digs his walking cane into the ground.

The day my husband sent elders to ask for me, my grandmother took me to her hut. "Gakenia, since you have decided to live up to your name and make the men of Matanya village happy on your backside, no man is likely to take you for a wife," she told me and cackled, her mouth like an empty pocket. "If it was our time, a woman like you who has given birth while still in her father's hearth, a *gichokio*[95], would be married as the second or third

---

94   "elder" or "elderly person"

95   a term from Kenya, referring to a woman who has given birth while still living with her father. It is used as a derogatory term in the context of marriage, indicating that the woman is not a virgin and has had a child out of wedlock.

wife. Now the men who wear *matonyo*[96] have been forbidden by the church to marry more than on wife. Nyokabi wa Mathu has sent elders to ask your father for you."

"Ask for me? How can she ask for me?" I asked.

"Among us the Gikuyu, there is a practice where a woman who has never had children and whose husband has passed on can take a wife."

Being born and raised in a settlement away from the original home of one's ancestors robs one of the cultural anchorage of her people. For me, even the original greetings of my people for each age set, *wakia maitu*[97]—how are you my mother—for all the women of my mother's age, *wakia awa*[98]—how are you my father—for all the men of my father's age, *wakia guka, wakia cucu*[99]—the former for the men of my grandfather's age and the latter for all the women of my grandmother's age, confuse me.

"How will I be a woman's wife?" I asked my grandmother.

"You will obey the woman as you would a male husband. She will still be the head of the home. What she needs from you most is children."

"How will I get children?"

"The same way you got your first one and the one in your belly."

My children called me Mami, the newer term for mother and they called my husband Maitu the more formal term for one's female parent. I had the freedom to choose my mates but if my husband was not happy with the man I had chosen she would tell me. It had worked well until Chege came along and slashed at the fabric of our lives.

"She is my wife but she does not share my bed," my husband speaks for the first time. I can see the effort it has cost her to speak out. In the time I have been with her she rarely raises her voice. Perhaps the years of being scorned as a barren woman then as a widow has rubbed off the edge of her voice. Her voice is lilting, soft like the pattering of rain on a grass-thatched roof.

"What are doing with her then?" Chege asks. He is facing away from me but I know his mouth is curving into a sneer, the upper lip upturned in one corner, the left eye narrowed. I rise up and stand in front of Chege, as if with my body I will shield my husband from Chege's scorn. The early afternoon sun is in my eyes and I squint to look up into Chege's eyes.

The barrenness of the land stretches before us. All around are shrubs and cactus bushes and the grass crumbles under our feet. When I was growing up Nyokabi and her husband Mathu's goats and sheep would raise enough dust to obscure a homestead while they were passing. Nyokabi was originally from the pastoralist Maasai and the only crop she planted was napier grass for her livestock. I plant a few maize and beans but the livestock provides for

---

96   a modern or Western-style clothing, particularly trousers, worn by men, seen as less traditional and less respectable.

97   "visit parents"

98   "visit relatives"

99   "visit grandparents"

our needs and we have never gone without.

"Do you think I cannot provide for you if you leave this farce of a marriage?" Chege asks.

Chege has worn the same pair of jeans since I first saw him. Sometimes when I meet him in the morning he smells strongly of soap and soot, and I suspect he washes his clothes at night and have to dry by the fire.

"She has four children and another one on the way," my father tells him.

"That one is mine! A boy to name after my father," Chege says. There is pride in his voice like a man who has found a purpose, something to strive for.

"And the other four?" my father asks.

"Gakenia and I can take care of them. Don't the Gikuyu say wealth is in one's hands?" Chege asks.

When we talk, Chege talks of two acres of land, telling me his father divided the land between him and his brothers before he died. He tells me a quarter acre of land goes for twenty millions now and in a couple of years the figure will double. He tells me the land is in Gachie, a place that borders Nairobi city.

As soon as my second born had lost his two front teeth my husband took us on tour of Nairobi. The buildings dizzied in their height and my eyes blurred at the sight of so many cars passing by. I got photographed outside KICC, one of the buildings in Nairobi that is so tall it seems to sway in the wind. The photographer had positioned me in front of the building and told me to raise my hand with the palm facing down. When the photo came out I appeared to be holding the top of the building. We had gone to Uhuru Park and had taken a boat round the manmade lake. While my husband had pushed the oars, I had skimmed the surface of the lake, letting my fingers trail the warm water while my children and squealed with delight and splashed each other with water. My husband had taken us to a restaurant for lunch where for the first time in my life I had eaten potatoes deep fried in oil, enjoying the greasy deliciousness liberally splashed with tangy tomato sauce. Then she bought us cotton candy which melted in our mouth into liquid sweetness.

"Come with me," Chege says. "Tell them you have chosen to go with me. We will leave tomorrow and stay with my mother for a while until I build my own house."

He puts his hands on my shoulders, gently rubbing them and I begin to feel the ripening of desire. I imagine how it would be, his long body wrapped around me every night, running his fingers lightly over my nipples. A flush of warmth passes through me, as if I am being drenched with warm water.

"Are you going to give back the twenty cows her husband gave for her?" Thige asks.

"Not now but I will repay everything with time," Chege says.

"I will not allow the children to go," my husband says.

For the last few months she has been the one who cooks for the children, bathes them and goes for school meetings. When my first born Ciira hurts herself now she runs to her Maitu to be soothed and Ciku my last born totters to my husband to be picked any time she sees her. Even when I stay away for two days, unable to tear myself away from the sweet torment that is Chege, my husband still welcomes me home.

"They are not your children," Chege says. "You cannot claim children who have not come from your womb."

"It was said there would come those who have cowbells in their ears and cannot hear," Mzee Gachibi says. "Nyokabi paid dowry for Gakenia and Gakenia's children belong to her."

"You can leave her children. We have already started ours and we will have more," Chege says. I look at him and wonder whether children are like the afterbirth which can be left and forgotten.

My husband rises stiffly to her feet. Lately her joints have been hurting her, pain that she describes as a grinding. When I am home I boil mahutia—a medicinal herb whose liquid when applied in a compress to an aching joint, provides relief.

"Do you want to leave our children and go with this man?" my husband asks me.

Life with Nyokabi has been soft, the harsh edges rubbed off and the ripples smoothened out. However, I have had a yearning for something that quickens the heart, something that sets the blood pumping. Chege reaches out for my hand and the smell of him, a mixture of wood smoke and the mustiness of a he-goat, is intoxicating. I feel heady, as if I have taken a few cups of my grandmother's kameera—a kind of fermented porridge that makes men sing of wealth in goats and cows that they don't have.

"Go and sit down old woman!" Chege shouts at my husband. Chairs and old bones creak as the elders rise to their feet. My father's cane makes a tap tap sound as he walks towards us. Instinct and painful experience tells me to jump aside. The walking cane gets Chege just below the knees and I hear his yelp of pain. "Crazy old man!" Chege shouts and starts walking away.

"You know where to find me Gakenia." He throws the words at me.

I watch him walk way. It is early evening and his shadow is long beside him. I am going to miss putting my arms around that slim waist, those thrusting hips. Already I can feel myself shrinking, enfolding into myself.

Mũthoni Wa Gichũrũ *is a Kenyan writer who has written several young adult novels and children stories. She is the Cordinator,* AMKA *space for women writers Kenya. Mũthoni is an awardee of the* Burt Award for African Writing, *2016 and 2018. Mũthoni is also a short story writer and was shortlisted for the* Commonwealth Short Story Prize 2015 *and* Africa Book Club Short Story Competition 2018. *In 2019 Mũthoni was shortlisted for the* Queen Mary Wasafiri Writing Prize—*Life writing category. Mũthoni is also a playwright and her play,* The Land Along the River *was on the list of commended plays for the category of English as a second language,* BBC Radio *play 2016.*

The Chicken League
Neema Komba

MY BREASTS started budding on the same day we had the final match for our street's Chicken League, where the winner was to win a live chicken. I was mortified, so, I lied to my teammates that my mother forbade me from playing football that Sunday.

"It's the final game, how can she do that to us?" Mchina, our next-door neighbour, complained. We called him Mchina because he had a fancy name we couldn't bother to pronounce, Valentino.

"We can beg mama to let you play. What if we offer her the chicken we win?" Abu, the youngest in the team, suggested, coming up with another idea.

I just wanted them to leave me alone, but they weren't going to give up.

Our team was made up of misfits, kids who couldn't make any other team. We were also known as sissies, mostly because of me, the only girl in the league. Yet somehow, we had fought our way to the finals, we beat Bondeni and Jeremeka, and we were about to play against Migoko, the most notorious team in our neighbourhood. Migoko got their name because of their super strong calves, long legs, and rough play.

"You need to sneak out." Juma, the quietest in our team whispered.

Everyone agreed. I had the strictest mom in our neighbourhood, so no one would be brave enough to ask her for permission.

It was one pm, three hours before the game. My mom was in the living room, reading some Sunday newspapers. The team had gathered outside, planning on the best way to sneak me out without my mom noticing. I was still wearing my Sunday dress, a puffy pink lace dress with a padded chest, thick enough to hide my impediment.

"You guys can still win this without me. Get Frank to play." I said. Frank was a new kid in our neighbourhood. He wasn't good, but he was the extra body we needed and could probably pass a ball here and there.

"No, we need you man! We need a strong midfield to win." Ngwengwe, the captain-coach of our team started to lecture. "We can't win on strength, we need speed and strategy. They got Deo and Matongo on defence, those guys are strong, we will never be able to play ten against eleven."

At 12 years old, I was this swift tall thing on the pitch. Everybody called me Peter Crouch, after the English player. I hated the name, but it stuck on people's mouths. I started playing football with my neighbours when I was five years old because I sucked at all the other games—jumping rope, *rede,*

I was even bad at playing house because I would change my character every five minutes.

Back when we could still count the number of houses in our street, kids used to gather in front of our house to play. Girls played rede and boys played one-touch football. The rede matches were intense. The players would divide themselves into two teams. They would get an old sock, fill it with sand and paper to make a ball. Two people from one team would stand on opposite sides and try to hit a player from the opposing team with the ball. The player would move between the throwers, dodging the ball while staying within set boundaries, counting how many times she successfully dodges the ball, and at the end of the game, the team with most dodges wins. Sometimes, to spice things up, the player would have to dodge the ball and fill an empty soda bottle with sand to win the game.

Rede was about athletics and attitude. My sister was the best player in the neighbourhood. She ran fast, dodged with attitude, and hit with gusto. One day she hit someone so hard that she threw up her lunch. She had tried to teach me her skills, but I always got hit on the first throw. I gave up on rede and played one-touch football instead. The rules of one-touch were simple, you could only touch the ball once, so you had to try and score with every kick. I was better at it, so I started playing football with the boys. Although football wasn't as popular as rede, we managed to make it entertain for ourselves. Sometimes, instead of one-touch, we switched things up and played *chenga*, a dribbling and scoring game where you are judged by how well you can trick a defender and score. Sometimes we played *tobo bao*, another dribbling game, but instead of scoring, we had to get a ball to pass between someone's legs (commonly known as 'the nutmeg' or in Swahili, *tobo*). Whoever gets nutmegged can be slapped by anyone until they touch a tree or whatever object we agree on to signify their release. Sometimes when more girls joined the game, the boys would switch from *tobo bao* to *tobo busu*, that way whoever gets nutmegged can be kissed by anyone, and all the boys circled around the girls they liked hoping to nutmeg them and blow air kisses at them. While *chenga* was exhilarating, it was one-touch that drew me to football and kept me there.

As our neighbourhood grew, the friendly one-touch games turned into intense football matches, almost as intense as the rede matches. Kids formed street teams and competed at various levels. The chicken league was the world cup of our street football, the be-all-end-all league.

To win the chicken meant to win respect of the entire neighbourhood, something we desperately needed. On any other day, I too would have been as pumped up about the game as my teammates, ready to strategize on ways to send a bunch of teenagers to hell. Unfortunately, I just happened to grow breasts that day. The breasts weren't much bigger than boiled lima beans, but to me, the slightly painful little mounds on my once flat chest felt as big as coconuts. What if they noticed? Being the only girl on the team was bad enough, but at least I looked like them. To be an actual girl with tits and everything was terrifying. It meant that I too would become a target of *tobo busu*, that my dribbling and passing skills would suddenly mean nothing, and I'd cease to be the best midfielder on my team and become something else in their eyes. So, while the team planned on ways to sneak me out, I thought of ways to get caught and stay in.

"Neema!" My mom called for me from the sitting room. I ran inside the house, leaving the boys to make their plans. Mama was going to visit her friend Mama Furaha for the rest of the afternoon. "Be home before dark." She heeded her usual warning.

"Mama said I can't leave, I need to do chores," I lied to the team once more as my mother pulled out of the house in her old Toyota pick-up.

"We'll do the chores with you, that way you'll be done before the game."

I glared at Ngwengwe for his suggestion, but felt a little hopeful that I could still get out of the game.

"She told me to clean the pig house before she returned."

Brilliant! The smell in the pig house was always disgusting, and we all hated it. Besides, half of the team was Muslim, so I knew they couldn't help me.

"We'll do it!" They chorused. Abu was the first to head to the barn.

"This is *haram* for you guys. Really, I can do this." I grabbed Abu's skinny hand. The team pushed past me toward the barn area, ready to clean the pig house. As we approached the barn, the smell of fresh dung and maize chaff greeted us. Isaac grabbed a shovel, Abu a broom. Amani pushed the old wooden door open. The concrete slabs were wet, freshly scrubbed. The pigs stretched out lazily on fresh dry grass, their bellies full of leftovers and maize chaff. Someone had cleaned the barn not too long before.

I lowered my head and waited for the team to start a screaming match, but they were all too happy to complain. We left the barn and Ngwengwe told us to meet in front of our house in one hour, at three pm, so we could all go to the match together. I simply nodded. I was out of tricks.

I dragged myself to the house and looked for different outfits I could wear to the game. I tried on different t-shirts, but nothing gave me enough cover. I wished I could go with one of my padded-chest dresses, but that too was out of the question. I shuffled through the bottom of my drawer and pulled out a black lace training bra my sister got for me for my twelfth birthday. It was an embarrassing gift then—and I thought I was never going to need it, but puberty was cruel and made an appearance anyway. My face flushed as I inspected the little lace that was to cover my little secret. Even though I had imagined wearing the training bra underneath one of my sister's grown-up dresses, I never once imagined I'd have to wear it to a football match. I stuffed the little bra back to the bottom of the drawer.

Time moved fast that Sunday. Before I knew it, it was already 2:30 pm, and I was still out of ideas. Tired of solving the issue by myself, I rushed over to Queen's house to get help from my best friend. Although Queen and I had been friends all our lives, we couldn't be more different—I was shy, she was feisty, I hated girlhood, she thrived in it. I found her playing rede with a bunch of other girls on the sandy road in front of her house, her lacy Sunday dress flowing as she ran and dodged the ball in the middle of two girls. I didn't have time to envy their freedom of running in the middle of the road in their padded dresses.

"You have to help me," I pulled Queen out of the game. "I can't go to the game today," I told her.

"Why? She paused for a second to catch her breath from all the dodging. It's the final game?"

"I-have-breasts," I said with disgust as I covered my mouth as if I had cursed.

"What? Show me..." she said, her right hand stretched out, ready to search for evidence. I pushed her hand away from my chest.

"I wish..." She folded the palms of her hands as if in prayer. "You are so lucky!" She smiled.

Queen has always been fascinated by breasts. She wanted to have them so much that on fifth grade, she dug out fukufuku, antlions, and put them on her breasts so that they would swell. Her breasts were yet to make an appearance, but she was more than ready for them.

"What am I going to do? The game is in an hour." I tugged her arm desperately.

"You can probably cover them, and no one would notice." She paused for a moment to consider some options then snapped her finger in excitement before running into the house. I was immediately excited by her finger snap. She used to call it the brilliance snap, when she thought she had a really good idea. Like the time she was convinced putting a leaf between crossed fingers and then leaving it on the doorstep would make your mom forget everything you did wrong, or when she hid me in her wardrobe after I beat up Amani so that my parents wouldn't find me. The snap meant that my problems were almost over.

I ran behind her. She went straight to her room and rummaged her cupboard. I stood by the door and waited for her to find whatever she was looking for. After a few minutes of frantic searching, she pulled out a crepe bandage and safety pins from a pile of things. I probably should have been skeptical but in my desperation, I let her unzip my dress and tie the bandage tightly around my chest, securing it with safety pins. The bandage was so tight, I could barely breathe, but my chest felt flat again. I walked out of Queen's room feeling a little more confident. I went to my house to get ready for the game. Despite the heat, I put on two t-shirts for good measure.

At three pm, the team gathered under the mango tree in front of our house. We talked formation as we headed to the football pitch by the river. "What are going to do with the chicken once we win?" Abu asked the team. "Let's sell it and buy a rubber ball." "Let's cook it." "Let's buy jerseys." Everyone in the team wanted to do something different with the chicken, but we all had one goal, to win.

We had started our team just a few months before after getting rejected by all the other teams. Abu was too young. Ngwengwe was too short. I was a girl. Amani was too fat. Ndutu's grandmother was a 'witch' and the rest just weren't good enough to play in their teams for one reason or another. So, we had gathered one day and cleared the plot behind Mchina's house whose owner hadn't started building yet. We made a ball out of plastic bags, a little bit of sand and sisal rope and started playing together every day after school. When the Chicken League started three weeks before, we signed up to play and made it to the finals. Winning the league was the biggest revenge we could take against everyone that looked down on us. We were ready.

We reached the football pitch early, kicked off our slippers and started jogging. We all played barefoot because none of us had football shoes. Migoko team arrived shortly after us. Their shins were scarily strong compared to our own. They jogged around the pitch, making hissing sounds to intimidate us. A crowd started gathering around the field. Queen and the girls had abandoned their rede game to watch the match. There was much anticipation—who wins, who gets injured, who cries? Migoko team was known for making kids cry in the pitch.

Shabani, who played for the older boys' team, was the referee. He held the trophy chicken in his arms, a white rooster with a bright red crown. He had tied a rope around its legs to keep it from running away. He called the captains to toss the coin to decide on who starts the game, and because we didn't have uniform jerseys, the coin toss was also to decide which team wore shirts, and which played shirtless.

"Heads or tails?" Shabani asked Ngwengwe and Matongo.

"Heads." Matongo answered first

"Tails, I guess." Ngwengwe shrugged.

Shabani threw the coin in the air and it landed on the bare ground. I bit my nails as he picked up the coin from the ground.

"Migoko starts. Sissies play shirtless."

My stomach sank when the referee announced. Migoko started laughing at our team. I searched for Queen in the crowd, hoping she would offer some kind of support from afar.

"Take off your shirts, you sissies!" some older boys shouted from the crowd.

"Ref, can we just keep our shirts on? We have a girl in our team!" Ngwengwe pleaded on my behalf.

"The other team has to yield since they won the coin toss."

There was no way Migoko team would agree to playing shirtless. Matongo, Migoko's captain, and Ngwengwe were sworn enemies. They both liked Queen. She didn't like either one of them, but every so often she allowed one of them to buy her Sunvita, frozen blackcurrant juice.

The boys took off their shirts and tossed them outside the field. Their small chests glistened in the sun. I envied the flatness of their chests— puberty was still a long way for them. All eyes were on me, waiting to see if I'd take my shirt off too. My hands shook, and I could feel a stream of sweat dripping in my armpits. That was the day the whole world found out I had breasts. If I kept my shirt on, everyone would assume I had them, and if I took my shirt off, everyone would know I had them.

I closed my eyes for a moment to pray. When I opened them, the crowd was still waiting for me to do something. I slowly peeled off the first t-shirt and tossed it in the pile of my team's t-shirts. I had just started pulling off my second t-shirt when I saw Queen doing her brilliance snap. I let out a loud sigh when she stormed into the field screaming at the ref.

"This is unfair! You can't make her take off her shirt."

"I don't make the rules, I just enforce them." Shabani wasn't about to yield to some screaming twelve-year-old girl.

"Boo! What kind of rules are those?" Queen never backed down from a fight.

"Girls-have-the-right-to-play-football!" Queen started chanting with her fist up.

"Girls-have-the-right-to-play-football!" Some people started laughing at her. I couldn't let my best friend take my punches. I joined her in the pitch with my fist up.

"Girls-have-the-right-to-play-football!"

The girls from Queen's rede group also joined in our march. The chants grew louder. We shouted with as much intensity and rage as we could find in our twelve-year-old lungs. We had all watched *Sarafina*, and Michael Jackson's, '*They don't really care about us,*' video. This was our moment to protest!

"Who-are-you-to-keep-us-out!"

"Girls-have-the-right-to-play!"

Abu was the first boy to join the march in the middle of the field. The rest of the team joined, and some boys from the crowd also joined. We marched in the field for almost five minutes singing the famous song from

Sarafina, '*Freedom is coming tomorrow!*'

Shabani blew his whistle to silence us!

"Okay, Migoko plays shirtless!" he shouted.

We all cheered. The crowd cleared from the football pitch and the match began. Migoko boys played hard. They pushed, pulled and kicked as if we were wrestling.

Seventy minutes into the game, half of our team was limping on the field. The score was still 0-0. Migoko's strategy was to tire us out with rough play, but we pushed equally hard, building defensive walls while finding opportunities to score. The pitch was silent except for the players' laboured breathing and the sound of kicks against the rubber ball.

The ball was in our court. Ndutu passed it to Ngwengwe. Ngwengwe passed it to Abu, Abu passed it to Mchina, Mchina to Athumani, Athumani to Amani. We were playing one touch, no one stayed with the ball long enough to be tackled or lose it. I ran and found the right spot. I was wide open. Amani made a long pass to me. The goalkeeper had left a whole left side open. I kicked the ball and it went right between the two wooden poles that marked the goals.

"Gooooooaaaaal!"

Our team erupted in cheers. We bumped chests, they carried me on their shoulders… and as it was my tradition when I scored, I took off my shirt and threw it in the air, completely forgetting in that moment, that I had wrapped my budding breasts with a crepe bandage.

Neema Komba *is a poet and writer from Tanzania. She is the 2014 winner of the* Etisalat Prize for Literature *in the Flash Fiction category. She is the author of* Mektildis Kapinga: a silent hero, *and* See Through the Complicated, *a poetry collection. Her work entitled, "The Search for Magical Mbuji", appeared in the creative non-fiction anthology,* Safe House: Explorations in Creative Nonfiction. *Her short stories have been featured in* Payback and Other Stories: An anthology for African and African Diaspora Short Stories; Adda Stories; and Index on Censorship. *She co-founded La Poetista, a platform for poets and other performing artists where she coordinated the* Woman Scream International Poetry and Arts Festival *in Tanzania from 2013 to 2015.. She is a steering committee member for the* Ebrahim Hussein Poetry Prize *and has served as a judge for* Project Sawti Poetry Prize (Swahili) *and* Andika na Soma short story competition (Swahili).

Seed Sowing
Regina Asinde

YOU STAND in front of the mirror and smile. You are gorgeous. With those red wine painted lips, perfect eyeliner and shadow, and trimmed eyebrows accentuated by black eye pencil, your face is the face of Lupita Nyong'o. You have sunk thousands of your hard-earned money from the international commercial bank where you work to keep your mahogany skin flawless. No one would guess that you are approaching your mid-thirties. In fact, come next month you will be celebrating thirty-four years. However, who knew that except your mother and yourself? No one. Not even Facebook. On that day, Facebook will be telling all your virtual friends that you are turning twenty-four.

You smile and turn sideways. The mini green dress fits you perfectly. Standing sideways, you check out your backside and smile wider. It had been worth investing in the Moonlight Butt Lifter Shorts. Your buttocks are slightly pushed up and to the sides giving them a firmer, younger appearance that beautifully fills out your clingy dress. You looked downright sexy. The urge to take a *selfie* overwhelms you and you pick your TECNO Phantom 6 Plus phone from its position on your pillow, open wider the single glass window curtain, walk back in front of the mirror and click away, turning and twisting your lips, head, buttocks, and legs to get the best shots.

"Phionah! Phionah!" the shrill voice of your friend Rose interrupts your *slay queen* moment.

"Just a moment," you answer back.

You pick up a yellow clutch bag and throw in your phone, and the toiletries strewn on the dressing table. Lipstick, lip gloss, the now blackened toothbrush you use to brush your eyebrows, eyebrow pencils, hand lotion, makeup kit. You pull open the dresser drawer and pick a sealed brown envelope. You stare at it for two seconds. It is bulky. On the bottom of its left corner are printed words in black bold letters:

MIRACLE ACHIEVERS MINISTRIES
P.O BOX 256, KAMPALA
"Come and achieve your miracle today!"

Running across the mid-section of the envelope are the words:

Seed sowing offering

You had printed in blue pen your name, Nakintu Phionah, where the name segment was. Your phone number and address were neatly printed in small letters. MARRIAGE was the prayer request written out in capital letters. You did not want to take chances that the prayer request might not be visible and so you wrote it in capital letters. Two million shillings only was the amount of money you had sowed. Yesterday the women in your savings group had finally given you the money you had asked them to lend you. You hoped that this time around your seed would be accepted so that your prayer request for marriage breakthrough is fulfilled. In April, two months ago, you had sowed 800,000/=[100] for the same prayer request. Pastor had told you that you could not possibly expect God to give you a husband when you only gave in such a paltry amount.

"Big blessings require huge sacrifices. Do you think if Solomon had not sacrificed over a thousand sheep God would have given him the wisdom he was given?" he had asked, holding your sheepish gaze. You stared right back—he hated it if you did not look at him directly when he was speaking to you.

"That's all I have Pastor. That's my entire salary. My Boss refused to give me a salary advance once again," you said, your tone demure. It was the third time you were sowing seed that wasn't acceptable.

Pastor had sighed. You could hear his exasperation in his voice when he next spoke: "Phionah, Phionah. Why is your faith so little?"

You had looked at him in confusion, not quite understanding why he said that. You believed in him; you had seen so many people receive their breakthroughs after he had prayed for them. Rose, your friend, had conceived after three years in marriage without a child. She had had to sow her car though, before she conceived. But Rose's husband had money so she could afford to sow the car as a seed. He was a *kubakyeyo* in the UK.

Your confusion must have shown because Pastor's eyes had softened, and he had said quietly, "Just trust in the Lord, he will answer your prayer. Remember what he said: ask and you shall receive!"

You had remained silent, wondering what it was you were missing. Why was your faith shallow?

Pastor had leaned over the mahogany table and rested both his strong muscled arms on the top. He spoke to you the way you saw your neighbor Taata Brenda speak to his six-year-old girl when he was convincing her not to cry because he was leaving home. "If we believe, we receive whatever we ask for. Don't you have any one you can ask for money?" he leans back into his black leather office chair and closes his eyes for a second. "*Rabashakareebabbabae* ish! I can feel your breakthrough is near, you just have to sow enough seed and you will receive it! *Rababababashahakaka...*"

New hope had flowed into your soul at Pastor's words. You knew the spirit had just revealed it to him. If Pastor said your breakthrough was near, it was near. But where could you get money from? You had closed your eyes too, thinking hard whom you could ask for money. Pastor continued speaking in tongues. You wouldn't possibly ask Rose for more money; she had been the one who had given you the first seed of 500,000/= that you had sowed. And your sister Doreen wouldn't possibly give you any more money; she kept telling you that Pastor was false, and she wouldn't give you anymore of her money to give to Pastor. You had tried explaining to her that what people and the media said about Pastor

---

100   Ugandan Shillings. The '/=' symbol is used to represent the currency.

was false, that it was the devil using those people to discredit Pastor, but she had refused to believe in you. The last time Pastor had told you to be careful of her; the church she prayed in had no Holy Spirit so how could she not be used by the devil to try to steal your destiny? So, these days you avoided her.

"*Rabababashahaloreebabbabaishhhhhhnakaka…*" Pastor's voice continued chanting.

The savings group! Yes! You had smiled, of course you could get money from your village women's savings group. You were a member in a savings group for about fifteen women. The members could borrow money from the group and pay it back with some minimal interest. Of course, you had hoped to borrow money from the group to buy a plot of land sometime towards the end of this year but then this was more urgent. Your thirty-fourth birthday was fast approaching and you did not want it to find you still single.

You had sat upright, pushing your breasts that had been almost popping out of the push-up bra back into place. Pastor had opened his eyes. You had smiled when his eyes remained fastened onto your chest. Standing up slowly, you let him savour the sight. "I will get going Pastor," you had said.

"Eh, come and we say a short prayer before you leave," Pastor had said. You had walked over to him and straddled his laps," ensuring that the hardness pushing against his ash-grey suit pants was nestled between your thighs. His coat was hanging over the coat peg behind the closed door. Your hands held onto his neck, pushing your firm breasts against his hard chest. His hands held your waist. This was the praying position. In this position, the Holy Spirit would easily work in both of you. You had experienced his power in the way your body temperature rose to feverish levels during the prayers especially when Pastor spoke in tongues, pushing you hard onto his hardness as you rode up and down his laps.

After twenty minutes or so, he had groaned hard before going silent and laying his head on your now naked breasts. Both of you had been breathing hard. You had felt the wetness in your silk panties and known that the Holy Spirit had cleansed you. Pastor said that every time he prayed and you released liquids from your body that was a sure sign of deliverance. You never questioned this however absurd it had sounded when you had first heard it for you knew that God's ways and thoughts were not man's ways and thoughts. As Rose loved to remind you, the righteous live by faith and you cannot please God without faith. Your desire was to please God so that He grant you your breakthrough.

"Go in peace. You will soon get your breakthrough."

You had gotten off him and entered the bathroom that was within his office. After easing yourself in the pristine white toilet bowl, you had taken off your wet silk panties and placed them in the plastic transparent bucket that was in one corner of the bathroom. There were other panties in the bucket. That was the rule; every woman whom Pastor prayed for left her wet panties in the bucket. You never asked why. You simply obeyed, for disobedience was like the sin of witchcraft. Pastor had told you the first time he had prayed for you and you had asked.

"Banange Phionah! What are you doing in that bedroom of yours?" Rose's voice once again interrupts your thoughts. You realize you had sat down on the bed once again. What's wrong with you? You walk out of the bedroom into the sitting room. Rose is standing inside the sitting room, her face showing her irritation. She is in a floral printed *kitenge* fitted at the high waist and flowing wide like a butterfly. Her pregnancy is barely visible through the dress. Her right hand jingles a black car key.

You smile at her. She smiles in appreciation, looking you over. "*Leero osazze wo kubakubba*?!"[101] It is both a question and a statement expressing admiration.

You smile. You slip on yellow high wedges. As an afterthought, you rush back into the bedroom and pick your well-thumbed Bible from the bedside table.

"Now what?" you hear Rose mumble in disgust.

"Isn't Pastor praying for you today?" Rose asks when you come back into the sitting room.

"He is. Why do you ask?"

"Look at the time, we are so late. I don't think you will be able to see Pastor. By the time we reach, it will be almost ten AM!"

"I will see him. I sent him a text yesterday and he said he would see me today."

You both move out of the room. As you lock your door, your neighbour, Mama Brenda comes out of her house.

"Eh, Phionah, *tojakuswaala kugamba ntino*[102] you are going to church dressed like that!" she says without preamble, her voice dripping scorn.

You keep silent.

"Good morning Mama Brenda," Rose chirps in, her voice honey sweet.

After locking the door, you turn and watch your nemesis. She is the reason you want to move out of this neighbourhood. You glare at each other, her forehead knitted in disapproving lines. You pull down your dress which had ridden up your thighs when you bent to lock the door. You see the disapproval lurking in her eyes, her lips curled in disgust. She is dressed in a plain sea green gomesi held together by a yellow sash tied round her generous waistline.

"What does it look like to you?" you say, your voice terse. She mumbles something inaudible. You don't catch the words but see her lips moving. Before you can say another word, her husband comes out of their house, holding the hands of their daughter Brenda. He smiles at you and you feel warmth flood your face.

---

101   "Where have you been to look so beautiful?"
102   "Why are you going to church dressed like that?"

"Good morning, Phionah."

You allow your lips to unfurl into a smile. "Good morning, Ssebo."

You stifle the urge to kneel down before him as you answer when you see his wife's lips tighten further. You remember her strict command delivered to you via Rose: "Never kneel before my husband again if you cannot wear decent clothes!"

You felt awkward, standing before a man while you spoke to him. If anyone from your village, Kyalokyalizo, ever saw you do so, they would tell you they now knew why you were still unmarried.

You grab Rose's hands and walk to her white Mark II on unsteady feet. Now more than ever, you have to see Pastor to present your seed so that you got your marriage breakthrough.

You slip into the second last seat at the main entrance of the vast church hall, careful not to make any noise and draw attention to yourself. You had left Rose still searching for a parking spot in the spacious compound filled up with all types of cars.

Pastor was preaching. His baritone voice booming through the imposing speakers placed at the four corners of the rectangular hall. You sat down and crossed your legs at the ankles, placing the yellow clutch bag on the seat to your right. You bowed your head and closed your eyes.

Father Lord, thank you for granting me the grace to come to your house today.

You felt tranquility settle over you and your mind cleared. For a few seconds, all you were conscious of was the sublimity you always felt when you first entered the house of God. Gradually though, Pastor's voice stole through your fibres, flowing like sizzling oil over your nerves, leaving you burning with ferocious sensations. You opened your eyes wide in a bid to erase the image of Taata Brenda smiling down at you that your mind had painted in a flash of light.

Pastor continued speaking. Righteousness. "The Word is very clear; you can only be established in righteousness. Do you want to be untouchable by the devil?" he asked.

A number of voices shouted, "Yes!"

"Become righteous!" was the immediate answer.

The keyboard pianist played a crescendo note to the sound of fervent clapping intermingled with shouts of "Amen" and "Alleluia" from the congregation.

You do not participate. Your mind is preoccupied with the vision of Taata Brenda that you had a few minutes back. The last time Pastor prayed for you, he had given you a handkerchief, which he had told you to place under your pillow each time you were going to sleep. He had said that you would dream about your prospective husbands. Since then, you had started getting these dreams of Taata Brenda. Since then you had started feeling tense whenever you were in his presence, noticing how good-looking he was.

You close your eyes once again and allow your mind to draw his portrait. He is about five feet tall, with broad shoulders that pulled taut the beautiful shirts he loved to wear. Today he had been in blue. Bright colours were one of his trademarks. His skin was the colour of dark cooking chocolate—under heat it melted to a silken smoothness that shimmered like a mirage. He had high bushy eyebrows over his wide set eyes. His most distinguishing feature though were the wide full lips, which was a canopy for ivory coloured teeth set in a blue-black gum with a gap in-between the upper front teeth. His smile always unfurled like a hibiscus flower, drawing the viewer in.

"Numbers 23:23…someone read that."

You kept your eyes shut and head bowed. You started rocking yourself back and forth in your seat and beads of sweat perched on your forehead. Your knees pressed hard together. Your lips moved as you mouthed silent words.

"I pull down every lustful thought in my head in the name of Jesus. I rebuke you Satan who is the source of every temptation. There is no condemnation for those who are in Christ Jesus therefore every weapon of the devil fashioned against be broken now in Jesus' name. Every sexual thought in my head and my heart be wiped off now by the blood of Jesus."

The sound of rustling paper distracts you from your feverish silent prayer and your eyes pop wide. You raise trembling hands to your forehead but jerk them back before you can touch your face.

A loud voice reads out: "There is no divination against Israel…"

"I need your help father, please help me!" you cry out in silence.

Pastor moves to where the praise and worship team sits. You follow his brisk movements with anxiety. "I feel a miracle coming!" he shouts before a young woman falls at his feet howling and thrashing on the tiled floor. Ushers rush to pick her up and carry her into the side door that leads to his office. She will be the first to be prayed for today. For a moment, you wonder who she is and what her prayer request is.

Pastor continues walking down the hall. His eyes searching through the congregation like a laser beam slicing through human flesh. "The spirit of God is here and he is pouring out blessings!" he shouts again.

Ululations and thunderous clapping receive his pronunciation. The choir breaks out into song. The congregation gets frenzied with some members howling, others speaking in tongues, young women falling at the feet of Pastor and thrashing around on the floor. Ushers carry away the ones Pastor points at. You know that they are put inside the prayer room, which was opposite Pastor's office. It was from there that the ones who had come with seed offerings would be chosen to go and see Pastor. If you had no offering, you never got to see Pastor in private. When Pastor was almost reaching you, you stood before him, clapping and shouting "alleluia" at the top of your voice. You had to see him today. You were tired of having the disturbing feelings about Taata Brenda. He stopped right in front of you and when you would have fallen, he held your hands. You stood swaying, your eyes closed until you felt the hands of the ushers lifting you up. They took you right across the room, down the long corridor that led to the prayer room and Pastor's offices, through his outer office into his private office. Everything blacked out.

When you next open your eyes, you are lying on a white cotton cloth spread in the middle of the room. The room is painted black. The only other colour is the cloth on which you are lying and the mauve tiles on the floor. The brown envelope that contains your seed is by your side. It takes you a moment to realize you are completely naked. You have been stripped of even the Moonight Butt Lifter Shorts. It is hot in the room. There is a ringing in your head. You sit up slowly, using your hands to cover your nakedness, keeping your legs spread out before you. You realize the heat from the room is from the blazing fireplace right in front of you. The smoke escapes through a chimney. The question as to where the wet panties of the girls whom Pastor prays for go, is answered. Instead of wood, the panties burn in the fireplace, giving off a gagging smell. You cover your mouth with your hands, feeling the first stirrings of fear. Pastor rises up slowly from his squatting position opposite you. You hadn't realized that it was him squatting in front of the fireplace, feeding the panties into the fire. He holds your gaze, a smile tugging at the sides of his mouth as he slowly untangles himself to his full height. You shake your head in a bid to clear it of the confusing images.

"Hello Phionah," he says, his voice nothing more than a whisper. It is the voice of Taata Brenda. You start. When next you look at him, he is Taata Brenda standing before you. He smiles. You shake your head.

"Today you will receive your breakthrough," he says, this time it's Pastor's voice. You stare, fear holding you immobile. He crumbles onto the ground, and you watch in astonishment as he crawls over to you, holding your gaze. You are mesmerized, not looking away from his eyes. When he reaches you, he remains on his belly. It's only then you realize that he too is stark naked.

"Give me the seed and receive your breakthrough," he whispers. You feel with your hands behind you until your fingers touch the envelope and draw it to you, still holding his gaze. You offer him the envelope with nerveless fingers, flinching from the coldness of his touch. With a whoosh sound, he pushes you onto your back and crawls onto you. His skin is ice cold against you and you break his gaze to look down at your body. The sight of a black snake, instead of Pastor, slithering over your lower body is the last you see before everything goes black again.

Regina Asinde, author of the poetry collection *Shards of Brokenness* (2019), has been published in a number of anthologies: *Fire on the Mountain* (Dovesong Educational 2018), *Wondering and Wandering of Hearts* (FEMRITE Publications 2017), *A Thousand Voices Rising* (Babishai Niwe Foundation 2012), *The BodaBoda Anthem* (Babishai Niwe Foundation 2015), *Moonscapes: An anthology of poetry and short stories* (African Writers Trust 2016), *Dear Nev, An anthology of Contemporary East Africa writings* (Word-O-Mart / AWT 2018) and various online magazines. Regina lives in Kampala with her husband and children. She is the Managing Director of Wordsmith Publications Uganda Limited.

Fish Skeletons
Dilman Dila

THE WAVES swept through the lake casting shells and chuff across the shore. Women bent washing clothes by the bay as children threw sand at each other diving into the lake naked. Boys stood by the rock cliffs with hooks immersed in water waiting for a catch. Fisher men cleaned their nets standing by the boats safely landed by the bay. The stench from the rotting wood in the now defunct fish market ruled the air. The noise went on like school children out to play at break time, each raising their voice to be heard. Different conversations were flying about in the space. Eseza sat by her mother's papyrus-roofed fish stall washing utensils as she switched listenership from one conversation to another. Mwalimu Juma was at his usual spot by the edge of the mosque veranda talking with Kyeswa who was cleaning his net by the bay.

"If they hadn't brought those men, I'd be having a new boat now," claimed Kyeswa waving up the tail end of his net. His small upper body, shirtless.

"You see that's a government policy and you can't challenge it."

"But it's our lake too. If they close us out, where will we eat?"

"That's the problem with the law. It looks at everyone not some people."

"We'll beat the system. They'll soon be jumping onto other things."

"Not when it's an economic gain," laughed off Mwalimu as he rolled up the hem of his ageing brown *kanzu*.[103]

Business had slowed down at the Bugonga landing site unlike before. Fishermen no longer came in big droves. Only the familiar faces stayed. There were scarcely any new random faces in the morning of traders rushing in to buy fish. Their noise had always woken Eseza up. Motorists had the advantage of taking the bigger fish since it could not be carried by an individual. Women from Kitoro market walked down Bugonga hill in their slippers and lesus wrapped around their waists to the landing site with buckets mounted on their heads in groups of not more than four. Only early birds could get big fish. No one ever picked small ones. They did not make good soup, they argued.

First were the big iced vans, the ones that never smelled of fish even when they were fully packed. They stopped coming. Even Farouq left. He was the only one who had the big weighing scales that could carry the big fish. Mulongo's boats always attracted the buyers from hotels. Her fish was a price higher than that of others. She had six white boats and the hoteliers thought she was cleaner than the other fishmongers who wore blood-stained fish smelling overalls. At the beginning of last month, she had come back to the site, something she rarely did, in fact Eseza had no memory of her ever

103   Traditional men's clothing worn: a white cotton tunic worn over a pair of trousers.

coming back in the afternoon. She went to the chairman's office and spent a long time there. When she came out, she ordered her fishermen to ignite the boats and take them to Kigungu. She was done working here. She went yelling out to everyone who cared to listen, "I'll find market somewhere else. This is our lake. You found us here and you'll leave us here."

She quarreled with her lean arms folding in different shapes in the air. It is said she would always be drinking in her bar after selling fish in the morning. It was hard to know when she was sober and when she was not. Eseza had once eavesdropped on a conversation between her mother and Maama Nyombi talking about her.

"How's she able to follow up on her business if she's always drunk?"

"She's a witch! Mulogo! Who doesn't know that?" sighed Maama Nyombi with her lips stretched backwards.

Then the other motorists followed suit. They no longer came on a daily. They would come thrice a week. They said better fish was at Kigungu. Even Mulokole left. Eseza found her to be the only sober person at the landing site. She had never seen her drunk like other women. She always stayed in her shop. At the beginning of this month on Sunday, a truck had parked in front of her shop in the evening around seven pm and they had loaded all her belongings. She left. Fish business ended earlier these days. This was an opportune moment to meet up at Maama Nyombi's bar to drink *waragi*.[104] At first, Maama Eseza would send her to get sachets of *waragi* from Maama Nyombi and drink them from home. But now that she also had some more time, she gave up on drinking from home. She went to the bar herself staying there even longer. "Lock the house," is all she ever said on coming back home drunk without adding another word.

The fishing site had become a shadow of its former self. There was not much fish to sell. The market was closed by ten am unlike before when it went on till midday. It became a common sight seeing people leaving, and no one asked why anymore. Only children gathered around the truck to run after it as it drove off. Other people showed up no more at the shoreline. No one bothered to ask. Kawooya had since turned into a barber. He did not bother much about fishing. In the afternoon, fewer men gathered at Lukyamuzi's workshop under the Mutuba tree to review the Champions League matches as they unveiled.

⋙⋘

KABUGO was the first victim. He had gone fishing that night when he was ambushed by the marine patrol. They confiscated his boat engine and fishing net. He was only seen after two days. His wife got a call from a person who identified himself as Afande. He called to let her know that her husband had been detained for fishing illegally on the lake without a license.

104   a distilled spirit made from bananas or millet, popular in Uganda.

However, she had to pay for his bail. Later that day, Kabugo was released. He sat at Lukyamuzi's workshop in the audience of a number of fishermen to narrate his experience.

"The men beat me. *Bali bakuba!*" He stared at his fellow fishermen as if he was addressing a press conference at Serena Hotel. His hands clasped together. "I didn't know how serious it was until I was dragged into their boat." With a breaking voice, he lifted his shirt and the cane straps on his back crossed each other like a crossword puzzle. "They beat me. Ho!" he paused. And sobbed. "The lake is no longer ours. They took it over."

There was a short silence before murmurs sprang up from the gathering.

"But how can they do that to us when our forefathers all lived on this lake?" one of them asked.

"Who do they think they are?" another shot in.

"So now, how will we feed our families?" inquired a cracking voice from behind. Few heads turned to look at him. Many of them were facing down as if they were following a script of what was being said.

"The government is taking full control of the lake. They say we've drained it and there is no more fish," mumbled Kabugo, his voice shaking as if he wasn't sure of what he was saying.

"Fish are a natural resource; they take care of themselves. Unless they are going to sell the lake," reasoned another man leaning against one of the abandoned boats under construction. By now, women from the shanty restaurants and bars had also joined. Eseza's mother too. The meeting carried on in measured tones as if they feared that the soldiers were nearer to tap what they said.

⸎⸎⸎

"I DON'T know what I will do," said Maama Eseza as she served dinner.

"What? Why, mama?"

"Things are getting harder by the day. Didn't you hear Kabugo tell his story?"

"Does that mean I won't be going back to school?"

"Go and ask your father that question. I am also trying. What don't you see?"

The lone solar bulb hanging in their one roomed wooden house was becoming dimmer by the passing minute. It hung on top of the long netted curtain partitioning the room. One side was the bedroom and the other, the general room where they kept the homeware and merchandise. A green bucket of deep-fried fish sat quietly in the corner next to the pole that had been eaten by termites. Mother and daughter ate the matooke served with groundnut stew mixed with fish as they talked. Bones were discarded on a side plate before they could be served to Police, the dog. No one ever claimed real ownership of Police. He was a public asset in which everyone had interest. Police was particular about homes where he would eat food and where he would not. He knew where he was welcome and where he was not. His evenings usually ended at Maama Eseza's where he was assured of something prepared for him to eat. Recently, when the municipal council was killing off all rabid dogs, the chairman had invited the veterinarian to vaccinate him. That's how he survived.

The last time Eseza heard about her father was when rumor was rich with word that he was marrying. Not just getting a woman. A wife. He had never visited them since they left. Being a lumberjack, he spent most of his time in forests, harvesting wood. Often times, he would be away from home for a month but he would eventually come back.

One day when he came, he was drunk. Much as Eseza's parents quarreled, they seldom fought. This particular evening was different. Eseza's father was speaking at the top of his voice beating her mother. He accused her of adultery and bringing shame to his name. He staggered into the house and threw out her belongings. He ordered her out of the house. Maama Eseza's pleas fell on infertile ground as he insisted on her leaving his house. Her mother told her to get her shoes and follow her. He sent them off.

Eseza and her mother spent that night at Mrs. Semakula's place at the trading centre. Maama Eseza used to refer to Mrs. Semakula as *senga,* her aunt. Eseza had never established whether she was her real aunt or not. Her husband was away. He had gone to attend the last funeral rites of a friend who had passed on sometime back. The two had some time to talk uninterrupted.

Upon entering the house, Maama Eseza had burst out crying letting her brown checked suitcase fall unattended. She hugged her. In between her sobs, she would remind Mrs. Semakua, "*Omusajja angobye.*[105] My husband has sent me away." And she would cry some more gripping her dress to dry the tears on her bowed head as if she was ashamed of the act. Eseza distanced herself from her mother and watched in grief as the two women spoke.

"Did you fight?"

"No! He came with a made-up mind and that was it."

"I thought he had stopped beating you."

"But he's been changing lately. I hear he got another woman."

"Is he still providing for the family?"

"Only when he's around."

"Have you talked to his friends?"

"Uhhm! Whom can you trust? They are all the same."

"Abasajja! Men! You can never know what he's plotting next."

"I thought yours was okay?"

"It's never as you think. Men carry secrets like us women."

"Uhm!"

---

105   "The man is coming"

"He keeps you around but never lets you in."

"At least yours keeps you around."

"If only I knew his next of kin."

They kept quiet. Eseza looked at the two women and wondered what more they were keeping away from each other. They had not bothered sending her to bed as they talked. She kept her eyes on the candle struggling to keep aflame in an empty Omo bucket. Their conversation had begun immediately the food had been served. She had hungrily eaten her food in silence as they talked. Her mother kept stealing glances at her until Mrs. Semakula addressed her as another woman. Whatever that was supposed to mean!

In the morning when they woke up, Mrs Semakula had already prepared tea. Eseza had not slept off fully. Her sleep had been interrupted by nightmares of her father chasing her and her mother. She had imagined him following them up to Mrs. Semakula's and beating them up. She feared her father for his strong arms. She remembered the incident that had happened during the previous long school holiday. It was a Tuesday afternoon when her mother was away. She went out to play *kakebe* at Namayanja's place in the neighbourhood. There were many children on holiday and that made it even better. The game was on and Mirembe was the one in charge of guarding the *kakebe*. Her role was to make sure no one flung it away and yet she had to dig everyone out of their hideout. For the past twenty minutes or more, she had not succeeded. Instead, Namayanja had stealthily come out of her hiding and flung the tin away giving another chance for those who had been singled out to go back and hide.

Eseza was hiding behind the kitchen at Namayanja's place. There were a number of banana trees that made her invisible. She hung in there as the game continued. She could inaudibly hear the goings-on. Later, Mirembe called her out, "Eseza, wherever you are come out, your dad is calling you." She went on about five times but Eseza thought this was a tactic to get her out. She refused to respond. After all, her dad was never home. At least not during daytime. Next was Namayanja, she also called her out. She repeated the same words as Mirembe's. Namayanja could be believed. She was older than they all were and she, most times, was serious. She crawled out of her hiding only to see her father summoning her from a distance. When she saw the candid eye, the straight face and his long hand beckoning her home, she knew all was not well. She felt her heart beat faster than she had ever imagined. She no longer felt her feet touch the ground. Her nose was profusely sweating, and for no justifiable reason, tears welled up in her small eyes.

"Why did you leave the house open? You want thieves to come and steal my property? Did you buy it for me? Lie down! Flat." He went behind the house towards the coffee trees and broke off two branches only to return plucking off the leaves. With his heavy right foot stepping on both her legs and his left hand pressing her head down, the rest was a heavy downpour of *kiboko*[106] on her buttocks. That was the last time Eseza ever went out playing with other children. She had a fear that her father would return when she was away and he would beat her again.

⁂

THEY arrived at Nakiwogo aboard the shaky yellow ferry. She had always wanted to have a feel of it. Her mother did not say much. She was staring away in the distance looking at the endless lake with her hands holding on tight to the suitcase. The ferry was so loaded with charcoal and firewood that there was hardly any space left to sit. They squeezed in with other people. "Make sure you don't fall," was all her mother said during the two-hour voyage. Mrs. Semakula had given her money she unrolled from a knot on her *gomesi*[107] as they left.

Aunt Kate did not know they were coming. She had moved from the place Eseza's mother knew. That was about two years ago when she last came by. They were directed to the fish market where she ran a stall. On arrival, she was so excited to see them. Aunt Kate asked her colleagues to help her out with her stall. She went with Maama Eseza to her home. It was a few meters away from Nakiwogo Primary School. Eseza saw the P.6 classroom and inside her heart she knew, she was going to study there. She did not tell anyone about it. And it came to pass. She studied the last two terms of P.6 there. Aunt Kate paid her fees. It was a government-run school and that made it affordable. In the evening after school, she would go to Aunt Kate's stall for the key so she could go and prepare supper at home. She did not have many friends. The only person she talked to was Phina. She was in S2 at Entebbe S.S. Eseza also wanted to go there after her P7.

Soon her mother got herself a stall at Bugonga. Aunt Kate had borrowed money as capital for her from Nakiwogo Tweyambe Women Savings Group where she was a member. Her mother had also become a member, but did not have enough credit to qualify her as a borrower for the money she needed to set up the stall.

The stall she bought used to belong to a one Nakazibwe who was moving-on to work in a salon in Wandegeya in Kampala. Having acquired the skill through her sister, Maama Eseza traded in fish as she attended school.

Eseza would help her mother run the stall on weekends and on holidays. In her long P7 holiday, she took up to manning the stall full time. The fish had now become scarce. There was rumor of the government taking over the lake. Fishermen no longer went alone but rather in groups to cast their nets.

Her mother had come close to paying back the loan until the incident of the market woman. The market woman she used to supply her fish to had

---

106   a whip made from hippopotamus hide, traditionally used in Kenya and Tanzania.
107   a traditional women's clothing worn in Uganda, typically made of brightly colored cotton or silk and worn with a headscarf.

stopped coming, disappearing with her money. She started taking the fish to Kampala herself. "The money won't bring itself to me. Enough of these fish skeletons." she had said.

One evening when she came back home from Kampala, tired, she joined Eseza at the stall while speaking to herself; "*Ekyo nakyo kiwedde!*" She was happy. She had finally paid off the debt. She would get lost in thought only to break into a smile. There was something more she wanted to say but would not come out.

Words have a tendency to be scarce when you need them in plenty. They come like a whirling wind. Stormy. They quickly leave as soon as they come. They go to places where they hide all the time. You would assume they stay in forests but that would be an overestimate. You send them to the desert but that is too long a journey for them to keep coming back. They have a tendency to move in rotation, lurking in the face of your mind but too hard for the tongue to say. That is what words do. They skulk around the neck like a beaded necklace; calm, poised and laid back. They keep looking at you. They leisurely creep into the mind when the thoughts are out playing. They tickle the brain membrane painting pictures of cities that visas have been slow at linking you up to. They drag you like dreams, from your point of interest to another. From that which is known to the unknown.

"I think you will be joining secondary next year, Eseza," she said with a calm voice.

The Shopkeeper Is Melting
Dilman Dila

OTONG wore a straw hat to ward off the heat rays from the sun. Every time a car sped by, dust rose like an angry cloud of bow flies and hung in the air for several minutes, painting the town red, turning the vegetation bloody, making it dangerous to breath. He wrapped a white handkerchief with yellow flowers on his nose to filter the air. This lent him a robber's costume, but no one wondered about the identity of the masked man, who was hurrying back to his shop at the extreme end of the street, after lunch in a cramped restaurant at the opposite end. The ill-fitting shoes made him waddle.

To make up the town, a dozen buildings straddled the dirt road like heaps of bricks in the ruins of a future civilization. Tailors, cobblers and idlers squeezed themselves into the tiny shadows of the verandas, a few had umbrellas fashioned out of cardboard boxes. Rickety stalls dotted the market with a struggle for survival. They overflowed with fresh fruits and vegetables, whose colourfulness the dry season had failed to wipe off. Similarly, the odour of dust failed to kill off the aroma of the traditional snacks and fast foods, kabalagala, bolingo, gonja, cassava chips. Nor could the heat subdue the chatter of the women who ran these stands. They gossiped at the top of their voices, speaking to each other from across the street, filling the town with laughter. The men, on the other hand, were gloomy in their shops, though they had fans to cool them down and radios to pass the time.

Sweat-drenched Otong. He looked as though he had fallen into a pond. His *kitenge* shirt stuck to his back like a filthy rag. Irritated, he ripped it off with such anger that two buttons jumped away. Still, no one took note of him. It was okay for men to walk about half naked. He flaunted his body for it had all the indicators of a successful businessman, the flabby breasts, the huge potbelly, the wag of his buttocks. However, even after taking off the shirt, the wet irritation did not relent. His trousers dripped, like that of a child who had delayed running to the toilet. His shop waited only fifty metres away, but, unable to bear the wet pants anymore, he took them off.

Now, the market stirred like water in a pan finally starting to boil. The women fell quiet, plunging the noon into a sudden hush. The petty craftsmen gawped, as Otong struggled to rip the pants off. He tried to do it without first taking off his shoes, or sitting down. He hopped about. He staggered. He fought to maintain balance. He fell, throwing up a cloud of dust. Pain shot through his back. The town held its breath.

Finally, the pants came off. He draped the clothes over his shoulders and hurried on to his shop. He did not feel naked. Having failed to find fitting underwear, he wore a pair of red soccer shorts. Footballers strutted in this kind of attire in front of thousands of people. He did not feel naked until the eyes of his neighbours unnerved him, as though he were in a World Cup final, a billion people watching, a question frothing on their mouths. Why does he waddle naked in the streets?

In response, to tell them that he was exercising to cut weight, he started to jog. He realized that he was instead dancing. His breasts, his potbelly and his protuberant buttocks vibrated to the rhythm of his feet. He waited for them to laugh. They did not. Pity glowed in their eyes, and he heard the phrase ringing in their heads—only mad people dance naked in the streets.

He stopped, a grin frozen on his face. He could not speak. A hot stone sat in his throat. He could not swallow it away to allow the words to come out, to explain that it was too hot to wear clothes. He pointed at the sky, blaming it, but they did not follow his finger. Their eyes stayed fixed on him. He thought the women were looking at his shorts, searching for the bulge of manhood, and, seeing nothing, finally getting an explanation for his loneliness.

The thought prompted him to run, very fast back to his shop. He fumbled with the keys. He could not find the right one. He felt his neighbours clustering, like crows gathering at the abattoir, watching him. He turned to yell at them to go away, but there was nobody behind him. Only their eyes had followed him. Finally, mercifully, the padlock snapped open. He vanished into the shop and locked himself inside, shutting off the world.

He staggered into the back room, where he lived, and collapsed into the bed. The window was closed, allowing in only a little light. Half of the room hoarded merchandise for his shop. In the other half he had squeezed in a wardrobe, a cupboard, a twenty-one-inch TV, a new Sony music system, and the bed, which was too small for him. He buried his head under the pillow, but he could not shut out the voices. They floated in from the street, faint and unclear, yet he understood everything. *He is bewitched! Why does he live alone? Where is his family? Why does no one ever visit him?* He thought he heard the nurse asking, *Why has he failed to find a woman to marry?* He once dated this nurse, but broke it off when he discovered that she was a Gishu, the same tribe as Sera, his dead lover. Maybe they were from the same clan, or same village. *Didn't you see him dancing naked? I tell you, he is cursed!*

He pressed the pillow tight over his ears. Still, the voices drilled into his head and echoed in his skull like the chatter of monkeys. They gave him a headache. He turned to the Sony for help, inserted a CD with his favourite song, his therapy song, *Dole W'omwana*, and played sweet sounds of a lonely housewife begging her husband to stay home and make love to her. It drowned out the voices, cured the headache, and it lured Sera out of her grave.

He used to sing it with her in a ragtag band. Panya Mziki. They played *kadongo kamu*[108], mixing oral storytelling with guitar tunes and raw percussions, crooning slow rhythms that nevertheless made their audiences to dance with vigour. He played a guitar, which he had found in a garbage bin and glued together. He had perfected his skill in those long, cold nights when he slept in the streets to escape from his evil mother. One such night, Sera heard him play. She was with her elder brother, Masaba, who had a biscuit tin drum. They were about his age, seventeen, but had been street musicians for nearly ten years. On hearing his guitar, Sera plucked sweet lyrics out of the thin air. The currents of her voice swept him into a sea of fairy tales. He could not take his eyes off the gap between her front teeth. Her skin shone in the moonlight like a pearl of ebony. Her sweat wafted to him like a perfume, bewitching him. She invited him into their band. She believed his skill would help her become a superstar. When her parents urged him to live with them, for his guitar would increase their income, he finally saw a chance to permanently escape from his mother. He found a new home, a new family, a friend, and a lover. Over the next three years, they enjoyed a wild and vagabond youth, riding from one obscure town to another, staging shows in the street corners for a few coins, he on the guitar, Masaba on the tin drum, Sera doing the vocals and the dancing, sometimes to an audience of one or two, sometimes to a hundred,

108 A traditional Ugandan music genre, typically played on a traditional string instrument called the adungu. It is a form of music that is played by the Baganda people, who are the largest ethnic group in Uganda. The lyrics of kadongo kamu songs are often in Luganda, the language spoken by the Baganda people, and the songs typically tell stories or convey messages about culture, history, or daily life.

often singing the crowd pleaser, *Dole W'omwana.*

Now, just over a decade later, the song was a time machine. In the nine minutes it ran, he relived those years in paradise with Sera and Masaba. He jumped onto the bed, playing an imaginary guitar, and he sang, and he danced, as he ripped off the hanky and the straw hat, as he wiped his body clean with a towel. He turned on the fan to soothe his body with a cool breeze. He drank an icy bottle of Coke, holding it like a mike, and he sang, and he danced, and he floated in clouds of long dead happiness.

The moment was short-lived, however. Another song blasted into the room, another song that they had loved to perform. *Dipo Nazigala.* It came from a long way off, booming from squeaky speakers that drowned out his Sony, a high-pitched noise that destroyed the cool sounds of his CD. He increased the volume of his system, but the squeaky speaker steadily grew louder as it moved toward his shop. He thought it was a hawker using the song to draw attention to his wares. It ruined his reverie of Sera. He hit the pause button, sat on the bed and waited for the hawker to pass by. To his horror, the peddler stopped right outside his shop, and *Dipo Nazigala* boomed into his ears like a hammer crushing a rock.

He stomped out, wearing nothing but the soccer shorts, to yell at the hawker to go away. He saw an old, rusty pickup, a huge pile of sweet potatoes on its bed. Two tattered speakers, strapped to the roof, spewed the hiss of a tape. Before he could scream out his rage, the hawker turned to him. Their eyes met. A block of ice formed in his stomach.

He fell back into the shop, dizzy, his vision blurred. He leaned on the counter for support. He closed his eyes, but he could not get rid of the afterimage, of the face that stared at him from behind the wheel of an old rusty pick up.

Was he hallucinating?

The rage he had bottled up for a decade oozed out of his eyes like the tears he had never shed for Sera, his first love. It could not be her brother out there. It simply could not be. It was a hallucination. A trick of the sun.

He wiped his eyes, braced himself, and peeped, like a thief. He saw the ghost standing beside the truck, staring back at him with the same kind of shock that he could feel on his face. He wore a striped tie and a threadbare coat, but not a bead of sweat showed on his skin. Only a ghost could wear a coat and stay cool in this heat. But it could not be a ghost, for the nurse danced as she admired the potatoes, as she spoke to the hawker. He was real. He was Masaba. Older, with a long goatee, but still the scrawny tin drummer who had once been his best friend.

Otong slunk back into the shop, dazed, his heart pounding like the hoofs of a zebra fleeing a lion. His hands trembled. His body shook with emotions he could not identify. He again locked the door, as though that would keep him safe from the ghost that came riding in an old truck full of potatoes. He tiptoed to the back room, afraid that Masaba would hear his footsteps, and collapsed onto the bed.

He had not been able to save his love, and now *Dipo Nazigala* smashed through the walls to fill the air with remorse. He floated in a dark sea of sorrow, of rage, the waves slamming against him, trying to smash him into pieces. He stuffed his fingers into his ears, but the song drilled in, making his brain to swirl in agony. He screamed. His legs kicked. His eyes closed tight. He wished he could close his ears as well.

Dipo Nazigala. I gave up drinking. Did alcohol kill Sera?

He crawled under the bed, seeking safety in the darkness, snuggling amid the shoes and basins like a child hiding from an angry mother. Still, he could not muffle the song. It hovered in the air like an evil spirit looking for a home. *Please God, please, please, stop the song.*

A miracle happened. God answered his prayer. The song stopped so suddenly that for a moment, he thought he had gone deaf. Gradually, he began to hear drumbeats, which he recognized as his heart. Sweat slipped off his nose and splashed on the floor. It sounded like the shattering of glass.

Did Sera's tears make the same sound?

Something happened in the night, something that had made her cry. He had not immediately noticed the tears when he awoke. A drop of sunshine painted her nose gold and made her cheeks to radiate. He picked up his guitar and played *Dole W'omwana*, hoping she would rouse from sleep and add her voice to the beauty of the morning. Only when Masaba tried to shake her awake did they realize that she was dead. There were no signs of the cause, just tear stains on her face. Whatever had made her cry had killed her. The tears left white, salty tracks running down her cheeks, which meant she had cried in an upright position, and another set running into her ears, which meant she had also cried while supine. Why? What killed her?

We cannot go to the police, Masaba had said. They will blame us.

Otong had nodded in agreement. She had died so suddenly, so mysteriously. Was it from alcohol? Was it a natural cause, like a heart attack, or a sickness they knew nothing about? Maybe a maniac had crept upon them in the night and raped her, and suffocated her?

Many years later, Otong attended a public seminar in which a doctor talked about alcohol misuse and sudden arrhythmic cardiac deaths. He never understood the big words, but they showed him another possible cause. Though barely out of her diapers, Sera drank hard, maybe in an attempt to wash away the anger against her parents, who had forced her into the street as a little girl, first as a beggar, and then as a musician. Otong used not to drink before meeting her, and that morning, as he watched the white tracks of tears on her face, he swore never to touch the bottle again. At that time, he did not think that it had directly killed her, but if he had not been drunk, maybe he would have heard her cry, and saved her.

But saved her from what? It had to be a murder. Nothing else could explain her sudden death. The police would think they did it, maybe accidentally, but that would not save them from jail.

She eloped with a stranger, Masaba told their parents when they returned home the following week, after they had secretly buried her. *We don't know where she is.*

Frowning, his mother had turned to Otong and said, *I thought she loved you.*

Otong heard those words long after he had run away from his second home. They gave him nightmares as he tramped from town to town, doing odd jobs, drifting six hundred kilometres from the east to the north, into this small town, where he started a vegetable stall, which then grew into a successful retail shop, giving him a new life. Putting an end to the nightmares. He thought he had escaped.

He rubbed his eyes to dislodge the image of her tear-stained face.

How had Masaba found him? That he came as a hawker meant he lived nearby. Had he also fled his home, or had he come searching, sniffing at Otong's trail all the way from the east? Had he been close by all this time?

Otong lay still, listening, waiting for knocks on the door. Surely, Masaba had to come knocking. He had to, after running into a face he had not seen in ten years. A face he had once loved. He had to come to the door. Otong turned off the fan, afraid that its buzz would muffle the knocks. He listened. His sweat splashed on the floor.

Did her tears make the same sound?

Please God, let him knock. He cried. Just as he had wished for the song to end, he now prayed for a knock to vanquish the silence. The longer it stretched, the louder the splashing became, each splash hit his eardrums with the force of a hammer pounding a nail.

Was it a coincidence that Masaba had walked back into his life after all these years, or had Masaba searched for him? Had he come for a happily-ever-after reunion, or had he come to explain the mysterious events of Sera's last night? Had he found out what caused the tears? Will he confess to making her cry?

Splash!

Please knock!

What will happen after he walks in? Will they fight each other in the apocalyptic battle that they had avoided for a decade? Will he tell Otong what happened after Otong had fled, that he had confessed and spent several years in prison? The questions whirred in his head like a grain miller.

Masaba did not knock.

Splash!

The sound of her tears falling on the floor. Then silence. Like the silence at the beginning of their performances, just after Otong had strummed on his guitar to alert the audience that a song is coming, just before she sang the first notes. That silence.

Her voice floated into the shop.

Otong stiffened, thinking her ghost had finally awoken. The streaks of light falling in from the cracks in the window looked like the beams on which she rode from the grave to his room. He watched the dust float in the sunrays. He saw her face in a particle, peering at him from a window at the other side. Smiling.

Otong scrambled from under the bed, and scampered out through the back door, into the back street, which was nothing but a bush, and he would have kept running if he had not tripped on a stone. He fell smack on the ground.

Her voice swirled all around him, in a high-pitched tone that could not be human. It came from the squeaky speakers on the potato truck. He had forgotten that song, one of their original compositions. *Amitho i kende*. I Love Only You. A fan had recorded it on his home stereo. The sound quality was horrible, and after all these years painful to hear, but her voice was still sweet. The notes of the guitar sliced through the fat on his chest and pierced his heart. The biscuit tin drum throbbed in his skull like a headache. In the duet she played a wife groaning for love, while he played a husband eloping with another woman. In one verse, she moaned that something was wrong with her because no man has ever loved her. On hearing this, Otong grabbed a log and charged at the hawker, her brother, once his best friend.

He had loved her. Masaba knew it. Why then should he play this duet in which she weeps that no man has ever loved her? Why?

Otong went round the building and burst into the street, brandishing the log like a medieval warrior showing off his club to intimidate the enemy. Masaba stood by the truck, serving potatoes to two women. One danced to the music, the other pressed her fingers into her ears, unable to bear the noise.

Otong stopped. The scene confused him. Masaba chatted up the women as he filled a bag, seemingly unperturbed that he had run into Otong, just as the heat seemed not to bother him. When the bag was full, he washed his hands with water from a bottle and wiped them on a towel before taking the woman's money. He carefully separated the notes from the coins, packed the notes in a coat pocket while the coins went into a pouch strapped to his belt. He might have been a teller in a cozy bank. Then he washed his hands again, meticulously, before proceeding to fill the second woman's bag. How can he be nonchalant while playing that song? He had kept the tape all these years. It meant he had not gotten over her death. He still mourned her. Why then does he continue his business as if he had not recognized Otong? Why does he play that song? That song in which Sera moans about a love she cannot have!

Otong charged. Masaba looked up. The cool demeanour, the picture of a trouble-free banker doing business in an air-conditioned room, collapsed.

His jaws dropped. But he did not run. The women fled, on seeing a naked fat man charging at them. The street froze. The seconds it took to reach the truck seemed an hour.

As Otong neared, Masaba regained his composure. He put on the cool face of a salesman, smiled broadly, and spread out both arms for a hug. Otong wanted to stop, to throw down the log and fall into Masaba's arms for a happy reunion. But the song kept playing, Sera cried to him from beyond the grave, urging him to avenge her death.

He swung the club, too early. Missed. Masaba fled.

Otong did not chase. He attacked the speakers. He smashed them off the roof of the truck. They fell on the road. He pounded them until his fingers hurt, but they did not shut up. Though in pieces, wires still attached them to the radio in the cabin. They emitted a stream of static that reached Otong's ears like the voice of Sera. Otong wrenched out the radio and pulped it too, finally plunging the street into silence.

He felt more than saw Masaba charging, as though activated by the sudden silence. Otong pirouetted, swinging the club. It smashed into flesh. Masaba fell.

Otong felt good. He had wanted to do it for a decade. He suspected that Masaba had killed her. It had taken him a long time to come to this conclusion. It solidified the more he thought about Masaba's quick decision to bury her, and then to deceive his parents. But why would Masaba have killed her? No motivation made sense. Still, Otong needed to blame someone for her death.

Masaba hurled a rock. Otong was too slow to dodge the missile. It hit his forehead. He crashed to the ground, seeing daylight stars. Next thing he knew, Masaba was sitting on his chest, pummeling him. The anger behind the blows told Otong that Masaba had also wanted to do it all these years, that Masaba blamed him for her death.

They fought, rolling about the dirt road, punching each other, trying to kill each other. The town folk did not allow them that luxury. Several men rushed in and separated them, and dragged them to the office of the Local Council Chairman, an elected civilian who helped the police to keep law and order.

The Chairman spoke to him, but Otong could not make sense of the words. They bubbled in his ears like a strange language. The Chairman then turned to Masaba, whose coat was torn and drenched in blood. Masaba replied. Otong wanted to understand their conversation. He tried to make sense of their words, but he had momentarily lost the intelligence to understand speech.

The Chairman took them to the police post. It being a new town, two shipping containers had been cut up to create office space and a jail. They were the only inmates. The cell had six tiny windows. The steel walls wrapped them in a blanket of heat. Otong felt his brains melt and plop about inside his skull like porridge in a gourd. The nearness of Masaba made his blood boil. He avoided looking at him, but he could smell him, could hear him breathe in the far corner like an animal that wants to gobble up an enemy.

They did not speak to each other. Otong wondered what would have happened if he had accepted the invitation to hug. Had he destroyed the only chance he had to reconcile with the past? Would they ever break the silence that now separated them? What would the first words be? An apology? The accusations they never uttered all these years, each blaming the other for causing the death of a sister, of a lover? Maybe it will be a remark upon the weather, or something about the inhumanity of locking people up in a shipping container? Would they tell the police why they had fought, or would they let the police continue to assume it was all because of a radio?

The hours passed. No one talked.

Darkness fell. The heat gave way to a chill. It evoked the atmosphere of their last night together, in the abandoned church in whose backyard they buried her. The broken windowpanes had let in an icy breeze. They had cuddled together around a fire, drinking and singing. It's all he could remember, the happiness in her voice, the laughter. Now, he could not sleep. The chill nearly loosened his tongue. He wanted to ask Masaba if he had made her cry. He wanted to hear Masaba deny it, or confess it. He wanted to know if Sera still lay in the secret grave, or if Masaba had confessed to his parents. Several times, he opened his mouth to speak. It ended up a cough, a clearing of his throat, a sigh. Each time he heard a similar sound from Masaba, he stiffened, and waited for words, but they both could not find their voices. They sat awake all night, their lips frozen shut.

Dawn broke. The sun rose, throwing beams of gold into the cell, reminding Otong of the way it had painted her tear-stained face. The door opened. A policeman walked in. Your wife is here, he said.

Masaba ran out, but at the doorway he paused, and turned around. Their eyes met, for the first time since they had become inmates. Otong saw a glimmer in Masaba's pupils. He saw Masaba's lips open and waited for the words. The moment stretched for nearly thirty seconds. The policeman broke it up when he shoved Masaba out and closed the door.

Otong ran to a window, his face pressed hard into the bars. He saw Masaba and a woman in a blue *gomesi*[109] walking to the gate. She had negotiated his release, maybe passed cash to the uniforms. How close did they live? Did she know about Sera? Masaba stopped at the gate, glanced over his shoulders, and once again their eyes met, for only a second, before his wife yanked him out of sight.

Otong remained on the window long after Masaba had gone. He saw

---

109   A traditional dress worn by women in Uganda and some parts of Kenya. It is typically made from brightly colored, patterned fabric and is worn with a headscarf.

visions of Masaba returning, his arms spread for a hug, a guitar in one hand, a tin drum in the other. This time, he would accept the hug. They would hit the streets again, just the two of them.... He waited for two hours, watching the gate, until the officer in charge of the police post, Sergeant Okello, a lanky man whose wife frequented his shop, walked in.

It wasn't about the radio, Otong said before Okello could utter a word. With his face still pressed on the bars, he confessed about Sera, about her strange death and her secret burial. Each word that came out of his lips reduced his weight by a kilo, until he was totally weightless. Something snapped inside his chest, flooding him with warmth, unshackling the chains that had enslaved him for a decade. When he finished speaking, he turned to face the policeman, expecting to hear something about murder charges. The officer simply shrugged, and said, this case is closed. Go back home.

As he walked back to town, wrapped in a sheet he had borrowed from the police, he wondered which case Okello meant was closed. Her death or the fight? Maybe both. He debated whether he should move to a new town, maybe in the far west, or if he should stay and hope that Masaba, who now knew where he lives, would return.

After reopening his shop, an answer came with a hawker on a bicycle, and a commodity no peddler ever touted. A guitar. A man in a potato truck sold it to me, the hawker said. He thought I'd resell it to you.

Otong's fingers tingled when he touched the guitar, for the first time since Sera had died. His hand shook as he looked for hidden messages, but he found nothing. For over an hour after buying it, he could not bring himself to play. When he did, he thought the strumming would awaken the ghosts. He waited to hear Sera's voice, to see Masaba's silhouette in the dusty heat. Nothing happened. Only the hot wind kissed his face, a dusty taste stung his mouth, and his neighbours gathered to hear him play.

Dilman Dila *is a Ugandan writer, film maker and a social activist. He is the author of a collection of short stories,* A Killing in the Sun, *and of two novellas,* Cranes Crest at Sunset, *and* The Terminal Move. *He was shortlisted for the* 2013 Commonwealth Short Story Prize *for "A Killing in the Sun", longlisted for the* Short Story Day Africa *prize, 2013, and nominated for the 2008* Million Writers Awards *for the short story "Homecoming". He was longlisted for the* BBC International Radio Playwriting Competition *with his first radio play,* Toilets are for Something Fishy. *His film* The Felistas Fable (2013) *won four awards at the* Uganda Film Festival *2014, for Best Screenplay, Best Actor, Best Feature Film, and Film of the Year (Best Director). It won two nominations at the* Africa Movie Academy Awards *for Best First Feature by a Director, and Best Make-up Artist. It was also nominated for the African Magic Viewers Choice Awards for Best Make-up artist, 2013. His first short film,* What Happened in Room 13, *is one of the most watched African films on* YouTube. *In 2015, he was longlisted for the* Inaugural Jalada Prize for Literature *for his story "Onen and his Daughter".*

Kissing Gordo
Muthoni Garland

REBECCA'S swollen stomach was encased in a sleeveless lacy dress that looked like a petticoat. Her pregnancy—his dead brother's baby—glowed at Steve. "Ta-imagin ee," Steve said, silently, trying to picture it in his mind, "I am looking at Gordo's son."

Steve and Rebecca were seated sideways at a ridiculously small table at the Burger Den in Nairobi West. Cash Money boomed on the music system. Steve sneaked glances at Rebecca. She looked thick and juicy. He willed his eyes to move up from the plump pillow of her breasts to focus on her face. The softness of her powdered skin, her flaring nose and pliant mouth contradicted her angular jaw line and pulled-apart cheekbones. She'd painted a black line along the edge of her squishy lips—a dark perimeter fencing shiny red lipstick. Bits of colour rubbed off as she bit into her beef burgher.

She moved her shoulders to the music. "Hey, I'm here. Look up, Steve. Talk to me."

He cleared his throat. "Ahem. Are you cold? You can have my jacket." What he really wanted was for Rebecca to cover up her breasts, her body.

Rebecca raised her pencil-thin eyebrows and shook her bob. The permed hair whipped back and forth exaggerating the movement.

She did not seem like the girl Steve had known and watched from afar these last twelve years. And it wasn't just the glowing pregnancy or the careless way she chewed or drowned her chips in tomato sauce. Rebecca seemed barely contained, soft yet hard. Undeniable. The words he'd rehearsed since Gordo's funeral disappeared. He felt anxious.

The waiter refilled their cups.

"Hey, *jaza kabisa*,"[110] she scolded the waiter, and turned back to Steve. "Even you should demand they fill your cup to the top. Why is this place trying so hard to be posh? We are Miros."

 Steve hated the way she debased the word Miro, implying anything Black African could never be posh. "It's not about race," he said, running his finger around the rim of his cup. "In an economic downturn, it's easier to maintain profits by reducing portions than by raising prices."

She slapped the side of her head. The pink and red sparkles on her oval nails glittered. "Aw. Let me guess. Nairobi University, second year economics." Over the booming music, she shouted at a waiter. "Chief, bring me another burgher. And don't hold back the beef and all the toppings. *Jaza kabisa!*" She laughed, mouth wide open shoulders shaking, breasts trembling.

Steve let embarrassment fuel negative thoughts. Barely ten in the morning and she was shovelling it in, he thought. Even if she was eating for two,

110   "completely fill" or "fill entirely"

how did she have space for two burghers and chips before midday? "If she ain't hungry, she's ain't for me, know what I mean?" his late brother, Gordo, used to say, in exactly the same mock American movie-cowboy-chewing-a-matchstick-from-side-of-mouth-way that Steve would say, "If it ain't 4D, it ain't a game, know what I mean?"

The coffee scalded his tongue. Steve's eyes watered. The pain drew his attention to Rebecca's discomfort. He noticed her shredded napkin, noted the way she kept patting her bump as though to calm the baby or, perhaps, herself. It occurred to him that she was probably being aggressive to camouflage her anxiety.

Steve's own mood echoed the sag of his trousers. He'd lost four kilos. Gordo would have said Steve's frame looked a duplicate of Dr. Patel's, he of no bum; the doctor who'd pulled the humane plug and filled on Gordo's death certificate exactly one month before: *Complications arising from a compromised immune system.*

Compromised.

Cut to size.

Steve had overheard relatives backbite Gordo in the days leading to the funeral. "Men are dogs!"

"Instead of cutting it off, they think they can cure it with virgins."

"Gordo dipped all over the place. Did he think he was immune?"

The weight of these depressing thoughts pressed on Steve's head. A burst of laughter at the next table put him over the edge. Steve had selected the Burgher Den for the meeting, thinking its noise would minimize awkward silences between them. He now realized it was not conducive to discussing the baby with Rebecca.

"We should go." Steve stood, tightened his belt. That created gathers so he un-tucked his shirt and thought to hell with the fact that he'd only ironed the part that showed. He dropped notes on the table to pay the bill and added coins to tip the waiter.

Without argument, Rebecca rose and then looked down and brushed away crumbs. An old man passing by, eyed Rebecca's generous cleavage and startled himself into a coughing fit. Rebecca grinned at him. The oldie's partner, a beefy lady whose red belt divided her stomach into two generous halves, sucked her lips at Rebecca. "Nkt. Nkt."

Steve could not suppress a chuckle.

Rebecca quipped, "Mmm! Some women are jealous for nothing. Ugly spirit. Woof-woof ugly?"

Her questioning inflection was an invitation to Steve, a nod to something shared. When he failed to respond to it, Rebecca excused herself, went to the toilet. Steve waited outside. He leaned against a shop, glad for the respite from her. It would give him time to recover from the stab of betrayal that had swallowed his tongue. The history of the expression, "Woof-woof ugly!" belonged to him and his late brother, Gordo. When Steve was six, a neighbour's Alsatian had chased him round and round Baba's frog-like Citroen, whose tires had been stolen long before they were born. In response to Steve's screams, his parents had rushed out of their three-bedroom home in the Ngong hills. In the vegetable patch that served as their front garden, Baba waved his walking stick at the dog, shouting, "Shoo, shoo!"

Mama rushed to the fence, calling for God, neighbours, anyone, Yesu Christo, to save her son. In her arms, Baby Annie, then two, wailed a gibberish that sounded like "Unfair, unfair!" though it could have been, "Air, air!"

Gordo had the presence of mind to grab Baba's walking stick (Baba was lame in one leg and promptly fell over). Like a domino effect, Steve lost his footing and fell too. He scrambled round, saw the beast's drooling mouth over him, its shiny canines about to tear him to pieces. Steve opened his mouth. Nothing came out. He heard a sickening thud, as Gordo whacked the dog with Baba's stick, yelling, "Woof-woof ugly!"

The dog yelped, and with tail tight to its belly, fled, tearing through Mama's rows of cabbage, courgettes and coriander.

"Woof-woof ugly!" Gordo and Steve screeched, rolling on the ground in relief and laughter, as the dog whimpered in its kennel next door. "Woof-woof ugly!"

But Baba, the ex-Mau Mau general who'd fought for Kenya's independence from the British and often shared stories of daring exploits in the forest; who wore his withered leg as a badge of honour, didn't laugh at all. "My son is a hero," he said, in all seriousness. "Gordo is a hero."

Baby Annie clapped and babbled what sounded like, "Godhero. Godhero."

Much laughter followed as Baba made her repeat it over and over. "Godhero. Godhero."

From then on, it seemed to Steve that Baba dedicated himself to highlighting and celebrating Gordo's manly virtues. As long as he didn't whine or show tears or surrender, Baba ignored, explained away or forgive Gordo all mistakes.

Perhaps Baba was mortified for not rescuing Steve himself, or preferred not to see the instrument that exposed his weakness, but it seemed that from then on, Steve became lost to him. And due to her focus on the baby's (and only daughter's) needs, Steve dropped from Mama's radar too.

The story of how Gordo saved his brother grew with the retelling. The Alsation became an ogre-sized beast that had its fangs on Steve when Gordo blasted it to the next world and crippled it forever. And other heroic deeds dotted Gordo's life, a charmed childhood. When a *matatu* drove into a ditch near the house, Gordo joined the crew that pulled it out. When a little girl almost drowned during a swimming lesson, it was Gordo who pulled her out. Even though she insisted that she had not needed help but by then, the accolades had stuck to Gordo.

When Gordo shot a winning goal in the most critical school soccer match of the year, a cheering crowd, including Steve, carried him home on their shoulders. Steve's chest felt full, his brother, his own brother was such a hero! To much laughter that night, their father recalled the game, play for play, over and over, until Steve finally mumbled, "Gordo is not Maradona."

In the puzzled silence that followed, Steve offered, "I was second in class this term."

His father replied, "Good, good keep it up," but after too short a time said, "And how about that goal, Gordo?"

Baby Annie babbled, "Godhero. Godhero."

To invite back the laughter, Baba encouraged her repeat it. "Godhero. Godhero."

Noticing that Steve was not joining in, Mama said, in a jolly voice, "God willing, you will be first next term."

This made Steve feel worse, smaller for trying to insert himself in Gordo's limelight. He felt confused, rebuked, unworthy, invisible, nauseous. He went to the toilet and puked. These new feelings about Gordo felt too raw and complicated to share.

Still, Steve continued to shadow Gordo. Unlike other older boys, Gordo not only tolerated his younger brother but encouraged Steve to hang out with him. It was Gordo who taught Steve how to pee in a perfect arc. It was Gordo who taught him how to walk in low-slung jeans, sauntering legs apart, extra wide. Gordo who taught him to moonwalk. Perhaps it was not surprising then that Steve felt pleased when his brother sent him on errands or borrowed something. He lent him the Timex watch he got on his eleventh birthday, and when Gordo swam with it causing it to malfunction, Steve took the blame. Baba immediately accepted the lie despite knowing that Gordo had borrowed the watch that day and how careful Steve was with his things. As a result, Steve refused to apologize and blurted that it was his watch to do with as he liked. Baba punished Steve by refusing to get the watch repaired. Steve still had that watch, its leather strap worn and its insides rusted.

During their teenage years, Gordo worked out, bulked up. When Steve gained weight, it looked like puppy fat, and when he lost it, became as slight as their father. Gordo grew a moustache and beard that needed regular shaving. Above Steve's top lip and on his chin emerged whispers of hair not worth bothering about. Gordo clearly expected people to look up to him. And they did. Everyone knew Gordo and those who didn't pretended to. Bullies didn't touch Steve because of the unspoken threat of Gordo.

It was Gordo, not their father, who escorted Steve to the Ngong clinic to be circumcised. When the doctor approached with his cutting instrument and pulled his foreskin, Steve turned sideways and stared into his brother's eyes. Gordo willed him not to cry. Not giving in to his terror that day was the bravest thing Steve had ever done, and the gratitude he felt as a result was intense. Afterwards, Gordo pronounced him a man and forced on him a beer that got him drunk for the first time.

Steve was the guy people squinted at, the nice-mannered one they couldn't quite place. Gordo acted, Steve watched. Gordo was noisy, Steve was not. Gordo would have many girlfriends. Steve never recovered from his first teenage crush, the one and only Rebecca, who'd smiled at him from the choir at the Baptist Church on Ngong Road. Steve had only gone to church that fateful day because their mother was being presented as an elected lay Elder of the church. Their father, who had an on-off relationship with what he called the white man's religion, had not attended the service. Steve sat with his sister, who, even at ten, was still referred to as Baby Annie. Gordo had slipped out of church as soon as their mother had gone to sit in the seats reserved for Elders.

It was that long-ago smile that started, complicated and eventually upset everything. After that smile, Steve arrived in church an hour early to bag a front centre seat. Too shy to approach, he found out Rebecca's name from another choir member, a girl, a class-mate addicted to Mills and Boons and clearly delighted to be part of the secrecy involved in delivering Steve's 'anonymous' love letters.

Gordo eventually teased the details out of Steve and dared him to ask her out. Steve invited Rebecca on what was supposed to be a double date to watch Jackie Chan in action at the 20th Century cinema. When she smiled and said yes, the thrill of anticipation kept Steve on edge for a week. She had read his letters, she knew it was him, she had said yes!

On the day, Gordo's girlfriend did not show up. While waiting for her, they missed the black and white panorama clip, the adverts, previews of forthcoming features and the national anthem—key parts of the cinema experience that Steve usually enjoyed. He did not mind that day, not with Rebecca in a yellow dress looking so lovely and smiling. And Gordo made it easy—he did the talking and sent Steve to line-up to buy chocolate and soda treats. Rebecca sat between the brothers. In the flickering light of the film, Gordo snaked his arm across the back of her seat. He pulled Rebecca to him, kissed her and winked at Steve. Steve had winked back, a silly, reactive, blink that he could never undo, did not know how to. He sat there too stunned to think until feelings grew and overwhelmed him. He dashed to the toilet, threw up. Then he marched the eight miles home and smashed the windscreen of the old Citroen with a rock until it shattered.

Not once did the brothers talk about that date. With that wink-back, he rationalized, how could Gordo have taken Steve's feelings for Rebecca seriously? In any case, Rebecca had not protested, and had in fact, gone on to date Gordo. Despite the charged look Rebecca sometimes gave Steve the few times he met her over the years, she had clearly chosen the hero over the average man. So Steve pretended their date had never happened. He convinced himself enough to live without the knowledge breaking him.

Gordo continued to live in the bubble of a heroic life until he didn't. Childhood ended, but Gordo stayed the same. When he dropped out of university, his old friends fell away. The new ones were more reckless and didn't stick around when problems arose. Although his outgoing personality landed him more jobs and opportunities, they did not last.

Steve's complicated feelings about Gordo reared their head more often. As soon as he landed a job after university, Steve moved away. He built a quiet life on a different tangent, but he could not stop Gordo occasionally roping him back into his excitements and dramas. And it seemed to make no difference how many times Steve denied himself or bailed Gordo from the stream of troubles that followed in his wake: bar fights, termination letters, overdue pay day loans, sparring girlfriends, jail; Steve was never allowed to forget that he owed his life to his only brother—a debt that, oddly, weighed heavier now that Gordo was dead. So those private words, 'Woof-woof ugly' tripping from Rebecca's mouth made Steve churn and froth inside.

"Calling on Steve. You there, Steve?" Rebecca was snapping her fingers in front of his face to wake him from his daydream. When she finally had his attention, she added, "I'm ready. Let's go."

"Yes," he said. To hide his feelings, he walked a step ahead of her as they made their way along the dusty pavement. Steve had loved his brother, but it was tainted with envy. If only he had half the self-confidence, the swagger. If only, he had the certain knowledge that the world rotated in his direction. If only Rebecca had chosen him.

"I'm so, so sorry," Rebecca said. "I know it hurts."

Steve heard the break in her voice and knew she was talking about Gordo's death. He stopped for her to catch up, slung his hand across her shoulders. She paused and faced him. Right there on the street next to the crowded bus stop where crab-like Kenya buses with broken chassis screeched to a stop, where *matatu* touts pushed in one more passenger, where pish-posh cars flew by or Sunday-trolled; and just as the church bells gonged, Rebecca held Steve and bent forward to give him a kiss. It was intended for his cheek but Steve instinctively moved. Her lips met his.

He almost screamed. An ache surged and settled in his body, and he weakly stumble-meandered ahead as crablike as the buses. Like the dong of church bells, sniggers of amusement and clicking of tongues followed them. Nairobians frowned on public displays of intimacy. However, Steve wanted to do it again, wondered if it would help obliterate memories of Gordo and Rebecca.

Rebecca held his hand, as they walked, helping and hindering his balance.

Without conscious plan, they arrived at Steve's block of flats in South B. It was quiet—no doubt most of his neighbours were exercising their throats in church. Rebecca huffed up the three flights of stairs. Steve ushered her in with an extravagant wave, and was embarrassed to realize that he'd not put away the remains of the previous night's *ugali*[111] and empty carton of *maziwa mala*[112].

"Ever the gentleman," she sighed. She sprawled on his brown sofa, and panting softly, closed her eyes.

Steve cleared the table, sat on a high-backed plastic chair and studied Rebecca. She was so different from the girls he normally attracted—cute and kindly carbon copies of his mother, slight background girls as unlike Rebecca as Steve was from his late brother. Even lying there in her unladylike manner, Rebecca had an odd effect on him, like his blood was flowing faster.

He searched for the language to carry them into the territory of Gordo and the pregnancy. This was difficult even though she was lying back, eyes closed, her bump defined and huge, leading.

Steve swung the chair back until his head rested against the wall, unconsciously mimicking her pose. He spoke up. "I hope you're taking necessary care."

Without opening her eyes, Rebecca responded, "Of course, I am."

He wasn't sure she'd understood where he was going. "Gordo wanted to sort things out with you before..."

"But he didn't," she snapped. "You can't change that fact just because he's dead."

"He was confused and too scared to..."

"Ah, please," she said. She rested her hands on top of her belly.

A silence descended and sat fat and heavy between them. It stretched until Rebecca said, in a weary tone, "Your brother was a fool."

"That may be true..." Steve started, and stopped himself from adding, "but you chose him, not me." He, Steve, had given her up without a word, let alone a fight, but how it had hurt, secretly and deeply, just like his complicated feelings for his brother. Over the years, Steve had relived that moment in the cinema, mythologized that kiss, masturbated fantasizing that Rebecca's lips were on him, burning here, there, everywhere. He was clearly in the grip of something he had to suppress. He tried to look at her dispassionately. He studied the remains of her greasy red lipstick and the green on her eyelids.

"You are beautiful," Steve said. "You don't need make-up,"

Rebecca opened her eyes, stared at him. "You'd be beautiful if you'd open up, you know."

Steve winced. And it came flooding back—how Rebecca always challenged Gordo; asked him why he bullied waiters, why he walked out on jobs, why he lied to his mother that he was on his way to see her. Gordo would call Steve, perplexed that Rebecca sought explanations in order to understand him, not to win.

---

111   a staple food made from cornmeal or other grains, popular in Kenya, Tanzania and Uganda.
112   "spiced milk" in Swahili; a popular drink in East Africa, made of milk with added spices such as cinnamon, ginger and nutmeg.

"Man, she's groping my insides," he'd say.

"She won't like what she finds in there! Haha," Steve would crack, bitter with jealousy. One night, Gordo had lied to Rebecca that he was at Steve's place. Rebecca had come to his flat, woken him at 4 a.m. to check for herself. Steve was too stunned to do anything but watch as she ranted. Afterwards, he'd gone back to bed and humped his mattress to the vision of Rebecca's angry breasts poking their way into his flat, demanding, demanding, demanding…

Steve pointed at the bump. "Gordo said you were trying to trap him."

Rebecca drilled him with her green-lidded eyes. "Steve, maybe you don't know this. You're shy with girls. But your brother and I had sex. We had sex many times." Like a biology instructor, hands waving, fingers pointing, thrusting, pumping, Rebecca showed no mercy. "A natural consequence of sex happened."

The words slithered through cracks in Steve's mind, stirring the old ache, hard and painful. He squirmed in the unforgiving chair.

Rebecca continued, "I knew almost right away. Told him. Guess what? He was cool about it. Bought me vanilla ice from SnoCream, masala chips, Kenchic kausha. Urged me to eat for two. Then, at three months, I began to show. I was living at home. Dad and Mum turned traditional, asked my aunties to find out who was responsible for breaking their favourite goat's leg, wanted to know about dowry."

"Gordo wasn't ready."

"You think I was?" Rebecca smelled of hot red earth steaming after heavy rain. "But I couldn't ignore this," she held the bump, "anymore than my parents could. I couldn't keep drifting, eating ice cream. I needed to know where things stood. So I asked Gordo and he said he had a headache and would think about it. He disappeared. Even when I found out about the virus, he refused to talk to me. I eventually cornered him in some other chick's flat, told him it was a boy. He gave me thirty thou, a note with the details of a doctor, and then shut the door in my face. Next I heard, Gordo was at his father's house. But none of you bothered to find out what had happened to me."

Steve rocked forward to stop himself from falling. He wanted to tell her he didn't know until the bitter end, when Gordo, folded over in his hospital bed, had gripped his sleeve and gurgled.

"Sorry, I'm so sorry," Gordo gasped for breath. "About Rebecca."

Steve was not ready to hear the apology but was in no position to reject it either. He had pretended to misunderstand.

"She is still pregnant," Gordo said, with a wracking cough.

"Fuck, you didn't tell me …" Steve started, but was stopped by the weight of despair encompassed in Gordo's coughing. It was too late to go down that track. When Gordo quieted, Steve said, "I guess you're not expendable until you have a duplicate."

A duplicate.

To emulate.

After a long silence, Gordo had mimed, slowly see-sawing his bony finger between the two of them. "Woof-woof ugly!"

The two brothers cracked up, mulling over their history, sweet and bitter.

Then Gordo said, in a surprisingly robust voice, the last thing he ever said to his brother. "Raise my son to be like you."

Steve had turned away, left the hospital, his eyes more feverish with fear than Gordo's.

Rebecca broke into his thoughts. "Your brother was a coward."

Steve jabbed his index finger at Rebecca and snapped, "My brother was a hero!"

Godhero.

Godhero.

But it was not true. Or not all true. The hero and the coward lived in the same body and waited for a call that sometimes never came for either or both. "Rebecca, please. Gordo was ashamed, too scared to face you. Now he's gone. We have to…"

Accept, forgive and carry on? Rebecca reached for her bag, and turned it upside down, scattering notebook, lipstick, tubes, powder, brushes, bits of Kleenex, cotton balls, bottles of pills, fat envelopes …

Steve read the labels on the bottles: Retrovir, Epivir, Paracetamol.[113]

"Steve, you're a coward too." Rebecca picked up a stuffed envelope and flung it in the air. Money fluttered about the room. Then she picked another envelope and another and threw them too. "Thirty thousand to get rid of our baby. Gordo never had this kind of money. He got it from you."

Steve buried his head in his hands. He remembered the afternoon Gordo had come to him for help. Standing outside Steve's bank that fronted the busy Mama Ngina Square, he'd sniped at Gordo, "So your misguided sperm costs a thou for every year of your life."

"Papa don't preach." Gordo sad, quoting a song that had scandalized parents and even been raised in parliament as an example of the foreign influences that were ruining the nation's children.

But Steve could not stop. "You have to swear never to come to me like this again. That is my only condition for giving you this money. It's the last time."

With a sneer, Gordo raised his finger to the sky and said, "I swear never to beg my brother for money again." Then, one after the other, Gordo pushed the three envelopes with the thirty thousand shillings Steve handed him, down his trousers, into his underwear. "Fuck you, bro. What do you know about life?"

"I know life is not about juggling spare wheels," said Steve. "It's not about impregnating chicks with kids you don't want."

"You're only upset because I cheat on Rebecca, bro. But you don't want

---

113   All medications to treat HIV infection.

like to face facts."

"You talk shit, smell like shit, behave shitty," said Steve, hotly. They stared at each other. With his dirty clothes, unshaven beard, and rough skin, Gordo looked like he'd not slept, eaten or bathed for a long time. He'd lost weight. Steve added, "And you look like shit too. Shit. Shit. Shit."

The sun glinting off a glass building cast brilliant light, illuminating the un-natural glitter in their eyes. Sensing a fight, the ever-ready-for-entertainment Nairobi crowd of the insane and unemployed gathered, surrounded, encouraged.

Gordo pushed Steve.

Steve stumbled backwards, shouted, "What the fuck is wrong with you?"

"Piga yeye," someone said, conversationally, and others in the crowd concurred, as though instructing one to beat another who did not know why he was being beaten was common-sense.

Gordo obliged with a backhanded swipe that only landed because Steve was too perplexed to move. Gordo coughed phlegmatically, as though to remove something deep and ugly within. When it subsided, the fight was gone out of Gordo. He stared into Steve's eyes with such intensity that Steve felt a different kind of fear.

"What?" Steve asked. "What?"

"You're my brother," said Gordo, loading it with meaning. "You know what's wrong with me."

But Steve really didn't know. Perhaps it would be more accurate to say, he chose not to know, did not have the mental strength to add the sum of the injured parts. At least, not until two months later when Gordo moved back into their childhood bedroom in the last stages of his shockingly fast deterioration.

During those final months, Gordo banned Mama from hosting prayers at home. To her and Baba, Gordo refused to admit pain, rejected their company. "I'm saving myself for you," he'd say when Steve wiped him down or gently turned him or helped him to the toilet.

Steve imagined the deathly microbes in the tissues Gordo dropped, spotted with blood and mucus, their huge teeth seeking entry paths into warm bodies. Really, the disease was like an extra character lurking in the room needing to be accounted for. In its presence Steve was always battling with the facts, that you couldn't catch AIDS by looking, being with, touching, even drinking from the same glass as the afflicted, for God's sake. He recognized the courage displayed in the celebrated image of Princess Diana hugging an AIDS patient. Still, Steve was revolted by the cancerous pustules that bubbled and opened on his brother's skeletal body. When Steve, with a gloved hand, covered the lesions with topical imiquimod cream, Gordo sighed, and smacked his lips in mock ecstasy. Afterwards, Steve would rush off to wash his hands. Gordo chuckled, knowingly, like an old man amused at the foibles of a world that took itself too seriously.

Sometimes Gordo looked at Steve pleadingly. Steve would ask do you want water, food, tissue, and Gordo would turn away, face the wall. Mostly they watched television, Gordo in bed, Steve in a chair beside him. A child in a commercial asked if the ocean existed because someone forgot to turn off the taps.

Gordo cracked, in a hoarse whisper, "Brotherman, I think someone forgot to turn on your life."

Perhaps Gordo was bitter that it was he, Steve, who'd survive instead of him who had had so much life in him. He attributed this along with the other hurtful things that Gordo said as arising from bodily pain and anger of being reduced to a hacking shell. Steve held his tongue. But Gordo knew how to stir things up.

Looking intently at Steve, Gordo said, "I never planned to bring a girl on that double date."

"You sick bastard," Steve retorted, and backed out of the room to hide his shock.

"It's a good thing I'm dying or you'd kill me yourself?" Gordo attempted to laugh it off, "Hey, I'm joking. I didn't think it would matter that much. I was young. She went along and and then it was too late …"

Shuffling sounds broke through Steve's contemplation. With ungainly movements, Rebecca rose from the sofa. She shuffled past him towards the bathroom. He heard her pee. She'd obviously left the door open. Steve heard her stream—a long burst followed by several short ones.

When he thought it was over, Steve said, "I'm sorry Gordo messed your life."

"My life is not over." She peed again, on and on, long and short, like it was part of the conversation.

Steve swung his chair back and forth, in tune with the peeing. When it stopped, he did too. He had a hard on. Embarrassed, he forced himself to remember that this meeting was about Gordo's son.

He heard Rebecca pour a bucket of water into the cistern to flush the loo—the water pressure too low on upper floors to auto-fill the system.

He asked, "How are you coping?"

"With what?" She waddled back into the room, wiping her hands on the flimsy dress. Stood over him. "Gordo's disappearance? His death? The pregnancy? HIV?"

Steve cracked his knuckles and said, "Yes."

"I curse every time I get gas or cramps. I pee too much, and too often. I eat for ten. My doctor says HIV/AIDS is just a disease, as though it's no worse than cancer or Ebola or whatever. My CD4 count is currently in the normal range but that is no guarantee that my child will not get it. My mother swears that by year 2000, there will be a cure but walks around moping as though I am already dead. My father talks politics, investments, foreign wars, anything to avoid my issues. My sisters joke to try minimize the pain. Other relatives either smirk or shake their useless heads at me. My friends find reasons to party without me. I cry too easily and too much. What else do you want to know?"

Her hostility was living thing, bristling in his direction.

"I read that HIV positive babies often turn negati..."

"Fuck wishful thinking!"

"I want to take care of you," Steve said, his voice unsteady. "I want to help you. I want to help you take care of the baby."

"Why?"

Steve felt immobilised. What did she want him to say? Clearly, for her, actions fueled feelings, not the other way round. No wonder she'd chosen Gordo over him.

As though reading his mind, Rebecca said, "Why feed on Gordo's dregs, Stevenson Musyoki Kilemi? Can't hook your own woman?"

Maybe it was the way she pronounced his full name, dragging it out. He didn't even know she knew it. She was so bitter! Perhaps, like Gordo, it was to distract from the real obsession in the room: fear.

He stood up, reached for her hand. "Rebecca, please let me be your friend."

She smirked, cupped her breasts, lifting them so they spilled over the lacy neckline. "What you really want is to poke me. You've been wanting since you saw me, panting since I got here. Let's do it. It will clarify your motives and get me out of your system."

That militant face, the injured tone, those heaving breasts, the heat of her smell—who the hell did she think she was, laughing at him, teasing? Steve pulled Rebecca, dragged her down on the mess she'd spilled on the floor. "Fuck you," he said, "And fuck Gordo..."

Steve could barely breathe as she tore his shirt off just like he did her dress. Then they were scratching each other, removing underwear. He could barely contain himself as she fumbled about, changing position so he was behind and at right angles to her. She whispered, "Careful. Wait...wait," as Steve, trembling, raised her leg to lever himself. It may have been painful for Rebecca, but he couldn't stop. Not even when she said, "condom condom," tried to buck away, before giving in, slick, churning, burning, thrashing her head from side to side, gasping, shivery gusts. He finally had her. She was his. She was his. Steve stabbed, again and again, exacting revenge on her, on Gordo.

Afterwards, he lay on his back, stared at the ceiling. A surge of hatred washed over him. All that love and jealously she showed for Gordo, and yet here she was naked, his come inside her. She was probably unfaithful in his life as in his death. Fuck, maybe she was the one who'd infected Gordo, killed him. Flashes of Gordo's face in the casket washed over Steve, followed by a sudden conviction that the body next to him, so warm and womanly, could soon be thin, marked with pustules that oozed—cold and dead. And that he too, could now be marked for death, the AIDS bullet shot through her into his body. His dick ached—microbes with huge teeth were already gnawing away his life. He imagined deadly little critters stalking and coiling themselves into his cells, sweeping along his veins, eating him away. He was surely finished. *Kaput.* His scalp crawled. Sweat broke out on his forehead. He moved away from her, sat up.

What is it?" Rebecca asked. She sounded frightened.

He ignored her, scattered her things, reached for the bottles. Without reading the label, he opened one, removed a couple of tablets… opened another. He threw them into his mouth and swallowed. "She was wet, lubricated," he told himself. He wanted to get up, run to the nearest VCT clinic. He didn't want to die.

Rebecca was crying, her big body heaving. Her weeping grew into howls of fear and distress like that dog of long ago. Had he hurt her? Damaged the baby? Or was she crying for Gordo?

He'd broken her. He felt sick. For years he'd hungered for this woman, and if Steve were brutally honest, probably loved and wanted her more because his brother had taken her. Perhaps the sex had been, for him and perhaps for her, a way to reach and touch Gordo now that he was quiet, dead. Rebecca had been their silent battleground, but also a kind of communion. Screwing her was at once a fuck you to Gordo, and an assertion of Steve's strength. He felt ashamed.

Placing his fingers at his temples, Steve pressed and rotated the skin. It struck him that one required empathy in order to discern truth, some basis of similarity. Now that he was exposed, no longer could his, "I'm sorry", also mean "I'm glad it isn't me". He was he. He was his brother. He was her. He was all.

Rebecca stopped crying. She blew her nose, wiped her face, and stood up. From the resigned way she reached for her clothes, careful not to look at him, he sensed that she'd come to the conclusion that, like his brother, Steve would run, disappear.

When he held out his hand, Rebecca flinched. Steve persisted, moved close to her. On his knees, he wrapped his hands around her belly, around his brother's embryonic son. He cried as he embraced everything. So much love, so much pain and death and life, and this child coming.

Muthoni has published over forty books for children, two novellas for adults and several stories published in literary journals. Her anthology, *Helicopter Beetles* is available on Amazon as an e- book. She is also a storyteller and has appeared on stage in several countries. Muthoni regularly runs workshops, incorporating storytelling, to help writers develop stories for children and teenagers. She is the chief judge of the Morland Writing Scholarships, and has also judged the *Caine Prize* for African writers. Muthoni is a founder member of the writer's collective, *Storymoja*, which publishes books for ages 4-16.

The Bigness of Littleness
Davina Philomena Kawuma

WHEN KATANA returned, the bats were gone. She pried off her gumboots and knelt, supposing that they'd crawled from where they'd dropped at night and concealed themselves, but there was nothing beneath the wooden table and chairs except old cobwebs and shed cuticles. She rolled the strings of web between her thumb and forefinger, and then sniffed the cuticles. Then she sat with her back against the wall and managed one last sweeping search of the room: seeing is believing. Or was it?

Although her eyes readily received confirmation of the missing bats, her hands preferred to scurry the information to the back of her mind. Now momentarily freed from her preoccupation with her erstwhile housemates, she realized that someone had dusted the table, swept the floor, cleaned the windows, and emptied the bin that squatted in one corner. Technically, anyone with access to this part of the research station could enter her sitting room. However, only one person could have tidied up.

Katana could imagine the satisfaction with which Bellden had scrubbed the cement and wiped the glass. To say nothing of all the stories she'd probably told all morning about the dead bats she discovered, which bats must have seemed the embodiment of magical powers—what you kept in your house to protect yourself against bad luck. Except Katana didn't believe in bad luck. Well, she didn't believe that bad luck hindered good research. She preferred to think that she didn't believe in spirits either, at least not to the extent that you could harness them to produce specific effects in the physical world. No matter how mysterious the incident with the bats, no matter their frantic appearance the other night, Katana believed there was a material explanation. Just because this explanation wasn't yet clear to her senses or obvious to her mind didn't mean that spirits, at least the kind in which Bellden believed, were responsible. Which is precisely why she left the bats on the floor in the first place.

The plan was to physically examine them when she returned from her morning round of point counts (when people joked about the eyes of some Africans being in their hands, they meant Katana). There should have been copious notes and revealing photos, both meant for Dr. Mace, who guest-lectured at the faculty twice every year and was interested in "the long-term monitoring of afro-tropical bat populations." The email about the dead bats was meant to be a cover, as she had no genuine interest in bats (the idea of airborne, mouse-like mammals seemed pretentious to her). But now the bats were missing, as was most of the dirt and dust which Katana had saved for close to two weeks. She'd planned to spend the rest of the day cleaning and then retire, physically exhausted but mentally refreshed, to her bedroom.

Until today, Katana hadn't seen the need for anything more than what she thought of as a "flexible passivity." For as long as all she had to contend with were mere words, she'd committed herself to peaceful resistance. However, now that Bellden had crossed the threshold, Katana might have to switch tactics. Although Bellden was employed by the research station to house-keep, Katana took the latter's intrusion personally. That the room seemed clean enough, cleaner than Katana might ever hope to make it, wasn't the issue. The problem was that Bellden left blatant evidence of her appearance. That she chose this morning was an unforgivable betrayal—a breach of the most important law Katana had imposed since her arrival.

For four and a half months, Katana had minded her business, which was to collect as much data (as ethically and efficiently as possible). She therefore generally avoided activities that were unrelated to and which might interfere with data collection. She didn't engage in the "politics of peopling," for instance, as this was something Prof. Bailey warned could have "adverse effects" on her research. The only person to whom she spoke at length was Sarah, her research assistant, and even then she was careful not to divulge personal information. Sometimes, come to think of it, she shared a joke or two with Issa, the chef. Otherwise, she maintained a polite but firm distance from the other staff. She often left the campsite as soon as the fire went out and rarely accepted invitations to any staff-organized merrymaking.

Unfortunately, despite her determination to avoid the "politics of peopling," some staff occasionally cornered her; the patrolmen, porters and other casual labourers, especially those that slashed the trails, were the worst. Mugabe, who patrolled the forest in the morning, was particularly fond of discussing the private lives of others. He was especially fond of "reporting" Bellden, so much so that Katana was compelled to inquire about what seemed like ill will on his part. When she asked if Bellden was once his lover—maybe, after their relationship soured, Mugabe committed himself to tarnishing her reputation—he laughed. He said he could never love a woman as dangerous as Bellden—the kind that worshipped both the white man's and the black man's Gods (she took communion in St. John's every other Sunday and sacrificed to the spirits in the forest every other Saturday).

Late one evening, Mugabe apparently saw Bellden and an unidentified man carrying many-headed barkcloth sacks into the forest. Two weeks later, attracted by the high smell of ripening fruit, he discovered the offertory site—there were sugarcanes, pineapples, passion fruits, mangoes, and bananas concealed within the buttress roots of one of the oldest Mutuba trees. There was also a *kataasa*[114] filled with eggs, he said, because for some reason the spirits in this forest manifested as egg-loving snakes. Mugabe and the other

---

114   From Luganda, one of the major languages spoken in Uganda, meaning "to twist" or "to bend". It can be used in different contexts, for example in construction, referring to the process of bending a metal rod or in cooking, meaning to bend a banana leaf to wrap food.

patrolmen are supposed to have eaten what wasn't too ripe and buried what was rotten.

For a while, after Mugabe recounted that story, Katana feared to venture into the forest alone; whatever gnarled root had previously amused her begun to frighten her. Her new-found fear surprised her as much as it surprised Prof. Bailey, who sent a one-line reply to her email about Bellden's offerings:

Magico-religious bullshit! You should know better than that!

Prof. Bailey's exclamation marks, and he rarely used exclamation marks, didn't dull the edge of Katana's wariness; she avoided Bellden even more than she had before. Bellden, thankfully, ignored Katana; she spoke only to the Bazuungu students—lingered whenever she brought their meals, used every opportunity to flirt with the Swedes Zac and Alex. Even after he'd learned what Bellden said behind their backs, Zac still flirted back and complimented her figure and legs. At worst, he complained—but always when Bellden was out of earshot—that she didn't wear deodorant. Unlike Zac, Alex took whatever gossip he heard personally; Katana reckoned he would never recover from the discovery that Bellden considered Bazuungu uncivilized—only uncivilized people doused themselves with perfume in lieu of bathing; only uncivilized people washed clothes in the same saucepans in which they cooked food. Although Alex still let Bellden do his chores, Katana suspected that he now did this more to spite her than to "supplement" what she'd told him was a meager salary.

Katana had heard worse from Mugabe, things that would make Alex seethe. But, always mindful of "the politics of peopling," she kept it all to herself; she merely listened, nodded sympathetically, took their side, when Zac and Alex grumbled to her. It never occurred to her to inform them that it wasn't just Bellden who considered them uncivilized, for she couldn't imagine what points that sort of thing was meant to score. Even when Mugabe shared what Bellden thought of her, Katana kept it to herself. It was Mugabe who said that Bellden begrudged Katana her independence—he's the one who recommended that Katana begin to display some sloppy habits about which Bellden could gossip to the other staff.

It hadn't occurred to Katana how much she took for granted until Mugabe pointed out that she was the only student who cleaned up after herself. She hadn't over thought the fact that she washed the clothes she wore or cooked the food she ate. It wasn't news on campus that Katana didn't leave unwashed utensils under her bed, clog the tub with her pubic hair, or leave skid marks in the toilet bowl. After what Mugabe said, though, and given what had happened this morning, she might have to reconsider. Perhaps Mugabe was right; perhaps, despite Emily's passivity, Bellden considered her aggressive. Perhaps now was the time to reevaluate her position in relation to the other students, who apparently let Bellden do everything from chucking out their used condoms to washing their underwear.

According to Mugabe, Bellden insisted that behind Katana's independence lay "a mean-spiritedness typical of Baganda." That Bellden launched an assault on Katana's tribe neither surprised nor bothered her; her tribe was after all something she hadn't chosen for herself. She was however amused to learn that the station staff thought her monied. She attributed their widespread misunderstanding of her financial status to her close association with Prof. Bailey, who wrote most of the grants that secured funding for the conservation projects in and around the forest. The truth, which was that the graduate researcher scholarship for which Prof. Bailey enrolled her did not cover a stipend, was less glamourous and scandalous. Even if she wanted to, she couldn't afford to pay Bellden to wash and cook for her. As there was neither enough motive nor suitable opportunity for Katana to clarify her financial status to anyone at the station, only Dr. Mace knew that her family faithfully subsidized most of her fieldwork costs despite their failure to empathize with her interest in wildlife.

("You're such a *Muzuungu*," they liked to tease. "Why couldn't you have been a normal Ugandan and studied business administration?")

She learned, while chaperoning him around Kampala, that Dr. Mace could be very expansive. They had plenty in common—a mutual interest in formula one racing; he was also single (or at least he said he was); an active interest jewelry ("I like your necklace…I'm a Pisces, too…I should be wearing fish all the time!"). However, one of their conversations left her in doubt as to the true nature of his motives, especially about future collaborations with Prof. Bailey. They were eating pork chops at a new restaurant in Kisementi after much panicky last-minute shopping at the craft village on Buganda Road, when he said: "So, you and Andrew."

Like most faculty, resident or otherwise, Dr. Mace referred to Prof. Bailey by his first name. She looked up from her plate and said, "What about us?"

"You two get along pretty well."

Because this was not the first time someone marveled at the smoothness of her interaction with Prof. Bailey, she had a ready answer. "We agree on things."

"He's a difficult man."

"He likes things a certain way, that's all."

"Hard to please."

"Aren't we all?"

Dr. Mace had merely smiled into his glass of juice. He said he would email her about opportunities for "bright African women like you." But that was at least three months ago and she hadn't heard from him since. And now that there were no bats to examine and photograph, she would have to find another pretext. Although she could always email to say she had finally read Lewis Hamilton's autobiography, it seemed more prudent at this point to limit their correspondence to something academic. Unfortunately, as they had no intersecting research interests, she might have to feign interest in restoration ecology, his other pet subject, which thought dampened her spirits enough to remind her that there were half a dozen other things in which she had to feign interest.

Katana rose, slid her socks off and shoved them into one gumboot. She nudged open the door into the small room that doubled as kitchen and store, and which on one side opened into a slim corridor. She could have sworn that there were some carrots and tomatoes in the food basket the last time she checked but as she didn't intend to cook supper today and tomorrow was market day she didn't dwell on the absentee vegetables. Instead, she extracted a matchbox from behind a line of plastic Tropical Heat spice bottles and lit the gas stove. While the beans warmed, she examined the crack through which red ants often entered; one night, finding herself with no insecticide, she'd had to boil several kettles of water with which to kill the ants. Sarah, who believed red ants in a house were a bad omen, had promised to speak to the caretaker. But come to think of it that was over a week ago and the crack remained unplugged. She would gather some ash from the *sigiris* in the kitchen and buy some paraffin, and she would keep both in the space beneath the sink. The next time the ants visited, she would set them ablaze, and she would watch while their tight bodies loosened and melted into the ash.

She turned off the stove when the beans boiled and poured them over a bowl of leftover *pilau*[115]. She grabbed a spoon, unlocked the door that opened onto the backyard, and sat on the top stair. Her house, the first in a series of two-roomed houses that snaked down to the mouth of the longest and widest forest trail, gave her a comprehensive view of what lay beyond the chain-link fence—tumpeco-shaped houses, blooming herbs, tire-chasing children, fruiting palms, hopeful cattle, and bold footpaths between shy homesteads. But it was the eucalyptus on the distant hills that she liked best; she admired their stoic invulnerability—how unbothered the trees seemed whether the sun shone or the rain fell or the wind blew.

She'd shoveled a few spoonfuls of rice into her mouth when Sarah appeared at the periphery of her vision. She approached Katana and set down the bucket she held. "Beans."

Unsure as to whether what Sarah said was a question or statement, Katana tried to match her tone. "Protein."

Sarah pulled a rug from the bucket and wrung it. "Have you emailed your supervisor?"

Katana had put off emailing Prof. Bailey for at least a week now. "Soon."

"What will he say?"

Prof. Bailey wanted a minimum of 500 birds caught, but so far they'd

---

115   "Pilau" or "Pilaf" is a traditional dish made by cooking rice with spices, onions, and sometimes meat or vegetables. It is a very popular dish in East Africa, particularly in Kenya and Tanzania, and it is often served at special occasions such as weddings and religious celebrations.

only caught two hundred and three birds and it didn't look as if they'd catch many more. Although Katana suspected he would suggest that she prolong her stay here, she said, "I don't know."

Sarah spread the rug on the grass and emptied the bucket into the drain. "I'm going to the market. Are you sending me?"

"Candles."

"Are we moving the nets tomorrow?"

"Unless you think we shouldn't."

"Let's go early because I'm going to town in the afternoon."

"First thing in the morning."

"Only candles?"

"And doom."

"Are you giving me the money now or later?"

"Later."

As she watched Sarah retreat, Katana wondered how much information Sarah shared about her and her research. But then she told herself that whatever people here thought about her didn't matter. Soon, she'd be back in Kampala, reprising her role as graduate research assistant in the biological and agricultural sciences department of her alma mater. And what would it matter then what anyone here thought?

She was halfway through her meal when Rodney appeared through a window in the trees that lined the fence. He was throwing pieces of watermelon at a couple of clucking hens. Despite the ridicule he'd earned from the station staff, he continued to share his fruit with the neighbour's poultry. He watched the hens while they happily pecked at the watermelon. Then he bent to pick up a bottle and walked round the fence through the small wooden gate. Rodney, who lived in the house next to hers, was a Brit with a rusty complexion that she found quite comical and a stiff-limbed walk that belied his laid back personality. They'd arrived on the same day, barely minutes apart, and had struck up a fast alliance (based mostly on the anticipation of similar hardships).

"You man," Katana said, as Rodney approached. "Give me some money."

"Hey, Muzuungu[116]!" Rodney said with exaggerated enthusiasm. He shook what she could now see was a Pilsner Lager bottle in front of her. "Take me to London."

Katana laughed. Without trying hard, Rodney had turned into a bit of a naturalized Ugandan; at least he spoke like one. Nevertheless, he was still, to the neighbours and station staff, just another Muzuungu researcher, which meant that people invariably charged him higher, among other things (he was constantly asking Katana if there was a "PLEASE RIP ME OFF" sign on his forehead). His field was human-wildlife conflict; he was currently studying the effects of forest fragmentation on crop-raiding by red-tailed monkeys.

116   In Swahili meaning "white person"

They used the same trails for their respective counts and feeding observations inside the forest.

"I didn't see you this morning," Katana said.

"I wasn't in the mood."

"Again? Lucky you." Katana had never been the sort of person that needed a mood to do something she considered important. Even on days when she felt unwell, she conducted counts. Meanwhile, whenever he "wasn't in the mood," Rodney entered that into his data sheet as "unfavourable weather conditions." "Watermelon and beer? What's the occasion?"

Rodney peeked into her bowl. "Bellden would say you're eating like a poor person."

Katana chuckled. "I'm certainly not rich."

Rodney sat on the bottom stair. "Nonsense. Everyone here knows you're swimming in dimes."

"Oba which dimes?"

"Don't pretend-pretend. I've heard things."

"Such as?"

"How your super has lots of dime. All along you've been having dimes but not wanting to tell me! Yiiiyii."

"I wish," Katana said.

Rodney waited for her to finish laughing and then held her gaze. "You know people think he's fucking you, right?"

Katana nodded.

"Bellden says maybe you're not so good in bed. Maybe that's why he doesn't give you enough money. Maybe that's why you can't afford to pay her to wash your clothes."

Katana put the bowl aside. She could feel her face burning. She looked away in case Rodney could see the heat radiating from her face.

"Let her clean."

"Is that what this is about? That I don't let her clean?"

"It's what she's here for."

Katana wanted to say that on top of being unable to afford help she also actually liked doing chores—that, for reasons she'd never herself fully understood, chores unclogged her brain. Whenever she reached a dead-end in her research, and in her time here she'd encountered many bottlenecks, she scoured and swabbed and cleaned. She might have explained this to Rodney if she didn't think it would take too much time.

Rodney offered his bottle to Katana. "Don't be a miser. Let the woman make some dimes."

Katana said nothing.

"Listen," Rodney said, "Kris and I are going out tonight."

Kristin, the dark-haired and blue-eyed Dutch student, was one of those Bazuungu that thought Uganda and Africa were the same geographical space.

Because she seemed unwilling to socialize with Katana in the absence of other Bazuungu, Katana rarely spoke to her.

("This is supposed to be a world class research station. Why isn't there any electricity here?" was the sort of thing Kristin offered as a conversation starter.)

"Where are you two going?" Katana asked.

Unlike the other students, who had found ways of slowly but surely acclimatizing to the inconveniences of living away from civilization, Kristin was bent on rejecting whatever compromises the station staff made. Katana could not imagine spending an entire evening in her company.

"To that pub."

"There are no pubs here. How many times must I tell you?"

Rodney rolled his eyes. "We're going to that bar we went to last time."

Katana took the bottle from Rodney. "It's cold," she exclaimed, after she'd managed a hurried swallow.

"Yeah, so?"

"I don't drink cold beer anymore!"

Rodney sneered. "Poseur!"

It was the only change she could completely attribute to her stay here— her preference for warm beer. "Takes one to know one."

"So, are you coming?"

"Is Katie going?"

Katie was the only American student at the station. Unlike most Americans Katana had met, Katie was neither loud nor brash. Even better, she did not act as if she knew everything.

"Good idea," Rodney said, before he trotted off towards Katie's house.

By the time Rodney returned, Katie's hand in his, Katana had licked the bowl clean and was wondering how much drinking water she had left in the kitchen. Samantha, who was gesticulating wildly into her phone, was following closely behind Rodney and Katie. It sometimes seemed as if Samantha was always on phone; Katana had meant to ask her how she always managed to keep a charged phone, what with the way the solar had been acting up. Samantha was Australian and at the tail end of her research into tropical forestry management practices; she was famous in and around the station for her hair, which she wore like a mantle (although she was only twenty-three, her hair had gone whitish from premature greying). Katana had tried, and failed, to talk to Samantha about more than the late Steve Irwin.

Katana moved to create space for Katie, who started off by apologizing for "like, borrowing some stuff." Since Katie discovered that Bellden bought fewer groceries for her than what Katana bought using the same amount of money, she'd been "borrowing" many things. Half a head of cabbage today. A pumpkin tomorrow. Several Irish potatoes the next day. Insect repellant the day after. And so on.

"Sharing is caring," Katana said.

Katie smiled profusely and then turned to Rodney. "What time are we heading out?"

"Oh shit," Katie added before Rodney responded. "I don't have anything to wear." She quickly turned to Katana. "Could I?"

Katana laughed. "But what do I have that fits you?"

Katie described one of two jumpsuits that she wanted to borrow. Katana said she would have to check, that she hoped the jumpsuit wasn't dirty. Katie screamed and hugged her. "You're, like, the best!"

Katana smiled but said nothing.

Samantha, now no longer speaking into her phone, was standing next to Rodney; her arms were crossed in front of her chest. The brief silence was made more awkward by how uneasy Samantha seemed; she seemed unsure of her role here. For a while, Katana had suspected that Rodney, Katie and Samantha run a three-way. Looking at them, now, however, a threesome seemed unlikely.

"Hi, Samantha," Katana said.

"Hey," Samantha said.

"You're good?"

"Yeah."

Katana stood. "I better go look for that jumpsuit."

"Right," Rodney said. "We'll see you later."

The trio left the same way it came; with Rodney and Katie holding hands and Samantha trailing them. Katana grabbed her empty bowl and ascended the short flight of steps back into the kitchen, thinking how interesting it'd be for her to establish how far Katie would go. Katie, who used her toilet the day before, had commented on how pretty Katana's underwear was. Mugabe told Katana that Bellden often found blood-stained underwear in Katie's laundry basket; apparently, Bazuungu would rather throw away their soiled underwear than wash it. She couldn't help but wonder if Katie might someday want to borrow her underwear.

She let some tap water run into the dirty bowl and saucepan and left both soaking in the sink. She took a key from her pocket and opened the door to her bedroom. She slipped out of her overalls and was about to take off her bra when the sensation of being watched overcame her. When she turned, it was towards a man chewing on a sugarcane; he stood next to the jackfruit tree in her neighbour's garden, about a hundred metres away. He didn't even bother to hide the fact that he was watching her. She smiled stiffly and waved at the man. After the man smiled back, she drew the curtains. While it was perfectly okay for Katie and Samantha to dress however they liked, no one stared when they wore shorts that barely covered their butt cheeks. There seemed to be a consensus that, except for her face and arms, the rest of Katana's body was a family secret that must remain unexposed.

When she'd undressed, she walked into the bathroom. Only after she had peed did she notice that the roll of toilet paper she'd left on the cistern was missing. She swallowed her rising irritation, turned on the tap, and stood beneath the shower nozzle. After close to five minutes of listening to gurgling noises that brought no water, she tiptoed along the corridor, hoping no one would choose that moment to walk in. She might eventually explain away the dead bats in the living room, but would she ever be able to explain why she was naked, at one in the afternoon, in her kitchen?

She heaved one of two jerrycans into the bathroom and filled a bucket. While she scrubbed herself, she wondered if the idea of going into town was a promising one. They'd have to take *bodas*[117] to the main tarmac road and a special hire to town, which seemed too much trouble to go to just to eat roast pork. Rodney and the rest would of course depend on her to haggle with the *boda* riders and special hire drivers. On top of which she'd have to watch them dance to dancehall music; how painful it was, watching them move ta-ta-ta to bom-dum-doo beats. (Honestly, how hard was it to dance according to the rhythm of a song?) She started to tell herself that she wouldn't go, let the Bazuungu learn to fend for themselves, that come to think of it she was tired and should stay in to watch Grey's Anatomy on her laptop. But then she recalled that her laptop battery was dead.

If she went out she might even sit by the counter and watch sports highlights. (She could take her laptop, too; the bartender was sweet on her and would let her charge it.) If she chose to stay in, on the other hand, the best she could do was listen to "love doctor" type shows on radio. Either that or while the night away in the interns' dormitories on the other side of the station. Although most of the interns were at least six years younger than Katana, she occasionally liked to spend time with them. Rather, she liked to lecture them—tell them how disappointed she was that they, like most of the villagers, behaved as if biological resources were infinite. She liked to say that, unlike diamonds, forests weren't forever, certainly not when the population within the nearby villages was steadily increasing. Anger gripped her when they offered responses like, "But, when my grandfather was alive, this forest was here." As if the fact of the forest's presence in the past somehow nullified the possibility of its absence in the future. As if the forest would survive and persist, of its own volition, through firmness and determination, via a resolute and unshakeable faith, regardless of what the people around it did.

She rinsed the soap out of her loofah and scooped water onto her body until she felt sufficiently clean. She looked around for a towel, only to recall

---

117   "Bodas" or "Boda-Boda" is a term used in East Africa to refer to a motorcycle taxi or a motorcycle used for transportation. It is a common mode of transportation in urban areas in countries such as Kenya, Uganda, and Tanzania. The name "boda-boda" is derived from the phrase "border-to-border" as they were originally used to transport people across the border between Kenya and Uganda. The service provided by the boda-boda riders ranges from short distance transportation to delivery services.

that she hadn't brought one. She dashed across the corridor and into her room. She bolted the door, toweled herself dry, and then slipped on a boob tube and underwear. While looking for the jumpsuits, she sniffed all her clothes, eventually sorting them into two categories. She left the dirty ones on the floor and threw the clean ones into the makeshift closet. She wavered between wearing a dress and harem pants; whatever she chose would have to do for now and when she went to town. She eventually settled on harem pants and a printed tied-front top, although dressing like this only reinforced the general idea that she was "like Bazuungu."

She turned on her smartphone. There were several missed calls from her parents, and a text message from her sister asking when she could visit. She checked for new emails in vain, then she turned her phone off again and went into the kitchen. She was washing up when she heard what she thought was a knock on the door. She waited until the knock turned into persistent rapping. Then she popped her head into the sitting room. She was momentarily immobilized by the half of Bellden that stood on the veranda.

"Just a minute," she said, after she'd finally found her voice. She retreated to dry her hands. Then she took several deep breaths and walked into the sitting room.

"Hello," Katana said with a calmness she was far from feeling.

Bellden moved so her body was in full view. She stretched her arm and what it held—a black kaveera—towards Katana. "I hear you want your bats."

Katana hadn't spoken to anyone about the bats. But it didn't seem wise to ask how Bellden knew. The shorter their interaction, the better. Katana found herself walking towards Bellden. She received the quivering kaveera. It took all the strength she had not to drop the kaveera when she loosened the knot and discovered a couple of bats stuck together in a squirming mass.

"They are supposed to be dead," Katana said.

Bellden wore a smile with a meaning Katana couldn't decode. "It's as if you don't even know the difference between dead things and alive ones. Didn't you go to school?"

"My bats were dead," Katana insisted.

"I used to think that people who went to university know everything," Bellden said. Before Katana could think of a proper response, Bellden turned and walked away.

Davina Philomena Kawuma, *a lifelong resident of Kampala, is the author of "Of Birds and Bees" which was shortlisted for the* 2018 Short Story Day Africa Prize. *Her children's and adult fiction and poetry have appeared in anthologies published by the* African Writers Trust, New Internationalist, the Uganda Women Writers Association, the Babishai Niwe Poetry Foundation, *and* Law-ino *magazine.*

In Transit
Abraham T. Zere

"I AM AFRAID you will have to wait," the immigration officer smiled at Thomas as she took his boarding pass and checked his name against his passport.

"Delay? How long?" He forced himself to smile back. He stretched his hand to claim his documents as the officer put them in her drawer.

"Not sure. Maybe hours... days... weeks... months... or it could be more. I can't be certain. No one can be so certain. We will try our best, but the matter is beyond our control. Let's all hope for the best." Her tone changed.

Thomas removed his eyeglasses and stepped closer to the counter. He shifted his coat from one hand to the other. "Excuse me; I'm going for a conference. I need to be there tomorrow. I have to present a paper and...." He ran short of words. Thoughts came to him in brief and explosive images.

For seconds he could only think of colors.

A serene voice brought him back. "Don't worry; I know no one wants to stay long in transit. But we can't help it and you must comply. I hope your stay will be short." With this, the officer resumed her typing on the keyboard.

"Can I talk to the manager? My case is urgent. I can't wait..." It took Thomas all the energy to compose himself and articulate his statement. His face turned red.

"Unfortunately, our manager is out of the country for a conference. We are hoping to see him next week. Let's all hope he returns safely." She typed on the keyboard while replying to him.

"Who else can I talk to?" Thomas persisted angrily.

"You have already reported it. That's all. Please go straight to the far hallway, then turn to the right and join the passengers waiting. Meet the coordinator; I will notify him, and he will provide you with all the necessities. He will take care of you." Her tone sounded an automated reply.

Past the officer, Thomas could see travelers strolling to catch their flights. Mixed feelings of nausea, angst, frustration, and anger overwhelmed him. He struggled to compose himself and make sense of the incident.

The officer slowly stopped typing and leaving her seat, took a few mechanical steps to show him the way out.

"But listen... you can't be serious. I can't understand what you are talking about...." As he looked toward her to resume the conversation, she entered her cubicle, slammed the door, and locked it from inside. He could see her through the glass doors, but it was obvious she would not entertain further questions.

For Thomas, everything turned white followed by complete darkness.

He felt suffocated and had to resist the urge to vomit. He exerted all his energy to look unperturbed. He put on his eyeglasses, checked his handbag. Unconsciously, he started fidgeting his right leg.

Standing still, he watched the departure and landing of the planes through the glass ceiling. Passengers who were rushing to catch their flights jolted him, but Thomas paid very little attention. The loud, monotonous voice on the intercom calling passengers to board irritated him.

He thought his layover was scheduled for two hours. He took out his ticket to check and threw it down as he found out that he was right. Shortly after, he picked up his ticket kept, thinking perhaps it could still be used.

In the plane, until he reached his connecting destination, he had been consumed with the idea of the conference and the presenters he was hoping to meet. As his dreams evaporated in the terminal, he stomped hard on the floor. He threw away his air-ticket, and quickly recollected it.

Despite putting all his efforts toward staying attentive and making sense of the whole situation, Thomas lost the capacity to stay focused. With a disturbing irregularity and speed, disfigured images started to cascade in his mind: Home. His bed. Two mismatched socks. The immigration officer with her smile. The passenger who was strangely pulling his handbag. Connecting flight. Airport. The inevitable concluding image of the officer who collected his passport. Then came the unhappy end—stranded. He thought of sneaking onto the plane but immediately dismissed that option as childish.

"I think you are a newcomer. May I know your name, please?" A soft masculine voice asked from behind. Thomas suddenly felt relieved to have someone to talk to. He slowly turned his gaze, but in a flash, he lost all desire to speak with anyone and just wanted to run away… somewhere, anywhere.

His words were already reverberating without him realizing how he uttered them: "Hi. I am Thomas. I arrived in the airport an hour ago. But they told me the transit will take…"

"It's okay! Don't worry; I feel you. You are not the only person trapped in this condition. Let's hope that we will leave soon. I am Mohammed."

Thomas was impressed with this stranger's manners.

"The officer told me that I might wait for weeks. Does she really mean it?"

"It would be a blessing if we can go home in weeks. It could take us months or maybe a year."

"I hope you are joking?" Thomas started to rethink his first impression of Mohammed.

"Maybe, maybe not, but how I wish to be a joke."

Mohammed carried Thomas' luggage and took him to the coordinator. Thomas followed him absent-mindedly. On the way, they passed passengers rushing with their luggage. Some were shopping, others relaxed or waited impatiently. For the first time, Thomas started looking around. Familiar franchise names, officers in their uniforms, impatient travelers—it was the usual airport routine he had experienced before.

Following Mohammed, he reached the waiting area. He was surprised to find an established office bustling with many passengers who were casually carrying out their daily routines. Some were feeding their children, others were playing cards, children were running and playing hide and seek between the luggage, and some were calmly sleeping.

Thomas sat at the coordinator's desk with his handbag on his lap.

"Welcome Thomas. God willing, we might leave soon," the coordinator said loud. "At least that is what we are hoping for. It is impossible to tell how long we will be here, but luckily, we provide all the necessities needed to accommodate you for the time in transit. Please fill out this form. I will give you a blanket, a cup, a plate, a fork, a hand mirror, a sheet, and a rug. There is some space in the next hall. You can sleep along with Mohammed's group. We also provide a Bible or a Quran, if you want. All expenses are covered by the generous support of the airport management in collaboration with some donors."

The man's composed tone and manners would have impressed Thomas had it been in a different setting.

"What? What?! What are you taking about?! What am I supposed to do with forks and plates? What the hell are you talking about?" Thomas suddenly became so furious his body started to shake, and he wanted to slap the coordinator. He kicked hard the chair in front of him, but the composure of the man on the other side of the desk made him feel stupid.

"This is not a big deal, brother. It is only a matter of hours. Otherwise, you will soon normalize it. We wish you all the best... But this is not the way to talk to authorities. I only spared you because you are a newcomer. Otherwise, I would have reported you to security."

Thomas started to get up from his seat, only to sink, sobbing, back into the chair.

The loud voice over the intercom brought him back. "Passengers traveling to...." He threw his handbag to the ground.

"Anyways, I wish you all the best," the coordinator said. "Who knows, you may go shortly. Keep praying." Thomas could hear the footsteps of the departing coordinator. He did not know where to go. Disheveled and disillusioned, he covered his face with his palms. He realized that he had no choice but to obey the rules of the game.

"Poor Thomas." Mohammed. "You are making all this fuss because you are a newcomer. I felt exactly like this on my first day. You will get used to this soon. Get up now; I will take you to your house, I mean our hall. We call the halls our house in here."

Mohammed helped him stand and carrying his luggage, led him to the hall.

The hall had about 78 occupants. It was makeshift compartmentalized in some sections using bags and luggage. The 10-inch ceiling had some graffiti. Seating himself in the corner of the hall and supporting his head with his palms, Thomas watched the surreal banality of routines in the hall. The occupants hardly paid him any attention, and he lacked energy to speak. He hated Mohammed and wanted to be alone. The hall was noisy, and children were running freely. Many of the passengers in the hall were sleeping. He could see a notice in bold letters: "NO COOKING IN THE HALL." He could not help smelling onions being cooked—where, he was not able to tell.

The wild and irritating noises, the disturbing games of the children, the smell of overcooked onions and spices—it all made him want to throw up, but where was a bathroom? He didn't want to ask, preferring to wait in agony.

To no avail, he tried to bury his anxiety and forget everything. He fetched his handbag, luckily found some Advil, took two pills and fell asleep. He had an uncomfortable sleep punctuated by unsettling dreams and woke up three times at night.

⬙⬗

EARLY the next morning when Thomas woke up, he was greeted by Okonkwo, the chief coordinator of passengers in transit.

"We should only think how to avert the damage that befalls us," he told Thomas. "The harm has already been made, but you still look at the future and dream big. There is no other way out."

Thomas nodded his head in affirmation, to please Okonkwo. In a muffled voice, he assured him that he was okay.

"I hope you will not wait like us," continued Okonkwo. "It is unfortunate that we have been trapped here for around two years. Here, and in the other three halls, there are around 250 passengers. At the beginning we were around 290, but now we are 250."

Thomas found it hard to distinguish between the solemn tone of the speaker and the message his words conveyed.

"Two years? Here, for two years… you mean?" His voice started to rise, but he lacked the strength to shout.

"Calm down. Everything is in hands of God, and everything happens for a reason. You have to thank the Almighty."

Thomas lost track of what Okonkwo was saying. Over the man's head, Thomas' gaze rested on the pile of luggage.

"Passengers traveling to… the boarding time," the intercom voice droned, although it seemed too slow.

Both men paused. Slowly, Okonkwo continued. "On the first day, we spent the night at this airport because our plane had an engine failure. It was not fixed immediately, and the rest of the aircrafts which stop here for transit are always fully booked. The hijacking of planes and the terrorist attacks did not help us. Most airlines lost confidence and they could not take any of our passengers. Thank God, things have improved dramatically now, and at least we succeeded to send one passenger every month. Some airlines were kind enough to take two. Priority is given to the deceased, the old, children, and women. The story is long. You will hear it from others in the terminal anyway."

Thomas started to imagine how long he could possibly wait in transit.

"Do you mean that there is no any possibility of going out?"

"I am not sure," Okonkwo replied. "No one can be certain. Keep praying. We are hoping to leave soon. Thank you, Lord!"

⚜

IT was the second day that Thomas had gone without food. Okonkwo readily noticed, and as a gesture of welcome invited him for coffee. Thomas did not feel any difference between staying in the hall and going out for coffee. Only to please Okonkwo, he agreed to accompany him.

They went together to a café in the airport. Thomas was envious when he saw workers carrying out their daily, natural routines. Through the glass ceiling, he watched the landing and taking off the planes.

Passengers, employees of the airport, and immigration authorities walked through the café.

"The owner is such a considerate man. He charges us half the regular prices. Friends and families outside also wire us money through him." He pointed at the café owner who was sitting behind the cashier. Thomas listened half-heartedly.

The waitress brought their orders.

Sitting comfortably, Okonkwo began telling his story: "I want to remind you of one thing… There are lots of mischievous people in this transit. They always depend on newcomers. I have already seen some of them with you. Please watch out. More importantly, you better start searching for a job as soon as possible. Never give up!"

"What are you talking about Mr. Okonkwo? What job?"

"My wife is working as a cleaner in one store, and I am a janitor here in the airport. In fact, we were lucky to get such offers. Some have jobs as dishwashers in the cafeteria. The airport management is cooperating. Job priority in the airport is given to us. It is kind of affirmative action." He smiled at his own joke.

Thomas wanted to put himself in their shoes but could not complete the picture as his mind struggled to focus on a single thought. He sipped from his cup avoiding Okonkwo's eyes and stared at the blank wall beside him.

"But I am going for a conference. I am only in transit, and I did not come to live here. What job are you talking about?" Thomas asked. He had to raise his voice as the coffee machines and music became louder. It physically exhausted him to speak louder.

"That is not a big deal, Mr. Thomas. You will soon adjust to it. I advise you to sell your laptop immediately, and I can help if you want. You are physically fit and young, and I assume you will secure a decent job either in the coffee shops or one of the restaurants."

"But the conference..."

"You told me. I am also... I mean, I was also a college professor at home. Thank Lord, if I go home, I mean my country, I will pursue my job at the college. If not, I will always thank God for His guidance and stay for the rest of my life here. We have to be grateful to God for saving us from starvation."

Outside the café, Thomas could see the flight schedule boards and passengers pulling on their handbags. His gaze moved through the small businesses and duty-free shops in the terminal, over the ads and the movement of the passengers.

"Is there a way to sneak out?"

Okonkwo smiled at his naivety and dismissed the suggestion with a gesture. "A long time ago we did a hunger strike, but the worst followed. Some of us were detained for three months. The only option is to accept your destiny make the best of it."

Okonkwo continued: "People in transit die so easily. You wake up early in the morning and you see people who were so healthy hours ago, sprawled out in one corner. In two years, around 30 members of our community have passed away. After some negotiation, the airport management is doing a very good job. They take the bodies to the graveyard and settle the payment. If family members want to send the body home, of course dead bodies are also given priorities according to our procedures."

Thomas was perplexed, but he realized what Okonkwo was implying. He glanced at the posters and ads on the coffee shop.

"May God bless their soul," murmured Okonkwo.

"But how come two years in transit?"

"Everything is in the hands of God. You can even stay for 10 years. I will consider it a miracle if we will be stuck here for only two or three years. I have recently heard—I do not know where—that there are also passengers who were stranded in transit for seven years. Two years is just a piece of cake in comparison to their situation. We have to thank the Almighty for not waiting that long."

"What can be...?"

"Let me finish... We drew upon lifelong lessons in here. It may surprise you that there were some who were traveling to attend the wedding ceremonies of their sons and daughters. The ceremonies took place a long time ago, and they are now waiting to return to their homes. My wife was pregnant, and she gave birth here. I do not have a talent for language, but there are some people who made use of this opportunity. For example, my wife speaks very good French now."

"How is that possible?"

"Her friend is from France. In fact, she is also teaching my younger daughter."

Thomas stared at the walls. "Passengers traveling…," the intercom's announcements continued over the familiar scene of passengers rushing, colliding, and pushing each other.

Okonkwo continued: "The manager of the airport is very cooperative. He always reminds us to pray. He says that if we are patient enough, we can have some of the best opportunities. Some passengers who were stuck in this airport a long time ago got a lifetime career. Some were flight technicians and later became pilots. I did not confirm it, but I heard the former airport manager was promoted to his position as he was originally stranded in transit here."

Okonkwo paused for a response.

Thomas was watching the planes taking off. Turning his gaze, he asked, "Have you ever submitted a petition? What does the management of the airport say?"

"Poor Thomas. You seriously think we could not think of a petition in two years? The former manager was really a tough man. With the new one, however, we turned out to be the beneficiaries. He allowed us a small prayer room for Muslims and Christians. There is a dramatic improvement in our living conditions." Okonkwo looked around furtively before continuing. "A lot of mischief was done by the former coordinator. Priority was given to the deceased, children, and women, but they took advantage of the opportunity for their own interests and left the airport."

"When exactly do you think we will leave?" Thomas realized that for the first time he used "we" instead of "you."

"There is a rumor that we may leave shortly. I met the manager the day before yesterday. He has sworn to me that we will all leave this airport within two years. He sounded confident about it. It is possible that we may also leave within eight months. But we have some obstacles."

"What obstacles do you have?" Thomas asked, but now he was starting to feel dizzy. He yawned and turned his face to avoid Okonkwo's gaze. The duty-free shops, the electric steps, and passengers pulling their luggage immediately reminded him that he was stuck in the airport.

"Some passengers want to stay. They have good jobs here and that's complicating our case," Okonkwo said, trying to smile.

"But how can you lead a normal life confined here? What do you do the entire day?" Thomas had unconsciously stood up and, coming to his senses, lowered back into his seat. He spat in his coffee cup. Immediately, he realized his lack of manners, apologized to Okonkwo, and attempted to look composed.

"Don't worry. You will adjust soon. Just in a week, you will see it as normal. In fact, some good rumors have been circulating."

"What is that?"

"The airport will be expanded to twice its size, and therefore job offers are also expected to be doubled. Who knows, you could also be the manager of one big restaurant that is opening soon," giggled Okonkwo. Before he could stop himself, Thomas smiled.

Some occupants from the hallway were waving at Okonkwo, and he waved and smiled back from his seat, only paying half attention.

IT was lunchtime. Okonkwo led Thomas to the dining hall. Thomas did not want to eat at first, but became hungrier as they walked. They went to their hall, where they collected forks, cups, and plates. For the first time, Thomas perceived the great number of stranded passengers. In the long waiting queue of the dining hall, Thomas saw passengers exchange greetings and updates about their works, while others pushed and nagged at each other. Some smiled at him, and others looked indifferent.

Thomas and Okonkwo waited in line for about half an hour before entering the cafeteria. Thomas felt even hungrier and grabbed a dish. Okonkwo whispered, "Wait for the prayer."

"I am not a believer."

"You will be eventually," Okonkwo said. "Anyway, it is the rule of the cafeteria, and you have to wait." He pointed him to the big poster: "KEEP PRAYING." Okonkwo explained that all the other notices were just translations of the prayer rule.

The prayer started. Only to avoid unnecessary attention, Thomas closed his eyes and stayed still. Similar prayers were recited for about half an hour in different languages: Arabic, Swahili, French, Russian, Urdu, Mandarin, Telugu, and others.

"Have a seat, Tom," whispered Okonkwo.

The long prayer had stolen Thomas' appetite. So desperate to rest, Thomas almost bumped into his chair. He did his best to hide his unease as he ate rice. He threw a confused glance at Okonkwo who apparently understood. "I was not a believer at home. But you need your religion and an identity here. The only thing that has kept us struggling is our faith. I know the prayer is too long, but we could not come up with a better solution. There are always arrivals who want to pray in their own languages. I am afraid that another ten minutes will be added; of course, the management is also obliged to accommodate their demands."

After lunch, they went to their hall. Noon was when all the passengers exchanged news and discussed their day. As customary of the transit, many passengers flocked to welcome Thomas. Okonkwo introduced them by name and respective country. The first visitors were Okonkwo's wife and his daughter. Thomas felt bad not having anything to offer to the child. Instead, he kissed her hand affectionately.

"What a lovely girl—what is her name?"

Okonkwo's wife explained: "I think we are little late in naming her. She is so popular in this transit, everyone hugs and kisses her. Some call her 'Transit'; others call her simply 'Okonkwo's Daughter'. Her dad and I call her 'Our Daughter'. Hopefully we will name her soon."

As Thomas was about to speak, another visitor joined.

He took a long look around the hall. Many were taking their naps after lunch; some were playing cards, many looking at their faces on the small hand mirrors –everywhere, he saw such relaxed faces. Only the piles of luggage made it sound as if they were ready to fly at any time.

"This is Mr. James the most versatile man, and this is Jessica, his daughter," Okonkwo said, gesturing at the two.

Thomas shook hands with Mr. James.

"Nice to meet you, young man," smiled James as he squeezed Thomas' hands hard. Thomas immediately concluded James was an athlete.

Mr. James launched into a lively conversation. His joking nature, simplicity and straightforwardness impressed Thomas. He made fun of their living conditions.

"I am only worried about my daughter; she misses her mom. Otherwise, I am very comfortable here." Mr. James drew attention as he laughed loudly.

"You are right, Mr. James. It is only a matter of acceptance," replied Thomas.

"I heard about you this morning. It is an unfortunate situation for many of us. I was heading from London to Johannesburg before we got stuck in this airport. My daughter was…."

"What did you say, Dad?" interrupted his daughter. "We were going back home from Johannesburg?"

"No! We were heading *to* Johannesburg for your summer break."

"Don't you remember it? We stayed two weeks in Johannesburg and were going back," his daughter said with confidence.

Mr. James asked Okonkwo for confirmation. The girl was right, said Okonkwo.

"Anyway, Mr. Thomas, whether we were going to the north or the south does not matter. The thing is," added Mr. James, "we have waited here for two and a half years."

A new debate ensued about their stay in transit. Others joined. Some said they waited for a year and six months. Some argued that they had waited for two years while others—including Mr. James—said as long as two years and six months.

"I never thought we stayed more than a year and six months," said a young man who stood up in front of Thomas. "I mean, that is a wild guess, and no one can be certain except the Almighty God."

"I know everything is in the hands of God. But you are having a honeymoon here and that is why you subtracted a year," argued Mr. James. "Okonkwo's daughter was born here. She can now walk and talk. At what age does a toddler talk? Just answer me this question." Mr. James raised his voice. He looked more confident.

Each of them looked absolutely convinced, and Thomas was confused.

He followed the heated debates and giggled at the some of the jokes. At times, he joined the conversation. Other times, he listened as an observer. He was repeatedly attempting to put himself in their position and thought he could not have done better than what they were doing.

Lost in his own thoughts, he took a deep breath in the middle of the back and forth, inhaling loud enough to be heard by others sitting next to him, while trying to focus and think clearly about his fate. He started thinking about the worst-case scenario—a plane crash. He realized he was in a much better position than others who had been hijacked. In comparison to many, he told himself, he was lucky indeed.

He inhaled and exhaled again, louder this time. He started thinking about how to make the best of what he was starting to think of as a "mishap."

On and off, Thomas joined the conversation as the notion of the airport providing jobs became a topic of discussion. He hadn't thought of getting a new job but now he realized that he could cover his daily expenses as long as he was in the airport.

"I speak five languages… if there is any vacancy for translation…" Thomas whispered to Okonkwo.

"Sure, if there are any new openings…," answered Okonkwo looking at the ceiling.

Everyone gradually withdrew to take their noon naps. Thomas comforted himself beside Okonkwo, facing the ceiling. As he stayed focused, Okonkwo's words struck him. He looked at the opposite wall. A new glimmer of light was emanating from the dark blue walls. Thomas raised his head, his face brightening with hope, and turned toward Okonkwo.

"Are you sure the manager promised that we will all leave within two years? Does he seem certain that we will go home in two years?" asked Thomas.

"Maybe," answered Okonkwo, barely audible.

Abraham T. Zere *is US-based Eritrean journalist/writer and founding executive director of* PEN Eritrea *in exile. Among others, his work has been published in* The Guardian, Al Jazeera English, The Independent, Index on Censorship Magazine, *and* Dissent Magazine. *His short story The Flagellates was included in* The Global Anthology (2017), *an initiative that gathers a short work of prose from every country in the world edited by Michael Barron. With* PEN Eritrea *colleagues Daniel Mekonnen and Tedros Abraham, he has edited the book:* Uncensored Voices: Essays and Poems and Art Works by Exiled Eritreans (Loecker Erhard Verlag, 2018).

How To Break
Tim Baroraho

THIS IS NOT a self-help essay. Nor is it meant to be gimmicky, nor trendy nor zeitgeisty. This is how I talk, how I think. I promise. But why would you believe me? Let me try to convince you while maintaining that I don't need your approval. Maybe your attention. Equally bad? Don't judge.

I stopped watching the news regularly after I got fed up of someone else setting the agenda. Some people deciding what our reality is and us letting them. Wasn't the point of being free from our darkness and sins that we could be free form others' as well? Or that we had the choice to engage or not? Whether we truly could or not is business for another day. We would have the freedom to find out.

I wanted to take back my entire life. What did I really like? What was pretending, appeasing? What was me? Was my life only about the price of oil? Another egomaniacal politician's incompetence? I wanted to find what was underneath firmly established frameworks. The possibilities which lay there for me. The version(s) of myself I could be. The lives I could lead. The (wave) lengths I could reach. The places I could run to and hide. Dimensions I could get lost in and never return. Where everything is molded by my hands. The less wordy account is that I want to create my own world. But who doesn't?

I didn't always want to because I didn't know how. There were fewer things as meaningless as finding yourself. Mostly because I saw things along the lines of how there's no way to know the real you untainted by the curse of upbringing, by the world around you. You make peace with that and negotiate the best deal.

Still, I have been stuck on this notion of stripping, peeling away to reach some depth within me. Of what? I don't know. Truth, I suppose. Some inherent worthiness. Shedding bits of yourself feels nothing like throwing off a fur coat (I wonder which part of me is a glamour pussy; a gangsta; a savage? Are words enough to draw him? It?)

IN the beginning was an egg; big enough to contain the entire universe. The details vary. There are tales attributed to Native American spirituality in which a giant egg is cracked, unleashing the Universe, Earth, Gods. Amongst the Bande and Yoruba, there are similar concepts. Within the Bantu too. In ancient Egypt is the egg from which Ra came out of. The Amma of the Dogon created an egg that was the source of the Universe.

In Chinese Daoist tradition, a deity named Pan Gu grew inside the egg. As this deity tried to get out, the egg cracked into halves. The upper half would become the sky and cosmos while the lower half became the earth and sea. Pan Gu got ever more powerful and large, widening the miles between earth and sky until, finally, they were hidden from one another, forever.

I GET a little carried away with beginnings. I want to know the exact origin of things. There's the obvious conclusion: a means to trace a journey, find the detours, re-route. Of course. Instead, I'm more interested in something more— fun? I want to find present elements in the genesis. I want to predict the future.

I've often thought of myself as psychic. When I'm being generous with myself, I will choke it down to intuition, to being an empath, looking beyond the surface. When I'm putting myself down it's something more sinister: I'm an over-thinker who obsesses over as many possible outcomes as I can. A control freak.

I began as the first child of a young couple in love who split the year I turned into a teenager. I was a happy kid who would become suicidal. A goody-two shoes who wouldn't handle his alcohol. What were the signs? What should I have known from the beginning, what had I missed? Could it have been possible not to? Must I regret? Before my missteps, before my reactions, before these questions, what existed? Is that my essence? Or am I formed by all of these things?

IT is said that Pan Gu had lived for 18,000 years in the egg. Things happened over time. There's more to the story than a bored god who broke an egg and created an entire world. In the egg it was dark, it was silent.

I KNOW a thing or two about darkness and silence. I have had a life-long dreariness of them. I'd lie awake at night staring at the ceiling, wondering what happened when we die. Such a morbid kid I was. I started off being comforted by a Heaven where everything would be perfect until I learnt the idea was that you spent Eternity bowing to the Lord. I mean, Sunday Mass was bad enough. I looked to Hell to end this troubling permanence. There, the burning would not stop. Back to Heaven. I was young so the assumption was that I would make it. If I remembered to pray, if I was a good boy, if I didn't tell lies.

I took after my mother who gave her life to Christ a few months after my sixth birthday. I learnt how to bind spirits and cast them into bottomless pits sealed with His blood. To give of yourself and your possessions. To detest things of the world. I learnt through the weekly fellowships she hosted and the church services I accompanied her to. I heard people speak in tongues. I listened to voices claiming to be demons speak through people. I watched my mother fast her life away. She turned the colour off and opted for a mute life. A simple one of meager pleasures without booze or extravagant dreams. A chaste life for Him. I hated being there.

Yet I knew it was the difference between unending boredom or suffering. I persisted. I took down my Britney poster and threw away my rock CDs. I crammed Hillsong lyrics. I learnt to hate sin. To stop kissing boys, to pray after I failed. I learnt to hate the parts of myself that loved sin. I discovered how to bribe those parts with Shame. Sometimes it worked, most times it didn't. I learnt how to contain my filth. Hide it and act like it wasn't there. I learnt how to keep secrets.

WITHIN the egg, yin and yang existed before Pan Gu was conceived. They were not in balance, or even separate. It was just some substances and energies reacting with each other. Pan Gu was the result. Yin and yang separated when he cracked the egg open. All that was light and clear rose up, making the Heavens. The dark and heavy shit sank down to form the Earth. That's why we're fucked. It wouldn't be a myth without some good ole' light is good, dark is bad symbolism, would it?

MY faith kept leaving and coming back to me, ebbing and flowing. I was continually having epiphanies and revelations that seduced me into new territories of being until I was too far adrift, along Road Less Travelled Upper Hill Lane, left only with the overpowering aftertaste of stupidity that novelty leaves after its glimmer wears off. I swapped the Lord for independence and sought a different kind of courage. I started drinking. The battle scars (quick-and-easy guilt, self-righteousness, occasional judgment) and war spoils (faith—albeit godless and fluctuating, compassion, humility) of my Christian days remained.

I feared becoming a fixed thing. Like the people I knew: a full-fledged person with a distinctive set of characteristics and shit. That guy people knew what to expect from. I wanted to be hard to pin down, free. I wanted to fly and be grounded at the same time. Roots sunk in by a weightless spirit. I wanted everything. Through it all I had an anchor keeping me tethered to some uninterrupted form of myself—my mother.

PAN Gu worried the egg would shut itself up. He stood between the two halves keeping them away from each other. Every day, the sky rose by ten feet while the Earth was hollowed by the same proportions. Pan Gu also grew by the same height, each day for 18,000 years. He became a giant.

IN writing about my mother, I'm vested in the politics of the metaphor I have been drawn to. The egg. Somewhere in my notes, I ask, is it anti-feminist? I don't know. Surprisingly, my initial attraction to the egg was for its shell. Boundaries. Something both my mother and I have struggled with. We have laid out red carpets to have our emotional spaces invaded. In Mummy's (I still call her that) case, it was her sisters that she was unable to request to move out when a short stay was lengthened to several years. Even when it became unliveable. With me, it was telling anybody who could listen how unloveable I felt; whenever I got drunk. Talking about feeling too wobbly, too here and there to ever impress. Thinking I needed to impress. Mummy and I have both been too concerned about being liked.

I laugh with my eyes closed, like I just recently learnt how to and now can't stop myself from giving into it, a friend wrote of me. My mother laughs the same way. We have each other's self-deprecating dark sense of humour. We love to look cute. We forget about how we look when we're down. We forget many things when we're down. I reckon that's another reason for the metaphor. Chicken? Egg? Who is influencing whom? Because my mother is older, the tendency is to say she has fashioned me in some way. Or I have fashioned myself according to her. I don't like the implication that we can't genetically be similar. As in, had I not grown up with her, wouldn't I still be like her?

As I said, I have a thing for beginnings. Root causes. I'm careful not to say blame because that is not what I am after. Nor do I have the right. I just want the why.

When I found myself in a major depressive episode, I was horrified. I had never experienced anything like it—a little time off stretched past months, into a year. I drank again after years, became reacquainted with Shame. Everything became soaked in it. I felt entitled and spoilt. I had wobbled again and fallen out of place. I sank. During this period, I saw a therapist. I wrote after a two-year hiatus. I saw my masculine and feminine aspects as complementary. A spiritual hedonist. A bohemian with "gentlemanly" posture that I felt pretentious about.

I looked at my mother. For a long time after things ended with my father, all she did was get up to take my little sister to school. Come see me on visitation days at boarding school. Visit family, some friends. She took things easy and withdrew from just about the whole ball of wax. She knew Shame. It was being seen as a failed woman because she couldn't 'keep' a man, being left out of church groups because she wasn't married and losing her place in the world. She watched too many Nigerian movies and played a lot of Judith Babirye. She made jokes about things, we (her, my little sister and I) laughed. We learnt the rules of our position—which was only one. Don't be offended when people called your home broken. We got hooked on *Desperate Housewives*.

One day Mummy got up and went back to school. It was twenty years since her diploma in Secretarial Studies and she re-did her O'Levels. Then her A'Levels. Got into Makerere and earned a degree in Social Administration. She took classes in feminist theory. It can be said that she has grown gigantically. Become some kind of patron saint for the single, even while still alive. She gave me the map to get out of where I was. You sink, you surrender, you float.

PAN Gu held on that long because he needed to be sure that the realms could stand on their own. He collapsed, exhausted. His last breath we know as the winds and clouds, his voice as the thunder, his left eye as sun. The right eye is the moon, his hair and beard are the stars. Limbs, hands and feet, the mountains. Rivers flowed from his blood. Flesh as soil, bones, teeth and nails as minerals. Skin as vegetation. Sweat as rain.

MY mother wants grandchildren from me. I mansplain about global warming and not wanting to bring children into this mess. She implores that things will get better, she's praying. I quote some 'key' figures: degrees, water levels, that kind of thing. We both know the conversation we are dodging. The reason she's looking down and avoiding my eyes. She offers to take care of them. I humour her: no, they would be in a boarding school, or not like her much. For those seconds her eyes light up as we take turns expanding the story, adding scenes, sharpening the tone. Her eyes glimmer and her smile is full. Then the routine drags and we stop.

She reminds me about a thing I have to do tomorrow. I thank her. We talk about her friend's daughter's upcoming wedding. We realize we're back to the same conversation and start to fade out the length of our responses. Soon, we're in separate rooms saying our prayers. She has a Bible in her hand and she asks for forgiveness and guidance. I write about my doubts and adventures. I am looking for connection. The less holier-than-thou account is we each find what works.

THE point is not whether the Pan Gu story is fact. It's that it can work. Notwithstanding my being an African writer set against the background of the impending so-called Chinese take-over. Take a pick: a pros and cons list on why I should not restrict myself to African mythology; a brief history on pre-colonial Afro-Chinese trade relations; a yin and yang dissection of how I can take inspiration from anywhere as long as I do so *incontextio*. Hashtag respect, hashtag honour.

The less sarcastic account is that a metaphor is less important than the real thing. It builds a world but is not the world itself. I began as an egg. I have cracked and broken. Transformed into a miracle. As we all do. It's an ethos for living. We're all fragile, we break, yet we can mend and always into something better. *Blah blah blah.* But in my own cheesy-to-everyone-but-me-which-is-the-point-I-guess way.

ON my jog one evening, I will run up a hill. I will slow down as I reach the top. I will walk. I will feel a presence behind me, turn, see a man running up towards me. He will stop when he sees me, go back down. A *boda* guy will be waiting for him. I will hear him speak into a phone, "Hit him on the head with a stone." I will look at them; they will look at me and leave. I will feel bad for whoever it was they were talking about. In that selfish human way, I will be glad they were not talking about me. I will feel relieved. I will continue up the hill and find another *boda* guy. He'll be parked and he will look at me. I will feel a very dark presence so much so that I won't feel like I'm exaggerating when I think his is the face of evil. I will cross the road and continue climbing the hill. I will not run. I will see him turn and leave in the opposite direction. I will feel safe.

I will look behind and see a car and *boda* approach, headlights in full beam. I will lose and regain consciousness. I will watch *bodas* come and go past me. I won't know why. I will look for my phone and fail to find it. I won't know where I am. I will be saved by a fourth *boda* who will lift me off the ground and take me to a clinic. I will realize I am bleeding. My head will need four injections to calm the swelling and be stitched. Strangulation marks will be found around my neck. A CT scan will show that I'm OK. I will feel buoyant as my parents take care of me. Childishly indulged. I will recover.

A few days later, I will play the radio I haven't listened to in years. I will dance. I won't take the radio off for weeks. I will accept my mortality. My smallness. I will relish the deluded fantasy that is my love of horoscopes and mysticism. A dance in cynicism and hope, knowing but still not knowing, shape-shifting into metaphors abundant enough for the season, wobbling on your own terms.

I will believe it when I call myself an artist. I will think maybe I have something to say with The Writing. I will read books no longer as indulgence but burning prayers that needed to come to life. I will think the same of writing. I will watch movies with the intensity of my grandmothers preparing Christmas lunch in Hoima. I will return to wearing clothes with the boyish vanity—playfully showing off my vision for my Self—I had at nine-ish, ten. Branding in Millennial. I won't find it excessive or non-consequential. Or it won't matter. I'll tire of explaining. I'll hope this lasts forever even when I know it most likely won't.

I'll finally finish this essay and wonder what it means that it took such dramatic circumstances to speak on all of this. How I could only do so once I required a supernatural sequence of events I could tolerate. I will remember that my soft underside is real. I will feel angry that I could have died and what had I been doing with this little Life of mine? I will take an honest look at things and want back a lot of time. The less sappy account is that the incident will make me want to be more intentional with my life.

I will believe in things again. A more rigorous description might be that after the void that is a death too soon, anything short of it would be somewhat thrilling. I would now be more easily, shall I say, moved? I will worry about my jelly-like wobbliness but I won't dwell on it. The sound of waves at any shore will release my Spirit into its surroundings. In cold weather I will refuse to stay in my bed alone. I will break. Many, many, many times.

Tim Baroraho *is a writer and human rights lawyer. He is a 2018 alumnus of the* Purple Hibiscus Trust Creative Writing Workshop. *In these times we live in, he is finding radical vulnerability a most crucial strategy. He's crazy about scented candles, making contact with aliens and long walks.*

Nobody's Child
Bob G. Kisiki

AMANDA Nakandha stood erect and listened… The faint knock came again. For one, she barely received visitors at her house. Anybody who came to the house had a definite reason to be there—delivering the weekly milk supply (but that man came every Monday, yet this was Friday; collecting the litter every other day, but the rubbish man had been only the previous day; or any other reason, but people always called first. So who was knocking? Secondly, it was late evening. What would anybody want now?

"May I go and open the door, mummy?" Nicholas tugged at his mother's arm. His eyes burned with enthusiasm. That was him; he spoke with bountiful gusto and acted with unrestrained fervour.

"Go sit down, Nico," his mother said, gently extricating herself from the boy. "I'll go check."

She nudged Nicholas to a seat against the dining area wall; the one that divided the dining area from the boy's bedroom, with her hand against the nape of his head. "Be good."

"Okay mummy."

Amanda could have sworn she knew the woman whom she found standing a respectable distance from the entrance to the house. Standing about five foot seven, with gentle features that made her look more than just tame, the woman was an obvious beauty. If Amanda found the general looks and overall disposition familiar, a closer study of the woman's eyes removed all doubt. It was like Amanda looked at… nay, looked *into* those eyes on a daily basis. Just who was she? Where had she seen her?

"I can see you're fighting to recognize me," the woman said. She spoke as gently as she looked, enunciating each syllable like the words cost her money, but she needed them anyway, so she used them with love and generosity.

"Welcome. How may I help you?" Amanda involuntarily planted an arm on each side of the door, like to block the intruder from getting in and disrupting their peace.

"Do you mind if we talk while seated?" the woman said, without taking any step towards the house. It was like she expected that they would just sit on the paver-fitted yard and talk.

Amanda stepped aside and swung her arm in a wide arc, motioning woman to get into the house.

"Thank you."

It was uncannily dry; bland and curt. Amanda thought that was a sudden, uncalled for change from the earlier geniality. The woman walked into the house and, before Amanda could tell her to, she had sat down in a chair. Amanda too entered after her and sat in the seat by the door. She fixed the woman with a demanding gaze.

"My name is Agnes. Agnes Wananda. I am—"

"Nice to meet you," Amanda cut her short, but she proceeded like there had been no disruption.

"Seven years are quite a spell, so I can't blame you for not remembering me… that's if you do not."

Again, Amanda wondered why the impolite tone, but chose to let her talk. The sooner she got rid of the woman, the better.

"Did you by any chance deliver a baby at Namungalwe Hospital seven years ago?"

Amanda sat bolt upright. "Yes. Why?"

"I too did. I—"

"Don't bother. Goodness, there's no way I could remember you. Been seven whole years. How could I remember?"

"No, you wouldn't. You wouldn't," she repeated the words, like emphasizing the fact that Amanda had no reason to take note of the passage of time.

Again there was something about her tone that bruised Amanda's inner tissue. She shifted tentatively in her seat, coughed and then said, "Wako ward?"

"Yes. Now you recall," the woman said. "It's been long."

"What happened then, besides us getting our babies?" Amanda was suspicious.

"Maybe not besides… maybe *after*…"

"I don't follow."

"Presently. Can you believe we have each raised the wrong baby?"

"Huh?"

"Either I have raised your child all this time, or you didn't get any child at all, for the baby you returned home with isn't yours." Wananda fixed Amanda with a stern, albeit lingering gaze. "That is precisely why I am here."

The finality with which this woman spoke bothered Amanda. She needed to make her stand clear.

"I don't know about you, but the child I came back home with was… is mine. No doubt about that." She spoke coolly, but decidedly.

"That is you saying so. I can fund a DNA test and I am sure it will return positive for my blood or his father's."

"Oh, that is indeed very confident of you. Aren't you scared of the repercussions of a possible negative?" Amanda tried to sound confident, but something told her this woman had a case.

"No room for that. I am sure of what I am saying. See, I too, like you, are a social media buff. So just yesterday, I saw your… I saw my son as he danced at their cultural gala… at school."

"At school?"

"Yes, at school… where you also were."

"You lose me. How is his dancing connected to his not being Col. Musoke's son? Oh, you probably mean to say that you at some point… um…"

"Slept with your man? No. Not a chance in five million. I have my man. Now I want our son. Where's my boy?"

"Which son do you mean? Which boy are you looking for in my house?"

Amanda's anger was beginning to rise. Wananda realized it.

"And even if I were to hand my precious boy to you, where is the one you insinuate is mine?"

"I am talking about my son. I am more than convinced that the medical staff at Namungalwe made a mistake. I am sure that they switched our babies; giving me yours and giving you mine. That picture you shared on Facebook is my saving grace. I had always battled the thought that the child I had was not mine, but there was no evidence of it. Oh, how my heart ached!"

Without saying a word, Amanda got up and headed to the inner part of the house, where her son was. But, reading Amanda's mind, Agnes also got up and followed Amanda.

"Where are you going?" Amanda barked at her, then recoiled immediately, as she realized what she had just done. She couldn't believe she had barked at someone. "Look, I am sorry. That's not how I talk, but…"

"No need. I too would probably react that way, if after seven years of raising a child it suddenly dawned on me that the child wasn't mine after all. So, may I have my boy? I am sure he's the one you were walking to… Maybe to hide him."

Just then, Nicholas walked into the room, stopping suddenly between the two women, each of whom reached for his arm. While Amanda grabbed his right hand, Agnes took hold of the left. Nicholas' alarm could not be hidden. He quickly extricated himself from the stranger's hold and held onto his mother's legs, like his entire life and future depended on it. The other woman tried to reach for him, but Amanda blocked her.

"Listen, Agnes Wananda. It will be best you leave my house. First, this is trespass. Nobody enters another person's house and begins to behave the way you're doing."

"Really? How did I think that you had actually led me in here? Anyhow, why don't you save us all the discomfort by surrendering my son?"

It was when Amanda looked angrily into the impudent woman's face that she was struck by what she saw. Truth is, she could as well have been looking into her son's… *Oh heck!* What was this? For, the thing that had disturbed her when she first saw Wananda… It was the resemblance between Nicholas and this woman who claimed him as her son. Especially those eyes… How could anybody explain that away?

"Listen, Amanda Nakandha—"

"Who told you my name?" she was stunned.

"The same person who directed me here. I have sought out my son for six years and eight months. I have asked questions. I have moved places. I have done homework… Till I got here this evening. And, Amanda, I am not spending the night. No, neither am I ready and willing to be retained any longer." Again she tried to grab Nicholas, but he eluded her. Amanda also stood before the boy, so that she stood akimbo between him and Wananda.

"I am not going anywhere, mummy. You're my only mummy. I am staying here," Nicholas cried, clinging onto his mother.

"Yes, Nico; you're indeed going nowhere. Mummy is here to protect you."

"His real mummy is here to collect him and take him where he belongs— at her home."

Again she made a dash for him, and a struggle ensued. When Agnes tried to sidestep Amanda to get to Nicholas, Amanda made a dash for it, shielding her. At the same time, Nicholas kept running round his mother, evading Agnes, who was reaching for him. Thus they went on, running in the same squeezed space, making a cacophonous noise and attracting the attention of neighbours, who crowded at the door but could not get in, for the moment she got the chance, Amanda darted to the door, turned the key, pulled it out and threw it out the window, into the lawn. Now they were all indoors, with the door locked and the key outside.

Outside, the noise of the gathered neighbourhood was overwhelming, too. Some pleaded that Amanda lets them in. Some urged the stranger to leave. Many inquired about what was going on in the house. It just did not make sense.

As Amanda tried to focus on the external noises, Agnes quickly rushed at her, sending her sprawling on the rug and grabbing Nicholas. Quickly getting up, Amanda tried to get the now wailing boy, but Agnes could not let go.

"I am going to call the police," Amanda said as she ran to her bedroom to collect her mobile phone—the same phone she had used to advertise her son on Facebook. When Amanda was gone into the inner rooms, Agnes pleaded with the throng outside to look for the key and open for her. That, though, only gave one of them, a neighbour and friend of Amanda's, to look for the key and then walk away. Nobody saw her pick the key; nobody noticed her slink away.

So when Amanda succeeded in getting through to the police, they told her they would be at her house 'in a jiffy'. The woman she had talked to knew her from the evangelical church where Amanda fellowshipped. And, true to Afande Mande's word, the cops were in the yard barely ten minutes later.

The crowd paved way for the two men and one woman, Afande Mande, as they strode towards the house. When she heard the car's siren advance, Amanda, relieved, walked to the door. Agnes, holding the boy with both hands, stepped away from the door, aware that the first thing the police would do was rescue the boy from her. She knew that the police would side with Amanda, whom they knew personally.

"Open the door," Afande Mande, the OC CID at the station that was only about five kilometres away, shouted.

"The key is out there," Amanda said.

"Out where?"

"In the lawn grass."

Amanda's desperation knew no bounds.

When they heard that the key was somewhere in the grass, all the people fell to looking for it. But search as they could, they could not find it. Afande Mande was getting really worked up. Amanda was getting frantic by the minute. Nicholas wailed his lungs out, but Agnes would not let go of him. The pandemonium was prohibitive!

"I am left with no option but to leave you in your mess, Amanda," Afande Mande said, exasperation lining his tone.

"No! please wait; those people will find the key. People, please search some more. You will find it."

The entire crowd, including the two policemen, fell to searching for the key again. And, as expected, they could not find it.

"I am going, Amanda. I am sorry."

"No, Afande Mande. Okay, break the door. Break the door please."

"I need a warrant to do that. Is this your house?"

"No. I rent it."

"I can't break it. It's illegal."

She called the two men to stop searching for what she called 'the elusive key' and they leave. When she heard that, Amanda began wailing like she had lost a relative.

"She will kill my son. I don't know why she has done this. Afande Mande, this impostor has my son in her hands. Please help me!"

When they heard that, the people now crowded at the window.

Ayayaya! Whose son is that boy?

Eh, eh, eh! People can look alike!

Wait a moment, is that Amanda's son like for real?
Ggwe, you. That… no, this case is clear!
Ye why did she put the boy on Facebook?
Facebook, you idiot!
Whatever…

"Afande Mande, please break the door," Amanda cried.

When she turned and saw that Agnes wasn't in the living room, Amanda became hysterical. She shouted at the top of her lungs. Just then, the crowd outside burst into rowdy shouting, with some turning towards the gate and giving chase.

There!

She's escaped!

No, it's the boy. He's escaped!

What had happened is, while the melee progressed, Nicholas suddenly got an idea. Whispering to Agnes, he told her they could open the rear door and escape. "I can see who my real mother is," he had told her and, blindly, she had let go of him, so he could open the door. But the moment he opened it, he took to his heels, making for the gate. Agnes gave chase, but she was no match for the young boy. By the time the crowd realized what had happened, it was too late; Nicholas had gone out the gate and into the open street. When Amanda realized what had happened, almost everyone had left her compound to run after the woman who had claimed her son as her own, and the boy of contention himself. The police too had followed the crowd. Darkness had descended.

Bob G. Kisiki *is an author with five published novels, as well as poetry and short stories in various anthologies in Uganda and beyond. The vice president of* PEN Uganda *responsible for publicity, he has also worked with the organisation to run writing workshops in three of Uganda's prisons, coming up with an anthology of inmates' writing, titled,* As I Stood Dead before the World. *Bob is also a columnist with* New Vision, *as well as a publishing consultant, writing coach and biographer.*

The Super Dancer
Josh Mali

"KIVUNDU'S voice bellowed through the alleys…" grandma began her long-awaited tale without warning, stopping momentarily as gossipy whispers went around the bonfire.

We had all been looking forward to this, all day long. At breakfast, my brother, Wafula, had declared his desire to be president one day—an appetite he had voiced again after our lunch gathering, prompting grandma to roll her eyes so hard that she could have won the world eye-rolling contest, had there been one. I wondered why these declarations coincided with mealtimes. After a brief consideration, grandma had asked for a bonfire to be lit in front of our house that evening, closer to the only avocado tree in the compound that bore the worst-tasting, watery avocados. A few metres from the tree, was a little fence that separated the lawn from our banana plantation.

Grandma had asked everyone to gather around the bonfire immediately after dinner. She'd an unmissable story to tell, she'd said. It was important that every youngling in the family brought their frame and mass of somatic cells before the bonfire, she'd stressed. We would all be engrossed in it, she had promised. But most importantly, everyone, especially Wafula, would learn an important lesson from the tale, she'd concluded.

My sister Bea, as usual, was late for the gathering. She'd sneaked off to go and see our neighbour's son—they'd recently fallen in love and were constantly swooning over each other. Surely, grandma's tale wasn't as important as quelling the tumultuous desires of the heart, my sister had decided in her hot-blooded teen wisdom.

And so, it happened that my sister Bea wasn't present when grandma rendered her opening line, nor was she done with her amorous escapades when grandma delivered the narrative that followed, as all of us listened attentively.

"Kivundu's voice bellowed through the alleys, journeying from the front to the rear," grandma resumed her narration.

"Ladies and gentlemen, good evening, and welcome."

Silence.

All the animated chattering suddenly ceased, transforming the theatre hall into one silent tube. The MC had caught his cue.

"Ladies and gentlemen," he carried on, "It's that time of the year again; on an evening that you're all familiar with, unless you were born only a year ago," he said, grinning, evidently amused by what he had just said, or about to say. "In which case," he went on, "you would be forgiven for being in the wrong place. But maybe your parents should be charged with child abuse."

Laughter. And then silence.

"Every year, for the last fifty years, our country has celebrated this special evening—an evening that defines who we are, and where we are."

Applause.

"It's an evening that brings out the titans that best represent our culture through dance. It's an evening when a few words are uttered—except of course by this chatterbox that is currently holding the microphone because it's the only way he knows how to feed his family…"

Laughter.

"…an evening, friends, when we celebrate the best in dance. On this night, every year, the very best of our dancing folk come onto this stage to tussle it out for the crown in the realm of dance."

"Today," the MC continued, "we will know whether the current reigning champion will be dethroned, or if he will retain his crown, to continue an unprecedented feat of taking the crown for what now seems like countless times."

Cheers. Murmurs, followed by looks of disbelief.

"Time to stop him," some in the audience shouted.

"Time to start the contest, ladies and gentlemen," the MC went on, ignoring the remonstrations. "But first, a quick reminder of the house rules," he said, like a school examination invigilator, sounding a little more stern that he had at the beginning.

"First, each dance contestant will dance to a maximum of two songs of their choice. Secondly, once their two songs are finished, a dancer must exit the stage for the next dancer."

"Yesss!" shouted some in the audience.

"Nooo," thundered others, betraying divided loyalty.

"You may applaud the dancers, but no talking on phone or to your neighbour during the dance," concluded the MC, to increasing anticipation.

"Ladies and gentlemen, without further ado, I would like to invite the first contestant on stage," declared the MC, before thundering, "Put your hands together, ladies and gentlemen for Wilton, the dance doctor!"

"Wilton! Wilton! Wilton!" the first dancer's fans chanted, with some whistling, some ululating in high-pitched voices, while a much more animated lady in red stood up to do a little dance of her own, wiggling her waist invitingly as Wilton walked onto the stage with a lot of pomp.

"We love you like money!" shouted one enthusiastic fan, to the amusement of the audience.

Wilton smiled, assured of more chants and cheers as he got ready to launch into his dance routine. He stopped mid-stage, and looked at the audience seductively, his eyes wandering through the hall in search of enamoured eyes. There were many, including the pair of cathode-ray bulbs on the frontal cranium of the lady who had wriggled her waist rather enthusiastically seductively. His eyes and hers locked into each other, as he momentarily forgot the purpose of his presence on stage. He brushed his left hand through his afro, and then repeated the same act with his right hand, in what one would perhaps interpret as an attempt to pull back his brains to the position they had occupied before the temptress in the audience tried to make them abandon him. That aside, it was clear that he had invested quite a bit of time in combing and moulding the woolly overgrowth on his scalp. And then he closed his eyes, and signalled to the DJ to play his first song.

Drums.

The first beat boomed through the hall with a thundering that nearly got everyone in the audience to their feet. But it was not their show, so they restrained themselves, keeping their place as cheerers. Wilton had the cue. He stepped forward with flair, deftly throwing his left foot forward and then, standing on his right, did a spin that set the crowd off, melting the hall into a congregation of boisterous cheers!

Wilton worked through what were evidently well-choreographed strokes, hypnotizing his fans with one move after another. It was amazing how he switched his dance strokes from salsa to rhumba with ease. He affected an aura of a polished performer, born to rule the dance floor. To him, dancing was an art, and he was the painter, transforming the canvas into whatever he pleased effortlessly. It was a fitting honour to have him as the opening act for an evening that had been long coming. He was a joy to watch.

As the first song wound to a climax, Wilton began working his way to whatever best strokes he had saved for last. Suddenly, to the disappointment of many, the music stopped. There was a technical hitch. A downcast Wilton waved to his fans affectionately, before walking backstage to refresh while the unexpected snag was fixed. The MC announced that the dance would resume as soon as the technical team had resolved the minor glitch that had crawled in to put a damper to a wondrous evening.

After a few minutes, the music boomed back to life. The MC stepped back on stage, ready to announce the continuation of Wilton's dance. But before he could reach the microphone, the next dancer majestically walked onto the stage and grabbed the microphone. Popularly known as Daddy Gamin, he was known to possess an impatience that had no breathing rival. Apparently, the technical hold-up had taken a bite into his time, and he could not wait on the sides any longer. He wanted to get on stage as soon as possible to do his thing, and he wasn't going to wait for the MC's announcement.

"Ladies and gentlemen," Daddy Gamin started. The hall responded with silent anticipation. Nobody knew what to expect, as Daddy Gamin had never participated in the dance competition before. Only a few, cautious whispers could be heard. But there was something about him that ebbed the little unease that had momentarily crept into the hall: his face beamed extravagantly and affectionately.

"It's my turn," he said curtly, before dropping the mic and beginning to rock to the now-fading tune of Wilton's first song, unabashed.

The DJ was clearly unprepared, so he scrambled through the collection of music CDs, looking for Daddy Gamin's CDs. Each dancer had been asked to submit two CDs with two songs. But Daddy Gamin had, for some unknown reason, submitted only one CD.

"I need two CDs with the two songs you'll dance to," the DJ had said to him, when he submitted what was supposed to be his music of choice.

"Everything I'll dance to, is in there," he had retorted impatiently.

The DJ remembered that brief conversation as he finally found Daddy Gamin's CD, examined it hurriedly, and slotted it into the player.

As the first beats of the song came to life, Daddy Gamin sauntered from one end of the stage to the other, and then started swaying his massive body from side to side. He continued grinning and waving to the audience. They waved back affably. Assured of their support, he launched into an energetic dance move that got the hall erupting into delirious cheers. Maybe it was the energy with which he did his thing. Or perhaps the clumsiness with which he executed his dance strokes. Whatever it was he was doing, his first strokes had struck the right notes with the audience and rallied them all behind him. He was a little overenthusiastic, one would say. He expended large amounts of energy on his first paces. Some in the audience wondered if he would last to the end, with that extravagant use of his calories. No one was sure whether he would win the dance contest, but he had certainly brought something new onto the stage. The audience momentarily forgot about the dexterity with which Wilton had been executing his dance. It was, suddenly, all about 'the new kid on the block' as some said.

What was supposed to be the first song transitioned into another, without the characteristic intermission that allowed the MC to announce the end of one dance and prepare the audience for the next. As it turned out, Daddy Gamin had mixed his songs to play nonstop on the CD he submitted. No one knew for how long his CD would be playing, and it seemed like Daddy Gamin would be dancing for a lifetime. But it wasn't too long before his energy ebbed. Fissures crept into his hitherto sprightly performance, slowing his stride and strokes withal. Daddy Gamin had promised so much at the start, and then had outdone himself with the nonstop dance. He had depleted his biological resources, just like that, and with that, the audience's animated enthusiasm for his performance. He lurched forward with a few laboured strides to try and reenergize the audience but was received with boos of derision instead. Some of Wilton's fans, perhaps a little nostalgic, started chanting his name again, while some pelted Daddy Gamin with little missiles of rolled entry tickets. Sensing the new hostility, Daddy Gamin hurried off the stage, escorted by more booing and celebratory chants. The audience was happy to momentarily take over the theatre again from Daddy Gamin's imposing presence and demand a real contest.

After a little confusion, and to the relief of many, the MC emerged again from backstage and reached for the mic.

"Ladies and gentlemen," he began his announcement, sounding a little less assured than he had at the onset of the dance contest. "Time to resume our normal programme after that rude interruption. Certainly, judging from the little foregoing episode, the man who thought he was the best dancer neither lived up to your expectations nor his own."

Laughter.

"But now that you've ejected him and reclaimed the dance floor, we shall waste no more time," announced the MC, followed by ear-splitting chants.

"Wilton! Wilton! Wilton!"

The MC understood.

"Okay, ladies and gentlemen. It seems only fair, that we let the first dancer complete his performance because he didn't get a chance to, following that technical hitch and..."

"Yes! Yes! Yes!" shouted some of Wilton's fans, drowning the MC's voice.

"And so, ladies and gentlemen, let's put our hands together once again, as we welcome Wilton back on stage."

The energy with which the audience applauded was telling! It was as though they had all been injected with new doses of adrenaline and were only awaiting a vent. And there it was, presented in the second coming of Wilton.

Wilton could feel the love in the air. He stepped forward as he had done when he first appeared on stage. He skipped all but one of the antics of yore: the hand-through-the-hair gesture. The audience loved it. And they responded with cheers and whistling. The DJ wasted no time, as he let the sound of Wilton's second choice song reverberate through the hall. Wilton was back in the act, quickly sliding into his dance element. It wasn't long though, before bouts of disruptive noises started emerging from backstage. Wilton ignored all that and continued working through his dance routine. He kept his focus on the audience, whose attention he sought to sustain. And sustain it, he did for quite some time, until the dying minutes of his dance. It was then that the speakers in the hall went silent once again, followed by darkness. The commotion backstage had resulted in the disconnection of the main cable connecting the DJ's machine to the speakers, while someone, who obviously disliked Wilton's dance, had deliberately turned off the lights.

When the lights came back on, neither Wilton nor the MC could be seen. The DJ had somehow managed to fix his cables, and started playing music again, just to keep the audience entertained. In the confusion following the blackout and Wilton's exit, one uninvited rookie dancer jumped on stage and tried to draw the attention of the audience to his dance strokes. Without words, he was telling them, "Look, I can dance, too. Maybe I should be a part of the competition." But his strokes were largely bland, and he was roundly ignored. And before he could go on, the commotion backstage resumed. This time, though, it didn't result in the outage of sound and sight. There emerged, instead, a man who, without a doubt, seemed like a competitive dancer. The audience had seen him before, when he appeared as a minnow in previous dance competitions. He was dressed in a costume reminiscent of Daddy Gamin's garments, although his was of more economical ornamentation. There was one peculiar thing, though: he had walked onto the stage with mean-looking bodyguards. He walked straight to the DJ and handed him two CDs. After whispering instructions to the DJ, he took the microphone and tapped it three times before he spoke.

"Ladies and gentlemen," he began, "My name is Joel Taguka. I'm sure many of you remember me. I'm here to restore the integrity of the national dance competition, with a short dance performance."

And just like that, as Daddy Gamin had done before him, Joel announced his own entry into the contest.

"For those who may not know, I'm a dancer too, and I bring something different to this theatre," he said, before launching into a spirited dance, with a zest unseen before.

Without any warning, Joel's song had started playing and he, without wasting time, had thrown his best foot forward and started moving in text-book uniformity with the beat. The hall moved with him, turning into one large bus, with the audience as the passengers, and him as the driver. He was in charge of the aesthetic odyssey, hypnotizing all in tow and effortlessly taking them with him. He swung to the left, and all bodies swung with him. He repeated the deed to the right, and the audience followed suit, like flags changing direction with the wind. He was the master enchanter, swinging everyone into an emotional rollercoaster. They had yielded to his charm. Or as the teenagers would say, they had *allowed*.

Joel pirouetted from one end of the stage to the other. He was, without a doubt, relishing every moment of his dance moves and the attendant applause. He swung his arms from side to side, his face beaming with satisfaction and anticipation. The dexterity with which he dropped his strokes was something the audience had not witnessed since the establishment of the dance theatre. Here then, was a man whose agility both rekindled the hitherto fading enthusiasm for the theatre and inspired promise for electrifying nights of enchantment and entertainment. Each time he stepped forward, the audience erupted in delirious applause. The women ululated, the men stomped their feet on the floor, little girls screamed with mouths agape, while boys tried to outdo each other with multi-pitched whistling. When this happened, Joel danced himself to a frenzy, teleporting himself to a trance. He felt invincible. He hopped forward, closer to the edge of the stage, and spread his arms. The audience got the cue and responded with outstretched arms. At that point, Joel flung himself at the outstretched arms, like a man assured of a safe landing—which indeed it was, as the audience wouldn't let him touch the ground. They adored him, and it would be an act of betrayal if they let him land on the floor. It was like a mass contest of loyalty. The front rows passed him onto the next row, who conveyed him to the next and the next until he reached the rear of the dance hall. At that point, he got down to his feet, and ran through the alleyway, touching the outstretched hands of those who clamoured to touch him. And just when the audience was expecting him to head to the staircase on his way back to the stage, he thrust himself forth and somersaulted onto the stage, sending the audience into an even bigger delirium. He had been dancing for a full ten minutes, but the audience didn't even notice it. The fact that he showed no signs of fatigue, made them want even more. His costume was now drenched in sweat, making him a bit uncomfortable. As the music continued playing, he made a dash backstage and, within seconds, changed into a different, bright-coloured costume. He returned to the stage and carried on, for another five minutes, and then another five. There was no sense of time in the theatre hall anymore. The MC, who had been gone since Wilton's exit, had reappeared on stage, dressed in the same colours as Joel's new costume. He just stood on the edge of the stage, grinning, mic in hand. There was no sign that he was going to announce the end of Joel's dance, as he seemed to be mesmerized by it, too. A group of animated women and men—wearing tee-shirts of the same colour as Joel's new costume—walked in at this point of the dance and took the front-row seats. The seats had mostly been unoccupied, as most theatregoers preferred mid-hall and rear seats. But the new fans were actually paid cheerleaders, and the aesthetics of the theatre had nothing to do with their presence there: as long as their pockets were full, any seat in the theatre would do. At that point, to everyone's surprise, Joel took a pause. He signalled the DJ to pause the music, and then reached for the mic.

"Gallant ladies and gentlemen of the theatre," he began, as everyone, except the newly-arrived group, waited with bated breath for what he was going to announce. The new group of fans had immediately started cheering and chanting his name loudly, even when Joel was not doing or saying anything worthy of ovation.

"I've been dancing for a while now, and you've shown incredible support for my dance," he said, as the overenthusiastic fans cheered him on. "I promised to restore the integrity of our dance competition with a short performance, but you kept wanting more," he said proudly. "At this point," he went on, "I'll ask for one more dance, and then I'll exit the stage and the competition—for good," he said, as a member of his entourage went to speak to the DJ.

"Yay!" shouted the audience in a deafening choral cheer. Ululation and whistling, starting from the front-row seats, travelled through the hall as had happened when Joel first stepped on stage.

The DJ inserted Joel's second CD into the player and pressed the play button. An eerie squeaking sound came out, lasting a couple of seconds. And then the music roared to life proper.

It was game on again for Joel who, despite the emerging signs of fatigue, still had a spring in his step. And with one spry stride, Joel relaunched his dancing feat. It was clear, at that moment, that he was going for the killer strokes—the stuff that makes dance champions. And indeed, he did do some eye-popping moves that left the audience entranced in wonderment. The audience had no doubt that the man they were watching was going to take the crown home. And they rewarded him with their support, carrying him through most of it with copious encouraging rounds of applause.

Joel just carried on doing his thing, trying different strokes at every turn of the minute. Save for a few flashes of variation, most of the strokes were similar to what he had displayed earlier. After about five minutes of dance, it was becoming obvious that fatigue was setting in, and the earlier-mesmerizing dancer had nothing new to offer their optical cravings. But Joel just continued dancing, his tempo dropping with every passing minute. There was something odd about time. Joel's song should have ended in about five minutes, but it didn't. The CD that he had given to the DJ was playing nonstop. A few in the audience exchanged curious looks. There was something uncanny about music CDs playing nonstop in the competition. Some kind of déjà vu.

"Daddy Gamin," a woman seated on the third row whispered to her partner. Maybe he was her boyfriend or husband. He smiled, before joking fondly, "*Clever* will be the end of you one day!" It was a trendy way of telling one they were too smart for their own good. The woman smiled, looking into the gentleman's eyes affectionately. He attempted to kiss her, but she pulled her face away teasingly.

The music played on.

Joel was now working through a laboured performance, but carrying on, nonetheless. His momentum had considerably dropped; his quick footwork had faded to duck-like shuffling. But he carried on. The hitherto energized theatre hall was now a shell of itself, with the only enduring cheers coming from the front row, where Joel's hired cheerleaders sat. But he carried on.

Minutes ticked by. A little boy in the sixth row dozed off, dropping his head into his mum's lap. She stroked his head as she watched in silence. She was disappointed. She had told her son, when Joel came on stage, that she was certain he was going to win the dance contest. Spurred on by his mother's judgement, the boy had been engrossed in Joel's earlier performance like he normally did with television cartoon programmes. But now he had lost interest. He wasn't alone. Not many in the theatre remembered much of Joel's earlier performance. They now wished he had stopped while his performance hit the climax. But now they just sat there, wondering why, as they watched him hobble through the dance. His dance shine had faded, and his star dimmed with it. Unable to sit through the self-humiliating experience of a promising champion, some got up to leave. A few people managed to get out—having just enough time to do so before an occurrence that both shocked and left theatregoers confused. Joel had noticed the fading enthusiasm of the audience and, somehow, anticipated this moment. When the five bored youth walked out, he made a thumb signal to Kivundu, who had all but forgotten what his job was.

Gunshot.

"Nobody leaves, nobody moves!" shouted Kivundu.

Gasps of fear rose in the air as another gunshot sound rang out. The mother in the sixth row held onto her son protectively, waiting for it all to end.

The mean-looking bodyguards Joel had arrived on stage with had moved to position themselves near all exits. One agitated youth got up in protest and made for the exit, but was roughed up and bundled into an empty seat in the front row—for all to see.

Another dance contestant emerged from backstage and walked to the DJ with his CD. He wore a T-shirt with his stage name inscribed in bold letters: Zika Bob. But before he could hand over his music, two of Joel's bodyguards came and whisked him off stage, amid protestation both from the removed dancer and the audience.

The front-row cheerleaders applauded the use of force to remove Zika Bob.

"Taguka! Taguka! Taguka!" they broke into a spirited chanting of Joel's name.

Joel danced on, shambling off the stage from end to end like nothing had happened. There was a growing buzz of voices of discontent in the audience. Yet, no one left. Three shrewd youth in the third row saw their opportunity. They moved to the front row and positioned themselves next to the cheerleaders. One cheerleader drew three brightly-coloured tee-shirts from a bag she had brought in with her, and handed them to the three youth. The youth held the tee-shirts, hesitant. Another cheerleader brought out a parcel—of three envelopes fastened together by a rubber band—and passed them on to one youth. The three youths smiled, and slipped into the tee-shirts, one by one. An older bloke, who had previously sat next to them, briefly considered what he had just witnessed. He got up and moved to one of the remaining few seats in front, and started cheering. He was quickly rewarded. A tee-shirt. An envelope.

Three cheerleaders got up with wands of envelopes, and started distributing them to the audience. One approached the panel of adjudicators, positioned immediately below the stage, and dropped three brown envelopes on their table. One pushed the envelopes away. His colleagues looked over their shoulders—to see if anyone was watching. Of course we were watching. They still slid the envelopes into their briefcases anyway.

The dance, or whatever was left of it, maundered on endlessly.

The audience started wishing for a power outage. Not the front row occupants and the new owners of brown envelopes, though.

And that, my grandchildren, is how the dance contest ended," grandma concluded.

"So, who won?" Bea asked. No one had noticed her sneaking back and surreptitiously depositing her little frame behind our cousin Nelly, her trusted accomplice in the realm of amorous escapades. Asking a question was her clever way of announcing her presence so everyone would think she'd been there all the time.

"No one," grandma had said decidedly.

"But grandma, I don't understand; what was all this dancing about if nobody won?" Bea pressed on. She had an obsessive penchant for everything about dance. She practiced in her room every day, hoping to hone her skill and get her figure on television as a popular dance queen.

"Indeed, nobody understands, my child. It is the story of our country's politics," grandma went on. "All dancers arrive on stage with so much promise, yet none wins," she said.

"So, how can one win?" Wafula, our president-in-waiting interjected after being lost in thought momentarily.

"When the ovation is loudest, my child. You want to be president? When the ovation is loudest. Have you never heard? "The Yoruba people say *it is when the ovation is loudest that one ought to quit the dance floor*"—the only way to win.

"The best dancer's prize has been waiting in a box, embroidered in our country's flag, for more than 50 years. I am now in the evening of my life; my lifetime ticket has expired. Will I see a winner before I check out?" she concluded, with a question no one dared answer.

There was an uneasy silence around the bonfire, which seemed to increase with the rising sound of twittering crickets.

I was knackered, and so I was already nodding involuntarily to the enticing beckoning of slumberland just as grandma was uttering her last words.

Josh Mali taught Communication Skills at Makerere University, and high school Literature and English (at Aga Khan High School, Kampala and St. Joseph's Girls Secondary School, Nsambya), before starting a career in journalism with the BBC in 2006. He is the author of a children's book, *The Bad Friends* (Fountain Publishers, 2003) and three plays, including *The Betrothal* (2019), and *God of Small Hands*. His first collection of poems, *The Women Are Here* was also published in 2019. *The Super Dancer* is one among a collection of short stories he is currently working on. Besides a degree in Education (Language and Literature), he holds an MA in Communications, Media and Public Relations from the University of Leicester.

A Tale of Two Husbands
Julius Ocwinyo

HER NAME IS BESIMENSI. However, for as long as anyone could remember, she has been called Bensi. And the happenings in her life have become the stock of conversation in her hometown.

Bensi's first marriage was to a man named Kasongo. Kasongo was tall, spare and sinewy, and had a triangular goatee that he loved to caress. His addition to *khat*[118] saw him chew cheekfuls of the leaves as he puffed away on cigarettes, every now and then spitting out a stream of thick, green liquid.

The local medical assistant, a bosom friend of Kasongo's had once told him that *khat* and tobacco were a deadly cocktail. "Do you know, my friend," the medical assistant had counselled, "that you will end up with a body so seriously wrecked that you won't believe it belongs to you?"

"Why should I really be bothered about what condition I'll be in when I die," he had retorted. "Those who die with their bodies perfect, don't they also decay? Just like the rest of us? In any case, as a driver, each time you get behind the wheel you are flirting with death. So, I don't even think about death at all."

Life can be boring and sordid, Kasongo frequently told himself, when your mind is clear all the time. Sometimes you need just a little bit of something that transports you into that strange heavenly world, where everything is so pure, and the soundless melodies sung by absent mouths soothe your jaded ears and massage your frazzled nerves.

Kasongo was a Muntalim, as a member of the Bintalim faith is called. Despite this, he felt there was no need for Bensi to convert to Bintalim. So he allowed her to retain her first name. People found this nothing short of strange since the Muntalim faith seemed not to countenance this sort of behaviour. Something that people found even stranger was that Kasongo had only the one wife, and didn't seem interested in marrying a second, and a third, and a fourth wife. For was Kasongo not only a Muntalim, a faith that set great store by polygamy, but he drove a water bowser, too? Truck drivers were believed to not only have deep pockets, but also to be insatiably promiscuous.

Some of his polygamous co-religionists wondered what he was doing leading a monogamous life like a pigeon. He usually gave the same, time-

---

118   "Khat" or "Qat" is a plant that grows in East Africa and the Arabian Peninsula. The leaves of the plant contain a stimulant called cathinone, and when chewed, it produces a mild euphoria and increased alertness. The habit of chewing khat is common among men in countries such as Ethiopia, Kenya, Somalia, and Yemen and it's often used as a social activity. Khat is illegal in some countries, because of its effects on the central nervous system and its potential for addiction.

worn answer: "Don't you know that driving a truck is like having a second wife? When you hold its steering wheel, you are caressing it. When you change the gears and go round a bend, you are wooing it. And by the way, when you are driving a truck, your hands are full, like the husband of a large woman. I don't need more than two large women in this life, do I?"

When the rail construction project for which Kasongo drove the water bowser wound up, Kasongo took to driving long-distance trailer trucks.

Between them, Kasongo and Bensi begot and raised four children, one girl, Zulfi, and three boys. The boys went into business early and, one after another, left home to establish themselves in other towns. The girl got married at thirteen, and went off to found her own family with her eighteen-year-old husband, Fudhuli, a fellow Muntalim with a calloused forehead.

When Kasongo died, his health wrecked by hypertension, diabetes and incurable gum disease, the children had all left home. Bensi was still not very old. She had got married at only sixteen, and still yearned for the things that make a woman feel woman. However, she had become rotund and dimpled all over. Her buttocks which, in her younger days, had jutted behind her far enough for a baby to perch on without much need for extra support, was even bigger now. It dropped away at the bottom like a precipice.

For as long as she could remember, other women had been envious of her voluptuous rear. She had even heard one woman whisper to another: "With a rear like that, I would have lured a minister into marrying me."

Grown men, on the other hand, leered at her like feral beasts. Occasionally they got so carried away that they got into trouble—and sometimes literally headlong. One day, when she was returning from the weekly market, a cyclist had become so absorbed in watching her walk with her huge backside jiggling that he had lost control and rammed into a roadside tree, ending up with a mangled front wheel and shredded, bloody lips.

Bensi loved her food, especially mutton. And her teeth, which looked like polished cow horn, were on show a lot of the time, for she loved to smile. Children loved seeing her roll around her compound like a huge and supple barrel whenever she was busy.

And oh how she loved the children! Whenever she had children around her home, she would be heard yelling out to them, in a vibrating, reedy voice, and, quite frequently too, letting off long, shrill gusts of laughter.

Bensi owned a large orchard lush with mangoes, guavas, lemons, oranges, papaya and jackfruit. Bensi firmly kept the kids away from her orchard when the fruits were still unripe. The moment the fruits ripened, however, she allowed them to eat their fill. The only conditions were that they didn't dirty her orchard or her compound, and that they didn't carry any away. She also insisted that not more than ten kids visit her orchard on any given day. The moment the specified number had turned up, she shooed the rest away, gently: "My children, I'm afraid today you are too late. Please come back tomorrow. The fruits will not have disappeared, my children." And she gave them her toothy smile, her teeth pearly and striped, and they believed her.

The neighbours sometimes asked her why she didn't sell her fruits to the children.

"I get enough money from the adults," she would remark, shrugging. "In any case, children belong to everyone."

⌾⌾

PANGRASIO was Bensi's second husband. Just a little older than her, he, like her, was a non-Muntalib. He was a famous butcher in the town and was widely known for his generosity. You wouldn't say he was tall, nor would you say he was short. He was sturdy, with a bull neck, broad shoulders and bushy eyebrows. Regular use of the machete to chop up bone and meat had tempered his arms into impressive masses of sculptured muscle.

When Kasongo died, Bensi had been gripped by paralyzing grief, loneliness and lethargy. After a while, however, she had started to feel a deep need for intimacy. Much as she had never thought seriously about Pangrasio as a possible mate, the way his muscles rippled each time she went to his butchery to buy meat sent a perfectly recognizable type of heat coursing through her body. It was not strange therefore that after their first lovemaking, a sweaty and tempestuous affair which took place in a seedy lodge on the outskirts of the town early one evening, she discovered that what had eventually brought them to this coupling was lust after many sightings. That evening, lying satiated and exhausted, she asked him: "What did you find so attractive in me that you decided we had to do what we've just done?"

He didn't respond right away. Finally, he coughed and spoke: "Your butt. Your smile. And your voice… And you?"

"Your arms," she had responded. "And your shoulders."

Before long, Pangrasio married Bensi as his third wife.

Despite being part of a polygamous triangle, Bensi discovered that she was happy. She had almost said "no" to Pangrasio's marriage proposal. One reason was that she felt that marrying Pangrasio would amount to a betrayal of the unquestioning trust Kasongo had had in her, of his unwavering affection. The second was that his wives might gang up against her since, from what she had heard through gossip, they were tight friends. As the locals said, the two wives were as close to each other as the eye is to the nose. Still, part of her needed Pangrasio, needed him very badly, and very urgently, too. There was a deep, abiding hunger in her that only he could assuage. She, therefore, still got married to Pangrasio despite the withering animosity that Pangrasio's two other wives showed towards her.

⌾⌾

PANGRASIO'S death was sudden. Pangrasio owned a large herd of cattle. His routine was to have one of his sons tend the butchery every Saturday so that he could take his cattle out to graze himself. In that way he could get to know how each of the animals was doing and also further bond with them. One such Saturday, a storm had suddenly brewed up. Thunder had rumbled angrily. And a tongue of lightning had lashed out and snuffed out Pangrasio's life like that of a bug. As custom demanded, like every victim of a lightning strike, Pangrasio was buried in the middle of a swamp after the performance of an elaborate traditional ritual.

THE dead are never dead. What is termed death is only a ceasing of breath, and later a dissolving of the flesh, a remaining behind of the bones and sinews. The spirit, long held captive in the body, is freed, and retreats into the world of the risen-dead. Then interacting freely with the living and, depending on how they were treated, or on whatever mood struck them, they either bestowed good fortune on those close to them or inflicted suffering. In the cyclical ebb and flow of time, marked by prosperity and happiness, or by want or calamity and unhappiness, the spirits were celebrated or condemned. They were also propitiated and their agony, whenever the need arose, salved. That was the old faith, the faith that held sway in the time of Bensi's fore parents.

Then the new faith, Ukristalim—whose adherents are called Ukristalimis—came. It closely followed the arrival of Bintalim, and its champions were greatly alarmed by the inroads the latter had made. While its tactics were stealthy, Ukristalim was also brash and swashbuckling. As a result of its arrival a lot of things changed, but a lot also remained the same.

The new faith came with a different worldview, which it imposed using the legendary carrot and stick. Everything about the old faith was wrong, it asserted. There was only one God, all-knowing and all-powerful; there was the Devil, smooth, slinky and cunning; and there were the angels. The Devil lived buried in the lowest and darkest depths of the earth. The angels, on the other hand, floated around on wings of muslin up above, blowing flutes and trumpets, and singing melodious songs with haunting lyrics.

The spiritualists' beliefs revolved around a pantheon of small gods. Among these were the hunchback god, the god of leprosy and the god of yaws. The new religion collapsed all these into one big God, called Obanga. Obanga lived up in the skies, and smiled upon you if you followed his will, and exacted vicious retribution if you didn't. Sometimes he was unforgiving, and demanded total and unquestioning obedience and respect.

The new faith also condemned as evil the building of the small shrines that represented the abode of the risen-dead, to whom libations of beer were regularly poured and morsels of food offered. Instead, the purveyors of the new faith set up bigger shrines, oblong, sometimes even grand, to which people streamed on specific days, to show obeisance to the new God.

Deep inside the hearts of many of the people, however, nestled a unique brand of the new faith. The natives picked bits and pieces of both the new and old faiths and spliced them into a faith that had a different texture and tenor, a faith that was a rough-hewn syncretic mongrel. Bensi was one such person.

ONE day, Bensi fell off a *boda-boda* motorbike with a basketful of bananas on her head. It was one of those freakish accidents. She was returning from the weekly market. She intended to use the bananas to bake pancakes. She was seated side-saddle on the Bajaj motorbike and was deep in conversation with the rider. The hem of her long skirt caught in the spokes of the motorcycle, hurling her heavily to the ground. When it was finally able to stop, the motorcycle had dragged her over a stretch of road riddled with rough stones the size of fists, with her head pounding the road like a mallet. The bananas on her head had smashed onto the road, the impact scattering and breaking them into shapeless, irredeemable pieces. There was also a trail of scarlet that marked the path her head traced, and where it finally ended there was a lump of congealed blood. An ambulance rushed Bensi to hospital, and the doctors said she was not dead but were not sure she would pull through. Bensi was to stay in this state of semi-death for a long time.

BENSI couldn't figure out how she got to be in this desolate land. The last thing she could remember was her butt perched on a *boda-boda* with a basket of bananas sitting on her head. And that was it. And here she was, alone, in this strange, inhospitable land.

The wind howled and skittered among the boulders. As far as the eye could see, there were caves, nestled in the sides of mountains that surrounded the valley on all sides. The sun seemed to stand still. The air was hot and stifling. The screech of owls travelled to the furthest reaches of the arid land. Shabby marabou storks and other scavengers, some neater than others, sat up in the trees, preening their wings. There were also creatures, some from as far back as prehistoric times, with long necks and large jaws and claws the size of ploughshares.

The sight of all these creatures and many more sent a chill down Bensi's spine. This is not what I was told the afterlife would be like, she told herself. I was told that the grass would be lush, the trees green, the land dark and fertile, flowers everywhere, the sun mild and soothing, the scenery stunning, and soft and haunting melodies everywhere.

Presently a man emerged from the bowels of a cave. He could easily have been twelve feet tall, his skin was green, and his eyes gunmetal. He was lanky, and wore a black, elegantly tailored, well-fitting suit. His shoes, very long and large, were also black, and of patent leather. He carried a giant brown clipboard, over which he held, elegantly poised, a giant pencil. He swung left, then right.

He reeled off a series of names, including Bensi's. People streamed out from inside the caves. People of all the three major races: the Kookazians, the In-Betweens and the Ebonies. Bensi feared that the creatures would attack the large assemblage of humans. However, they looked vacuously into space, seeming not to be interested in anything.

Bensi looked around, swinging her eyes slowly around the throng to determine whether there was somebody she could recognize. For some time, all she could recognize were the different human colours, shapes, sizes and ages. Then she suddenly saw someone familiar. Her gaze fastened on his face, and her eyes bulging with surprise. The man—for it was a man—smiled at her, and started walking, slowly, his feet dragging, towards her.

Bensi instantly remembered the man, whom she had met before the transition.

The man had become part of the garbage dump across the road from her house and lay there limp and unyielding, day after day, never leaving. And he spoke in an endless monotone, murmurous and subdued, in languages he alone seemed to understand.

One day, she asked him about himself. Eyes unfocused, he pondered for a long while, then answered: "It saddens me. They didn't see the whiteness of my soul, the purity of my spirit, the intensity of my purpose. All they saw was the blackness of my skin. And they didn't make any attempt to go deeper than that."

And he gave her a half-smile, half-grimace, like a funeral mask, his teeth turned yellow and a mottled-green by long periods of not-brushing. His hair, long and tangled, like creepers, bore witness to a prolonged not-washing and not-combing. His skin was an ashen-charcoal colour, striped by days-old sweat. The clothes, tattered and misshapen, were stiff and brittle with dirt.

She asked, "But what is your name?"

His answer was quick this time: "I have no name. I am a man without a name."

The man was just as shabby as he had been before the transition.

This time, in the afterlife, Bensi wanted to know the fate of the people who had been summoned by the green giant she had decided to call the

Green Guy.

She wanted to find out from the Man-Without-A-Name why they had been summoned.

"So," she asked, "what are we doing here?"

The Man-Without-A-Name smiled and responded, "The transition has two phases. This is the first phase. The man with the clipboard is called The Sorter. He knows everything about us. Before you arrived, he had already told us that you were widowed twice and that you were not very clear about which faith to follow. You were neither a spiritualist, a Muntalim nor an Ukristalimi. Besides, you got married to two different men of different faiths. That makes it difficult for you to be placed with people from any of the faiths."

"And you?" she asked.

"Good question," he answered. "That is why I'm still here. I'm an atheist, so I have to wait here until enough Ebony atheists join me."

"What do you mean?"

"In the not so distant past, everybody who made the transition was settled right here where we are. But the divisions that existed in their earlier life re-emerged here. People wanted to live close to those they understood, those whose ideas thy found acceptable, those of their own religious faith, those of their social class. Soon a war broke out here, and the land was laid waste. That is why it looks like this."

"What? War even here?"

"Yes," the Man-Without-A-Name answered, "so it was decided that this wasteland, the valley, should become some kind of holding area, where you wait to be processed before you are allowed to move on to the next phase. Like a refugee."

"And that means?"

"In my case, I'm in a dilemma. Not enough Ebony atheists are coming here. Therefore I have to wait for a while before the atheist quota is filled. Almost every Ebony who comes is either an animist, a spiritualist, a Muntalim or an Ukristalimi. Apart from those who want to return to the other life, these are easy to place. Among the In-Betweens, every time there is a huge number of atheists, so they get out of here no longer than a week after they arrive. A huge number of In-Betweens also come from a faith where there are castes, and you retain your caste even here. There is no equality. And being an Ebony means that you can't joint the non-Ebony atheists either. You have your own segregated territory, and you can't risk getting out of it. There is a lot of hostility beyond the boundaries of the territory As far as those out there are concerned, you're an intruder."

"You mean, there is the option to return to the other life?"

"Yes, from the holding area. Once you have moved on to the next phase, you can't back out."

"Would you take up the offer to return to the other life if it was offered?" Bensi enquired.

"No!" The answer came out pat. "I wouldn't. I suffered too much in the other life. At least here nobody spits at me, chases me, throws stones at me. And worse."

"I used to see you in the other life. You didn't look normal; you didn't sound normal. But here, much as you're still shabby, you're very clear-headed."

"Something terrible had happened to me. I went to study engineering in one of the countries of the In-Betweens. I was treated so badly that in the third year, I lost my mind. Only I didn't know that I had lost my mind until I reached here and became normal again, at least mentally."

"So what happened?"

"I don't remember. One moment I was on the other side, the next I was here. It is only later that The Sorter told me that I died of food poisoning."

"How does one get out of here? All I can see is caves all around us."

"There is a giant door that opens at the right time and allows people to go to the next phase."

"Attention!" The Sorter called out. "Attention! Today only a few people have arrived. I still don't have sufficient information on all of you to allow for your admission to the next phase. I will give you an update as soon as possible. The newcomers are required to go to Holding Cave Number 6." Then The Sorter wheeled around and loped back towards his cave.

A huge murmur of disappointment swelled up from the throng of post-terrestrial humans. Those humans who had arrived earlier melted back into their respective caves. Bensi sought out Holding Cave Number 6 and entered it gingerly, not quite sure what she would encounter in there.

⋙∞⋘

BENSI had lived in the holding area for two weeks now. She hadn't eaten anything. She had not had a bath. She had not visited the toilet. She had not had a change of clothes. There was no need to do any of these things because you didn't feel hungry, you didn't feel the need to go to the loo, and you never got dirty. In addition, there was no day and no night. Still, one felt the need to sleep. So one got out of bed only to witness yet another day that looked exactly like the previous one.

It was after the two weeks that she was summoned by The Sorter. She approached the door of his cave-office with trepidation. It was a slab of rough-hewn rock that seemed impossible to move. Bensi was astonished to see the rock-door move to the left and slide all the way into an aperture in the side of the cave. It was slow and soundless.

Bensi hesitated for a few seconds before entering.

The Sorter sat hulking on a highly polished rock chair behind a gleaming rock table. To the left side of the door, facing the right-hand wall, was a single chair. It, too, like The Sorter's, was highly polished. The contrast between the appearance of the office and that of its surroundings was stark.

The Sorter beckoned Bensi onto the chair.

"How are you feeling today?" The Sorter asked.

"No different from the day I arrived," Bensi responded.

"What exactly do you mean?"

"Anxious."

The Sorter fixed her with a greyish gaze for a few minutes. Finally, he let off a sigh. The sigh whooshed out of his huge chest as if out of a Hoover.

"Well... well... well! I believe that we will bring that anxiety to an end today?"

"How?" Bensi asked, leaning forward.

"Well, our investigation is now complete. One, we have established that though you are a syncretist, you tended, in your earlier life, to lean more to the purer form of Ukristalim, so you qualify to be placed with the Ukristalimis – of course, the Ebony Ukristalimis. Is that OK with you?"

Bensi nodded.

"Now, you will find Pangrasio there. The rule in the afterlife is that you must join your former spouse. I hope you have no problem with that."

"No problem at all," she responded.

"Now, your case is a little complicated. You had two husbands. Furthermore, they were of different faiths. That means they live in separate territories here. Now… now, it happens that when you come here after you've had two husbands in your earlier life, and both of them are here, we have to ask which one will want to live with you. Of course, we will have told them that each of them that the other is also now here—if, that is, they haven't already met. Life here can be pretty lonely without a companion."

Bensi nodded.

"In a lot of the cases we have handled, one of the former husbands has quite readily conceded his stake in the former wife." Bensi nodded. "In your case, however, both Kasongo and Pangrasio have refused to let go of you."

"Now what does that mean?" Bensi felt elated by the fact that both men were still interested in her. She, however, was also a little bewildered.

"The policy here is that, to avoid bitterness, since this is meant to be a life of bliss, we can't deny the men their wish. Especially since they live in separate territories."

"You mean… you mean…" Bensi stammered, "I have to be shared by the two men?" Her voice was shrill.

"Yes," The Sorter responded. "Yes…that is our policy. You will have to alternate between them." His expression was deadpan.

"Do I have another option?" Bensi asked.

"Yes."

"What is it?"

"To return where you came from."

"You mean, to my former life?" In her panicky state, Bensi had forgotten what the Man Without A Name had told her two weeks earlier.

"Yes."

"How do I get the permission?"

"You only have to say the word."

ZULFI screamed. She screamed again, her hands tightly holding the sides of her head. "Doctor! Doctooooor! Mummy has sneezed! Her eyes are open! She is moving her legs! She is moving her arms! Mummy is alive! MUMMY IS ALIVE!"

Zulfi ran hither and thither, now wildly beating her breasts with her fists.

A number of doctors and nurses came tumbling into the ward where Bensi had been laid up, unbreathing, for six months. Zulfi, her only daughter, had spent more time looking after her mother at the hospital during this period than living with her husband. She had now returned to the bed, and stood at its head, gazing down at her mother. Her eyes glowed with love.

Dr Karim, the chief neurologist, took one look at Bensi and remarked, "She is alive. Yes, she has come back to life."

Julius Ocwinyo *was born in Teboke, a township in Apach district, Uganda, in 1961. He trained in both a Catholic seminary and secular institutions. After qualifying as a teacher of English and French, he taught at various educational institutions. Eventually he quit teaching and took up book publishing as a career. Currently he is Associate Editor at* Fountain Publishers, *one of the leading publishing houses in the Great Lakes region, Africa. Ocwinyo is the author of* Fate of the Banished (1997), *a novel that has won national acclaim. It has also been on the Ugandan A-level Literature syllabus and is currently taught at a number of universities in Uganda and Kenya. Another novel,* Footprints of the Outsider, *has just gone on the Ugandan A-level Literature syllabus and is also taught at university. Furthermore, Ocwinyo has written works of prose targeted at youth and children and his poems have been published in a number of anthologies.*

Ceilings

Acan Innocent Immaculate

THE WATER DAMAGE had painted a hallucination across the bedroom ceiling. A hallucination with no single shape, shifting in the way things that are not real always do. On some nights, it was a forest of pale-yellow trees. And then, on other nights, nights like tonight, it was the sneering faces of Babirye's family, their silent open mouths calling her stupid for marrying Sula. On nights like tonight, they were her only company while she lay on her back and passively performed her wifely duty, pretending that the man moving roughly over and inside of her was as real as the faces in the ceiling.

Babirye and Sula met in a nightclub when she was in her final year at university. She didn't know he was Muslim then; her friends introduced him as Sula—a common enough name among even Christians—and he was drinking a Nile Special. They spent the rest of the night seated at the bar while their friends danced into daylight, trading memories and flirtations over their ever-filled glasses of beer. When the time to part ways came, they did so with the knowledge that one had the other's number and that the end of the night was merely the beginning of this thing that had sprouted between them.

When Babirye found out he was Muslim—by accident, bumping into him on campus on a Friday and exclaiming at the *kanzu*[119] he wore—she was blinded enough by love that she believed him when he said it wouldn't be a big deal.

It really wouldn't, she thought. Sula was funny and smart and good-looking, and he came from a good Muganda family too. Her parents would love him when they met him. Something as comparatively insignificant as religion would never get in the way of them being together.

When Babirye's sisters asked her what she would do if Sula decided to take other wives as his religion allowed, Babirye, blinded once again by love, believed Sula when he said she would be the only one for him.

When her family refused to host her *kwanjula*[120], Babirye smiled and endured the indiscrete questions from Sula's family asking why the *kwanjula* was being held at an aunt's home—were her parents dead?

When Sula's mother brought in a second wife for him just days after the birth of their third daughter, Babirye smiled through that too. It was the selfless thing to do for the man she loved. Her body had failed to provide a home for his Y-chromosome, and he needed an heir. This was the thing Babirye's life

---

119   A traditional garment worn by men in East Africa, particularly in Tanzania, Kenya, and Uganda. It is a long-sleeved, ankle-length robe that is typically made of lightweight, white cotton material. The kanzu is worn with a headscarf and is considered formal attire for special occasions such as weddings and religious ceremonies. It is also sometimes worn by government officials and other dignitaries.

120   Kwanjula is a traditional Ugandan ceremony that marks the introduction of a groom to the bride's family before the wedding. During the kwanjula, the groom's family brings gifts to the bride's family, including items such as cows, money, and traditional clothing.

had become since she'd met Sula—a series of concessions chipping away at her soul until she had no identity left but that of wife and mother, neither performed satisfactorily enough for her husband and his family.

His knock at her door that night had come as a surprise. It had been months since his shadow had darkened her door, longer even since he'd sought her out for sex. She'd floundered for an excuse to beg out of something she no longer enjoyed, a headache, a period, something, but nothing had risen to her lips quickly enough, and that had led her to this moment; nightdress pushed up to her waist, the duvet rough against her back, her unaroused body stretching painfully to accommodate her husband's desire.

"Not inside," she said when his pace quickened. "I'm not on the pill."

It was like she'd spoken into the ear of a deaf man. He finished inside of her, grunting and shaking, then he moved off her and sat on the side of the bed, his naked back to her. "You're my wife," he said after a moment of tense silence had passed. "When I come to you, you should always be prepared for me. It's your duty, as my wife."

He spoke in the same tone Babirye's father used when he was displeased with her—low, even, deceptively calm—and it made her feel worse than shouting could've, like she was the one who'd done something wrong. She watched him pull on his clothes with shame burning under the skin she concealed with a bed sheet, and when he turned to speak again, she flinched.

"I don't want to hear you telling me where to come next time," he said. "If you don't want to carry my child, don't get off that pill of yours."

As the door slammed shut after his exit, Babirye wondered whose bed he'd spend the night in.

Munira's? She was the youngest, the favourite. But she hadn't visited the bush in her childhood, so her privates were not as warm and welcoming as those of a woman who had pulled. This, Sophie had whispered to Babirye one day in the communal kitchen, when Munira wasn't listening.

Ah, Sophie! Second wife, with a tongue as sharp as a new knife. Sula had fallen upon its cutting edge enough times that he learned to give her bed a wide berth when she declared she would neither push out another of his daughters nor get on the pill.

So it would have to be Hanifa...Hanifa of the soft voice and the gentle hands, who had given the household its first son, who had remained kind even after this, who had nursed Babirye through her second miscarriage. She was the much-needed calm in the storm that was Sula's family, the only one who could bring their husband down from the simmering heights of his anger. Yes, Sula would go to her tonight.

What did it mean, Babirye wondered, that this didn't bother her at all?

ONE month passed. Babirye, accustomed to the sporadic nature of her period since she'd got on the pill, did not panic at the absence of red stains on her underwear. Even when the nausea started, she ignored that. It could be anything, she thought. She wanted it to be anything but a new life forming in her. Eventually, when the vomiting started, she visited her doctor on her own.

"Babirye, the urinalysis results are back," Doctor Nassali said with a sombre unsmiling expression. She placed the paper face-down on the desk and sat back. "Have you been taking the pill regularly?"

"Am I pregnant?" Babirye asked. But she knew the answer. Of course, she knew the answer.

"Yes. I'll have to start you on antenatal care immediately," Doctor Nassali said, flipping through the pages of Babirye's thick file. "You know we have to be careful since the last two pregnancies didn't go well."

They didn't just *not go well*, Babirye thought. Neither had stayed longer than a couple of weeks. What would the good doctor think of her if she said she'd been relieved when it happened? She didn't want to bring more children into her loveless marriage.

"Babirye? Babirye?" Doctor Nassali was calling her name. She'd been lost in her thoughts. She blinked and focused her gaze on the doctor, who now looked concerned.

"I thought we'd agreed to start you on the pill," Doctor Nassali said carefully.

"Yes," Babirye said. "I forgot."

"Don't worry about that. It happens to the best of us."

"Does it? Am I the best of us?"

The doctor's gaze softened. "Babirye, do you want to keep this pregnancy?"

"I… I don't know. Does it make me a bad person that I might not want to? That I wish I could get rid of it?"

"You can't make decisions about your body under the influence of societal expectations," Doctor Nassali said. She leaned forward and pinned Babirye with a serious look. "As your doctor, it's my responsibility to ensure you're in the best possible physical and mental health. You are my patient, not the foetus you carry."

"What are you trying to say to me?"

"I think you understand what I am saying, Babirye."

"I'm a religious woman, Doctor. A good woman! What you're suggesting is terrible and, honestly, offensive!" Babirye said. She pushed back her chair and stood up, gathering her things up and trying, very hard, to morph the consideration in her expression into anger.

Doctor Nassali stood up too, leaning over the desk to grab Babirye's hand before she could leave. "Take this," she said, pressing a small hard rectangle into Babirye's hand. "When the courage finds you, go and see this doctor. She will help you."

Later, after she'd walked out and found a taxi to take her home, Babirye looked down at the thing she'd held so tightly in her clenched fist it had made indents in her flesh. It was a card, with a name and an address. She shoved it deep into her bag and looked straight ahead. She'd figure something out.

EVERY Saturday, the wives gathered in the quadrangle of the homestead with their basins and the week's laundry and, in pairs, they washed and rinsed and hung up the clothes to dry on the wires crisscrossing the compound like a metallic cat's cradle.

This Saturday, Babirye was washing with Sophie, her attention miles away while the younger wife jabbered on about this and that. She *hmm*'d and *ahhh*'d in all the places she thought she heard the inflection of a question and scrubbed at the clothes without really seeing the dirt in them. "Ah ah, give that to me," Sophie said suddenly, snatching a white shirt from Babirye's hands. "Your mind is not here! You be rinsing the clothes. I'll wash."

Babirye opened her mouth to protest; Sophie came from a rich family— the kind that had a washing machine and a dishwasher in one of its many kitchens, maids to do everyone's bidding. Even after nearly a decade of marriage, her palms remained soft in that way of people who have never had to do housework. And she wasn't very good at washing clothes. But she nudged Babirye out of the way and took position in front of the washing basin.

"Not just today," she said, pointing at Babirye. "You've been distracted this whole week. What's wrong? I saw you vomiting the other morning. And even yesterday. And... oh. Oh, Babirye, are you pregnant?"

Babirye could have laughed at how easily Sophie had come to the correct conclusion. Instead, she gave her a look that said everything and nothing all at once. Sophie pushed back from the basin and clapped her hands together.

"Does he know?" she asked in a low voice. Babirye shook her head. Sula didn't pay enough attention to her to notice things like her vomiting, losing appetite, getting a little thicker in the waist. Sophie laughed. "You know it's going to be a girl, right? Why do you put yourself through this?"

"It was a mistake," Babirye said with a sheepish smile. It was hard to maintain any sort of gravity when discussing anything with Sophie. She lived life like a grasshopper in an eternal spring, flitting from leaf to leaf without a care in the world, never having to consider the rainy season.

Even now, she moved closer to Babirye and nudged her in the side, a sly smile on her face. "Sula is incapable of having sons," she said.

How? Babirye wanted to ask, when Hanifa's two boys had their father's broad nose and dimpled chin.

Sophie's sly smile broadened. "Only a woman knows her child's father," she said, and suddenly, Babirye thought of Sula's cousin Najib, who everyone said looked so much like Sula, whose loud laughter filled the home every time he visited and managed to pull a response from even Hanifa...

Babirye slapped a hand over her mouth and breathed, "No!"

"Yes!" Sophie said with a giddy smile.

Babirye shook her head. Sophie had always enjoyed gossip far too much.

"I DON'T want it."

Four words, so carelessly said, and yet they were both Babirye's salvation and her doom. She was standing next to the dining table, at her husband's beck and call while he ate, her emotions in turmoil. She'd expected this—his disappointment, his callousness. Maybe some of what she was feeling was relief that she wouldn't have to lie about this life having existed at all. But a part of her wept, wished he would raise his fists and beat this life out of her the way he had the last one so that she wouldn't have to bear the burden of killing it alone.

"You're just going to push out another girl," Sula said, biting into his chicken. "I don't care how you do it; get rid of that thing."

Her silence was a roar inside her head, loud enough that when Sula slammed his cutlery down on the china plate and pushed back his chair, she didn't really hear him. She was only jerked from her own mind when he tossed a small plastic rectangle at her and said, "You already wanted to do it anyway, not so?"

Babirye got down to her knees and picked up the card. He'd been going through her bags again. She wanted to release the burning anger that suddenly flared up inside of her at his invasion of her privacy, but the bruises on her arms, on her belly, all those places her modest dresses concealed had barely healed, and the memory of Sula's violence pulsed within them. So she remained on her knees, silent while he finished his meal, silent until he walked away.

The ceiling in the abortion clinic was white, spotless. While Babirye lay on her back with her legs up in stirrups, she wondered what she'd expected it to look like. Splattered with the blood of all the innocents who'd lost the possibility of existence her? Stained with the innocence of girls far too young to be mothers? Streaked by the tears of women who had become unmothered by no choice of their own?

She felt so exposed, spread open this way. It felt nothing like childbirth, the pain of her uterine contractions not nearly intense enough to make her lose her inhibitions. The doctor who, a few hours back, had slipped white tablets into her vagina, walked into the room with a leather apron over his white coat. Without saying a word to her, he rolled the equipment trolley toward her and slipped on his gloves. Another doctor walked into the room with a file in his hands, his youth betrayed by the straggling hairs on his chin and the shake of his voice when he started reading the details from Babirye's file. "Thirty-five year-old female from Kawempe, Muganda by tribe, unemployed, unmarried," he said, and Babirye closed her eyes against it all—the clinical way she'd been reduced to words in a file, the lie she'd told to soothe her already bruised ego.

Again, without a word to her, the doctor with the gloves pushed her thighs further apart, and she felt the coldness of a wet cotton swab, too rough against the delicate skin of her vulva. She bit her lip against the discomfort of a metal speculum spreading her open, yelped only a little at the sting of the needle when the doctor administered what his younger companion told her was an anaesthetic, to take away the pain.

But when something pushed into her cervix, she screamed at a pain so visceral it felt like she was being ripped open from the inside out. Her body convulsed on the table, and one of her legs slipped from the stirrups. The doctor cursed and pushed back in his chair, barking at his subordinate to put Babirye back in the correct position.

"Women of these days," the doctor grumbled, loud enough for Babirye to hear. "You go out and get pregnant for a man who isn't your husband, and when you come to abort, you pretend that you can't bear small pain. Now if she makes the cannula touch the unsterile table, she'll come back with a septic uterus and they'll blame the doctor."

And, while he went back to meting out what he obviously thought was her due punishment, Babirye's eyes darted around the room, looking for something, anything, to anchor her to the reality the pain threatened to rip her from. Her searching gaze landed on that of the young doctor, who had her file clutched to his chest and was staring at her with horrified eyes. Help me, she wanted to say, but the words wouldn't come, held hostage by the knot in her throat that wrung tears from her eyes. But, by some small mercy from the universe, her message reached the young doctor.

"Maybe we should give her some pethidine," he said to his senior, his voice shaking. "She looks like she's in too much pain."

"Ah, it's not that much," the doctor between Babirye's legs said, like somewhere in the depths of his android pelvis, there was a cervix opening into a fist-sized uterus, like he'd ever know the pain of clotted blood pushing out into a pad, like he'd ever known what it's like to mould, carry, deliver a life from one's own body.

"But she's paying for it," the younger one said. "Let's just give."

There was silence then, in the air, in the screaming pain in Babirye's gut. It was as heavy as water on the decks of a sinking ship, and for a moment, Babirye felt like she couldn't breathe. Then it lifted on a sigh—whose, she couldn't tell—and the older doctor said, "Fine. Give her 100mg, IM. And make it quick."

It felt like an eternity passed between the time of the order and the prick of the injection in Babirye's arm. Almost immediately, a haze like heaven's clouds fell over her consciousness, numbing her to everything. The chill of the air, the pain in her gut, the pain in her chest—it all floated away, lost to the fuzz of her medicated mind. Her gaze focussed on the ceiling. White. Spotless. And eternally stained with the invisible pain of all the women who'd come before her.

Acan Innocent Immaculate *is a Ugandan writer and doctor-in-training. She won the* Writivism Short Story Prize *in 2016, and has been published by* AFREADA *magazine,* Omenana Magazine, Brittle Paper, *and in* Selves: An Afro Anthology of Creative Nonfiction. *Her most recent work is a children's book titled* The Pearl Trotters in Black, Yellow, Red. *She loves to write fun stories and stories that force people to look within themselves for answers.*

Chief of the Home
Beatrice Lamwaka

This story will take me way back. Back to the time before my father's land in Alokolum village became home to thousands of displaced people because of war. To the time we lived in our home, farmed our land, fetched water from the well, cut and gathered wood, and told stories at the evening fire. To the time all Acholi was family, when we ate malakwang, vegetables with our neighbors, *puru awak*, farmed with assistance from the villagers. When we used the word *omera*, brother, and meant it although you were from another village. All this is now changed. Alokolum village now hosts iron-sheet houses where people peep through the window to see them drive through. Greetings are now a thing of the past. Villagers walk as if they are suspicious of one another. We now talk about *magendo*, how to make money, not how the family is fairing.

This story is about you, Lugul. I am telling your story because I think your story deserves to be heard. Many people may have talked about you, but they let your story be buried with the dead. Your story is not the kind of story that is told from generation to generation at the fire. But it is a story that must be told. So, I will tell it the way it is; only I am not at a fire. We no longer tell stories at the fire. And I live in Kampala, three hundred kilometers away from the place I once called home. I only come to Alokolum village once a year. I come to the graves of the people I love, and my tears won't stop flowing because I remember their stories and I may never tell their stories because of the pain it will bring to me. I will tell your story. Your story deserves to be told because you could never tell your story. Everyone watched what you did. You never told your story. And sometimes I wonder what moral is at the end of your story.

Nobody knew which village you came from but everyone called you *omera*. Some people said you were from Paminyai village but nobody confirmed it. Some people said, "Lugul is lapoya, a mad man." Others said you were possessed by *cen*, spirits. You didn't tell anyone where you came from or why you moved to Alokolum. I only saw you during the day and never got to know where you spent your nights. You didn't have your own home but everybody welcomed you into their homes. You became part of everyone's home. My mother's hut is where you had most of your meals.

My father said boys should not be close to you because you will teach them how to cook.

That you didn't know that being near the cooking fire will burn your penis. Whatever anyone said didn't deter you from doing what you enjoyed most. You continued to fetch water and gather firewood for whoever asked you to. The women loved you. Regina, the woman who had no food in her granary, called to you to help her every day. But soon you realized that she wouldn't give you food at the end of the day, so you went to other homes.

Some people said Regina had no morals and soon she would make a man of you. Others said you only had a penis but that wasn't enough to make you a man. I never understood what that meant. I still question what that means.

I always admired how easily you cut wood but the other girls said, "He is a man so he has a lot of energy to use." I wished that the men in Alokolum would cut the wood and that we would carry it. Something that the men shunned because they had been taught that cutting and carrying firewood is a woman's work. My mother never asked Okello, my elder brother, to fetch water. It was also a women's job, so I never expected that of him. You were familiar with the path to the well because you carried water in jerrycans every day. Something that my mother wanted my father to do but it was only wishful thinking. Like her mother, she had been told to provide whatever her husband needed. I watched her toil each day as my father drunk lacoyi, local brew with other men in the evening. At the end of the day, he complained he was exhausted, and my mother never said a word.

My mother called you to our home every day when we were about to eat. She knew you needed a place to call home. She called you her assistant because you helped when she needed something done. I would look for you until I found you then we would eat. You always said *apwoyo*, thank you, after every meal. My father never said thank you to my mother and it was funny to hear you appreciate my mother's cooking. My father always complained about the salt or the *odii*, groundnut paste, but you never did.

I remember the day you came to our home because you heard my mother screaming. She was being beaten by my father because she said there was no money to buy his lacoyi. I was glad you came to help my parents stop the fight, although that wasn't the last time they fought. You became the *latek*, a peace builder of the village. Whenever there was a fight between a husband and wife, you came to help the woman. I don't know why you decided to do that but I am sure a lot of women were grateful to you. You had begun what a lot of people didn't bother to care about because to them a fight between two lovers wasn't anyone's business.

I was about ten years old when you appeared in Alokolum. I saw you carry firewood on your head. I asked my mother why my father didn't do that. Her only reply was, *"En rwot gang*[121], he is chief of the home." And when I asked her why you were not *rwot gang* she scolded me for asking too many questions. That day, I decided you were my friend and I wanted to know why you were not *rwot gang*.

I sneaked from home when my mother was cooking the evening meal. I looked for you. It was not hard to find you. You were at Korina's house splitting firewood with an axe. I watched as you lifted the axe easily and the wood separated. Korina paid you with *arege*, the local brew. You sat close to her hut while other men sat under the mango tree and drank arege. You didn't join like other men did when they arrived later. You were more interested in what the women were talking about. Even though the men called you, *"Lugul bin imat arege ii kin coo*, Lugul come and drink alcohol with your fellow men," you ignored their call. You didn't say anything when one man drunk with *arege* said, "Lugul is a woman man." You seemed not to mind whatever people called you. You never answered the men when they insulted you. You murmured and walked away. Some men called you a coward. I didn't think you were a coward. I just wanted you to say something mean to them. You didn't seem to notice me as I followed you down the village path. You never once stopped, and I asked why I followed you around. You only turned and looked at me, and then I saw a smile appear on your lips. I knew that was our connection. You were my friend, and I would be yours.

When the new government came into power through a coup d'état you went to Gulu town. Many people in the village moved away. My father said Alokolum was our home, and we would stay there. We watched as people carried their luggage on their heads to safety. We heard the gunshots and the bombs, but we stayed in Alokolum. At night we left home and slept in the bush. I never complained because I felt safe although I worried about finding snakes in my bedding. I was happy when we moved back home because as nothing had happened in the village.

Nobody talked about why you left. You may have left the same way you came. We didn't see you around Alokolum anymore. One of the villagers saw you there. You were helping to clean around. You swept the streets. Picked up rubbish as you did in Alokolum. The soldiers shot you with six bullets because they suspected that you were a spy. Today, I stand at your graveside here on my father's land. Your grave is well maintained. Somebody has pulled up the unwanted plants. I remember when nobody wanted your corpse buried at their home. You did work and helped people do what most people hated to do. A lot of people thought you were mad. Some said you were not comfortable with your sexual manhood. That doesn't matter now.

---

121 "En rwot gang" is a phrase in Dholuo language spoken in Kenya, meaning "the chief of the clan" or "the leader of the community". It is a title given to a respected leader in a Luo community, who is responsible for the welfare of the community members.

When the news of your death came to Alokolum, my father said he would give you a home where you would rest. He said you were a good man, but the world didn't treat you well. I never understood his change of heart. Maybe he knew that deep down in his heart, although the harsh words never stopped coming from him. He now lies next to you. He died during the war because he wanted to treat people who were injured, sick. He wanted to stand by the people of Alokolum. He didn't stop when he received warnings from the soldiers that he was supporting the rebels even though the rebels came into his home and stole his medication. The soldiers shot him in the head and left him to die. My father may have been inspired when he saw you help people. He died helping people.

But this story is not about my father. It is your story. It is a story about the man that villagers didn't get to know. I wish that a lot of men could do what you did. Nobody knew where you came from. You have found a home in a new world. Nobody wanted to call you a man because you fetched water from the well, carried firewood on your head. Today, I will call you my hero because you did what you wanted to do. You were *rwot gang*.

Previously published in the anthology, Queer Africa

Beatrice Lamwaka teaches writing at *The North Green School* and writes for *Global Press Journal*. She is the Vice President of PEN Uganda and has facilitated workshops in prisons in Uganda and edited prison's anthology. Her collection of short stories, Butterfly Dreams and other stories was published a few years ago. Her short story is featured in the acclaimed, *New Daughters of Africa: An International Anthology of Writing by Women of African Descent* (2019) Safe House: *Explorations in Creative Nonfiction from Africa* edited by Ellah Wakatama Allfrey, *Caine Prize Anthologies: African Violet and Other Stories*, and *To See the Mountain and other Stories*, New Writing from Africa 2009: *Winning Stories Selected by J.M Cotzee; Original Short Stories by Young African Writers* Selected by the South African Centre of International PEN, among others.

Till We Find Our Voices
Hilda J. Twongyeirwe

THE WHOLE village was silent. People stood in small groups along the village footpath. They looked at each other with sullen eyes, suspicious even of the grass that lined the footpath. There were more questions than answers. Who did it? Was it a stranger? But how would a stranger manage to do such a thing in a village so knit together? Was it one of them? But how possible could it be for a man to eat his own eye? Ezra, like the other children that had disappeared before him, was an innocent boy. He had just celebrated his twelfth birthday. It was not likely that his kidnapper had anything against him. It was similar to the disappearance and discovered murder of three-year-old Shanice, six-year-old Kukunda, ten-year-old Medie, five-year-old Kato, seven-year-old Laila and many other innocent children.

This was the third day of searching and waiting. The first day had ended in emptiness. The second day had ended in more or less the same way but the policeman had said that there was a lead to something.

"Due to the sensitivity of the issue, we shall not tell you anything now," he had announced.

As the villagers stood together, they each thought anxiously about this lead. Who could it have been? What could have been the motive? Wealth? Power? Popularity? Health? Politics? Revenge? Religion? What was this lead?

Occasionally, the women crossed their hands over their breasts and wiped their tears. The men looked at the women and looked away, afraid of their own unshed tears. Five, six or more women sat under the huge *Mvule* tree that had once been the village shade. The resilient tree that had stood in this spot for hundreds of years suddenly looked tired and unable to provide enough shade. Sweat glistened on each forehead. A few voices could be heard, muffled.

The Police patrol car passed a fifth time. Or was it the fourth or sixth time? It was a grey double-cabin. The woman in the middle followed the car with her eyes. Every time it passed, she stared at it. Her red headscarf hung loosely covering her ears and neck. She shook her head occasionally and passed her tongue over her dry lips. She narrowed her eyes as if to focus on something beyond her reach. She seemed to see what others were not seeing. The woman next to her kept patting her back and mumbling inaudibly.

The double-cabin stopped near the crowd. Everybody moved forward. The officer took his time before he stepped out. And when he emerged, his eyes were looking above the people gathered. He did not want to drown in the sea of expectant eyes that surrounded him.

"Go home," he announced suddenly.

His voice stunk of an unexplained anger. The people searched his eyes for some explanation, but he looked away. He turned towards the car. With his left foot, he kicked at the hind tyre of the double cabin pick-up. He then turned and addressed the motionless people.

"Go home. Tomorrow we shall start from where we have stopped today."

The woman with the red headscarf moved forward, slowly, quietly. She knelt in front of the officer. She looked at the officer and raised her arms. Her lips quivered with scores of unspoken words. Her chest heaved in a slow laboured movement. Her arms in mid-air, begging.

The officer yanked spectacles off his face but he did not speak. Neither did he look at her nor at the people that surrounded him and her.

Silence.

Two women edged forward and held the arms of the woman with the red headscarf. One held the left arm, the other, the right. She did not resist. They helped her back on her feet.

"Surely you must have an answer," a voice came from behind.

"Please, do not make this more difficult than it already is," the officer said.

"Then you must understand how difficult it is for this woman, and for us."

"Sir, you are the investigator. We trust you," another voice cut in.

The officer did not respond to any of the concerns of the people. Instead, he stepped back into the grey double-cabin and it moved away. A heavy cloud of dust rose and fell, as if to cover traces of whatever had gone on that day and the day before.

The woman with the red headscarf did not sit down again. She walked ahead of the rest, her body stooping forward. Women walked close to her but they did not speak. The men did not follow. They broke into smaller groups again, talking indistinctly until dust covered their faces and forced them homewards.

⸙

IT WAS the village dog that no one cared about that stirred the village spirit on the morning of the fourth day. The black dog, which everybody called Buraka, emerged from the swamp with a blood-stained shirt. The young boys who were playing football at the village square saw it first.

"No," the first boy said.

"Yes," another added.

"It is Ezra's shirt," the third boy said.

The boys suddenly turned away from the banana fibre ball in the middle of the pitch and one by one they followed Buraka. Slowly at first, then faster.

"What are you chasing after?" Kamondi, the village madman, asked the boys.

"It's the dog," they answered.

"Has the dog stolen anyone's bottle of Waragi? Leave Buraka to go!" he shouted at the passing children but they continued their chase.

Even the boys knew Kamondi's seasonal madness which attacked him especially when the moon was full and high. It was the season.

The boys closed in on Buraka. As soon as Buraka realised that he was being chased, he increased his speed, too, but the boys' noise must have threatened him for he soon let go of the shirt and swerved back into the swamp.

The lead boy stopped. One by one, the other boys stopped too and gathered around the blood-stained shirt. It was the shirt that Ezra wore on that fateful evening of his disappearance. Earlier in the day, he had been at the pitch with the boys. After the games, all the boys headed to their respective homes but Ezra never arrived home. It was not clear at what spot he disappeared. There was a lot of speculation, and none had been confirmed yet. But Buraka was confirming something with the blood-stained shirt.

"It is your shirt Ezra," One of the boys whispered and two large tears ran down his left cheek and down his neck. It was Daudi. Daudi and Ezra had had a small fight the day before Ezra's disappearance. It was over the banana fibre ball that they were making together. Ezra had said that Daudi's knots were not tight enough to make the ball durable.

"You never appreciate my work," Daudi had responded.

"I do appreciate your work but that does not mean that you should not improve it," Ezra had said. "Okay Mr. Know-It-All. Do it yourself, then," Daudi had retorted.

"I gathered all the fibres, remember?"

Their argument had built up until Daudi threw the ball and fibres at Ezra, hitting him on the belly. Ezra picked the ball and hit Daudi back. Daudi was taller and stronger than Ezra. He was also very short-tempered. All the boys knew that. When Daudi launched forward to attack, Ezra knew what a fight with Daudi entailed and so he quickly swerved and ran towards the other boys, screaming for help.

"Do not joke with me next time," Daudi had said with a subdued smile.

"I won't, I promise. We are friends, aren't we?" Ezra had responded and offered his hand, which Daudi took and they laughed as they settled back to the task of completing their ball. Though Daudi was short-tempered, his anger never lasted more than a few minutes. And he was great friends with Ezra.

As Daudi and the boys stared at the shirt, Daudi realised there was never going to be a next time for Ezra, and he regretted the small fight. He felt relieved that they had forgiven each other and had forgotten the little fight by the time they headed back to their homes. Another tear came. And another. Heavy lumps stood like thorns in his throat as he sobbed uncontrollably. Other boys joined in. They sobbed for their friend. None dared to pick the shirt up. None dared to walk away. They just stood there; their innocent eyes set on the stained shirt.

Soon, Kamondi caught up with them.

"Why are you crying?"

The boys did not answer him. A few of them pointed at the shirt in the middle of the cycle.

"And what is that?"

"It is Ezra's shirt," one boy said between tears.

Kamondi looked from the shirt to the boy that had just talked, and to the shirt again. In wonder he held his mouth with one hand and pointed at the shirt with the other. Without another word, he broke into a run. He ran like the madman he was. Some children made to follow him but they stopped when they realised that others were still standing. In a few minutes, Kamondi returned with Banaga, the village Defence Secretary.

"Quick, call the LC Chairman," Banaga told Kamondi.

As they waited for the Chairman, the boys told Banaga about Buraka. Banaga turned the shirt over and over, with a bamboo cane as if looking for more evidence of the crime.

∽∾∽

VILLAGERS gathered and stood in a line along the edge of the swamp. This time, the woman with the red headscarf was not among them. "Go. I will stay here," was all she said when she heard the news.

"Let us comb the swamp," the Chairman announced. "Do not leave any track unsearched."

The villagers did not need to follow every track. As soon as they started searching, Buraka emerged again, and they watched him disappear back into the swamp. Shortly afterwards he returned and focused his misty eyes on the people searching. After a few minutes, he raised his hind leg and urinated. He then vanished back into the same direction.

"Buraka is telling us something," Kamondi said laughing. "Dogs urinate on a track they do not want to forget. Let's follow him."

"Dogs just urinate. Do not distract us, Kamondi," It was the Chairman.

The villagers looked at one another silently but they surged behind Kamondi as he followed Buraka's track. A few metres from the edge of the swamp, they found Buraka squatting next to Ezra's body. Ezra's head had been chopped off. It hung on a tree stump, next to the trunk.

The boys edged forward to see their friend. Lumps formed in their throats. Emptiness filled their stomachs. Fear gripped them. They shook from within.

They each nursed a pain that the killers would never understand.

A stench of their friend's body hit their nose. They felt guilty for smelling it. For smelling their friend. Daudi rested his hands on his knees and retched until there was nothing left in his stomach. The smell of his vomit, mixed with the smell of the swamp and that of Ezra's decomposing body, rose and wrapped the village.

It was the Chairman who broke the spell of silence that ensued.

"Let's call the Police at once," he said.

"Mmh, mmh mmh…" the women murmured, cupping their mouths. The men fidgeted with their arms that had suddenly become too heavy for their shoulders to support.

"Someone call the police, I said," ordered the Chairman. "We shall wait for them here."

"No," Kamondi protested. "Don't call those policemen! Why hadn't they discovered the body up to now? Should we dress all the stray dogs in uniform? It took Buraka to find this body!" Buraka looked up at Kamondi and he indeed removed his tattered court and threw it over Buraka. Buraka shook it off and walked away. Kamondi picked up his court and put it on again.

"Do I speak French? Someone, go to the road, jump on a bodaboda and call the police."

"Why don't you go, Mr. Chairman, if you are so interested in police?"

"After all what is the difference between you and the police?"

"Go and call them if you want. Gooooo!"

Several voices shouted at the Chairman in protest.

"That is not the point! And stop shouting at me!" the Chairman retorted.

"You are shouting too, Chairman!" Kamondi screamed back, small bullets of saliva shooting out of his mouth. "I don't think the police should be called here. This is our son. This is our body. This is our Ezra. We should not let anyone desecrate him with their bloody hands. We have been desecrated enough! I don't see why the police should be involved now, after they failed to find him."

"What you are saying has no meaning, Kamondi," answered the Chairman. "We are not here to blame anyone. The sacrilege is already done."

"That is what I am saying. Mr. Chairman, it is already done. It is already done! Is this the first ritual murder case we have witnessed in this village?"

"No. But remember they have all been handled by the police. Or have you forgotten?"

"Thank you, Mr Chairman. Thank you! Thank you for answering yourself. And which of these murderers have been charged with murder? Tell us, which of these murders have been resolved by police?"

"You are talking too much, Kamondi. policemen are not judges of the High Court."

"There is a problem, my friend," Kamondi quickly said as he tore off his shirt. "Today, I shall seek justice." Foam was gathering on the corners of his dry lips. People wiped their own lips.

Before anyone could stop him, he scooped Ezra's head and rolled it into the piece of shirt he had just torn. He put on the other piece, one sleeve and a bit of cloth that covered only his neck.

"This is a perfect gift to our president. Our most able Police Chief will deliver it to him." We goooo, we go! We go we go we go. We go we go we go!" Kamondi called upon the villagers dancing in small circles.

"I can see you have all lost your tongues! Anyone willing to deliver the gift?" Kamondi swung the head from one person to the other as they each moved backwards. More guilt gripped them for moving away from their own son.

There was silence. Banaga spoke in a subdued voice.

"Kamondi, sometimes your madness is beyond our understanding. Do you really find this situation comic? Please listen to the Chairman."

"Fine. But I will not listen" Kamondi said as he secured the head with his left arm and waved with the right arm. "I will deliver this if no one else will. When police come here, show them that body. Or have you forgotten it is also there?"

"Fellow villagers, the police will not return our son to life. The police will not find the murderers. Let us go and bury," one woman said, stepping in front of the group. "We shall not run away from what is our duty."

"This is a police case woman," the Chairman said. "When we are alive, we belong to ourselves. But when we die in such a manner, we belong to higher authorities. We cannot bury. We have to report to the police. Someone run and call the police. Or find the Muluka Chief. He will call the police to come and fetch the body. Can someone run or are you all deaf!" The Chairman was shouting again.

More voices sprung up, each offering a different suggestion. Some voices were buried beneath others and were not heard.

"Will you all stop whining and listen to me?" It was Kamondi again, his voice sweeping other voices like a whirlwind. "If none go with me, I still will go. If we let the policemen come here, they will whip us into more silence. Are we imbeciles? Why should we wait for them as if we do not have legs? Aren't we men or are the tails between our legs just for decoration!"

"Stop it. Can you stop it, Kamondi? You are simply confusing us the more with your irrelevancies."

Kamondi looked at the Chairman and roared with laughter. When he stopped laughing, he moved towards the Chairman and swung the head at him. The Chairman raised his arms in fear and resignation. Kamondi laughed again before he suddenly broke into a song as he matched out of the swamp:

Though none go with me I still will go
Though none go with me I still will go
Though none go with me I still will go
No turning back
No turning back

Sweat glistened on his bare black back. More foam continued to form on the corners of his mouth. The nerves on his forehead pushed against the surface. They throbbed with each step. He moved across the village square and kicked the ball that the boys had abandoned in the middle of the square, sending it across the swamp. He joined the footpath that headed towards the road.

When the crowd finally followed him, it was to stop him. But when they caught up with him, they were no longer sure which side they belonged to: stopping him or going with him. When they reached the village church, the catechist and a few believers tried to stop them, but they would not listen. "We have prayed and prayed but God does not seem to listen to our prayers!" the villagers shouted. "If there is no God, let us be our own gods!"

"That is not true," the catechist said as he tried to keep pace with the rowdy crowd. "God is there."

"Surely God could strike all the killers dead if he wanted to."

"God is not a killer."

"Then why are you asking us to pray to him if he won't kill the killers?" it was Kamondi asking.

"I am telling you to pray because we are heavy laden. Our state is heavy laden. God says that those that are heavy laden should come to him for rest. They should cast their burdens unto him." This burden of child sacrifice can only be dealt with by God, the Omnipotent. We are too powerless to do anything."

"We are not too powerless, catechist. We are not. Do not provoke our anger. We can do something. We can. Like now I can just bite off your lips if you do not shut up!" Kamondi shook his free fist at him. The catechist shut up.

Each village they passed added more people to the crowd. The young children were excited by the crowd. They jumped and danced with excitement as their parents sent them back to remain at home. Old women who could not join the procession held onto their walking sticks firmly, their other hands clasping their backs. "Let Rugaba, God the giver, lead your way," they said to the people passing by. Old men looked on and scratched the skin under their greying thin hair. Young men and women walked briskly to keep pace with Kamondi.

Close to the police headquarters, teargas canisters begun to rock the air. Kamondi held on to his load firmly as Chairman stepped forward.

"We come in peace," Chairman pleaded.

"Yes! We come in peace" the crowd roared.

"Please hear us out."

The policemen uncorked their guns and listened.

"Sir, we have come to…to…to…" Chairman stammered.

"We have a gift," Kamondi took over.

"Not a gift sir. We have come to…to…to report. To report murder."

"Sir, we have a gift for the president."

"Quiet, Kamondi! Sir, we have come to report that this morning we found the missing boy."

"The truth is that we have a gift for the president. We have come to petition him about the ritual murderers that have finished our children. This endless sacrilege in our village has robbed us of our voices. But today we have come to stand here till we find our voices again."

"Yes, yes! It's all about our children," the crowd murmured in unison.

"It is about us, sir," Daudi joined in, his voice feeble but audible. "It is about our brothers and sisters. It is about our friends. We are all going to die if you do not help us."

"Ezra was our friend," another boy said but he soon began to sob and could not continue.

Kamondi edged forward and placed his load on the ground.

"Sir, this is our gift." he said. "Please tell him that we are in pain."

"The president works, with or without your gifts!" one policeman shouted as he cocked his gun. "We have given you the breast and you have relaxed to breastfeed. Now go! We have heard what you had to say! Now go."

"This man is mad, chief, please don't listen to him."

"Take him away then," the policeman shouted and raised his gun. Kamondi protested as he unrolled the shirt to display Ezra's head. Ezra's eyes stared at the policeman.

The policeman shook with rage. He wanted to silence the stare. To silence Kamondi. His gun rose higher. He rose with it. He wanted to urinate. Kamondi cleared his throat and spat. The policeman's urge to urinate intensified. His legs jerked. He released the bullet into the air.

The crowd moved backwards.

"Move!" it was an order.

Another bullet tore into the air. A new order rose above the noise. It was madder. Wild.

"And don't you dare! Don't you dare leave that damned…damned head here!"

But Kamondi did not pick up the head, nor did the crowd.

"What is going on here?" It was the Police Chief just arriving at the station. Can someone explain what is going on?"

"It is the villagers, sir. Tell them to go away."

"What do they want?"

"They wanted you, sir. But let them go. We have dealt with their issue."

"*Munataka nini Wanainchi?*[122] We are very friendly people. Talk to me. *Tabu gani, hmm? Munasema nini? Eeh?*[123] I believe in dialogue, not shooting," he addressed the officer welding the gun.

"Kamondi stepped forward, bowed his head and pointed at the head on the ground.

The Police Chief stepped backwards; his face suddenly murky. He looked at the head and at the crowd and back at the head. He looked at the police officers and then back at the head. Something bothered him about the head. It was no longer one head but many heads. Small heads, big ones. Unkempt heads, clean shaven ones. Fresh heads, decomposed ones. Each head narrating its story. What troubled him more was that it was as if he recognised some of the heads.

"Have you seen it?" It was the crowd asking.

Hilda Twongyeirwe is an editor and has also published creative and non-fiction works in different anthologies and Journals. She is currently the Executive Director of *FEMRITE - Uganda Women Writers Association.* She is a recipient of *2018 National Medal* and *2018 Uganda Registration Services Bureau (URSB) Award,* both for her contribution to Uganda's *Literary Heritage and Women Emancipation.* She is also a recipient of a Certificate of Recognition (2008) from the National Book Trust of Uganda for her children's book, *Fina the Dancer.* She has edited fiction and creative nonfiction works, the most recent one being, *This Bridge Called Woman: A Cross-cultural Anthology by Ugandan & U.S. Women* (2022). She has also edited others including: *No Time to Mourn* (2020) by South Sudanese women. *I Dare to Say: African Women Share Their Stories of Hope and Survival* (2012) and *Taboo? Voices of Women on Female Genital Mutilation* (2013). She is a member of *The Graca Machel Trust Women in Media Network, Action for Development* and *FEMRITE.*

---

122   Swahili, meaning "What do the people want?"
123   Swahili, meaning "What is taboo? What do we say? Hey?".

Glossary of Common Terms

agbada	a traditional Nigerian outfit worn by men on special occasions, ceremonies and traditional events, it is an oversized, flowing robe with wide sleeves.
aki	a traditional children's game played with stones
alhamdulilah	an Arabic phrase meaning "praise be to God"
ama	a traditional game played by children in East Africa, similar to tag
anakutafuta	looking for in Swahili
azan	the Islamic call to prayer, usually recited by a muezzin, that summons Muslims to perform the five daily prayers
bali bakuba	a phrase in Luganda, a language spoken in Uganda, meaning "you should be careful"
biashara	business in Swahili
bodas	a slang term for motorcycles or motorbikes
chakula	food in Swahili
chakutumaini sina	I don't have confidence
chapati	a type of flatbread commonly consumed in East Africa and India
dera	dress
devos	a traditional game played by children in East Africa, similar to hide and seek
duksi	an Islamic boarding school or madrasa
ekyo nakyo kiwedde	a phrase in Luganda, meaning "I'll see you later"
gibendi	a traditional game played by children in East Africa, similar to hide and seek
githeri	a Kenyan dish made of corn and beans
gomesi	traditional Ugandan clothing worn by women
gorofa	A Swahili slang term that could be translated to mean 'elder brother' or 'big brother'
hakuna	A Swahili phrase that means "there is nothing" or "there is none"
hakuna haja	no need in Swahili
hakuna ma	no problem in Swahili
haraka	hurry in Swahili
hebu	a Swahili word meaning "let's" or "come on"
igirichi	a traditional game played by children
jamaa	man or fellow in Swahili
jaza kabisa	a phrase in Swahili meaning "completely finished"

jikos	charcoal stoves
kakebe	a type of drum used in Ugandan traditional music
kanzu	traditional men's clothing worn in East Africa, particularly in Tanzania, Kenya, and Uganda.
kataasa	a phrase in Luganda, meaning "to be careful"
katy	a traditional children's game played with a bladder or ball
kegondi	a type of grass
khat	a plant that grows in East Africa and the Arabian Peninsula. The leaves of the plant contain a stimulant called cathinone, and when chewed, it produces a mild euphoria and increased alertness.
kibaki tena	a campaign slogan used during the 2002 Kenyan presidential election
kiboko	a whip made from hippopotamus or crocodile hide
kifafa	Swahili for "epilepsy". Also a slang term for someone who is lazy
kimani	a name
kiondo	a traditional woven basket commonly used in East Africa
kipanzi	love
kivambara	a traditional game played by children in East Africa, similar to hide and seek
kwanjula	a traditional marriage ceremony in Uganda
maajanga etenga kinam-gozi ibiniga	a traditional game played by children in East Africa, similar to hide and seek
mabati	sheet metal in Swahili
mandazis	doughnuts in Swahili
masala	a mixture of spices used in East African cooking
matatu	a minibus used for public transportation in East Africa
matatu	a minibus used for public transportation in East Africa
maziwa mala	a type of sour milk commonly consumed in East Africa
mboch	a derogatory term used to refer to a poor person
mi si mlami	I am not the boss in Swahili
mkeka	a traditional mat used in East Africa
mlazo	a traditional game played by children in East Africa, similar to hopscotch
mnafanya nini	what will I do
modi	mode of transport
mugombero	a traditional game played by children in East Africa, similar to tag
mum imejaa wa	mother is the boss in Swahili
muntalib	a male given name of Arabic origin meaning "the one who seeks help"
muzuungu	a slang term for a foreigner, particularly of European descent
mzungus	a term used in East Africa to refer to white people
ngoja	wait in Swahili
nyama	meat in swahili
omena	a type of small fish

omusajja angobye	a phrase in Luganda, meaning "the man is coming"
pilau	a type of rice dish with spices, commonly consumed in East Africa
pishori	rice
riaruka	to come back
saa nane na forty	9:40 in Swahili
sambakhalu	a traditional game played by children in East Africa, similar to tag
seveve	The act of showing off or boasting
shauriyako	a traditional game played by children in East Africa, similar to marbles
shiba'd	a traditional Sudanese dress
shimwero	a traditional game played by children in East Africa, similar to hide and seek
sigiris	a type of traditional East African drum
sindio	a traditional game played by children in East Africa, similar to hide and seek
sufuria	a type of cooking pot
tsimbare	a traditional game played by children in East Africa, similar to hide and seek
ugali	a type of porridge made from cornmeal, a staple food in East Africa
ugali mwiko	A type of Ugali (a staple food in East Africa made from cornmeal) that is cooked using a stick (mwiko) instead of a cooking pot
vuhindi	a traditional game played by children in East Africa, similar to jacks
wallahi	an Arabic expression of emphasis or oath
waragi	Ugandan moonshine made from fermented bananas or millet.
yako	yours in Swahili

About the Editors

BEATRICE LAMWAKA

Beatrice Lamwaka teaches writing at *The North Green School* and writes for *Global Press Journal*. She is the Vice President of PEN Uganda and has facilitated workshops in prisons in Uganda and edited prison's anthology. Her collection of short stories, Butterfly Dreams and other stories was published a few years ago. Her short story is featured in the acclaimed, *New Daughters of Africa: An International Anthology of Writing by Women of African Descent* (2019) Safe House*: Explorations in Creative Nonfiction from Africa* edited by Ellah Wakatama Allfrey, *Caine Prize Anthologies: African Violet and Other Stories*, and *To See the Mountain and other Stories*, New Writing from Africa 2009: *Winning Stories Selected by J.M Cotzee; Original Short Stories by Young African Writers* Selected by the South African Centre of International PEN, among others

She was awarded by Uganda Registration Service Bureau for her literary contributions in 2018. She is a recipient of the 2011 *Young Achievers Award*, was shortlisted for the 2015 *Morland Writing Scholarship* and the *2011 Caine Prize for African Writing*, and was a finalist for the 2009 *South African PEN/Studzinski Literary Award*. The anthology of short stories, *Queer Africa* (2013), to which she contributed, won the 26th Lambda Literary Award in 2014.

She was fellow at Stiftung Kunstlerdorf Schoppingen (Germany), Rockefeller Foundation's Bellagio Center Residency (Italy), Le Chateau de Lavigny International Writers' Residence (Switzerland), Femrite's Regional Writers Residences (Jinja, Kampala and Entebbe) and Caine Prize writer's workshops (Cameroon and South Africa) and Miles Morland Foundation's workshop in Zanzibar (Tanzania).

JOSH MALI

Josh Mali taught Communication Skills at Makerere University, and high school Literature and English, before starting a career in journalism with the BBC in 2006. He is the author of a children's book, *The Bad Friends* (Fountain Publishers, 2003) and three plays, including *The Betrothal* (2019), and *God of Small Hands* (unpublished). *The Women Are Here*, his first collection of poems, was also published in 2019. He is currently working on a collection of short stories.

Besides a degree in Education (Language and Literature) from Makerere University, he holds an MA in Communications, Media and Public Relations from the University of Leicester.